SEASON OF THE DOVE

SEASON OF THE DOVE

MARIE Q ROGERS

Namai Press

Published by Namai Press

ISBN 978-1-7342413-0-3

Typesetting services by BOOKOW.COM

To my Great Grandchildren:

May you grow up in a world that has no resemblance to the one in this story.

"To cherish what remains of the Earth and to foster its renewal

is our only legitimate hope of survival."

Wendell Barry

PROLOGUE

"Mr. Hardman, there is something you must see." The set of Kramer's jaw and the unnerving look in his eyes told Gregory Hardman the business was serious enough for him to leave the safety of Hardman Hall. Of all days—Sunday, the morning he planned to honor his youngest son for completing college and earning National Citizenship.

Greg shut down his computer screen, but not in time to prevent Kramer from glancing at the weather report. He saw fear flicker through the eyes of his chief of security. He didn't like to inform staff about approaching hurricanes too soon. It affected efficiency. But in a day or so he'd have to order them to begin storm preparations.

Kramer asked no questions. He drove his employer out of the residential compound, down the lane past the agricultural fields, to the perimeter fence. The guard opened the gate to let them through. Greg set his face in hard lines to disguise his anxiety. Already, a small group of beggars drifted up the road toward them. Greg patted his holster to reassure himself of the presence of his sidearm.

Kramer turned the jeep off the road and followed the fence line for a quarter mile. "It's only getting worse, sir. More of 'em every day. You'd think word would get around that we don't give out charity, but they come looking for it anyway."

"Are you sure none of your staff are giving them anything?"

"If I catch 'em—hell, if I suspect them—they're gone. I don't tolerate pity." He jutted his chin toward the ten-foot-tall fence. "Even that doesn't stop the riffraff from tryin' to get in. Sometimes we don't catch 'em till they come out with as much produce as they can carry." He stopped the jeep by the orange grove.

Greg climbed out and walked to a slit in the fencing just large enough for someone to sneak through. "Isn't it electrified?"

"Yes, sir, but we must of got a bad batch of Syntat switches. They burn out as fast as we replace 'em. The thieves take advantage of it. We're always having to mend fences. Don't worry." He ducked through the hole. "I shut off the juice before I picked you up." He held the fence open for Greg to pass through. "We put out booby traps, like you told us to, in the most vulnerable places. Like this."

Greg looked apprehensively at the ground.

"It's safe, Mr. Hardman. We removed the punji traps. Wouldn't do for you to step on one."

Greg cringed at the thought of sharp spikes piercing the soles of his shoes.

Kramer led the way between rows of trees. "The whip trap's behind this tree. Gotta warn you, it's pretty grisly."

Showing no emotion, Greg stared down at the body impaled by sharp blades. "Looks like you got two with one blow."

"Yes, sir." Kramer stepped aside to vomit.

"How long's it been here?"

Kramer wiped his mouth. "A few days, I guess. Don't know how we missed her. We patrol every day. But it's a big plantation."

The body was swollen and putrefying, but it was obvious the woman had been pregnant. The arm of an impaled fetus hung through a slit in her belly.

"So, what do you plan to do?" Greg asked.

"Whatever you say. By law, we should report it to the sheriff, but they've been complainin' about so many vagrants getting injured out here. Last time, the sheriff himself warned me they're thinking of filing charges on us."

"For defending my property? Don't worry, I own a piece of that sheriff." Greg frowned. "But if word got out about this...." A simple death by booby trap was one thing. A starving woman stealing food, a pregnant one at that… "Who else knows about it?"

"Just the guy that discovered the body. I told him to keep quiet."

"Give him cash to shut him up. Has anyone come looking for her?"

"No, sir. Probably no family, just a drifter."

"Dismantle the whip trap, then get someone you trust to help you take the body out to the longleaf pine plantation. Bury it where it won't be found. Then come see me. You've earned a bonus."

CHAPTER 1

A sunbeam edged through the blinds in Rob's bedroom and perched on his eyelids. "Ah, a new day is dawning," he murmured. "But I want to sleep. Command: close blinds." Almost silently, the slats turned, darkening the room. But that small act roused him, and remnants of last night's celebration danced through his head.

Yesterday, the first of May, 2123, had seen his initiation into manhood. First, graduation from Hayes University. Robert Michael Hardman was granted his Baccalaureate in Business Science, and the State of Florida had bestowed Citizenship on him. Afterward, at a lavish reception in the ballroom of the Beauchamp Hotel, Rob's father announced that, due to the family's status as national shareholders, Rob qualified as a National Citizen. A representative of Interstate Consolidated presented Rob with his National Citizenship ring. The cheers that rose when the dignitary slid the ring onto Rob's finger still resonated in his ears.

Rob raised his hands to examine his rings. He'd worn the gold Birthright ring, engraved with the family crest, as long as he could remember. When he was a child, it fit his ring finger. Now it adorned his pinkie. At thirteen, upon completion of religious training and his dedication to the Loving Spirit, he'd been granted the Third Covenant ring, of bronze with a simple cross. Worn on his right hand, it symbolized Rob's position at the right hand of God.

The two new rings weighed heavily on his left hand. The Citizenship ring on his middle finger was silver, embossed with the shape of the State of Florida overlaying a four-point star. On his ring finger, the

National Citizenship ring, of platinum, displayed an enamel bald eagle. *How long before I get used to them?*

After the reception, he'd partied with friends until very late. Andreu, the family's chauffeur, had brought him home where Leonard, his valet, put him to bed.

Rob stretched luxuriantly. A glorious future lay before him. When his brother Doug graduated, Father had endowed him with a few of the family's business holdings. He looked forward to being his own man.

Hammering on the door of his suite brought Rob back to earth. Father shouted, "Are you going to sleep all day?"

A soft rustling near the door, the ever-attentive Leonard materialized from the dressing room and said, "Coming, Mr. Hardman."

Rob grunted, sat up, and leaned against the headboard. "Father, it's Sunday. I want to sleep in."

"It's almost eleven. You should be dressed for chapel by now."

"Can't I skip it? I'm a Citizen now."

"As long as you're under my roof, you'll answer to me." He grabbed Rob's left hand and yanked hard. Rob slid across the silk sheets and tumbled to the floor. "Get up and put on some clothes. Proper clothes. I expect you in chapel in ten minutes." He left without shutting the door.

Leonard quietly closed it. "I'll have your clothes ready in a moment, Mr. Rob."

Rob collected himself from the tangle of bedding and staggered into his bathroom. He couldn't figure Father out. Last night, he'd acted so proud, but this morning he was treating Rob like a child.

Rob smeared shaving gel on his face and stepped into the jet shower. Within seconds, he was clean. He ran a comb through his hair and went to his dressing room where Leonard had a Sunday suit laid out. "Thanks, Len." He allowed Leonard to help him into the foundation garments and layer the suit over them. He adjusted the collar and cuffs and slipped his Nebula onto his wrist while Leonard dressed his feet.

The Nebula buzzed. Father's angry face appeared.

"I'm coming!" Rob shouted at the screen.

Leonard deftly adjusted Rob's tie and stepped back. "You look splendid, Mr. Rob."

"Thank you, Leonard. I'd rather look comfortable."

"Mr. Hardman wants you to look like a prince of industry, which you are. You can change clothes later."

"The old man's in a worse mood than usual. Especially for a Sunday. I wonder why?"

"I don't know, sir. He went out with Mr. Kramer earlier. Some bad business, I hear."

Leonard followed Rob downstairs, through the mansion to the hologram room, which on Sundays was programmed as a chapel. Rob slipped into the family pew. Leonard sat in back with the other servants. Rob looked around for his brother's family. Doug had mentioned going to the mountains. Maybe they left early to get out of Sunday services.

Father stood at the podium, taking note of everyone. Other than on-duty security, all employees were required to attend chapel. In a pious voice, Greg announced, "We are gathered here this fine morning to give praise to our Lord and Father, to thank Him for His blessings, and to ask forgiveness for our sins. Furthermore, on this day we endow our son, Robert, who has completed his formal education, with the status of National Citizen of the United States of America. Robert, please stand and receive your ring."

Rob glanced at his left hand. How did Father get his National ring? When he pulled him out of bed? Slick! He joined his father on the dais.

Greg held up the ring. "With pleasure and pride, I, Douglas Gregory Hardman, Jr., confer the honor of National Citizenship upon my son, Robert Michael Hardman. Wear this ring with integrity and pride." He slipped it onto Rob's ring finger and hugged him. Under his breath, he hissed, "You're late. We had to delay the broadcast. The first part won't be live."

Everyone in the room applauded. Rob forced a smile and thanked them. Then he stepped down and hugged his mother. "How are you this morning?" he whispered.

She sobbed. "I'm so proud of you, Robbie!" Her secretary, Amaline, handed her a handkerchief.

Greg took his seat next to Amaline. From the stage, a gong sounded, organ music swelled, and the stage lit up with pillars of color. These condensed into larger-than-life 3D images. A woman in a shimmering gown threw out her arms with, "Welcome to the Sanctuary of the Loving Spirit! We come to you from beautiful downtown St. Louis!" Accolades boomed. "And may I present—the Apostle Raphael!"

A man in a golden robe took center stage. Rob zoned out, uttering the required responses. Apostle Rafael ran through his script of praises, admonitions, and readings from the Holy Bible and the writings of the Prophet Joachim. He marched across the stage, punctuating his words with grandiose gestures. A hymn was announced. Rob stood beside his mother, opened the virtual screen on his Nebula to display the hymn, and held it in front of her. Mother didn't sing, only uttered an occasional sound. *She's not having a good day.*

After his initiation into the Third Covenant, Rob had been schooled in the mysteries of the Loving Spirit. Before long, he'd become disillusioned by the hypocrisy. He attended chapel only because it was an unspoken requirement for anyone who wanted to advance in his father's world. His stomach rumbled, reminding him he'd missed breakfast.

Finally, sweating profusely, the image on stage declared intermission. Greg returned to the podium. After leading a prayer, he gave announcements, followed by orders, then admonitions and public shaming.

Rob squirmed. Who would be today's victim? Even he had been the subject of public chastisement a few times.

Father ordered Gracie, the head cook, to stand. "Grace Underwood, you have been accused of stealing food from the kitchen of Hardman Hall and removing it to your home. Is this true?"

"Yes, Mr. Hardman, but..."

"The Word of God says, 'Thou shall not steal.' Are you aware of that?"

"Yes, sir, but I didn't..."

"Furthermore, stealing is a crime, punishable by fines and/or imprisonment."

Blood drained from Gracie's face. "Mr. Hardman, please..."

"How shall I punish you?"

"I won't do it again."

The corners of Father's mouth rose in a predatory grin. Rob shuddered.

"We can be benevolent. We will not report this crime to the police. The cost of the stolen goods will be deducted from your wages and you will be put on probation. Any further transgressions will result in your dismissal from our service. Is that understood?"

Gracie sobbed. "Yes, sir, Mr. Hardman."

The transmission resumed. Greg took his seat as Apostle Raphael reappeared. Rob could hear Gracie's quiet weeping. He resolved to talk to her later.

The preacher droned on with exhortations to work hard, uphold the law, and be charitable to fellow Christians. Rob mentally grumbled retorts to the Apostle's advice to refrain from enabling those guilty of laziness, irresponsibility, and vice.

In truth, Gregory Hardman had made a fatal error in parenting Rob. He had focused his attention on Doug, the golden-haired heir apparent. After Rob's mother had become an invalid, servants assumed the parental role. Rob had been immersed in their worldviews. Their values had been instilled in his psyche, and his fine education hadn't been sufficient to counter them.

When Rob grew tired of mental debate with Raphael, his thoughts wandered in a more pleasant direction. Rosa, with her Latinx complexion and startling blue eyes, smiled into his mind. Where was she and what was she doing? He'd seen her and her parents at graduation but had no opportunity to talk to her. Her family wasn't invited to the reception, and Rob wouldn't have wanted her there anyway. His friends would not have treated her courteously.

* * *

Rosa Ortiz sat in the back seat of her parents' Runabout on their way home from church. She hadn't seen her brother Ramon since graduation last night. He'd skipped Mass but was supposed to join them for dinner.

Grandmother had stayed home that morning because she felt poorly, but when they returned, she was cooking dinner. Rosa's mother scolded her. "You go lie down and rest. Rosa and I will do this."

Instead, she took her crocheting to the front porch and sat in her rocking chair. Before long, she called out, "Ramon's here."

Rosa heard her brother whistling up the front steps. He kissed Grandmother on the cheek, then greeted his parents and sister with hugs. Rosa said, "You're full of affection today."

"Yes!" Ramon grinned. "I am full of love."

Mama narrowed her eyes. "Were you with that girl all night?"

"What if I was? We're going to get married."

Grandmother said, "Her father will not allow it."

"Who cares? We're both Citizens. We're free to do as we please."

Papa said, "Not all Citizens are equal, son. You have the right to marry anyone you choose, but that girl's family won't let her marry you."

"How can they stop us?"

Grandmother shuddered. "That girl will bring trouble."

Ramon's smile faded. He turned to Rosa and ruffled her hair. "When do you start work, sis?"

"Tomorrow. The summer semester starts next week."

"You'll be a great teacher."

"I hope so." She looked at her grandmother. The old woman's eyes were deep and dark. The peace that had followed Rosa home from Mass dissipated. *Something is amiss, and Grandmother knows.*

After dinner, Grandmother returned to the porch and Rosa joined her. It was quite hot, but the ceiling fans made a pleasant breeze. "Are the mosquitoes bad today?" Rosa asked.

"Not yet." Grandmother picked up her crocheting. "We could use rain. The cistern's getting low. Not a hurricane, though. We don't need one of those."

Rosa shivered. Hurricanes hadn't bothered her so much when she was a child. Her parents always assured her that their solid little house had weathered many a storm. She'd sleep contentedly under their watchful care, but they didn't sleep. Rosa would half-wake to hear them pacing. During the last tempest, she was at school in a safe building. She spent the hours worrying about her family.

Grandmother rocked to the rhythm of her crocheting. Rosa sighed. "It's been so long since I've had time to just sit out here and relax."

"You've been busy with school and work."

"Uh-huh. From now on, I'll only have work."

Grandmother looped yarn over her hook. "You won't be a teacher all your life." The hook pierced a stitch in the previous row.

Rosa shrugged. "I don't know. I enjoy teaching. I'll have to teach five years, anyway, to satisfy my scholarship. After that, if I go back to school, I could qualify for jobs that pay more."

Yarn over. Grandmother pulled a loop through the stitch. Yarn over, she pulled this through two loops on the hook. Yarn over. Through the last two loops. Stitch complete, Grandmother set the work in her lap and looked at Rosa. "You'll want to get married and have a family."

"There's no one I want to marry right now. And I need to finish five years of teaching before I can think about kids. It's a requirement."

"You'll still be young enough." Grandmother resumed crocheting.

Rosa relaxed into the afternoon. It was good to be home. Mass had been a welcome respite from the Sanctuary services she'd been required to attend at college. She surveyed the neighborhood. It was an old community, built in the early twenty-first century. Despite being in a low-lying area, it had been dubbed Palm Rise. The homes were well kept and roofed with solar panels. Many had vegetable gardens in raised beds, and some back yards housed chickens and the occasional pig.

Behind the houses were canals which once ran to an intercostal waterway. When the neighborhood was new, residents owned pleasure boats, but no one in Grandmother's memory had been able to afford one. The canals had deteriorated into long shallow ponds with no outlet to the ocean. Breeding grounds for mosquitoes, they were prone to flooding. Most of the houses had been lifted above the high water level and cisterns built under them to collect rainwater for washing and irrigation. Composting toilets provided fertilizer for vegetables.

Rosa looked down at their garden. Mostly, Grandmother tended it. What she grew supplemented the grocery bill. The spring vegetables had been harvested, but okra and sweet potatoes thrived in the heat.

Grandmother had lived here all her life. She used to tell Rosa what it was like when she was a child. Then, the house sat on the ground and was surrounded by trees, azaleas, and a lawn. Floods had killed the grass and flowers, which were replaced by salt-tolerant plants. Storms had destroyed the trees. The last one had crashed through the roof in a thunderstorm. Only palm trees remained. Rosa recalled watching them during a hurricane. They bent so far she was sure they'd snap, but they survived. If only all living things were as resilient as palm trees.

Rosa closed her eyes and listened to the neighborhood sounds. Children were playing outdoors. Families conversed on front porches. A radio played popular music. The sound of a hammer. In the distance, a mourning dove cried, "Who-i-who-who-who." The refrain lulled her into contentment.

Rosa yearned to someday buy a home here, close to family. Occasionally she looked at houses for sale and dreamed of living in one. But she was in no hurry to move out. Her added income would help buy things they presently couldn't afford. She looked at her left hand, at the new Citizenship ring. It represented much sacrifice on her parents' part. She'd told them she didn't need a ring, only the certification, but they wouldn't have it. Unable to go to college themselves, they banked on their children's accomplishments. Well, she had five years to work off before she could make other plans.

A bird flew onto the porch and disappeared into a corner of the ceiling. "It must have a nest up there," she said. Grandmother didn't reply. Rosa looked over at her. She was asleep.

Marriage. In college, Rosa had seldom dated. Scholarship students were discouraged from fraternizing, and a strict curfew was enforced. She'd been too busy, anyway. When not working, she studied. Occasionally she had lunch or attended evening functions with young men, but she'd built a wall around her heart because she couldn't afford the distraction of a boyfriend.

One man had made a chink in her wall—Rob. At the thought of him, she flushed with pleasure. Not exceptionally handsome, he had a pleasant face, brown hair, and hazel eyes. His wealth made him popular. Why did she like him? Perhaps because he was unattainable. She could indulge in a schoolgirl fantasy with no threat of complications, as long as she didn't let him know how she felt.

They'd met in their sophomore year. Rob was running for student government and asked her to vote for him. "I'm sorry," she said. "I'm a scholarship student. I can't vote."

Instead of turning away with indifference, he'd said, "That's something we should change. Why shouldn't you vote? You're part of the college community. In fact, most of you are smarter than we are." He smiled. "That's how you got in, right? We just ante up the money."

She had smiled back and felt a spark between them. She hoped he didn't notice.

Rob added scholarship suffrage to his platform. Needless to say, he lost the election, and scholarship students still couldn't vote at Hayes University.

They shared a few classes. He usually sat in the back row, she in front. He was a mediocre student with little desire to excel and a reputation as a playboy. When elected vice-president in their senior year, he told her, "I'll look important, but I won't have to work too hard." Being a son of Hardman Aquatics, which supplied potable water to much of the Southeast, his future was ensured.

They'd never dated, never kissed, not so much as held hands. Only talked. Not about their feelings—she wasn't sure how he felt about her, but they could talk about anything and everything else. Unlike most of his social class, Rob took her seriously. He showed interest in what she thought, respected her opinions, and didn't resent her superior academic achievement. He seemed intrigued by her lifestyle, her family, so different from his.

Why did he want her friendship? He had plenty of friends. Although class differences prevented their relationship from going further, she enjoyed his companionship. Rosa closed her eyes and allowed her heart to swell. She wondered where Rob was now and what he was doing.

CHAPTER 2

After the formal Sunday dinner, Rob tarried in the dining room, toying with a glass of wine while the servants picked up the remnants of the meal. The house seemed empty without Doug and his children. Mealtime conversation had been more strained than usual. Amaline said little, Mother even less, and Father wanted to talk about nothing but business.

Rob's eyes wandered to the expensive artwork adorning the walls, then above to the gallery of family portraits, which displayed the Hardman pedigree over the past two hundred years. When they were children, Father would drill Doug on the names and histories of each ancestor. Although Father ignored Rob, he always listened attentively. The men in the pictures were handsome and distinguished, but there was not a kind face among them.

One of the kitchen girls, Cisli, came in to remove the tablecloth. "Did you have enough to eat, Mr. Rob?"

"Yes." He handed her the empty wine glass. When she bent down to take it, her curls fell across her forehead and her blouse gaped open above rounded breasts. Rob stood up, encircled her in his arms, and murmured, "I could eat you, though."

She giggled. "Oh, Mr. Rob! I have work to do."

He whispered, "Where is everybody?"

"Ms. Hardman's sleeping. Mr. Hardman told Ms. Amaline to give her a sedative, then come to his office for further instructions."

Rob released Cisli. His father disgusted him. No one believed the story that Amaline Reed was his mother's secretary. She did handle social matters for Rhea and acted as companion and nurse, but her real role was that of Greg's mistress. Greg Hardman could never divorce his wife. Too much of his money was in her name. Even if he were widowed, which Rob suspected could be arranged, he couldn't marry Amaline without losing social standing. The only way to keep her on was to keep Mother alive. Rob thought about Cisli and other servant girls. True, he had his faults, but he didn't have a wife to cheat on.

Rob followed Cisli into the kitchen. "I need to talk to Gracie." The door to her office was closed. Rob knocked.

"Come in." Gracie wiped her eyes. "Oh, Mr. Rob, you don't need to knock."

"It's the polite thing. May I speak with you?"

She nodded and he sat down.

"Gracie, what was all that about?"

She stifled a sob. "Mr. Rob, I ain't no thief."

"I know."

"There's this old man lives by me, an old veteran. He has a pension but it ain't enough. He was starvin'. I started givin' him food, but things is so tight at my house, I couldn't give him much. An' I'm gone all week an' the rest of the family don't always remember to feed him. One day I was cleanin' up, puttin' scraps into the pigs' bucket, an' I thought, the old man would like this, so I put it in a dish to take to him." She looked up at Rob. "I didn't think it was stealin'."

"It's not."

"After that, I started takin' him food that was just goin' to the pigs anyway, and Mr. Hardman caught me. He wouldn't listen. He said the pigs need to eat, too."

Yeah, thought Rob. Pigs are more important than a starving human. "How much is Father fining you?"

"Five hundred dollars."

For pig food?

She began to cry. "I don't know how I'm gonna pay my bills and feed my family."

Rob had his own money, but if he transferred that sum to Gracie, Father would notice. "Gracie, if I give you cash, would that help?"

She nodded and whispered, "People where I live would rather have cash."

"When's your day off?"

"Tuesday."

"I'll get you some cash tomorrow. I can't help you feed the old man, but I can help you pay the fine."

"Are you sure, Mr. Rob?"

"Yes. See me before you go home tomorrow."

"Thank you, Mr. Rob!"

Now how do I get cash? Cash wasn't exactly illegal, but only the underground economy used it.

On the way to his room, Rob looked out the windows. A beautiful sunny day, but Sundays at home were boring. Father didn't allow work on the Sabbath. "You shall not do any work, or your son, or your daughter." He left out, "Or your manservant or your maidservant." His rationale was that they had a day off during the week.

It was a perfect day for horseback riding, but horses were included in, "Or your cattle." Rob enjoyed tennis but, with Doug and Little Greg gone, he had no partner.

Leonard was unpacking his belongings from school. Rob grabbed a T-shirt and shorts. "I'll take these."

"Don't you want them laundered first?"

"Why? They're clean." He sniffed to be sure. "By the way, Leonard, do you know how I can get my hands on some cash?"

Leonard froze. "Did you say cash? Money?"

"That's right."

"Why would I know about that?"

"Well, I just don't know who to ask." He lowered his voice. "Don't tell Father. I told Gracie I'd help her out."

"That's nice of you, Mr. Rob. When I'm home tomorrow, I'll ask around the neighborhood. Maybe I can find some. If I do, I'll call you. You won't tell on me, will you?"

"Of course not!"

After changing clothes, Rob went to his mother's sitting room. Rhea Hardman had never recovered from the nervous breakdown she'd suffered when her youngest daughter was killed. She wasn't asleep. She was fingering a frayed piece of cloth which she hastily stuffed behind the seat cushion.

"How are you feeling, Mother?"

"Fine."

Apparently, the sedative was too mild to knock her out. Rob was suspicious of the amount of medication they gave her. He sat beside her. "Mother, it seems like we haven't had much time to visit in—I don't know when."

She stroked her son's cheek. "You're so grown up, Robbie. Are you still in school?"

Rob bit his lip. "No, Mother. I graduated yesterday."

"Oh, that's right. I forgot." She'd been too ill to attend the ceremony.

"I won't be away so much now. I'll be able to spend more time with you."

"That's nice."

"Mother, it's a beautiful day. Let's take a walk outdoors."

"Oh, that would be nice. Let me ask Amaline."

"No, Mother. Amaline is your servant. You make the decisions."

She giggled like a little girl. "Of course."

On their way out, Rob peeked through the window of his father's office. Neither he nor Amaline were there. He and his mother went out the front door to the veranda. Rob inhaled the fresh air.

Mother sighed. "I need to rest a little. It's hot."

She sat on the glider. Rob turned on the cooling system, sat beside her, and gazed out at the park. The well-kept lawn was dotted with trees. The paved drive circled the fountain in front of the house, then wended among shrubs and statuary toward the gate. Brick pathways wound among flower beds. A mourning dove sounded its plaintive cry. Such an inviting place, Rob thought. It was a shame they seldom took time to enjoy it.

Despite the efforts of the grounds crew, the gardens fell short of perfection. Little bloomed in the late spring heat. Shrubs and forbs with variegated leaves provided color. Rob looked up at the trees. Even the most skilled gardener couldn't mask the damage to the canopy from last month's hurricane. It hadn't been a direct hit, but it spawned tornados, and one bounced over the Hardman estate, stripping branches nearly bare of leaves.

His mother pushed the glider back and forth with her feet. The gentle rhythm lulled Rob to sleep.

A shrill scream jerked him awake. Mother no longer sat beside him. Rob bounded down the veranda steps and raced to the back yard. There, his mother crouched on the ground, wailing and tearing up sod with her fingers. Servants flew from all directions, reaching her before Rob did. Gracie pulled Rhea to her feet and enveloped her in a tight hug.

Rob said, "Let me," and took Mother into his arms.

"What the hell!" Father shouted from an upstairs window. "Who let her out?"

In no time, Amaline hurried out the back door, buttoning her bodice as she ran. "I'm sorry, Ms. Hardman." She touched Rob's elbow. "Mr. Rob, please let me."

By now Father had joined them. "What do you mean, leaving her alone?" He slapped Amaline across the face.

"I'm sorry, Mr. Hardman. I'll take care of her now."

"Father! It's not her fault! It's mine. Mother was with me."

Greg snarled, "I'll deal with you later. Get out of my sight."

Rob reached the gate to the swimming pool before he noticed how he was trembling. He fumbled with the latch but couldn't get it open.

Sinking to the ground, he leaned against the fence and forced himself to breathe deeply until his heartrate slowed. He wiped sweat from his eyes and thought about going somewhere cool.

"Mr. Rob…"

A strong dark hand reached down. Andreu, the chauffeur, pulled Rob to his feet.

"Let's get you somewheres to cool off."

Andreu deftly opened the gate and led Rob to the gazebo. Rob sat down and Andreu switched on the cooling fan.

"I'm sorry, Andreu. We were sitting on the porch and I fell asleep. I didn't notice her leaving."

"It happens. Whenever she can, she gets away and goes to that spot. Don't matter who's with her. She even gets away from Mr. Hardman. That's why Amaline doesn't like her to go outside."

"But she needs to get out once in a while."

Andreu nodded.

Rob drew a deep breath. "Andreu, were you here the day it happened?"

"No, sir. It was my day off."

"I was at Aunt Edwina's. They didn't tell me anything until I got home. They didn't even bring me home for the funeral."

"You were just a little boy."

"I still don't understand what happened. Nobody'll give me a straight answer."

Andreu cleared his throat. "All I know is what I was told."

"That the dogs got her."

"That's all I know."

Rob nodded.

"I beg your pardon, Mr. Rob, but there are things I need to do before the evening service."

When Rob returned to the house, he looked at "that spot." Other than a few pieces of recently shredded grass, there was nothing to see.

It was an unremarkable piece of lawn, but somehow his mother always found it.

The story given to the public was that Rhea Hardman suffered from some unspecified physical malady. She hadn't always been like this. In the depths of Rob's memory lived a mother who was cheerful and outgoing. Also in those depths dwelt a little girl whom Mother doted on. A little sister who was here, then gone.

Rob once asked his brother what became of Michaela. With an adolescent sneer, Doug said, "We had watch dogs. Mean ones. One day she was in the yard by herself and they got out of their cage. They ate her."

Rob had suffered several nights of bad dreams before he asked his sister Sophia.

"Don't believe everything Doug tells you. He wasn't even home that day. Neither was I. All I know is, the dogs killed her, but they didn't eat her. Mother found her body. That's why she took it so hard."

* * *

Rosa heard the family's phone ring. Grandmother said, "Rosa, it's for you. Your classmate, Salli Stubens."

"Thanks." She opened the screen and smiled. "Hi, Salli. How are you?"

"On top of the world. Rosa, you should get a Nebula. You're a Citizen now."

"I don't have enough money. Maybe when I get paid."

"I can help you get an advance."

"No, that's okay. I'll wait."

"Hey, Daddy told me you're going to teach at Bayview Academy. You know he owns it, don't you?"

"Yes."

"Why didn't you tell me? This is so exciting! I'll be running the school someday. Daddy's going to start my training tomorrow. You're coming in tomorrow, right?"

"Yes."

"Sweet! We can do lunch. Why don't you come home with me afterward? We can spend a few days together before summer school starts."

"I have to work all week."

"Well, then, you can come home with me for the weekend."

"Sure. That'll be nice."

After they hung up, Rosa's frowned. Salli would be her boss someday. How would that affect their friendship?

At first, Rosa had viewed Salli as a spoiled snob. Though stylishly pretty, blue-eyed and blond, Salli was emotionally needy and struggled with her weight. She had no friends among her sorority sisters. Rosa was used to being looked down on by those girls, but she was surprised to see them treat one of their own that way.

One day after statistics class, Rosa had found Salli in the restroom, crying,

Salli wiped her nose with her hand. "I just can't get statistics. I'm going to fail!"

Rosa handed her some toilet paper.

Salli cleaned her face, then washed her hands. "I'm terrible at math. Statistics is even worse." She sobbed. "You don't seem to have any trouble with it."

"It's not easy, but I get it."

"I wish I could."

"I can help you."

"Really?"

"Sure. I don't have another class until this afternoon. Let's go to the library."

"Thank you so much! I can pay you to tutor me."

Rosa shook her head. "That's not necessary. I'm studying to be a teacher. This will give me practice."

With Rosa's tutelage, Salli passed statistics. Their time together morphed into friendship. The other girls in Salli's house, at first indignant at this intrusion of a scholarship student into their domain, grew to tolerate Rosa, even treat her with respect.

Salli introduced Rosa to a world she otherwise would never have known. Some weekends, Rosa went to Salli's house. But when Rosa returned the invitation, Salli declined. Her father wouldn't let her.

Salli never resented Rosa's superior academic ability, but a professional relationship would be a different matter. Rosa hadn't asked to teach at Bayview—she'd been assigned, and she'd have to make the best of it. She wanted a Nebula, a wrist device with expandable virtual screens, a connection to the wider world, but she would not accept a salary advance on the basis of friendship with Salli. She'd play by the rules.

* * *

Rob dared not miss the evening service, or there'd be hell to pay. He showered and dressed as casually as permitted. Quietly, he entered the chapel, avoiding eye contact with his father. Mother was absent—no surprise. She was probably heavily sedated. Amaline sat stiffly in the pew, makeup covering a bruise on her face. Rob was grateful that Amaline, not his mother, was the target of Father's anger.

Only servants who'd been on duty that morning were required to attend the second service. With the smaller crowd, Father didn't bother to preach, but he took the opportunity to "deal with" Rob. "Robert Hardman, stand up and face me."

Rob stood, fists clenched behind his back.

Father started out softly. "I am disappointed in you, son. You know how fragile your mother is." His voice rose. "Yet today, without permission, you took her outside the house and allowed her to wander around without supervision. And she suffered. Greatly!" He pounded the podium with his fist. "You may think you're grown now, but you lack the judgement!" Pound. "Knowledge!" Pound. "And understanding!" Pound. "To make decisions about your mother." Pound. "Only I have that authority. Only I can delegate that authority. I have delegated some of my authority to Ms. Reed, but it'll be a cold day in Hell before I delegate any authority to you!" Pound.

Music softly interrupted.

"Now take your seat."

Amaline stared ahead woodenly.

When Apostle Raphael appeared on the virtual stage, Rob tuned him out, but his mind remained active, thinking of the many ways he could, or wished he could, exact revenge on his father.

CHAPTER 3

Rosa woke at 5:30. Her parents drove her to Bayview Academy before they went to work at the uniform factory. She was reminded of her schoolgirl days. In fact, she fidgeted in the back seat like a schoolgirl. But now she was to be the teacher. She arrived early and stood at the front door until a custodian let her in.

"I'm Rosa Ortiz. I'm a new teacher."

"Yes, ma'am. I can tell."

Rosa looked down at her uniform and laughed at herself.

"The office will give you the door codes, so you can let yourself in after this."

Rosa walked through the halls until she found a classroom with her name on the door. With a thrill, she entered and felt immediately at home.

The building might have been new some eighty years ago, but it was in better shape than the schools she'd attended before her test scores qualified her for private school. The classroom size was the same, though, forty-eight desks with older model workstations. Much of the instruction and testing would be electronic. She was expected to monitor the students' progress and provide enrichment. From experience, she knew maintaining discipline would be her greatest challenge. If she could keep them interested, they would be easier to manage.

Voices down the hall told her staff had arrived. Rosa reported to the office where Ms. Green, the secretary, gave her the codes for the doors and the in-house network.

Mr. Hadley, the principal, convened staff for orientation. He concluded with, "Someone from Corporate will be here this afternoon. I'll meet with each of you Friday morning to approve your lesson plans."

Rosa returned to her classroom. She was to teach American History, but which history should she teach? The textbook version, certainly, but would she have the nerve to teach the true history?

When she was in tenth grade, Rosa's teacher, Ms. Barton, occasionally digressed from the official version to drop hints about what had actually occurred. Rosa hung on every word. One day, Ms. Barton said, "Rosa, we have a little history club that meets at my house Tuesday evenings. Would you like to come?"

A new world opened for Rosa. Ms. Barton's house had a room dedicated to study. Shelves of old print books lined the walls. A handful of students, mostly from previous years with Ms. Barton, gathered to read and discuss the untold version of the past. Books on science and other disciplines were included, because their histories were pertinent to the flow of time. Ms. Barton let the young people take some of her books home to read, but others didn't leave her study.

She swore Rosa to secrecy. "What we're doing isn't illegal, but were the wrong people to learn about my books and what I teach here, there could be consequences."

Rosa gasped. "Would you go to jail?"

"Probably not, but my books would be confiscated, and I'd lose my job."

Rosa faithfully attended meetings of the history club until she went to college. Ms. Barton's inspiration led Rosa to major in history and education.

"Be aware," Ms. Barton cautioned, "you'll be fed the official version and you'll have to dig to find the truth."

Rosa longed to tell her charges what she knew, but how much dared she risk?

* * *

Monday, Rob woke again to banging on his door. Sunlight filtered through the blinds. He reached for his Nebula to check the time, but the battery was dead, even though he'd left it on the charger.

"Command: Open blinds." Nothing happened. Was the power off again? More pounding. Where was Leonard? Oh, it was his day off. Now Father was yelling. Rob got up to let him in.

Father gave him a going-over with his eyes. "It's after nine."

"My Nebula didn't wake me. What happened?"

"Some problem with a battery switch. Phillip's looking into it. Get dressed and come down to breakfast. We have business to tend to."

Father turned and left. Rob muttered, "Good morning to you, too." He dressed and went down to the breakfast room. While he wolfed down a cold breakfast—no coffee—the ventilation system shuddered and the lights came on.

Father was in his office, talking with Phillip, the household bursar.

"We don't have any spare components," Phillip said. "Haven't been able to order any. I took this one out of the stable. If another one goes, we'll have to get one from another building."

After Phillip left, Father turned to Rob. "When we're done here, I want you to locate a supply of Syntat switches. I don't care if you find them on the black market."

"Yes, sir." Father must be desperate to resort to black market goods. "Um, for that, I may need cash."

"That can be arranged. Now look at this." Greg turned to his wall screen. "Command: Storm." The wall lit up with a satellite image of the tropical Atlantic. Halfway between Africa and Florida swirled an angry mass of clouds with a clearly defined eye.

Rob froze. "What's the projected path?"

"Command: Storm track." A wide red arrow appeared, stretching in an arc from the ocean to Alabama. "It could to go right through here."

"When?"

"Depends. It's about a week out, unless it picks up speed."

Rob swallowed. "I hadn't heard about this one."

"It wouldn't hurt to check the news once in a while."

"Usually someone mentions things like this."

"It hasn't been released to the public yet."

"Why not? People need to prepare."

Greg snorted. "The minute they're told, they panic. They clog the roads, create chaos."

What about the chaos when they have no time to evacuate? Rob kept his mouth shut.

Father switched to another map. "We need to protect our holdings. The water plants on the coast will be shut down. Maybe the ones inland as well. I'll let Doug handle that." He looked at Rob. "The beach resort will be your inheritance. I want you to go over there today and see that it's prepared for high winds and storm surge."

Rob nodded. At last, Father was giving him some responsibility.

"Also, Mort has a school he wants to sell me. I'd like to close the deal before the storm hits. It's located inland, so it shouldn't sustain much damage."

"Why do you want another school? You always complain they're not profitable."

"This one could be, if managed right. It's near the Osceola Forest. We could convert it to a trade school for forestry workers. Tomorrow we're playing golf with Mort to work out the details."

Father didn't even like golf. "You're going to Mort's tomorrow?"

"No, you and I are playing virtual golf with him."

Rob grimaced. He hated golf even more than Father did.

"Whether you like it or not, golf is good for business. The schools will be your inheritance. You need to be in on the deal." He turned away. "Andreu will take you to the coast. You know what needs to be done."

"Yes, sir." He'd shadowed Father in the past to prepare for hurricanes. "By the way, what happened yesterday morning? Leonard said you and Kramer had some bad business to tend to."

His father didn't turn around or look at him. "Nothing that concerns you."

Rob shrugged. He returned to his room for his Nebula. Then he went to the breakfast room for coffee. It hit his stomach like lead. Why did hurricanes frighten him? He usually slept through them or watched their fury from the safety of the house. But as a child, he'd picked up on the servants' anxiety and listened to their stories of death and destruction.

He poured a glass of orange juice for his mother. He liked to see her in the morning before the drugs took over. Amaline answered his knock.

"Is that Robbie? Let him in, please." Rhea was still in her nightgown.

"Mother, I brought you some juice."

Amaline interrupted. "She hasn't taken her medication yet."

"She can take it with her juice." Rob took his mother's hands. "How are you feeling this morning?"

Her eyes filled with tears. "I miss her so."

"I know. So do I." Rob embraced her. "Mother, I'm going to the Dongtian today to do a few things for Father."

"Oh, Robbie, please be careful!"

"I will. Andreu's going with me." He kissed her cheek. "I'll see you later. I love you."

Andreu had the car in front of the house. He opened the back door for Rob. Once outside the gate, Rob said, "Andreu, pull over. I want to sit in the front seat where we can talk."

"Yes, sir."

From the passenger seat, Rob said, "This is better. I don't know why Father insists on your driving me. I know how to drive a car."

"It's a dangerous world out there."

"It's not like I haven't had self-defense training."

Andreu smiled. "Well then, we're doubly safe."

They passed a group of vagrants. To Rob, they didn't look dangerous. "Speaking of safety, what about that hurricane?"

"What hurricane?"

"I think it's named 23A6."

"A new one?"

"Yes. It's a few days off the coast, probably headed our way. A big one. You'll be safe at Hardman Hall, but I know you have family. I don't know when they plan to announce it to the public."

Andreu grunted. "I may be showing my paranoia, but it seems they do that deliberately."

"Why?"

"So they can cull out some of them on the bottom."

Such rumors weren't new. "Maybe they're unsure of the storm track and don't want to alarm everyone unnecessarily."

Andreu remained silent for a moment. "Still, I appreciate you telling me. I'll let my people know."

On the turnpike, Andreu relaxed and let the radar pilot take over. Rob looked out the window and watched scenery fly by. The road was built for speed and, since it required a Sharepass, there was little traffic. They passed agricultural fields, mostly fallow for the summer, and pastures with cattle. As they approached the city, rows of modest houses gave way to apartment buildings and a few factories. Beyond a stretch of parkland were business towers and, near the St. Johns Channel, luxury apartments. The highway arched over the water. A handful of ships and barges cruised below. "Somebody told me this was once a freshwater river," Rob said.

"Yes, sir. That was a hundred years ago."

On the other side of the channel, houses stood above the marsh on pilings. Rob could see the muddy bottom. "The tide must be out."

"Yes, sir."

"Where do your relatives live, Andreu?"

He tilted his head. "Upriver mostly. But it's low lying. I suspect they'll want to evacuate."

"Where will they go?"

"We got family up in Georgia. High and dry. If they don't have trouble getting across the border."

"Why should they? Aren't they Citizens?"

"Mostly. But not National Citizens like you."

Rob didn't ask what would happen if they couldn't leave before the storm. If he were master of Hardman Hall, he'd welcome Andreu's people to shelter in the outbuildings, but Father was boss.

"I know a girl who lives around here, in Palm Rise. I think she'll be okay. Last month, when A5 hit, she said their house was old but it'd been through lots of storms and she wasn't worried about her family." He glanced at his Nebula. *I could look up her address.* "Maybe next time we come this way, I'll stop in and see her. You wouldn't tell Father, would you?"

"Not if he don't ask."

Rob chuckled. Gregory Hardman seldom asked. He just gave orders.

In the distance, the blue ocean spread wide, giving no hint of the monster storm less than a week away. The causeway descended to ground level. Ahead rose a pastel pink tower, a castle on the sand, Dongtian Palace. Every time Rob saw it from this perspective, it gave him a thrill.

The hotel had been built by the Chinese years ago, in their classical style with columns and friezes, originally red and gold. When foreign investors had been forced out of the country, the first Douglas Gregory Hardman had bought it and repainted it to appeal to American tastes.

The resort covered one hundred acres. Besides a private beach, it had three swimming pools and other amenities, including a school for children of guests who came at the beginning of winter and stayed until spring. There was little business the rest of the year. The Dongtian closed the first official day of hurricane season, May first, and didn't reopen until Thanksgiving. This year they'd closed early due to the pre-season storm.

The expanse of green surrounding the high-rise was irrigated with water from a Hardman desalinization plant. The golf course was planted with salt-tolerant grass. Wind-stunted cedars and oaks provided shade over promenades, and solar panels shaded the tennis and handball courts.

The gate sensor recognized the Hardman car and opened for them. Although the resort was closed for summer, a skeleton staff remained. Angus Wilson, the manager, came out to greet Rob and ushered him into a cool lounge. Andreu drove the car to the parking garage.

"Can I get you anything?" Angus asked.

"A cold beer would be nice."

A maid waiting in a doorway disappeared and came back with a beer for Rob and a glass of water for Angus. "What brings you here today, Mr. Rob?"

"Are you aware a hurricane may be headed our way?"

Angus choked on his water. "Hurricane?"

"It could miss us, or it could be a direct hit. Either way, we need to prepare."

"Yes, sir. I know what to do. But it would be helpful if I could view the forecasts. I don't have access, you know."

Rob took off his Nebula, opened it, and expanded a virtual screen. "You get decent reception here, don't you?"

"Yes, sir. For the guests."

Rob brought up the weather map and handed the device to Angus.

"Holy Sanctuary! Um, I beg pardon, Mr. Rob."

"No offense taken." They studied the projections.

"It's gonna be a bad one."

Rob nodded. "It's a Category 4 right now, but it might strengthen." Rob closed the screen and returned the Nebula to his wrist. They spent the next hour going over what needed to be done. Angus drew up an order for supplies, and Rob approved it.

"Mr. Rob, I wish I could get this weather information after you leave. It would help to know what to expect. If it hits at high tide, I don't know if this building will survive."

"It was built to withstand a Cat 7." Forty-foot pilings under the foundation, reinforced concrete and windows... Rob looked out past the white sand to the rolling surf. Despite the strength of the building, he wouldn't want to weather such a storm here. "If it looks like it might be too dangerous, I want you and the rest of the staff to get out, go somewhere safe."

"What would Mr. Hardman say?"

"I'm making this decision. If it gets that bad, your staying here won't save anything. I don't want anyone's death on my conscience. Is the communications center operational?"

"Yes, sir, but I don't have access."

"Well, I do."

They went upstairs. Angus unlocked the room. Rob turned on a console, entered his thumbprint, and brought up the weather site. "I'll leave this running for you. Just don't tell anyone."

"I won't. I don't want to get in trouble."

"Can you think of anything else I can do here?"

"No, sir."

"If you do, call me."

"Thanks, Mr. Rob."

Back downstairs, Rob couldn't help noticing anxious faces among the staff. When Andreu drove him through the gate, Rob said, "You told them about the storm?"

Andreu straightened his back. "Yes, sir, I did."

"Good. By the way, do you know how I can get my hands on some cash?"

Andreu cut his eyes at Rob and grinned. "I might could find out."

"I promised Gracie I'd make up for Father's fining her. She's off tomorrow. I wish I could get some today."

"How much you want?"

"Can I get seven hundred?"

"I think so. There'll be a fee."

"That's okay."

The car drove silently for several miles. Then, without a word, Andreu disengaged the radar pilot and exited the turnpike. He winked at Rob and said, "I think we have a low tire. I'd better check." He drove down a side road, turned into a lane, and stopped before a vacant store.

"Here?" Rob asked.

"Not exactly. Let me check the tires." Andreu walked slowly around the car, making a show of examining each wheel. Then he stretched his back, walked around to Rob's door, and opened it. "Let me do the talkin'."

Rob felt like a puppy, following Andreu across the street and down the block. They turned onto a path between two houses and into a backyard where a man wearing only shorts sat under the shade of a tree.

"Mornin'," he said. The man studied Rob while he and Andreu made small talk. Finally, he said, "How much?"

"Seven."

"Fee's twenty percent."

Andreu looked at Rob, who shrugged his shoulders. "Okay."

The moneychanger pulled a banking device out of his pocket and handed it to Rob.

"Make the transfer," Andreu said. "Plus a hundred forty."

Rob did so. After he handed the device back, the man studied the screen, pocketed the instrument, and went into the house.

"Can he hack my account?" Rob whispered.

"Possibly, but he won't. Bad for business. Besides, you'd lose money, but he'd get locked up for life."

Rob watched the back door. The house listed on its foundation. The roof and siding had been repaired with scraps of metal and wood. The yard was covered with wedelia. "Does he really live here?"

"Maybe. But it might just be his business location."

The man emerged with his hands in his pockets. He pulled out a paper sack and handed it to Rob.

"Count it when we get in the car," Andreu said. Before they left, he told the man. "By the way, there's a bad hurricane comin'. Less than a week out. Spread the word."

For the first time, the man showed emotion. His eyes flashed and he said, "Thanks."

Rob couldn't get back to the car soon enough, but he made himself match Andreu's leisurely pace. He wasted no time counting the money. "It's all here."

"Of course."

"I wonder how soon Father will discover this."

Andreu smiled. "It'll show up on your records as some kind of investment. He won't suspect a thing."

Rob examined the bills. Other than being dirty and crumbled, they looked just like the ones pictured in history books. "Andreu, how did you know where to go?"

"Mr. Rob, you don't need to know everything."

He was glad Andreu told the moneychanger about the hurricane. When he got home, Rob sought out Gracie and slipped her five hundred dollars. "Let me know if you need anything else."

"Thank you, Mr. Rob!"

He wished he could do more.

* * *

At Rosa's school, a staff assembly was called when the representatives from Corporate arrived, none other than Salli Stubens and her father. Mr. Stubens approached Rosa, took her hand in both of his, and said, "Good afternoon, Ms. Ortiz. It's a pleasure to have you join our faculty."

Inwardly, Rosa squirmed. Salli, however, maintained an aura of professionalism, pretending not to know Rosa personally. After Mr.

Stubens welcomed the staff to the new semester, Salli gave a prepared statement about the mission of Bayview Academy and a pep talk on what a wonderful semester they were about to embark upon.

During Salli's talk, Rosa heard a soft snore. The teacher next to her had fallen asleep. Rosa nudged her.

"Thanks," the woman whispered. "I've heard this speech so many times I have it memorized."

Afterward, Salli managed to break away from her father to visit Rosa's classroom. "Rosa, I'm so glad you'll be working with me. Are you going home with me Friday?"

"Yes," Rosa said. "I can leave after Mr. Hadley approves my lesson plans."

"Good. I'll come for you."

Rosa had qualms about the weekend. Salli treated her almost like a sister when she visited, and Salli's mother was gracious. Salli's father was another story. Rosa recalled the one time she was alone with the man. He'd put his arm across her shoulders and said, "You're such a pretty girl. And rather smart, too. I could set you up in a good job."

Rosa had shrugged her shoulders, but he continued to hang on.

"No, thank you, Mr. Stubens. My advisor will assign me a teaching job when I graduate. I need to teach five years to satisfy my scholarship."

"Maybe something can be arranged there, too." He'd given her a little squeeze.

Rosa tried to wriggle away, but he held her too tightly.

"How about marriage? I could introduce you to some suitable prospects."

At that moment, Salli entered the room, saving Rosa from further embarrassment. After this, Rosa was careful never to be alone with him. She suspected he had orchestrated her assignment to a school he owned.

After school, Rosa waited an hour for her parents to pick her up. When they arrived, she said, "I'm sorry you have to go so far out of your way for me."

"There's nothing else to do," Papa said. "We can't afford another car."

Mama sighed. "When I was your age, we still had public transportation. Oh, well, it's a thing of the past."

"Humph," Papa replied. "Anything to help working people is a thing of the past."

CHAPTER 4

Rob woke on time Tuesday, but apparently not soon enough for Father, who barged in while Rob was showering and shouted, "We meet with Mort in twenty minutes!"

"I'll be down in a few."

Leonard laid out golfing clothes. Instead, Rob dressed in jeans and a tee shirt. "I'll be damned if I dress for golf when we're only playing over the TV."

Father scowled at Rob when he entered the breakfast room.

Rob poured himself a cup of coffee. "How's Mother?"

"As usual, I assume. Hurry up. It's almost time."

"I'm sure Mort can wait a few minutes."

"He wants to finish before it gets too hot. Besides, punctuality is good business."

Rob gulped down a small omelet and followed his father to the holo room, which had been reprogrammed to display a tee box. Mort lived in a community that encircled a golf course. Rob hoped the morning would heat up quickly so the game would be short. Father and Mort didn't compete to win. Both knew Mort was the better player.

Mort's image appeared. "Hello, Greg. Robbie."

"Morning, Mort."

Mort teed off and his ball arched over the greenway. Next, Greg. The program sent his virtual ball where it would have gone if they'd been on the course. Rob's first ball flew nearly as far as Mort's. He glanced at his father to judge his reaction. Greg showed none. Mort walked down the greenway while the program moved for the Hard-mans.

At the second putting green, a large area of grass was brown and shriveled. Mort grunted. "The desalination plant went amok a few days ago and they watered the course, anyway. With well water."

"What made it go down?" Greg asked.

"Faulty part and there wasn't a replacement. They had to fly one in."

With a grin, Greg said, "I know a reliable company that could supply you with fresh water."

"The homeowners insist on having our own."

Rob spoke up. "Why don't you plant salt-tolerant grass? Then you could use well water."

"Because Louisiana Bio holds the patent to the grass," Mort answered. "They'd charge us an arm and a leg." One of Mort's companies was a competitor.

Mort shouted off stage. "Tim, get your ass over here and do something about this disaster."

Tim appeared with a small rake and smoothed the dead grass as much as possible.

"That'll do," Mort said.

Greg and Mort talked about Olustee Academy. Rob spoke only when his father asked for his input. They discussed terms and price and shook hands, virtually.

"I'll finalize the agreement and send it to you when I get back to my office," Mort said. "I'm trying to get out of the education business. It's too much of a headache."

The sun climbed and the sky grew hazy. Mort sweated profusely. Finally, he said, "That's enough for me today. What about you two?"

"Well, I hate to see you suffer." Father winked at Rob.

"I'm good," Rob said.

Father shut down the holo program and they put away their clubs. "After Mort sends me the agreement and the lawyers look it over, I'll have you sign it with me. Meantime, I need to get with Doug about our coastal plants."

"Yes, sir."

* * *

Rosa carried an armload of antique books to school. Ms. Barton, her high school history teacher, had given her one as a graduation present. Folded up in this precious tome had been a list of out-of-print volumes of forgotten history. All through college, Rosa had added to her collection. Mostly through word of mouth, she located old book collectors and junk stores which yielded one or two treasures at a time, paid for in cash. A few were history textbooks, but many were writings on events of the past. Rosa had been surprised that some of the books Ms. Barton listed were novels. None were available in electronic form today. Ms. Barton had strongly cautioned Rosa against searching for them on the internet, lest she attract attention as a possible dissenter.

Ms. Barton kept a small shelf of books in her classroom, "To show students a piece of history," and Rosa had always dreamed of doing the same. So Tuesday morning, she took the least controversial ones with her. When Mr. Hadley stopped by her classroom, he noticed her books.

"What have you here, Ms. Ortiz?"

"Old books about history."

He thumbed through one. "I have no objection to these books myself, but you need to be careful. Sometimes Corporate sends inspectors. If they find something they consider non-educational, they might confiscate them." He lowered his voice almost to a whisper. "What's worse, if they consider them subversive, your job could be in jeopardy." He returned the book to Rosa.

She hugged it to her chest. Her heart pounded. "Thank you, Mr. Hadley. I guess I'll take them back home."

He nodded.

After he left, Rosa glanced at the book—*Emily Nugent*, a novel about a young woman in the early twentieth century who joined the suffragette movement. This story had been an eye opener. Although fiction, the novel revealed a society in which only men could vote and it showed the struggles of women and other marginalized groups to attain the same privilege, education and property notwithstanding.

From here, Rosa's research had uncovered a thread of history spanning the past century and more. Citizenship gave one the right to vote, but citizenship had been eroded by a series of laws. Few law-abiding people had argued with felons being denied voting privileges. Or the mentally ill, which eventually included anyone suffering from depression or learning or behavior difficulties. That led to educational requirements and property ownership. Rosa looked at her Citizenship ring and wondered if she should be proud or ashamed. Even she was restricted. Lacking National Citizenship, she couldn't vote in national elections.

She returned the book to her bag. As she took each one off the shelf, Rosa gazed at it briefly, as a mother would a precious child. When the shelf was empty, she set the bag on the floor beneath her desk.

* * *

Rob called Angus Wilson at the resort.

"Is anything wrong, Mr. Rob?"

"No, Angus. I just wanted to see how things were going."

"We're moving everything we can up to the second floor and shuttering the windows. I've ordered more supplies to tide us over in case we can't get out after the storm. I hope that's okay."

"Of course it is. Send me the voucher and I'll approve it."

"Mr. Rob, once we get everything taken care of, some of the staff want to go home to their families. Will that be all right? Not everybody. There'll be enough of us here to run things."

"Why, certainly."

Angus hesitated and looked down.

"What is it?"

"Um, some of us have families whose houses aren't strong enough ..."

"Angus, if anyone needs shelter, bring them over. As long as there are no criminal elements, that's fine."

"Thank you, Mr. Rob. That's a big worry off my chest."

"But if you have to abandon the resort, do you have somewhere to go?"

"We'll manage somehow."

After he hung up, Rob wondered what his father's policy had been in such circumstances. Well, he was running Dongtian now. How could his employees take care of the place if he didn't take care of them?

He turned to his next task, locating Syntat switches, a vital component of the solar electric system. Yesterday, Rob had searched the internet for a supplier. Syntat had gone out of business and no one manufactured their components due to patent restrictions. Surely someone had a stash of them, waiting to capitalize on the need. So far, no luck. What about a substitute? Rob wished he knew more about electrical engineering. Didn't Hardman Enterprises employ engineers?

Rob called the personnel department. Yes, they had a consultant but he was on vacation. Rob left a message that he had an urgent need.

* * *

A message came to Rosa's workstation, "Ms. Ortiz, you have a visitor."

She froze when she saw Salli's father waiting in the office.

"Ms. Ortiz, I'd like to see how you've set up your classroom."

"Y...yes, sir." Rosa turned a pleading eye to Ms. Green, who surreptitiously nodded. Rosa led Mr. Stubens to her room. When she heard Ms. Green's footsteps following, she relaxed. She opened the door for Mr. Stubens. As he entered the room, he put his arm around Rosa's shoulders, pulling her in. Rosa stepped away from him and gestured around. "What do you think?" She had taken pains to display maps and pictures of historical figures in a way that would spark the students' curiosity.

Mr. Stubens looked at Rosa, not the room. "Very clever." He started to move toward her when Ms. Green came in. "Sorry to bother you," she said, "but I need to check your net connection. It doesn't seem to be working." She pretended to pay no attention to them but made herself busy at Rosa's workstation.

Mr. Stubens made small talk and kept glancing at Ms. Green, who appeared to be having difficulty with the connection. Finally, he told Rosa goodbye.

After he left, Rosa let out her breath. "Thank you so much."

Ms. Green stood up. "No problem. That man makes a nuisance of himself to every new female teacher we get. If he comes when I'm not here, make some pretense to ask one of the staff a question so they can chaperone you. I'll remind everyone to be on the lookout. We don't want to make him mad, but we don't want to feed him victims, either."

Rosa had second thoughts about going to Salli's that weekend, but she assured herself he was less likely to harass her around his wife and daughter.

* * *

Having completed the tasks he'd set out to accomplish, Rob went down to his father's office. Father was busy talking to Doug and waved him away.

Rob's Nebula chimed. His friend Gene appeared on the screen. "Hey, Rob, what'cha doin' today?"

"I was just thinking about that. Want to join me for a game of tennis?"

"No, I don't have time to go out to your place. My old man has plans for me later. Why don't you come here? My sister has a friend over. We can play doubles."

"Sounds great. I'll see you in about an hour."

Rob walked to the garage where Andreu was cleaning a windshield. "Hello, Mr. Rob. What can I do for you?"

"I want to go into the city."

"I haven't heard from Mr. Hardman yet, what he wants me to do today."

"That's okay. I'll take the Sparkler and drive myself."

"Well, I'll have to run it by Mr. Hardman."

"Damn it, Andreu, I'm an adult, and I know how to drive."

"Yes, but if I let you take it without your father's permission, he could right out fire my ass."

"You're right. I'll go ask him." But Father wasn't in his office. "Shit on this! I'm a full Citizen. I can do as I please."

Andreu was in his alcove doing pullups. Rob walked behind the garage where the sports car sat in the sun. The gage showed full charge. The electric motor was as silent as a summer breeze, but when he reached the front gate, Father stood there with his hands on his hips. "Where do you think you're going with my car?"

"Into town."

"Not today and not on your own. Take that car back to the garage."

"Why?"

"Because I said so."

Rob's gut twisted into knots. "Gene invited me to play tennis. I've checked on the resort and put out feelers for the Syntat switches. If you don't have anything else for me to do, I'll be back later this afternoon." He nudged the car forward but his father didn't budge.

Rob jumped out and stood up. "I'm an adult. I've got the right to come and go without asking your permission for every little thing."

"As long as you're under my roof, you will obey. Now put my car back."

Rob slammed his fist on the hood. "Maybe I don't want to be under your roof anymore!"

"Fine. There's the gate. But you're not taking my car. Nothing but the clothes on your back." With that, he commanded, "Gate open."

Rob looked through the gateway to a world not entirely controlled by his father. He took off running. Seconds before he reached it, the gate slammed shut.

Father jumped into the car. "Get to your room. I don't want to see you again until you come to your senses." He spun the Sparkler around and returned it to the garage.

Rob stood in the driveway, clenching his fists until his palms bled. He stalked through the grounds, kicking anything in his path. He looked up at the fence. His father had surely locked all the gates and was probably monitoring him on the surveillance system. Rob wondered if he could find a way over the wall despite the electrified razor wire concealed along the top. He would not be a prisoner in his own home.

His home? Everything was in Father's name. Did he have any say over his own possessions? His own life?

Rob glanced at the sky above the fence. What would it be like to be out there with only the clothes on his back? Pure freedom! But at what cost? And what about Mother—he couldn't leave her in the clutches of that loveless man. Why did he let Father reduce him to such infantile frailty?

Rob returned to his room. Why wasn't he allowed to take the car? Because Father needed to maintain control. Rob had seen him treat Doug the same way, even after Doug was married. As heir apparent, Doug had no choice but to live in the ancestral home, but the lesser son had no such obligation. He would bide his time, make plans. At least he had a little cash, but it wouldn't go far. Somehow, he had to get his hands on his money. Father controlled that as well. If he couldn't get his money, he'd have to work for a living.

Rob paused. His education and upbringing had prepared him to manage his father's businesses. He had no clue how to earn money otherwise. The only skills he'd been taught were to boss other people. Greg Hardman could ensure Rob got no employment in the business world.

Who could he count on? Mentally, he listed his friends. They were all in the same boat as he, young and still financially dependent. If only he had somebody to talk to, but who? None of his friends would care to listen. He couldn't confide in any of the employees. Their livelihood depended on obedience to Gregory Hardman.

When he was calm enough, Rob called Gene. "Hey, sorry, something's come up. I can't do tennis today."

"Too bad. Maybe another time."

"Sure."

Rob clenched his fists again. The nails dug into the wounds they'd made earlier. But he didn't care. He wanted to unload his frustration on a sympathetic ear. Rosa came to mind, not as someone who could help him, but as a rational, caring listener.

He checked the weather. The satellite showed a huge spiral of clouds with a well-defined eye inching toward the coast. He hoped Rosa and her family would be safe. He knew little about her parents. Once she'd introduced them to him at a school function. They wore clean but inexpensive clothing and had been polite, without the self-effacement of the servant class. He was intrigued by such people.

The law demanded that a certain number of them attend private school on full scholarship, to be trained for jobs the business class wouldn't do. Entrance requirements were high. Rosa had exceeded them. He wished he could call her. He thought about mailing her, but his father would be monitoring his communications. His powerlessness chafed him.

CHAPTER 5

Wednesday morning, Father summoned Rob to his office. Rob was still in turmoil from the previous day's ordeal, but as usual, Father acted as though nothing had happened. How could he compartmentalize his emotions like that?

Greg was studying the storm. Without turning to face Rob, he said. "I'm concerned about this fire station." He flipped his screen to a map of the city and pointed at a red square. "It's too close to the St. Johns Channel. The foundation's getting less stable with each flood. There's a potential buyer in Minneapolis. I'd like to unload it before the storm hits."

"Is that fair to the buyer?"

He waved a hand. "He should do his homework. Besides, he can get compensation for any damage."

"Then why sell it? You'd get compensation, too."

"I have enough to worry about. I don't need a piece of property that's more trouble than it's worth. I'm telling you this because it was to be part of your inheritance. Do you have any objection to my selling it?"

Why did he bother to ask? "No. I have no objection."

Father turned his chair. "Well? Are you ready to apologize?"

So, here it comes. "Father, I'm sorry…"

His father pointed to the floor.

Rob shivered, recalling beatings he'd suffered in the past. But he was grown now, wasn't he? He knelt down and lowered his head. *I should be an actor.* "Father, forgive me. I just want a little independence. I know I went about it the wrong way."

Greg patted his head. "I know. I was young once. You'll get your independence. When I think you're ready."

The screen chimed. Doug's face appeared. His eyes flickered at Rob, still kneeling, and said, "Father, is this a good time..."

"Yes, it is. Rob and I just need a minute to finish."

Rob climbed to his feet.

Greg opened a small corner screen and beckoned Rob. "Here's the agreement for the school. It's ready for your signature."

Rob pressed his thumb to the signature square. Without smiling, he gave his brother a perfunctory greeting and left.

Back in his suite, he made efforts to calm himself. There was a message from the engineering consultant. Rob called back and told him about the Syntat switches.

The consultant said, "I have a woman who's pretty good at devising replacement parts. I'll put her on it. Maybe we can bypass the switch with a substitute." He gave Rob the technician's information. "You should hear from her today or tomorrow."

"Thanks."

* * *

Ramon gave Rosa a ride to work on his scooter. She looked forward to when she could afford her own transportation and not have to inconvenience her family. She went to the employee's lounge to tidy her wind-blown appearance.

One of the teachers said, "I see Mr. Stubens paid you a visit yesterday."

Rosa nodded.

"You don't like him, do you?"

"It's just...he makes me uncomfortable."

"You're not alone. You have to walk a tight line. You don't want to offend him, but you're wise not to welcome his attentions. Last year, we had a new teacher who thought she could get somewhere by giving him what he wanted."

Rosa bit her lip. "Did she get fired?"

"Not by Mr. Hadley, but when his wife found out, she was gone."

"That's too bad. Did she get another job?"

"Probably not."

Rosa thought about all the years of education the girl had invested and not yet paid for.

That afternoon, Ms. Reynolds, the lead history teacher, came to Rosa's classroom. "How are your lesson plans coming?"

"Pretty well, but I'm having a problem with a few things."

Ms. Reynolds sat down. "What sort of things?"

"Well, a lot of inaccuracies in the textbooks, things that aren't what I was taught in school."

"They do research all the time. They uncover new evidence, then they have to modify the books to agree with the new information."

"I know. I helped with some of that research. What I'm talking about…"

Ms. Reynolds held up a finger. "Excuse me." She called the office from Rosa's workstation. "Please turn off the power to Ms. Ortiz' room for ten minutes. We need to reset the system." The room and equipment went dark. "Now we can talk."

Rosa gulped.

Ms. Reynolds leaned forward. "Rosa, there are academics who have sold their souls. They rewrite 'history' to support the viewpoint of the pudientes. They want a narrative that backs their policies. They don't want a populace that thinks for themselves." She sat straight. "It's the same in science. The textbooks have been rewritten to support the teachings of the Third Covenant. That's one of the reasons print books have become obsolete. Electronic writings are easier to change than ink on paper, and the alterations are harder to trace."

She glanced around the classroom. "Mr. Hadley told me you have some old books. Keep them, protect them, but never let the pudientes know you have them. You see, this current régime is unsustainable. The day will come, things will change, and the pudientes fear this.

They will do anything they can to maintain the status quo, but it can't last forever. When change comes, the knowledge in your books will be invaluable."

Rosa was glad the room was dark so Ms. Reynolds couldn't see her tears. "That's what I was afraid of. But what do I do?"

"If you want to keep your job, you need to teach what's in the official textbooks. That's what students will be tested on. Your career depends on how well they swallow those lies and regurgitate them on tests. After you've been here a few years, you won't be under such close scrutiny, and then you can start telling your students a little of the truth. We must hold on to the hope that when the regime changes, there will be people who can recognize the truth, and it's our responsibility to ensure it isn't buried so deeply they can't find it." She laid her hand on Rosa's arm. "Remember, this conversation did not take place."

The lights came back on. Rosa's workstation came to life. She wiped her eyes. "Thank you, Ms. Reynolds. I'll do my best."

Rosa was surprised to hear Ms. Reynolds use "pudientes," the derogatory term for the rich and powerful. *She must not have friends in that class. Or she was badly hurt by them.*

Rosa thought back to the research she'd done in college. The history department acquired electronic copies of documents from around the world. Naively, Rosa thought this knowledge would be highly valued, that records would be set straight based on new evidence. It had been exciting to uncover new facts and ideas and pass them to the professor who, she thought, was spreading enlightenment. Had he sold his soul? Had someone above him squelched the information? Or had he, like Ms. Barton, secretly preserved the knowledge until the right time came to bring it forth?

One assignment had been particularly unsettling. Brought up with the belief that her country was the apex of civilization, admired by the rest of the world, she found instead a crumbling society, mired in isolation, shunned by other countries with standards of living superior to theirs.

The twentieth century had brought innovation at a rate unseen before in history. She'd been taught that industrialization had been the salvation of the world. Instead, it had triggered climate instability which caused human suffering as well as irreversible losses to the natural world.

The inventive nature of mankind had risen to the challenge. Advances in solar power mitigated a century of pollution. Solar roofs removed buildings from the power grid. Solar vehicles freed drivers from dependence on fossil fuel.

But in the end, salvation came too late. Too much damage had been done. Those with means withdrew to relatively safe places and built fortresses that could withstand much of what nature threw at them. In parts of the world, people suffered even more than in the United States, and some nations had been destroyed by rising seas.

It didn't help that every improvement was delayed by pushback from those who benefitted from the status quo. Rosa found descriptions of inventions which were never put into production, patents acquired and suppressed by those who stood to lose economically by their manufacture. The United States even enacted laws that prohibited importing advanced technology from elsewhere. With innovation thus repressed, a half-century of progress was retarded, and her country had deteriorated to an ignorant, backwater republic.

Meanwhile, foreign entrepreneurs ignored American patent laws and took advantage of technologies squelched in the United States. This and other factors spurred the nation, already moving towards isolation, to close its borders in 2077 to all but a privileged few.

Dutifully, Rosa had conveyed this information to her professor, believing he would pass it on to those who could use it for the common good. Now she wasn't so sure. What happened to the original writings? Had they been preserved? Or purged because of what they contained? Hope remained. Rosa still had her handwritten notes. Her intuition had told her to keep them, and she was glad she did. She kept them in a notebook with her collection of history books.

The gravity of the task Ms. Reynolds had laid on her was sobering. She'd never dreamed it would be her responsibility to keep the lore of civilization.

* * *

Thursday, the technician called Rob about the Syntat switch. "I've devised something that can temporarily bypass the original switch," she said. "I'll fly over and install it. Then I'll take the failed component back with me and see if I can invent one to replace it."

"Fantastic!" Rob wished he were so clever. And she was only a technician, not an engineer. Probably a scholarship student like Rosa. He looked out the window and thought about Rosa. He missed talking with her.

He found his father studying the storm. "This will drive all sorts of riff raff inland because they don't have the foresight to build houses that can withstand the weather. The streets won't be safe. There'll be muggings, rapes, murder... Who knows.... Afterwards they'll beg the government to feed and shelter them and rebuild their miserable shacks."

Rob took a deep breath. "Father, that's why I wanted to go into structural architecture, so I could design buildings that would withstand these storms."

Greg waved a hand. "That's why we give scholarships to the lower classes. So they can go into fields like that. It's a step up economically for them. For someone like you, it'd be a step down."

Why would doing something to help others be a step down? In some ways the working class had more freedom that he. "What I came to tell you is, we have a solution for the Syntat switch." He related his conversation with the technician.

"Good. If she invents one we can patent, and it works, we can put it into production. I may add that to your inheritance."

"Will she earn royalties from it?"

"Of course not. She works for us. Maybe we'll send her to engineering school under contract to continue with Hardman Enterprises when she's done."

After this, Rob needed fresh air. He left the compound and walked to the stable where his horse, Cricket, was galloping around the paddock. A stiff breeze made it a perfect day for a ride. Cricket trotted over and nuzzled Rob for a treat. "Sorry, ole boy. I forgot to bring you anything." He stroked Cricket's neck. "You're pretty frisky today. Are you feeling the weather?" Rob climbed the wooden fence and slipped onto Cricket's bare back. The horse took him around the paddock.

Steven, the groom, came out. "Morning, Mr. Rob."

"Thought I'd take Cricket for a ride. Would you like to join me?"

Steven shook his head. "I got lots to do before that storm hits."

"Anything I can help with?"

"Oh, no, Mr. Rob. That wouldn't be appropriate."

Rob slipped off Cricket's back and led him to the stable. He gave Cricket a quart of oats and saddled him.

"Mr. Rob, let me do that for you."

"No. You have enough to do."

Once Cricket finished his oats, Rob took him outside and mounted. Steven opened the gate. "You be careful, Mr. Rob."

"I've been riding since I learned to walk."

They cantered up the lane. The breeze in Rob's hair and the sun on his face cleansed him of his father's negativity. They crested the hill behind the stable. At the pasture gate, Rob dismounted to open it and lead Cricket through. He paused. From here, no buildings were visible. Ahead, for as far as he could see, lay rolling hills, a patchwork of cropland, pasture, and forest. He closed the gate and rode among a scattering of live oaks which cast a pleasant shade. From somewhere came the song of a dove. Rob smiled. He would trade all his inheritance for this ranch, and all his comforts for the privilege of sweating on it.

But Doug, not Rob, was slated to be lord of the manor. The sad thing was that Doug cared only about money, not the land.

At the far end of the pasture, Rob turned Cricket toward home and loosed his hold on the reins. Cricket took off at full gallop. They reached the gate all too soon. "Whoa, there, boy. What's the hurry? You think I'm gonna feed you more oats?" Rob walked Cricket the rest of the way to cool him.

Steven was mucking out a stall. "Mr. Rob, let me rub him down for you."

"No thanks. I can do it." He let Cricket drink and began to sponge him off. "Steven, do you have family somewhere?"

"Yes, Mr. Rob. They live over near Palatka."

"Do they know about the storm?"

"I don't know. Today's the first I heard of it."

"Why don't you call them?"

"I will soon's I get done here."

Rob took off his Nebula and opened it to telephone mode. "Here." He handed it to Steven. When he was finished, Steven gave it back. "Thank you, Mr. Rob. You don't know how relieved I am."

"What are your plans? Will you go to them?"

He shook his head. "Mr. Hardman wants me to stay here in the stable with the horses, to make sure they'll be okay."

Rob studied the structure. It was designed to withstand 175 mile-per-hour winds. This far inland, the storm shouldn't be quite that intense. Again, he regretted not being able to pursue his passion. Not only had his father discouraged him, when Rob tried to go behind Father's back to major in structural architecture anyway, the University wouldn't let him. The field was open to scholarship students only.

Still, no matter how sturdy the building, Rob wasn't sure he'd want to weather a major hurricane here, with only horses for companionship. But he didn't give the orders. With a twinge of guilt, he acknowledged he wouldn't even want to keep Cricket company under such conditions. Steven must be braver, or more desperate, than he.

What did horses do before they had strong stables? They weathered the storm wherever they were. Perhaps intuition guided them to places of relative safety. The cattle in the pastures—what about them? They had no stables. At best, they could shelter under trees. But storms blew trees down. Father probably had them well insured. "Humph."

"Sir?" Steven asked.

"Nothing. I was just thinking about the cattle. About how they could survive the storm."

"I guess all creatures that don't have shelter just do the best they can and hope God will look out for them."

On his way back to the house, a flock of birds flew over and settled into a sycamore tree. What about the birds and other creatures? Did God look out for them? Years ago, Jamis, the groundskeeper, told him about a hurricane after which the birds disappeared and didn't come back until the following spring. Where had they gone? How many had perished?

Their welfare was beyond his control. Also beyond his control were all the human beings who lacked adequate shelter and were not given time to prepare.

* * *

Salli arrived at Rosa's school mid-morning on Friday. She persuaded Mr. Hadley to go over Rosa's lesson plans early so they could begin their weekend. She told Rosa, "I'll hang out in the teachers' lounge until you're done."

"I'm sorry, Mr. Hadley," Rosa said. "Salli and I...I mean, Ms. Stubens...we went to school together."

Mr. Hadley held up his hand. "Say no more."

"I won't use our relationship to get special treatment."

"I know."

Salli had driven her family's Sparkler. Instead of returning directly home, she took Rosa shopping. When she pulled up to the Emporia gate, the security guard waved them in.

"He must know you," Rosa said.

"Of course."

Salli stopped the Sparkler by the parking valet and didn't wait for a receipt. Rosa gawked at the mall's façade. Salli snatched her hand and pulled her through the front door. "You act like you've never been here before."

"I haven't."

Several shopping assistants waited in an alcove by the entrance. Salli pointed at one who stood up and followed the girls at a courteous distance. Rosa still wore her uniform. Other shoppers paid no attention, but Emporia employees gave her quizzical looks. "I'm not dressed for this," Rosa whispered.

Salli held Rosa at arm's length. "You're right. Let's buy you something appropriate."

"I can't afford it. I haven't been paid yet, and even so, I can't afford this stuff."

Salli put her hands on her hips. "I didn't mean *you* should buy anything, silly. I owe you a graduation present."

Rosa shook her head. "I didn't get you anything."

"Yes, you did. You got me through statistics. Let's see what we can find." They entered a dress shop.

"Salli, I don't have any place to wear such things…"

"How about something casual, for the weekend."

"That would be better."

They settled on a summery dress, a pair of shorts, and two blouses. Rosa changed into the dress—powder blue, sprinkled with forget-me-nots. Salli smiled. "That brings out the blue in your eyes. Now, how about something to go with it?"

"No, Salli. This is more than enough. Thank you."

The assistant carried Rosa's clothes. Salli breezed in and out of shops, Rosa in tow, purchasing clothes, cosmetics, and accessories for herself. When her arms were full, the assistant called for a cart.

"Salli, your car isn't big enough for all this."

"No problem. They'll take it home for me."

The Stubens mansion was in the same golf community as Mort Cooper's. Each residence was an estate to itself, covering several acres. After they arrived, the girls went swimming. Rosa's new clothes waited in her room when she went back to change.

At dinner, Mr. Stubens opened a bottle of champagne to celebrate "graduation and a new life" for both girls. Afterward, they watched a movie in the holo room. Rosa sat as far from Salli's father as she could.

She watched the story unfold on the three-dimensional stage. It was a historical drama about young reporters in the early twenty-first century, battling misinformation from a rogue news agency. Perhaps because she had been focused on misinformation all week, Rosa suspected the movie was as much propaganda as entertainment.

By 2037, all major print publications had been taken over by three companies. The public was assured this provided healthy competition while streamlining the dispersal of information. A few years later all major media, including TV, radio, and movies, were under those companies' control. With the rise in power of The Third Covenant, censorship began, aiming at pornography and other "immoral" material. Print media fell by the wayside. Those in power heralded its disuse as a solution to "save the trees." As libraries switched to digital, books disappeared from their shelves. Printed material became archaic. Although not banned by law, it was viewed with suspicion and became nearly non-existent.

In 2042, the internet was privatized and fees were charged, making access unaffordable for many, which gave rise to protests. Cut off from the internet, activists organized by phone. As a result, laws were passed requiring a license to own a phone. The invention of the Nebula—phone, computer, and more on a wrist device—became instantly popular, but ownership was restricted to full Citizens and their heirs. Rosa looked forward owning one. It promised to open the world to her.

These thoughts spoiled the movie for her. She loved movies, especially if they were well done, which this one was, but the inaccuracies were glaring. Were the screenwriters unfamiliar with life in the twenty-first century? Some things, such as costumes, were correct, but overall it appeared the movie was produced through a lens of censorship.

Rosa tried to put this aside and enjoy the experience. It was bittersweet. Only the wealthy could afford 3D entertainment. It had been available at college in the dorm lounge, but at home, her family had to be content with an antique, two dimensional screen.

Rosa knew that in the past technology became affordable for the masses a few years after it hit the market, but times had changed. The buying power of middle and working class people had dwindled. Her family watched broadcasts from bootleg stations that flourished temporarily until the authorities shut them down. These typically featured old videos which were censored due to their depictions of unsanctioned history. Rosa wondered how the low-level officials who raided these stations felt about it, since even they couldn't afford 3D.

The girls sat up late, talking and sipping cocktails. When they decided to retire for the night, Rosa said, "Can you help me get to my room? I'm afraid I'm a lightweight drinker."

Salli giggled.

Rosa made sure no one was lurking in her room before Salli left.

CHAPTER 6

The sun was up when Rosa woke. She stretched luxuriantly on the satin sheets.

Salli knocked. "Rosa, are you awake?"

"Yes, Salli. Command: door unlock."

Salli was wearing her bathing suit. "Let's go swimming. I told Maddie to set our breakfast out by the pool."

Rosa quickly changed into her swimsuit and brushed her hair. The girls emerged into the warmth of the morning. Maddie put the finishing touches on an elegant breakfast table set under the shady arbor. Giorgio, the groundskeeper, was tidying up around the pool. Both withdrew as quickly and quietly as possible, but Salli shouted, "Thank you, Giorgio!" to his receding back. He half-turned and shot her a short wave and smile. Salli giggled. "Isn't his name wonderful? Gee-or-gee-oh." She wiggled. "Sooo sexy." Salli took a sip of her mimosa. "I could set you up with Giorgio."

Rosa nearly choked. "Set me up? I thought he was married."

"I'm not talking about marriage. Besides, he's not a citizen. But he's fun." She glanced around to be sure they were alone. "I know you won't say anything to Daddy. Giorgio is the best I've tried."

Rosa knew Salli was free with her affections, but to suggest... Rosa tried to wrap her mind around it. "Why, you could get him fired!"

Salli shrugged. "He's a good groundskeeper. With my recommendation, he could easily get another job. I know lots of women who could convince their husbands to hire him."

Rosa shook her head. "I'm not looking for that kind of relationship."

Salli laughed. "I know. You're a good girl. You're looking for love and marriage." Perhaps the mimosa had gone to Salli's head. "But they don't always come together, do they." She began to prattle about her fiancé, John, a man of wealth and influence. "He's an eldest son, too, so I'll be set for life. And you could visit any time."

Rosa knew John wasn't likely to welcome her into his home as an equal. Possibly as a tutor to his children, a role that didn't appeal to her. As his servant, she'd be subjected to the privileges such men expect. Behavior she'd witnessed in Salli's father and brother toward household staff. Did Salli love John? Did he love her? The more Salli talked, the sorrier Rosa felt for her. At least she was free to be her own woman.

After a fruit cup and pastry, they went swimming. The pool was cool enough to be refreshing yet warm enough to be pleasant. Rosa floated on her back, gazing at the clouds. She thought about Rob. If things had been different, if he'd been a scholarship student like her... She wasn't likely to see him again. He'd marry a woman of his own class. Time would cool her yearnings, and someday she'd move on to a more suitable man.

Rosa felt a drop of water on her face, then another. Salli, at the opposite end of the pool, was moving languidly. Suddenly she jerked her head and looked up. The blue sky dotted with soft, white clouds had been replaced by an angry band of dark gray.

"The storm must be moving in," Salli said.

Rosa snapped to attention. "What storm?"

"There's a hurricane off the coast. It's supposed to hit us this week-end."

"For real?"

Rain splattered the pool area. The girls scrambled to the shelter of the arbor. Salli handed Rosa a thick towel. Maddie and a young woman hastily moved the breakfast spread inside. Salli called, "Maddie, we'll go change. Set it up in the breakfast room."

"Yes, Ms. Salli."

Rosa couldn't direct a servant like that. Hers would be more a request between equals. "Salli, may I use a phone to call my family?"

"Sure. You can use my Nebula."

While Salli changed, Rosa called home. Ramon answered.

"Have you heard about that hurricane?" she asked.

"What hurricane?"

"It may hit this weekend. Salli told me about it."

Ramon snorted. "How long has she known?"

"I don't know. She talked like it wasn't anything new."

"Sanctuary! Why hasn't anyone been told? Never mind. I'll tell the folks. If you find out anything else, call me, will you?"

"Should I come home?"

"Why? Weren't you planning to stay there all weekend?"

"Yes."

"Then stay. Their house is probably as safe as any."

"What about you all?"

"We'll be fine. Don't worry."

Salli followed Rosa to her room and whispered, "I could ask Giorgio to pick you some flowers and bring them up here if you like."

Rosa's face flamed. "No."

"It's okay. I have sheaths in my room, I could bring you some."

"I have an implant." *Now, why did I say that?*

"You should use a sheath anyway, with a non-citizen. You never know what they might carry."

Could her face get any redder? "No, Salli. I don't want to be with Giorgio. It might not mean anything to him, but it does to me. He's married."

Salli grinned. "Okay, but if you change your mind..."

* * *

A hurricane is a massive cyclone that can be hundreds of miles wide. Spinning out from its center are storm bands interspersed with periods of relatively nice weather. As the storm approaches, these bands become stronger and more frequent.

Saturday morning, when Rob woke, he looked out his window at gray swirling clouds. His neck stiffened. *Here it comes.* By the time he finished breakfast, the sky was blue again. Later, a blast of wind and rain shook the shutters. Something outside fell with a clatter. Rob looked out. A ladder lay on the ground and Jamis struggled against the wind to pick it up. Rob ran to the door and called him.

Jamis scrambled to the porch, dripping wet.

"Come in and dry yourself off," Rob said.

"No, sir. One of them shutters won't close automatically like it's s'posed to. Mr. Hardman told me to close it before it's too late."

"Well, you can't do it when it's blowing like this. Wait till this band blows over and I'll help you."

"No, Mr. Rob, I can't let you do that. It's too dangerous."

Rob looked closely at Jamis. The man had aged. "You shouldn't be on that ladder. I'll get Steven, or somebody, to help. Come in the kitchen, out of the rain."

Before lunch, Rob's Nebula pulsed. Gene appeared on the screen.

"Hey, Rob, Morty's having a hurricane party at his place. He asked me to call you."

"Just a minute." Rob ducked into his room. "I didn't want Father to overhear us."

"Well?"

"I don't know. He's been squirrely lately. One day he sends me out to do a man's job, the next day he treats me like a baby. He and I played golf with Morty's dad the other day, so maybe…"

"Tell you what. I'll have Morty call him. Better yet, I'll get his old man to call. Morty's going to pick me up with his copter. He can pick you up, too."

"Thanks." The tension in the house would escalate with the storm. Father would become a powder keg. Rob thought about his mother. She'd be physically safe and they'd probably drug her to the point of insensitivity. There was little he could do to ameliorate her situation, so it would be better if he left.

At lunch, the screen in the dining room chimed. Father growled and started to suppress the call, but when Mort's face appeared, his demeanor changed.

"How's life treating you?" Mort said.

"I'll tell you after this storm's over."

Mort talked business for a few minutes before broaching the reason for his call. "My boy's having a hurricane party and would like Rob to come."

Father looked dubiously at Rob. "The weather's getting pretty stiff. I don't want him out on the road."

"We'll pick him up in the copter, between rain bands. The engine's powerful enough, and Mike's a good pilot. I trust my own blood with him."

"Who else is coming?" Rob asked.

Mort rattled off a list of names. Rob watched his father's face. The guests were offspring of his business associates. Rob could see plans germinating in Father's mind.

"Okay, I just don't want him out in bad weather."

"I'll have him indoors before the winds pick up again." Mort looked at Rob. "Be ready. When the sun comes out, look for Mike."

* * *

After lunch, Salli received a call from a friend across the golf course. After she hung up, she said, "Hey, Rosa, wanna go to a party tonight?"

"Party? Where?"

"Across the way, at Morty's house."

"I don't know..."

"He's having a hurricane party. It'll be safe. His house is strong."

"Who else will be there?"

"Probably all the neighbor kids. Come on, it'll be fun. We'll be there all night. We won't leave until the hurricane does."

Rosa thought about her family, hoping they were safe. She didn't really want to go a party full of strangers, nor did she want to disappoint Salli. At least she now had clothes suitable for such a gathering.

The wind and rain picked up. "How will we get there?" Rosa asked.

"We can take the golf cart over when the weather clears again. In the meantime, how about some ping pong?"

After Salli won three games in a row, Rosa threw up her hands and started laughing. It was contagious. Salli went into a giggling fit and Rosa joined her.

After they settled down, Salli looked out a window. "Oh, dear, I forgot to watch the weather. We better go soon."

Salli's father met them in the hallway. "I've just had some disturbing news." He looked at Rosa. "Come with me."

Salli started to follow, but her father said, "I need to talk to her alone."

Rosa's heart pounded in her throat. She looked desperately at Salli, who shrugged her shoulders. "I'll wait out here for you."

Mr. Stubens led Rosa into his study. He sat on an easy chair and motioned Rosa to sit on the couch facing him.

She tried to keep her voice steady. "Yes, sir? What is it?"

"I've just learned that your brother has been arrested for rape."

Blood roared in her ears. "What?"

"Ramon Ortiz, your brother, right?"

Rosa jerked her chin up and down.

"He forced himself on the daughter of one of my associates."

"No, that's—that's his girlfriend. They…" The look on Mr. Stubens' face silenced her.

"Under these circumstances, I cannot allow you to continue as a guest in my house, or as a companion to my daughter."

"Mr. Stubens, I haven't done anything…"

"Doesn't matter. You need to leave."

"Okay." Her brain was reeling. "I…I'll get my things. Um, can your driver take me home?"

He shook his head. "I'll allow you get your things, but once out the door, you're on your own. And your employment at Bayview Academy is terminated."

Rosa looked at the window. The storm was the least of her worries.

Then Mr. Stubens smiled and his voice softened. "Perhaps we can make other arrangements." Before she knew it, he was seated beside her, twining a finger through a lock of her hair.

Rosa jumped to her feet. "I'm sorry, Mr. Stubens. I'm not that kind of girl."

"What kind of girl? One who wants to remain employed? Or one who wants to be thrown out into the street?"

"The street, I guess." Rosa rushed from the room.

Salli sat in the hallway sipping a drink. "What's wrong?"

Rosa hurried past her and up to her room. Salli followed. Rosa broke down into tears. "I have to leave. Your father said my brother's been arrested, and he doesn't want me here anymore."

"No! I'll go talk to him."

Rosa packed her things. When she opened the door, she heard Salli arguing with her father. She ducked back into the room.

Ms. Stubens came in. She looked at Rosa's bag and said, "What are you taking?"

"Just my clothes."

The woman snatched the bag from her and dumped it on the bed. She rummaged through the clothes and pulled out a blouse. "What's this?"

"Salli bought it for me."

"We'll see." She took the blouse downstairs.

Rosa heard Salli shout, "That *is* hers. I bought it for her."

A few minutes later, Salli and her mother returned. Ms. Stubens handed the blouse to Rosa and said stiffly, "I'm sorry things turned out like this. I had such hopes for you."

"I'm sorry, too. Can I at least call my family to come get me?"

"No. I can't have such influences in my home."

"Mother," Salli screamed. "We can't just put her out in a hurricane!"

"She's a grown woman. She can handle her own matters."

"But it's dangerous!"

Ms. Stubens took a deep breath. "All right. She can stay with one of the servants until the storm's over." She looked at Rosa. "But then you must leave. If I see you, I'll have you arrested for trespassing."

Rosa nodded.

Salli led Rosa downstairs, through the kitchen to the staff entrance, out to the back porch. The wind and rain had picked up again. Salli hugged Rosa and clung to her. "I'm so sorry. I'll talk to them tomorrow. They can't blame you."

"I just don't understand."

"Neither do I." Salli handed Rosa an umbrella and pointed at the row of servants' cottages behind the house. "Just knock on a door and one of them will let you in. Please be careful."

Like an automaton, Rosa took the umbrella and stepped out into the storm. A gust of the wind blew her sideways. She struggled to reach the first cottage. She knocked on the door but got no response. Could they hear her over the racket of the hurricane? She pounded harder but got no answer. Gripping her bag tightly, she let the wind carry her to the next cottage. Halfway there, the umbrella was ripped from her hand and flew up into the wind. As she approached the door, a gust bashed her against it. Before she could regain her balance, the door opened. Strong male arms caught her. Rosa looked up and recognized Giorgio.

* * *

Morty's house was the perfect place for a hurricane party. Overlooking the golf course was a large game room with windows of shatterproof glass on three sides. By the time Gene and Rob arrived, nearly every neighbor of college age was present. The bar was well-stocked, the kitchenette had enough food to feed a small city, and hired musicians were playing popular tunes.

Morty greeted Rob with a shot glass. "You'll need this. We're going to be up all night."

"What is it?"

"Cathine." Morty's father, like Rob's, had a strict prohibition against recreational drugs, which didn't stop the young people's occasional use. Rob poured the bitter liquid down his throat and chased it with a beer.

Soon he was dancing with a girl, one his father approved of. Susan was seventeen but looked older. When the musicians took a break, Rob asked, "Can I get you a drink?"

"Sure. Surprise me."

Rob had no idea what she liked, so he fixed two Margaritas.

Susan took a sip. "Mmmm. How does it feel to be finished with college?"

"Good, I guess. It's only been a few days."

Morty came over. "I heard you played golf with my dad the other day. To close a deal."

"Oh?" Susan said. "What was the deal?"

"Nothing you'd be interested in."

"Try me."

"Morty's dad had a public school in Olustee that's not turning enough profit, so he wanted to sell it." He sipped his drink. "Father likes to add to his collection. He thinks he can teach the students the wood products trade. It'll amount to nothing more than a sweat shop."

Susan drew back. "I disagree. Even public school students—especially public school students—need some kind of work. The younger they learn, the better. Teach them responsibility, give them a good work ethic, and they won't be a burden on the rest of us. But owning a single school doesn't make much sense. You should have a chain of them, like the Stubens do."

No wonder Father approved of this girl. "I didn't come here to discuss business."

"Speaking of the Stubens," Morty said, "I invited Salli..." Outside, the wind screeched. He shrugged his shoulders. "I guess she's not coming."

* * *

Giorgio closed the door behind Rosa.

Have I left the frying pan for the fire?

A woman stepped up beside the groundskeeper. "What's going on?"

"It's Ms. Salli's friend."

"They kicked me out."

"In this storm? You poor thing." The woman led Rosa into the small living room. "Do you have any dry clothes?"

Rosa went through her bag. Although it was waterproof, rain had seeped in. Everything was damp.

"Let me find you something to wear and I'll dry them for you."

"Thank you." Two small children peeked curiously at Rosa. She looked around. The cottage was smaller than her parents' house.

The woman handed Rosa a set of pajamas. "Why don't you take a warm bath?" She led her to the bathroom. Rosa stripped off her soaked garments and handed them to her. The lady had hot soup waiting for her after she was clean and dressed.

The wind shrieked. In the interior hallway, away from windows, the couple laid blankets and pillows on the floor. Giorgio told Rosa and the children to stay there while he and his wife put together sandwiches, drinks, and snacks. Something hit the side of the house. They closed the interior doors and hung a heavy curtain across the end of the hall. The sound was muted to a low moan. The parents took their children in their arms and hummed softly to them.

Hunkered down with the family, Rosa looked from Giorgio to his wife and wondered, did the lady know about her husband's arrangement with Salli? He acted the perfect gentleman to Rosa, and attentive to his wife. Had Salli lied?

The cottage creaked and swayed. Rosa hoped it was as sturdy as her parents' home. She thought about the Stubens' safe, strong house. If she lived in such a place, she would invite her employees to shelter with her. But they were less valued than the family dog.

The couple had a reader and took turns reading to the children. Although Rosa tried to listen to the story, the words were drowned out by other worries. From time to time, the wife handed out food. That boosted Rosa's mood. She offered to take a turn reading.

The children fell asleep. In the middle of the night, the power went out.

"Something must've hit the system," Giorgio said.

In the dark, the hammering wind was even more terrifying. Rosa's personal fears were compounded. What happened to Ramon? Was her family safe? What about her job? What was she to do? The darkness hid her tears.

A window shattered. Giorgio jumped up and turned on his flashlight, but his wife stopped him. "It can wait till morning." Wind gusted through the broken window and whipped the curtain.

Rosa wished she were at home but was grateful to this family for giving her shelter, food, clothing, and protection. She lay down on her blanket. At the moment there was nothing she could do but pray, so she did. The sounds of destruction produced a wry thought: if it's bad enough, it could make all my problems moot.

* * *

The music resumed. Rob was relieved when Susan chose a different partner. Dancing was interrupted when a large limb slammed against a window.

"Whoa! Did you see that?" someone shouted. Party guests ran to the windows. Outdoor floodlights showed trees unmercifully beaten by the gale. The branch scudded across the ground, flew against the swimming pool fence, and shivered for several seconds before another gust scooped it up and sent it flying, nearly taking the fence with it.

Rob studied the grounds. Mort's servants had surely secured everything they could, but the water in the pool was sloshing over the edge and the gazebo quivered. "I wonder how much stress that gazebo can take before the wind tears it apart?"

Someone said, "Who cares? It's insured."

"No, I mean, can they be built strong enough...?" Nobody paid any attention.

A dark form flew up and snagged on a light fixture. At first, Rob thought it was a large bird, but no, it was an umbrella. Who would be out in such weather?

The hours wore on. The wind whistled over the din of festivity. Occasionally the building shuddered and everyone cheered. Rob couldn't help worrying about his family. Hardman Hall was built to withstand such forces but, as in this party room, the elements made themselves known.

During lulls, Rob longed for good conversation. His companions only wanted to talk about the latest soccer game or political scandal. He thought about Rosa and how they could talk about meaningful things. He hoped she was safe. She'd told him her family's house was sturdy, but was it enough? It was old, built before modern construction codes. Next time he went to Dongtian, he'd check on her.

The storm raged. The musicians completed their gig. Morty turned on recorded music before he left the room with a girl. Someone dimmed the lights and turned up the volume. Rob, quite inebriated by now, found himself with a girl, not Susan, in his arms and took advantage of the situation. The act was mechanical, lacking the playful passion he experienced with girls like Cisli. He fantasized about Rosa. They'd never so much as kissed, but he believed making love to her would be just that, making love.

Chapter 7

The wind abated. Rosa fell asleep. It was daylight when she woke in the hallway with the sleeping children. Giorgio and his wife had cleaned up the broken glass in the living room and covered the window with a sheet of cellophane. Now they were preparing food for the children and getting ready for work. Rosa wished she could help these kind people, but she didn't dare stay.

She changed into her clothes and handed Giorgio's wife the pajamas. "I need to leave before the Stubens see me here. Can I use your phone to call my family?" The call went through. "Mama, I want to come home. Can you come get me?"

"Rosa, we can't go anywhere. The roads are impassable. Aren't you safe there?"

"Yes. I'm safe. I've been worried about you."

"We're fine. Ramon left yesterday and went to his girlfriend's. Stay where you are until the roads are cleared. And stay in touch with us."

"Okay. I love you."

"I love you, too."

So, they didn't know about Ramon. If, indeed it was true, not a ploy on Mr. Stubens' part.

"Are they coming for you?" Giorgio asked.

Rosa hesitated. "Yes. But they can't come here. I have to go meet them. How can I get out without going by the Stubens' house?"

"The back way. I'll show you. Do you want something to eat first?"

"Can I have a sandwich to take with me?"

They picked their way around puddles and broken limbs. The back gate opened to a service road which was littered with dregs of the storm.

"Are you sure you're going to be okay?" Giorgio asked.

Rosa forced a smile. "Oh, yes. I'll be fine. Thank you so much." She wanted to hug him, but thought better of it.

The alley took Rosa to the highway. Workers from the golf community were already clearing it. Home was two counties away. It was going to be a long walk.

Then she saw the butterflies. Roadside wildflowers that hadn't been blown away were covered with them. Such delicate creatures— how did they survive? Where had they found shelter? Yet here they were, dancing in the sunshine as though all were well with the world.

Rosa shouldered her bag and set out.

* * *

Around 10:30 a.m., Morty's father knocked on the door. "Everybody up! Church is at eleven."

Rob woke and dressed hastily. Around him, other sleepers did the same. They talked and joked about surviving the storm. Rob looked out the window. The torrential wind and rain had ceased. The grounds were littered with debris, but he could see little damage. Even the gazebo had survived. *Maybe I didn't need to go into structural architecture after all. Maybe they've got it figured out.*

Most of the guests' families were members of the Sanctuary of the Loving Spirit. Many, like Rob, had parents who were strict about church attendance. He had little choice but to follow Mort along the covered drive to the chapel. On the golf course, employees were already cleaning up. During the two-hour-long service with a live preacher, much praise was given to the Savior for delivering His faithful righteous safely from the storm. Rob prayed silently for the victims of the disaster, living and dead, and wondered how many of them had also been righteous and faithful. When it finally ended, Rob was more than ready for breakfast.

Mike, the copter pilot, flew Rob, Gene, and a few others home. As the craft rose into the air and glided across the countryside, Rob watched the scene below him unfold. Beyond the golf community, roads were choked with downed trees and other rubble. Flooding was widespread. This was the first time Rob had surveyed such devastation from the air. Where had all that wreckage come from?

Crews were already clearing roads, but in the poorer neighborhoods, where the destruction was worse, there were no repair crews. Rob felt guilty that, while he could afford leisure, those men and women had to work for someone else before they could restore their own neighborhoods.

Rob scanned the horizon for a glimpse of Hardman Hall. How had the estate and its inhabitants fared? Finally it appeared, mostly unscathed. The grounds had suffered the expected wind damage, and staff was out cleaning up. Mike deftly set the copter down in the parking area.

On his way into the house, Rob spotted Steven. "How are the horses?"

"They're okay. The stable held up. We lost a few fruit trees, but I haven't had time to see about the livestock yet."

Rob went to check on his mother.

Amaline said, "She's sleeping."

"How did she do during the storm?"

"She slept through the whole thing."

Of course. Probably drugged. He spoke to his father and went to bed.

Hours later, Rob woke, showered, and went down for something to eat. Gracie served him a quick lunch. Her hands shook when she laid it before him. He glanced up. Her eyes were red. "What's wrong, Gracie? Is your family all right?"

"Yes, sir. The family's fine. But, you remember that old veteran? He died."

"Oh. I'm sorry. What happened?"

"He went outside during the storm. Nobody knows why. They found him laying in the street this morning."

Rob bit his lip. *How many more?* "Is there anything I can do?"

"No, sir. At least he's at peace now."

After he ate, Rob thought about riding out to check on the cattle, but Father's voice came over the PA system. "Robert, report to my office at once."

When Rob walked in, the fire chief was on the screen, pleading. "But I haven't been able to contact my family. I need make sure they're okay."

"Finish what you're doing first. I'm sure they're safe. There's nothing you can do if they're not. I'll have one of my crews look in on them and let you know when they report to me." He ended the call.

"Father, can't someone else take over while he sees about his family? There shouldn't be any fires after all this rain."

"I'm waiting on a FEMA contract for rescue and relief. He needs to get his staff ready for that. Besides, if I let one go, they'll all want to leave. If his family was prepared, they should be fine. If they didn't prepare, it was their own fault."

How much advance warning did they have? Rob cleared his throat. "Are you going to check on his family?"

"When someone in the vicinity is finished with what they're doing, I'll send them by."

"So, you weren't able to sell the firehouse."

Greg swiveled around to face Rob. "That's not why I called you in here. Have you called the resort?"

"I was going to after I ate…"

"Do it now."

Rob was unable to contact Angus Wilson at Dongtian. When he returned to report this, Father was talking to the headmistress of Olustee Academy.

"We're going to need some relief," she said, "but the roads are closed."

"Can you hold out another day or two?"

"Certainly. I'm sure there are others worse off than we are."

"We'll send help as soon as possible." He turned to Rob. "Well?"

"I can't reach them. I've tried everything. Do you have a crew in the neighborhood that can go by?"

"No. The roads are flooded and blocked. I can't get anyone over there. Keep trying."

"I wish we had a copter we could send over."

"Well, we don't."

No, thought Rob. Even though we could well afford one. He'd never known his father to fly anywhere. Even when he went to Tallahassee to serve in the legislature, he had Andreu drive him. Why was he afraid of flying?

Rob returned to his suite and looked out a window. Every employee was on the grounds working, even Leonard and other house servants. And this was the Sabbath. What happened to Father's convictions?

On Monday, Rob was still unable to contact anyone at the resort. He tried calling police and emergency departments, but the few who answered were too busy to help. A satellite view of Dongtian Palace showed the building still standing, but no details were visible.

In his office, Father was glued to news reports.

Rob cleared his throat. "I still can't get any information about the resort. I need to go over there myself and see what the situation is."

"It's too dangerous."

"I can take Andreu with me."

Father shook his head and gestured at a video of police trying to subdue a riot.

Rob looked closely at the caption. "Why, that's not even around here. That's up near the Georgia border."

"It's the same all over."

Back in his suite, Rob called Mort. "Father and I need a favor. We can't contact the staff at our beach resort. Times like this I wish we had a copter. Could you give me a ride over there so I can see what's wrong?"

"Sorry, Rob. I have my own problems, and my copter's busy. Maybe in a few days."

He sighed. "Thanks. We'd appreciate anything you can do."

An hour later, Mort called back. "You're in luck. I can't take you to the resort, but Mike was in the neighborhood and flew over. He took some footage of the area. I'm sending it to you. The place looks undamaged, but deserted. A lot of roads are blocked, but the turnpike's in good shape."

Rob called Andreu up to his suite and showed him the video. "Do you think you can get me to Dongtian?"

Andreu studied the layout. "Won't be easy, but I think I can." He traced a maze of roadways that appeared passable. "Probably will need four wheel drive. We'll take the Backpacker."

"Right. Let's run it by Father."

Rob brought up the aerial video on his father's screen. Andreu pointed out the route he could take. The streets were unusually empty. There was no sign of unrest.

Greg still had his news reports open. His attention shifted from the picture of the seemingly abandoned resort to the riots near the Georgia border. "Andreu, are you confident you can get there and back safely?"

"Why, I wouldn't consider taking Mr. Rob if I wasn't. We'll both be armed, just in case."

"All right. Be careful. Don't put yourselves in any danger. If you run into trouble, turn around and come right back. And keep me informed."

"Yes, sir."

Andreu made sure the Backpacker was fully charged. He stowed water, food, and weapons in various compartments. Then he added a chainsaw, two shovels, and other tools.

"What are those for?"

"If we're lucky, nothing."

The highway had been cleared, but the radar pilot system wasn't functioning. In a few places, barriers had been erected where pavement had caved in. Low areas of agricultural fields were flooded. Andreu shook his head. "If that's salt water, those fields won't be fit for growing anything after this."

"There might be salt-resistant crops. I wish I knew more about it." Rob had taken the only class Hayes University had on regenerative agriculture. That course of study wasn't offered at Hayes, even to their scholarship students.

In the pastures, trees had been uprooted. Cattle crowded around them, nibbling on the leaves. Rob spotted what looked like a fire on a hilltop. When they drew closer, he saw a knot of people, a few tents, and what looked like a cow's carcass. "What are they doing?"

"Looks like they're having a barbecue. Probably camping on high ground 'cause their houses are flooded."

In residential areas, trees had fallen across streets and through roofs. The siding on some buildings was green from being blasted with leaves. When they reached the luxury high rises, those streets had been cleared. Some factories had damaged solar panels. Others appeared to be in operation. Rob frowned. Those workers had no time to repair their homes. They probably came to work under threat of being fired.

The causeway over the St. Johns was intact, but the channel was twice its usual width. Buildings close to the water had horizontal brown lines, showing how high the water had risen. Debris still clung to the siding. Some of the houses on stilts had collapsed. Rob thought about Rosa. He searched for her address on his Nebula. *When we get done at Dongtian, we'll go by her house.*

Andreu interrupted his thoughts. "I don't know how much longer before the rest of this state just washes into the ocean."

"What do you mean?"

"How much Florida history did they teach you in school?"

"It was a required course."

"Did they tell you about Miami? Naples?"

"I've heard of them."

Andreu shook his head. "Once upon a time, they were major cities, bigger than Jacksonville. They died out even before they went under-water. They stopped rebuilding after hurricanes. Nobody wanted to live there anymore. Besides, there wasn't enough fresh water and it was too expensive to pipe in. That was before your family's water plants."

"How do you know this?"

"My granny told me. I didn't learn it in school, either."

Rob looked out at piles of fresh sand that hadn't been there before the storm.

Andreu continued. "A hundred years ago, this state was growing. Granny said everyone wanted to come here, especially the Yankees, to get away from the terrible blizzards. Now, nobody in their right mind wants to live here. That's why Georgia fortified their border. To keep people from moving there."

"I thought Florida fortified it, to keep the homeless out in winter."

"That, too."

Rob had been taught Florida was a desirable place for those who were industrious, but vagrants, who crossed the border illegally and set up tents and shacks, were unwelcome. They were a drain on everyone else. They didn't work but expected to be provided with water and food. Somehow, droves of them crossed the border every winter and left when the weather warmed. Neither state wanted them.

"We need to get off here," Andreu said. "Our usual route is impassible."

Andreu drove slowly, avoiding wash-outs. Rob heard the buzz of a chain saw. A half dozen men and women were struggling to move freshly-cut chunks of a tree that blocked the road. "Stay here," Andreu said and got out to lend his strength. The people thanked him and he climbed back into the driver's seat.

"I wonder who they work for," Rob said.

"Themselves. They live here. If they didn't clear the road them-selves, they'd be stranded for weeks." They came to a place where the pavement was covered by sand. Here, Andreu engaged the all-wheel drive. He drove through a maze of streets. Most had only a single lane cleared, fragments of trees and ruined buildings piled along the edges. Rob suspected this had been a respectable neighborhood, but it had been reduced to ruin.

The closer they came to the beach, the greater the destruction. The first and second floors of older high rise buildings had been gutted. Houses had been crushed, washed off their foundations, or gone al-together. A few people sat hunched on what remained of stoops and porches—residents? How did they survive? They stared at the Back-packer with blank faces, as though too exhausted to move.

"There's the resort," Andreu said.

Rob stretched against his safety restraints. The hotel stood high above the rubble and, other than broken shutters, appeared unscathed.

Andreu wove among debris and sand dunes. "The bird's eye view from Mike's video was a help. I hope it's no harder to get to than it looked." The Backpacker lurched to the left and stopped. Andreu tried backing up, but the wheels spun. "Oh, Sanctuary!" He jumped out and bent down to examine the situation. "Mr. Rob, I need your help." He opened the back and took out shovels.

Rob caught a movement in the corner of his eye as he stepped out of the car. Almost immediately, they were surrounded by people. Rob started to reach for his gun but Andreu laid a hand on his arm and shouted, "I have a bottle of water for everyone who helps me get out."

A sea of hungry faces stepped closer. Two grabbed the shovels.

"Rob, get in and take the wheel." Andreu put his shoulder against the passenger door frame and said, "Now ease on the accelerator." The Backpacker lurched forward. Andreu jumped into the passenger seat and said, "Drive to that bare spot, then stop."

The mob followed with cries of protest. When Rob stopped, Andreu got out and shouted, "I wasn't going back on my word." He took out a case of water bottles. "First, I want my shovels!" When he had them, Andreu started handing out water. "Only one. Move aside when you get yours." He ran out of bottles before the crowd ran out of people. He held up his hands. "That's all I got. You'll have to share." Disappointed, they hung their heads and dropped back.

When Andreu took the wheel again, Rob said, "There's more water in the compartments."

"I know. We may need it later."

The beach road was washed out in places and covered by sand in others. One wash-out had water running through it. Andreu waded in to check the depth and speed of the water. "We can make it," he said and drove through.

When they reached Dongtian Palace, the gate stood open and parts of the fence were down. A large number of people, more than the summer staff, were picking up trash. "Where were they when Mike flew over?" Rob asked.

Andreu laughed. "Hiding."

The Atlantic Ocean had washed completely over the grounds, distributing salty sand over everything, including the golf course. Rob was thankful for salt-tolerant grass. Other landscaping was badly damaged and would have to be replaced. Only the sabal palms survived. Their fronds littered the sand.

Instead of letting Rob out at the door, Andreu drove into the parking garage. "Too many people I don't know out there." Andreu drove up to the second level. A handful of battered vehicles, probably belonging to employees, were parked there, above the storm surge.

Angus Wilson met them.

"How are you making out?" Rob asked.

"We're making do. Trying to repair the electrical system, but there's no running water. We have to carry it up to flush toilets, and we're bathing in the swimming pools."

Rob nodded. "Doug shut down the plants. Now he's making repairs and will get them back in operation as soon as possible. What are you doing for drinking water?"

"The cistern's full. We've been filtering and boiling the water."

Rob looked at the crowd. "How many are here?"

"I lost count. About a hundred. Staff and their families, and…" He lowered his voice. "I let some of our neighbors come in. Only ones we can trust. They didn't have anywhere else to go. Their houses were destroyed. I hope you understand."

"I do," Rob said. "I won't tell my father."

"Thank you. I need my job now more than ever." Angus led Rob and Andreu to the upstairs ballroom. Open sliding glass doors let a good breeze flow through. He took them out on a balcony where it was cooler. "We're staying on this level and higher, above the mosquitoes."

A line of people on the beach stretched from surf to hotel, passing buckets of water.

"We're pretty well organized," the manager said. "We have to be."

"Do you have enough to feed this many people?"

"No, but I was afraid to ask for more."

The reason Rob hadn't been able to contact Angus was that phone and internet settings had been disrupted by the storm. He rebooted them and called his father with a brief report.

Angus invited them for lunch. Rob opened his mouth to say they'd brought their own, but Andreu said, "We'd be honored to join you."

"I'm afraid it's only black beans and rice. We've run out of everything else."

After Rob tasted it, he said, "It's the best black beans I've ever had."

"We cooked it in broth made of fish bones. Sometimes there are advantages to living by the ocean. Normally, the water's too polluted for fish, but that storm churned up clean cool water and washed the fish right to us."

After lunch, Rob set Andreu up in the communication center to document every person on the property and run background checks. Then he began the monumental task of assessing the condition of the hotel and grounds. Angus accompanied him. Rob expanded a screen on his Nebula to take notes. The buildings were strong, but they'd suffered cosmetic damage. "There's so much to be done," Rob said. "I'll get workers out here as soon as possible, but I'm afraid we won't have this place operational before November."

"If I may make a suggestion…" Angus said.

"Sure. I need all the advice I can get."

"There are a lot of people out of work. Why don't we hire them? The ones with the right skills, of course. Another thing, some of them have no place to live. If we can put them up in the hotel until November, they'll have time to make other arrangements."

"Sure. I'll let you decide who to hire, as long as they pass background checks. You know them better than I do. But this isn't a charity project. My father won't go for that. And everyone who isn't supposed to be here needs to be out before November."

Angus nodded. "As you can see, I've already started them cleaning up the grounds. We'll do what we can with what we have until you can get us the equipment and materials we need."

Equipment and materials? "Angus, I'm afraid I'm out of my element. Do you know what you need?"

"I've got a pretty good idea. I've been through this before. Not quite as bad, but bad enough."

"Then make me a list."

Andreu joined them. "Mr. Rob, as soon as you're finished, we need to go. It might not be safe on the road after dark."

"I'm almost ready." Rob thought about the people in the shattered cities at night. How safe were they?

Once they were in the Backpacker, Rob pulled up Rosa's address. "Let's go here first."

Andreu said, "Let me see that aerial video so I can scout a course."

Rob thought he had seen the worst of the destruction, until they reached Rosa's neighborhood. Andreu's maneuvering couldn't bring them within a half mile of her street. "I suggest we turn around and go home," he said.

Rob shook his head. "I want to see them. They might need help."

Andreu parked the Backpacker and handed Rob the mosquito repellant. "Strap on your sidearm." He took two rifles from a compartment. "Never know what we might walk into."

Rob felt a thrill of bravado and fear. They climbed around downed trees and mangled pieces of solar roofing. Even with repellant, mosquitoes attacked him. "What's that smell?"

Andreu sniffed. "A mixture of things. None of them good."

They made their way around a pile of splintered wood and concrete that had once been a house. A non-descript dog crawled out of the wreckage. Rob stiffened.

Andreu reached out his hand. The mutt sniffed it and rubbed against his leg. "It's okay, Mr. Rob. She's just hungry."

The street came to an abrupt end by a house tilting over a bank. "What happened here?" Rob asked.

"Washout. Looks like they were doubly hit. Storm surge from the Atlantic, and from the channel. You can see the high water mark." He pointed at horizontal lines of mud on buildings and trees.

Rob's bowels felt like they were turning to mud. "I wonder where everyone is."

"Probably hiding."

Rob looked at the firearm he carried. "Oh."

They picked their way down the bank and waded through knee-deep water. "I think it's this way," Andreu said. A twisted sign bore the name of Rosa's street. Using a fallen tree as a handrail, they climbed up.

Rob looked for her house number. A rustle in the bushes—the back of his neck tingled.

A man in dirty clothing crept forward cautiously, eyeing their guns. "Can I do something for you gentlemen?"

"We're looking for the Ortiz family," Rob said.

He pointed at a pile of wreckage. "That's where they lived."

The house had collapsed into the washout.

"The wind was bad enough," he said. "But the rain—the canals here-about filled up—it was like a dam breaking. Last night. Come with no warning."

"Do you know where the family went?"

"Some of them's still in there. I don't know where the girl and boy are. I saw the parents yesterday morning and they said the kids spent the night with friends." He sighed. "Nice people. Just talked to them yesterday. Now they're gone."

Rob edged toward the ruined house.

"Mr. Rob, don't go in there."

"I need to know…"

"I already been in there," the man said. "They're dead."

"But Rosa and her brother—you haven't seen them?"

"No. They're not here."

"I'll give you my number. Have them call me, okay?"

"You'll have to write it down for me."

Rob looked around. A layer of silt covered the pavement. With a stick, he scratched his name and number in the mud.

The man looked again at their guns. "Are they in some kinda trouble?"

"Oh, no. I went to school with Rosa. I wanted to see if she was all right. Maybe there's something I can do to help."

Andreu said, "One thing you might do is have someone get the bodies out and give them a proper burial."

Rob nodded. "I hadn't thought about what they do with bodies."

"Burn them. Or mass graves. There'll be so many." He nodded at the Ortiz house. "I suggest having them cremated and store the ashes 'til the kids can make arrangements."

"That's a good idea. Thanks, Andreu." Rob paused. "I'm not sure how my father would take this. He doesn't even know about Rosa. If I give you the money, could you handle it for me?"

"I'd be proud to."

Rob turned to the neighbor. "When Rosa and her brother come back, tell them, will you?"

"Sure will."

They returned to the Backpacker. The dog followed. Andreu gave it his uneaten sandwich. Then he took out the chainsaw and set it in the street. "The folks here are gonna need this more than we do."

On the way home, Rob said, "Andreu, would you prefer cash?"

"Probably the best thing, if you don't want Mr. Hardman to find out."

"Let's stop by that moneychanger, if we can find him."

When Rob got home, Father was in the holo room watching a news report out of Folkston, Georgia: "While early spring sees droves of Florida homeless trying to cross the border into Georgia, this storm has hordes storming border entries along roads and trying to climb fences in rural areas." A video clip showed people climbing an eight-foot fence, border guards trying to push them off and arresting any who got over.

Father grunted. "They ought to just shoot them."

Rob's stomach quivered. The 3D depiction of people in distress was too real. Why wasn't Father watching it on the flat screen in his office?

Another news clip showed a raging river teeming with human bodies, some swimming, others carried by the current: "Many have resorted to swimming the St. Mary's River, which is overflowing its banks. This has proved fatal to some." The camera focused on a woman holding a baby. She was crying so hard her words were unintelligible. The newsman faced the camera. "Here is a victim of the river. She said her husband and young son were swept away and she has no idea where they are, or if they're even alive. She swam across with her baby strapped to her back, but when she reached safety, the infant had drowned. There are no paramedics here. This mother doesn't know CPR. This is a cautionary tale to prevent further tragedy. If you're thinking of crossing into Georgia but lack transportation, money, or the proper paperwork, do not try it. Stay where you are. FEMA is working hard to alleviate the suffering of Florida residents."

"That's disgusting," Father said. "If they're that stupid, the world's better off without them."

Father's words hit Rob like a cold stone. "But, Father, those people's houses have been destroyed. They have nowhere to go. I saw it—whole neighborhoods uninhabitable. And I didn't see any evidence of FEMA."

"They'll get there eventually. I've seen it before. Instead of taking responsibility for themselves, everybody demands to be taken care of. Right away. Some of those neighborhoods won't be rebuilt. As it should be. It's God's will."

"God's will!"

"If those people lack the foresight to build for the climate, God will make it so they have to relocate."

"But where?"

"Other states. Planned communities built on higher ground." He rested his chin on his fist. "Perhaps that tract of land along Trail Ridge could be developed. They'd need jobs, though. Move a factory there …" He nodded. "With foresight and industry, this catastrophe might play to our advantage."

Rob remained stone-faced.

Father frowned. "Well, what do you have for me?"

Rob reported on the condition of the resort and Angus Wilson's plans to restore it.

"Keep a record of everything you do and every cent you spend. We can get reimbursed from FEMA."

"Why? Isn't the resort insured?"

"Insurance won't pay for everything. Besides, if we're employing storm victims, we're doing the government a favor."

The queasiness in Rob's gut increased. Father's plans might be legal, but they weren't honest. He didn't mention how many were staying at Dongtian.

Back in his suite, Rob's thoughts turned to Rosa. How could he find her? He opened his school yearbook and scrolled down the list of their graduating class. He'd need a cover story. He wrote a short message purporting to inquire about everyone's safety. He asked them to respond and to inform him if they knew the whereabouts of any classmate who might not get the message, communications being down in some areas. Then he sent it to everyone.

Within minutes, messages flooded in. Rob began to map who responded. Most were of his social class, living in safe homes like his. A few had gone to the mountains immediately after graduation. A few scholarship students responded and indicated they were safe. No one reported on Rosa. Perhaps the friend she had visited was another scholarship student with no access to the internet.

Andreu knocked on the door. "I contacted the funeral parlor my family uses. They'll hire somebody to extricate the bodies, then they'll cremate them and store the ashes until Rosa or her brother can claim them."

"Thanks, Andreu."

CHAPTER 8

Tuesday, after Rob checked with Angus at the resort, he sent a list of the "unaccounted for" to his classmates, hoping to get news of Rosa.

Father called him to his office. "Andreu will take you to Olustee Academy for an onsite inspection. I've had a report that the roads are clear."

Piles of wood lined the roadsides. Further inland, they encountered less storm damage.

Ms. Marshall, the headmistress, gave Rob him a tour of the facility. It was basic, clean, and well maintained, serving some 500 students in eight grades. There was less educational equipment than in schools he'd attended, but these students were not college bound. They had to know only enough to get into trade school.

Most of the staff and many students were present. Rob said, "I thought the school would be closed."

Ms. Marshall said, "They're very dedicated."

Andreu spoke up. "You can trust Mr. Rob."

"We canceled classes, but these children's homes have been damaged. There's nowhere else for them to go, to get out of the heat and mosquitoes." She took a deep breath. "A few have been spending the night here. Teachers, too."

Andreu asked, "How are you feeding them?"

"Mostly with imagination."

"Make me a list of what you need," Rob said. "I'll send you supplies tomorrow."

Rob spoke with some of the staff. He'd assumed teachers in schools like this were poorly qualified, the better educated getting better jobs elsewhere. To his surprise, they seemed as professional and knowledgeable as those who'd taught him.

Most of the children were reading. Rob looked over the shoulder of a girl engrossed in her workstation. "What are you reading?"

"*Jane Eyre.*"

A classic? He peered closely at the words. The language was archaic. She was reading the original, not a dumbed-down version. "What's it about?"

"Jane was an orphan who lived with her aunt and cousins, but they were mean to her. She got in a fight with her cousin, then her aunt sent her to a boarding school where the teachers were mean. Jane's friend Helen got sick and died. That's where I am now. If you want to know more, maybe Ms. Marshall will tell you."

Rob smiled. "Or I could read it for myself. What grade are you in?"

"Sixth."

"What do you want to do when you grow up?"

"I want to be a teacher. A nice one, not like the ones in the story."

"Are your teachers like the ones in the story?"

"Oh, no. They're nice. They never hit us or cut our hair off."

"That's good." Rob looked at Ms. Marshall. "Do these children have any prospect of becoming teachers?"

She shrugged her shoulders. "Some have the potential, if given the chance. I've referred this young lady to be tested. We do our best, but there's no school nearby where she can get the proper education. If she can get a scholarship to a boarding school, who knows what she could accomplish?" Then she laughed. "Not a boarding school like Jane Eyre's!"

Rob smiled but didn't let on that he hadn't read the book.

When he got home, Rob sent a truckload of supplies to Olustee Academy. Afterward, he checked messages from his classmates. To his first inquiry, Salli Stubens had replied that she and her family were safe. He now found a curt response, "Rosa Ortiz was here but left Sunday to go home."

Sunday? Rob had been at her house Monday. Not only was she not there, the neighbor hadn't seen her. Where was she? An uneasy dread crept over him. He called Andreu. "How many bodies did they take out of the Ortiz house?"

"Three."

Rob's heart froze. "Have they been identified?"

"Yes. It was the parents and the grandmother."

"Are you sure?"

"Yes, sir. You can get the death certificates from the funeral home."

Rob pulled up the documents. *Thank God!* A middle aged couple and an elderly woman, no young person. He hadn't even known Rosa's parents' names or anything about her grandmother. Where could Rosa be? He sent a message to Salli, "Who took her home? Have you heard from her since?"

Salli answered, "That's all I know."

Was she was embarrassed that a scholarship student had been her guest? Did Rosa go somewhere else, or encounter some mishap? He spent most of the day performing various tasks for his father, but he couldn't stop worrying about Rosa.

* * *

Rosa hardly recognized her neighborhood—broken trees and storm litter everywhere, street signs uprooted and twisted into unreadable scraps.

She'd been traveling for three long days, walking, climbing, wading, backtracking, battling mosquitoes. Water everywhere. Wildlife displaced. She'd dodged possums and raccoons and worried about snakes. Fire ants were the worst. Their hills had been flooded, leaving them scattered and angry.

Saturday's events plagued her. The terrible news about Ramon. The treachery of Salli's family. The loss of her job, career, dreams. At times, she broke down and cried. The belief that her parents and grandmother were safe, waiting for her, sustained her. Once in their arms, she'd find a way to rebuild her life.

Sunday night she spent under the canopy of a fallen tree. Other nights she sheltered with strangers. She picked through a plundered store for food and salve for insect bites. Journeying alone, she spotted a gang of rogues taking advantage of widespread lawlessness. She eluded them and joined a band of displaced families traveling together for safety. To where? At least she had a home to go to. The few times she had access to a phone, she tried calling but got no answer.

The road she thought led to home had been washed out. The only way forward was to slog through a muddy gully. She climbed up to what she thought was her street and saw a house the color and style of her own, fallen into the canal behind it.

Rosa stared at the ruin. Body and brain went numb. She was mistaken. This was not her home. Many had been built in the same style. It was a popular color. She looked around. Nothing was familiar. She was in the wrong place.

She saw a man standing nearby. Maybe he could tell her where she was.

He spun around, a knife in his hand. Rosa gasped and dropped her bag. The man lowered his arm. She looked at his face.

"Rosa?" He stepped toward her.

"Ramon!" She collapsed into her brother's arms.

He sobbed. "They're dead."

"Who?"

"Mama, Papa, Grandmother. They're..."

"No! They can't be! I called them. They said they were safe."

He hugged her tightly. "I just talked to a neighbor. She said they died when the house fell into the...uh...It happened after the storm."

Rosa's head swam. "What..." She shook her head. "What...do we ...do?"

"I don't know."

"I mean, about their—the bodies?"

"They're gone."

"What?"

"The lady said an undertaker came and got them. Before that, some men were here looking for us. They called the funeral home. I got the name of the place."

"What men?"

"I don't know. Maybe police. She didn't know. Her husband talked to them. They wrote their name and number down in the mud, but the funeral people must have trampled over it." He held her at arm's length. "Rosa, you can't go with me. They'll be looking for me. Somebody opened up the jail and we all got out. I'm...I'm a fugitive." He grimaced. "I'm sorry, you don't know what happened..."

"Salli's father said you were arrested."

Ramon beat his fist on a tree trunk. "We were going to get married! Her father found out. He called the police, said I forced myself on her. Rosa, I swear..."

"I know. That's what those people are like. The Stubens kicked me out. In the middle of the hurricane! And he fired me, too." She gulped air to keep from sobbing. "I have no job, Ramon. You're all I've got. I have nowhere to go. What are we going to do?"

"I need to get out of Florida."

"Okay, I'm going with you."

"No. I'll take you to Aunt Josephine's. Maybe you can sleep on their couch..."

"No, Ramon. I don't have a job, and no prospects for one. I have to pay for my education, job or no job. They'll demand the money back. Do you know what they do to people who don't pay off their scholarships? Besides," she fished into a pocket of her overnight bag and brought out a gold chain with a ruby pendant. "I didn't know if I should throw this away or mail it back to her."

He took the necklace. "What is it?"

"It belongs to Salli's mother. Yesterday, I found it in my bag. I think her father put it there to incriminate me."

"Why would he do that? I thought her parents liked you."

"So did I. I probably shouldn't tell you this, but he said he could save my job if I gave him what he wanted."

It took a moment for this to sink in. "That son of a bitch! I'll—"

"No! Ramon, let it go. But you see, I'm a fugitive, too. He'd like nothing better than to be able to pressure me again. When they start looking for you, they'll try relatives. If I'm at Aunt Jo's, if he's filed charges…" She shook her head. "We need to get going. Where's the car?"

"They parked it in that garage up by Sea Oats Avenue. I'll need the claim slip." He picked his way over broken concrete and wood and cautiously slipped through the gaping front door. Rosa started to follow. "Stay out here. It isn't safe."

She said, "The funeral home people went in."

"Doesn't matter. The only reason I'm going in is to get the receipt."

Rosa stood by the door, wringing her hands until Ramon came back.

"It's more stable than I thought. I'll get the car. Cross your fingers the battery isn't dead. When I get back, we'll go in for a few clothes. Wait for me. Out here."

Rosa waited until he left, then crept inside. It was as though a dollhouse had been thrown by an angry child. The floor had broken over the concrete wall of the cistern, walls were buckled, ceilings caved in. A stench rose from the back of the house, which had fallen into the washout. She noticed the TV was missing. The Ortiz family had few possessions of any worth, but other things were also gone.

She tried to reach her room. She slipped on the sloping floor and grabbed the doorjamb to keep from falling. Pulling herself up, she squeezed inside. She and Grandmother had shared the room. Their belongings were tangled together, all sense of order lost. Rosa stifled a sob.

Her suitcase was still under the bed. After leaving college for the last time, she thought she wouldn't need it anymore. She yanked it out and began to gather clothes, careful to take only the most essential. Then she lugged it outside and added the items from her overnight bag.

She listened for Ramon. The neighborhood was eerily silent. Most of the residents must have left. In the distance, a saw buzzed. By habit, she wished she had something to read while waiting. Her books! She couldn't leave them. In the living room, she picked her way around broken furniture to the bookcase. Its contents had spilled onto the floor, but they were mostly undamaged.

She made her way to the back of the house to look for boxes. Everything was soaked and covered with mud. Her parents must have drowned when their room fell into the washout. But Grandmother? What happened to her? Had she slipped and fallen into the flood? Or gone to their room in a vain attempt to rescue them?

A rat ran across her feet. She shrieked. After her panic subsided, she made her way to Ramon's room where she found several dry boxes. Had he been preparing to move out?

Now she was forced to choose which books to take and which to leave. Her favorite books, including poetry of Dickinson and Robare? Or her history books? There was no choice. The others existed in electronic form. The history books were irreplaceable.

She was pulling the second box through the doorway when Ramon returned.

"Whatever are you doing? I told you to stay out of there."

Rosa put her hands on her hips. "I'm capable of making my own decisions."

Ramon shook his head. "What's this?"

"My books."

"We're not taking books. Only a few necessities."

"Fine." She threw her suitcase to the side. "I don't need clothes."

"Rosa…"

"These books are valuable."

"We can't get much for them."

"They're not to be sold. These are the true story of our civilization. We lose these books, we lose ourselves. Where are you parked?"

Ramon shrugged and pointed. He picked up her empty overnight bag and disappeared into the house. Rosa carried a box to the car. It was heavy. She was tempted to ask Ramon to carry the other one but decided not to give him an excuse to leave it. When she returned for her clothes, he emerged from the house with his things.

"Someone's been in there," he said. "Stuff is missing." He handed Rosa a doily their grandmother had crocheted. "I found this. Thank goodness they didn't know where the cash was hidden. At least we have some money." He turned back to the house. "It's hard to leave."

"I know. We're leaving our whole life behind."

They decided to go to their cousin Hector's for the night.

"By the way," Ramon said, "how's your money situation? I don't dare use my bank account."

"I have a little in mine. Do I dare use it?"

"Only as a last resort."

Hector and his girlfriend Greta had an efficiency apartment in the hills outside Green Cove Springs. "We'll be happy for you to stay here," Hector said. "But you'll have to sleep on the floor."

"That's better than where we've been sleeping," Ramon said.

After she bathed and put on fresh clothes, Rosa felt human again. Over supper, she and Ramon told the couple what they'd been through.

Greta snorted with disgust at each bend of the story. "I could of told you not to get mixed up with those pudientes. I know what they're like."

"Tell you what," Hector said, "me and my buddy Jem been thinking about leaving the state. This storm's put me out of work again, unless I want to clear roads. Last hurricane, the boss skipped town before he paid us. FEMA paid him, all right, but there was nothing we could do to get our money." He looked at Greta. "Only thing, Greta still has a job."

"Not much of one. If you go, I'm going with you. I can find work anywhere."

"There, you have it. I'll go get Jem." Hector left and soon returned with a short black man.

After he was introduced, Jem said, "There's five of us? We're not gonna all fit in one car."

"We have a car, too," Ramon said.

While the others made plans, Rosa nodded off. "I'm sorry. I'm just so tired."

"Get in my bed," Greta said. "Hector can sleep on the floor. That is, if they don't talk all night."

When Rosa woke, Ramon was studying a hologram projected on the table in front of him.

"What are you doing?"

"Looking at my road atlas from work. Fortunately, I left it home when I went to see…" He swallowed. "Her." He took a deep breath. "Anyway, I'm glad I still have it. I'm plotting a course that isn't likely to draw attention. Mostly back roads."

"Where are we going?"

"Jem's family owns a place the other side of Baldwin. Nobody's living in it right now. We'll go there and lay low for a few days. After Greta gets paid, she and Hector will join us. Then we'll find a way to get across the border and head north. Maybe we can follow the harvest, work for cash, no questions asked. After that, we'll think of something."

* * *

Wednesday, Rob stood outside his father's office, watching him talk to Josei, the farm manger. *The report must not be good.* His father beckoned him in.

"What is it, Father?"

"We're missing a lot of cattle. Josei found fences down. He doesn't know if they died, escaped, or were rustled. I want you to ride out with

Josei and get a record of our losses. If you suspect any foul play, come back and get Andreu."

"Yes, sir." *At last—get out in the fresh air.*

Josei asked, "Do you want to take the Duck or horses?"

Given a choice between the amphibious vehicle and horses, the decision was easy. "Will you saddle Cricket for me while I change?"

Steven had three horses ready. "Mind if I join you? I've been worried, too, but Mr. Hardman had me doing other things."

Rob nodded. "Let's hope we don't run into any 'foul play.' Andreu doesn't like horseback riding."

They laughed.

"I'm surprised Father took so long to ask about the cattle."

Josei said, "As long as Mr. Hardman has enough for his table, he has little interest in the farm. I've been concentrating on the greenhouses and orchards. We lost a few pecan trees. Besides, the creeks have been so flooded it wasn't safe to cross them. Even with the Duck. Water's gone down some now."

As they approached the pastures, Rob began to detect the odor of rotting flesh. Songbirds were conspicuously absent, but buzzards were abundant. The dairy cows in the first pasture grazed contentedly. In the next pasture, the farm road forded a creek which was overflowing its banks.

"Maybe we should've taken the Duck," Rob said.

"No, we'll be okay. It's a low-water bridge." Josei rode to the edge of the stream and paused by a concrete post. "The other post must've washed out. Follow me. Stay to the right."

"Are you sure?"

"Yes." He pointed to the opposite bank. "I recognize that tree. It's on the other side of the bridge."

Rob wondered how he could tell one tree from another, especially since so many leaned over the creek, ready to topple in. Josei urged his mare forward and let her pick her way until she found the concrete.

The water came up to her knees. Rob nudged Cricket. "Go ahead, boy. Follow them." Steven took up the rear.

On the other side of the creek, the stench increased. A handful of cattle trotted over to them.

"They're hungry," Steven said. Much of the pasture was under water.

Josei pointed downstream at a carcass washed against a tree. "I bet we could of saved a lot of them if we got out here sooner."

"I wish we had a copter," Rob said. "At least we could've seen what was happening."

On his Nebula, Rob recorded live and dead cattle, fences that needed repair, and other damage.

"Well, we're not missing as many as I feared," Josei said. "Some of them may be wandering in the woods."

They didn't ride into the woods, but Rob observed many pine trees that had been blown down, twisted, or snapped off. They would have to be harvested before insects and decay took their toll.

"Let's head back," Josei said. "I need to get a crew out here to round up what's alive. We may have to feed them hay until the water goes down."

"You didn't really need me for this," Rob said. "You could have done it yourself, couldn't you?"

Josei laughed. "Your daddy's not a very trusting man."

Steven grumbled. "Seems to me the safety of the animals should have been a priority over picking up branches in the yard." He looked sharply at Rob. "I'm sorry. You won't say anything, will you?"

"Of course not."

That afternoon, still with no word of Rosa, Rob told his father he needed to go check on the resort. "I know Angus will do all he can, but I'll feel better if I can see for myself."

"Sure. I don't have anything else for you right now. Take Andreu."

At the resort, cleanup and repair were underway. Angus seemed pleased to see Rob. "I've brought in some equipment and hired a few workers for things nobody else here could do."

"That's fine. Just keep a good accounting of everything."

"I appreciate the interest you're taking in the place. Barring another hurricane, we could have it ready for the winter season."

After they left, Rob said, "I'd like to go back to the Ortiz's neighborhood, see if there's any news about Rosa."

Andreu smiled. "You're pretty smitten with that girl, aren't you?"

"Huh? No, just worried. We went to school together. She was pretty interesting. Good to talk to."

They were able to drive within a block of the house. "Let's not take our guns this time," Rob said.

The man he'd talked to before came out. "I didn't see him, but my wife said the boy came by yesterday and she talked to him."

"What about the girl?"

"She didn't see her."

"I wonder if anyone else saw them?"

"Not many people still here. So many houses unfit to live in, and there's no running water." He directed Rob to the few neighbors who remained.

Most people hadn't seen Rosa or her brother. One said, "I saw a girl going down the street carrying a box."

"What did she look like?"

"I didn't get a good look. She had curly dark hair like the Ortiz girl."

Rob relaxed. That must have been Rosa. At least she was alive.

When he reported on the status of the resort, Father said, "Are you keeping careful records of expenses?"

"Yes, down to the penny."

"Good. Are you listing our cost or retail?"

"Both. I wasn't sure how you wanted it."

"Retail, of course. That's the only way to turn a profit. By the way, be sure to include Andreu's time and mileage,"

"Yes, sir." *How could Father charge FEMA for his own employee's work?* He knew better than to ask.

CHAPTER 9

On the way to the house Jem's family owned, Rosa drove and Ramon navigated with a map projected in front of him.

Jem leaned over the seat. "Where'd you get that?"

"I work—worked!—for the road department. I monitored the condition of roads." He grunted. "Not that they paid much attention. Seems the only roads that got proper maintenance were where the pudientes wanted to go. By the way, how can your family afford a house no one lives in?"

"It's an old farm, been in the family for generations," Jem said. "Now it's planted to pine trees. My grandparents were living there, but they got too old and moved in with my aunt. The whole family chips in to pay the taxes. Someday the timber'll pay off. We still go out there to hunt, and for holidays."

Jem directed Ramon onto a dirt road. They had to move a fallen tree that blocked the way. At the end of the lane was a locked gate. Jem got out to open it. "I'll leave it unlocked for Hector and Greta."

The vacant house smelled musty. They opened windows.

"Let's sweep the leaves off the solar panels," Jem said. "Then we can turn on the electricity. We shut it off the when no one's here."

"Do you have water?" Rosa asked.

"Yes, we have a good well."

While the men cleared off the roof, Rosa cleaned the house enough to make it comfortable. A pantry yielded a few canned and dry goods. Once the electricity was working, she cooked a pilaf of rice and canned vegetables.

* * *

Rob was in Father's office Thursday morning when Doug called to report on the desalination plants. "I've got most of them back in operation," Doug said. "The Flagler plant took a direct hit, lots of damage to the infrastructure. That one's going to take a while."

"Doesn't that one supply the resort?" Rob asked.

"Yes."

Rob frowned. "I've got a lot of people working on repairs. We're hauling in drinking water. They're using ocean water for everything else."

Doug shrugged. "Have patience. I'm doing what I can."

Father spoke up. "Do your best. If there's a delay getting the resort open, we can recap our losses from FEMA."

"But the people who work there depend on it for their livelihood," Rob said.

Father gave him a stern look.

Doug grinned. "I have some good news, though. We're going to have another baby."

Father's expression didn't change. "What sex?"

"A girl."

"You already have a girl. You need another boy."

"Why? I have an heir for you."

"You need two sons. If something happens, you have a spare. Another girl will only dilute your legacy."

Doug's face fell. "Wannis wants another girl, and I can afford plenty of children."

"I'm saying do something about it. Get another boy first."

"Well, about the plants…"

Rob paid little attention to the rest of the conversation. He was reminded that he was a "spare." Do something about it? He shook his head. The Third Covenant had a strict prohibition against abortion.

* * *

While they waited for their friends, Rosa, Ramon, and Jem made preparations for a trip. Jem took two tents and five sleeping bags out of the attic and Rosa helped him air them out. Then he sorted through his tools, choosing mostly compact, multi-purpose tools to stash in his belt. "Never know what we might run into."

Ramon studied his maps. "We can follow Old Highway 441 that used to go from Lake City to the mountains."

"How up to date are your maps?" Rosa asked.

"Florida's are current. I hope the others are, too. Right now, I'm going to scout a way to cross the border without taking a main road."

He returned hours later. "I can't find a way into Georgia. Every road between here and Lake City is either guarded or blocked off. Even the dirt roads." He began to pace. "I can't take the chance of guards stopping me. If they find out I'm wanted…" He shook his head. "We'll have to go beyond Lake City. Maybe security won't be so tight there. If it is…" He went outside and stomped around the yard.

"He's really worried," said Jem.

Rosa nodded. "With good reason."

Hector and Greta arrived late that night. "Our car isn't going to make it much further," Hector said. "The differential is making noise."

"Can it be repaired?" Jem asked.

"Sure, but it would take time, and more money than we have."

"Sanctuary!" Ramon said. "Our car's too small for all of us, plus belongings. Maybe we could squeeze in if we put a rack on top. Only thing is, we'd look conspicuous."

"Maybe we can get another car," Hector said.

"How?"

"It's too late to do anything now. Let's see what we come up with in the morning."

* * *

Rob was coaxing his mother to eat when Father came into the breakfast room. While he appeared outwardly calm, his face wore what Rob called his evil little smile. "I've been given some disturbing news."

Rob waited for the ax to fall.

"One of my deliverymen tells me he took a load out to Olustee Academy and people were living there. Can you explain that?"

Was that all? "Yes, sir, some of the staff and students needed a place to stay because of the condition of their homes."

"Who gave them permission?"

"I did, sir. I listed all the expenses as disaster relief."

The smile turned feral and Father's eyes shone with a cold light. "That is not a declared disaster zone. That will come out of my profits."

"I...I'm sorry, sir. I didn't know...I'll pay for any loss. You can take it out of my funds."

His father banged his fist on the table so hard silverware clattered to the floor and glasses toppled. Mother ran from the room, screaming.

"I'm running a school, not a fucking homeless shelter. You're damn right you'll pay. So will those lazy, shiftless, squatters! And you're going out there right now to clean house. And you can take names and inform those bastards that I'm charging them hotel rates. I won't be taken advantage of like this."

Rob shook so hard he could barely speak. "Father, it's not their fault. It's mine. I...I thought I was doing the right thing."

Father lowered his voice. "The right thing? And how many other 'right things' have you been doing?"

"It's all there, in my records. I haven't kept anything from you."

He backhanded Rob, knocking him to the floor. "Get out of my sight. You disgust me. Get out there and straighten things out."

"Yes, sir."

"Take the Backpacker and bring back as much as you can cram in it. I'm not running a damn soup kitchen."

Rob rushed to his room and looked in the mirror. His mouth was bleeding. He dabbed it with a washcloth. After hastily changing clothes, he went by the back stairs to the garage. Andreu said, "The Backpacker's fully charged."

"You're not going with me?"

"No. He said you're to go alone. I'm very sorry about this. I feel like I led you into it."

"No, Andreu, I got myself into it. Now I'm afraid I've hurt a lot of people I was trying to help."

"I put a case of water in the back." Andreu handed him a handgun. "And I put a rifle and ammo in one of the compartments."

Rob shook his head. "I don't think I could shoot anybody."

"You don't have to. Just threaten them. Unless they're armed, too. Then sometimes it's better to hand everything over. Anything to save your life. Remember what I've taught you." Andreu gripped his hand. "Good luck. And stay safe."

"Thanks, Andreu." As Rob drove through the gate of the compound, he thought how, just over a week ago, he'd itched to go out without a bodyguard. Now here he was. Last week he wanted to get out of his father's grip. Today that grip was tighter than before, an ever-constricting vise that threatened to crush him.

When he turned onto the road, a horn blared and a car he hadn't noticed swerved around him. He was in no shape to drive. He pulled over and gave into his feelings. How could he face those innocent people at the school and give them the bad news? Maybe he could reimburse them with cash, like he did Gracie. He wished Andreu was with him. Once he was calm, he looked twice for traffic before getting back on the road.

After several miles, he stopped for a truck that blocked the road, with a crew loading storm debris from the roadside. Suddenly, Rob felt vulnerable. He locked the doors and waited. Why was he afraid? Because he was alone in a lawless world where his money and his father's name afforded little protection? Where, because of that name and wealth, he could be a target for desperate people? Andreu must think so—he'd armed him. Rob had seen small pieces of that "other" world in the past week, but he'd had Andreu's protection. Now what might he encounter?

Remember everything I've taught you. Andreu had taught him how to handle weapons, martial arts, hand-to-hand combat techniques, and how to disarm an opponent, both literally and psychologically. He'd used some of those mental skills in dealing with his father. Indeed, those skills occasionally helped him avoid beatings. He often wondered if Gregory Hardman, the supreme manipulator, was aware of his son's attempts at manipulation.

The equipment pulled out of the way and a workman waved him on.

Olustee Academy was buzzing with teachers and students. Rob met with Ms. Marshall and told her what his father said. He watched the color drain from her face. "You can't know how sorry I am. I'm afraid I've done more harm than good."

She shook her head. "It's not your fault. I knowingly broke the rules. I thought I could get away with it, too. I should have known better."

"I'll do everything in my power to alleviate the situation." Everything in his power? What power? One minute, he was a respected young businessman reaching out with the hand of charity. The next, he was a naughty child being reprimanded. Sitting in front of the desk of this school principal, he crumbled into that child and actually began to cry.

Ms. Marshall came around her desk to comfort him. "Rob, I don't know your father personally, but I know men like him. He doesn't see the human side of things. He views me, and my staff, and my students the same way he views a machine in one of his factories. You are different. I can see that. I'll probably lose my job, but I'll survive. You'll survive, too. All I ask is that you don't surrender your generous spirit to the demands of this society. Someday, you will hold the power your father has over the fate of others. I know you'll wield it more compassionately than he does."

"I will. God strike me dead if I don't!" He managed to collect himself and asked where he could wash his face.

When he returned, Ms. Marshall led him to a storeroom where staff were separating out several crates and boxes. "These are the most expensive and least necessary. I hope this placates your father, somewhat."

Rob disengaged the door locks so they could load the Backpacker.

Ms. Marshall noticed the rifle and said, "Some schools have armed guards, but I've never felt the need for any. The community around here recognizes this school's value. Even the criminal elements respect and protect us." She hugged Rob before he left. "Good luck. Stay safe."

Rob's tears had dried, but he still cried inside. Man up, he told himself. That woman has more to lose than you do. Did you see her crying?

A fallen tree blocked the road. Was he going in the right direction? He looked at his compass. Yes, he was heading east. The tree wasn't there earlier. The bank where the tree grew had collapsed into the ditch, bringing the tree down with it. There was no way to drive around it, even with all-wheel drive. Rob tried to push the tree out of the way, but it was too heavy. He thought about using the Backpacker to push it aside, but that would likely scratch the vehicle, and he was unwilling to incur more of his father's wrath.

Perhaps he could find another route. He missed Andreu, who seemed to know every road in this part of the state. He turned around and took the first right he came to. After two more turns on unpaved roads, he was lost. He opened a map on his Nebula. He should have done that first. But it didn't show the back roads.

The next road ended at a gate. Before he could turn around, something darted across his rear-view mirror. Then someone opened the passenger door, slipped into the seat, and said, "We need to borrow your car. Just drive straight ahead, through that gate."

Rob jumped out of the Backpacker and was confronted by a short black fellow. Rob whipped out his handgun. The man raised his hands. "Tell your friend to get out of my vehicle." The friend got out and, raising his arms, stood by the black man. What now? Rob faced two strangers whose intentions couldn't be in his best interests.

The friend smiled and said, "I think we can come to an agreement."

"Yeah. You agree to leave me alone and I agree to leave."

The man's smile grew wider. "I don't think violence is necessary if we can be so agreeable."

Before he knew it, the man sprang to Rob's side and snatched the gun from his hand. The shorter man grabbed Rob's arms and held them behind him while the other frisked him. "That's all he's got." To Rob, he said, "Now, let's try this again, only you get in the passenger seat, and I'll drive through the gate."

Blood pounding in his ears, the irony was not lost on Rob. His first excursion without a bodyguard, and he was in trouble. What happened to his self-defense training? His assailant had disarmed him psychologically before taking his weapon.

The man waved the gun. "Get in."

Should he tell them who he was? Who his father was? That might make things worse.

The dirt track led to a handful of farm buildings. The man pulled up in front of the house. "Get out. Don't try anything stupid. You can't run away and you can't fight. If you cooperate, we won't hurt you. But if you don't…" He put on a menacing face and waved the gun.

A third man came out of the house. The tall one said, "We got us a vehicle."

With wide eyes, the third looked at Rob and then at the gun. The short one said, "We had to. He was gonna shoot us!"

The third man looked in the Backpacker. "What's all this?"

Without thinking, Rob said, "These are supplies for Olustee Academy."

"Well, this ain't the road to the school."

"There was a tree in the road. I had to take a detour."

"This ain't no detour," the tall one said. "What's your name, boy?"

"Rob."

"Rob what?"

"Smith."

"Okay, Rob Smith. Why don't you start unloading this stuff."

He complied. The tall man watched Rob while the others carried the boxes to the porch.

The short one looked at a label and said, "What are haricot verts?"

The third answered, "Fancy green beans. Funny thing to take to a school."

After everything was unloaded, Rob said, "What now?"

"You've got more cargo space than this." The short man opened a compartment and pulled out the rifle. "Hey, look here!"

"Supplies for the school?" the tall one said. "Do you have any more weapons, Rob Smith?"

Rob shook his head. "Only a box of ammunition." They'd find it, anyway.

The man pointed the rifle at a box labeled beef stew. "Take that in the house."

The house was a cement block building that must have been a hundred years old. Rob carried the case in and set it on the table.

A girl walked into the room. "What you got there?"

The tall man grinned. "A car and a chauffeur."

Rob stared at the girl. That voice, that wavy dark hair, blue eyes…

CHAPTER 10

Rosa had refused to believe their situation was hopeless. The primary concern that morning was transportation. The men tried everything they could think of to make Hector's car roadworthy, but it was no use. Jem found a small utility trailer in the barn, but they had no trailer hitch.

"Let me ask my neighbor," Jem said. "Maybe they have one we can borrow." He and Ramon walked down the road.

Greta took the Ortiz car to a store for groceries. Hector stayed to help Rosa tidy the house. "Even if they get a trailer hitch," Hector said. "Your car may not be powerful enough to pull it."

Something's got to give. It just has to. "Help me with my books. I may have to leave some of them here." They put both boxes on the table and Hector helped her sort through them. She boxed up the fiction. "Will you put these in the attic for me?"

"Sure." Hector peeked out a window. "Jem and Ramon are coming back. They look empty handed."

Rosa sighed and packed the rest of her books. As she carried the box into the bedroom, she heard a car door close. Hector came down from the attic. "Someone's here," she said.

"Greta's probably back." He headed toward the door.

Rosa heard voices on the porch. She set her books in a corner and returned to the front room. Instead of Greta with groceries, a man set a heavy box on the table. A question for Ramon left Rosa's lips, but she didn't hear his answer.

The man straightened up. "Rosa?"

Blood roared in her ears—this couldn't be real! "Rob?"

"What are you doing here?" he asked.

"What are *you* doing here?"

Ramon said, "You know this squirrel?"

"Uh, y-yes, we…we uh, went to school together." Every nerve in her body flared. "What on God's green Earth is going on?"

"This is our ticket to Georgia." Ramon crossed the room and laid a rifle and handgun on the kitchen counter. His hands were shaking.

Rosa stared at the weapons, then at Rob. He looked petrified. "What in Heaven's name…?"

Rob whined, "They took my car."

"What?" She zeroed on Ramon.

He turned away. Hector and Jem looked at the floor.

"No! Ramon! Do you have any idea what you've done?" She pointed at Rob. "Do you know who this is?"

"Rob Smith, so he said."

"Hardman, Ramon. Rob Hardman! Gregory Hardman's son. Hardman Aquatics!"

"Oh, shit!"

Heavy silence filled the room.

Rob cleared his throat. "Let me go. I won't tell my father. You won't get in any trouble."

Ramon barked a laugh. "Oh, we're already in trouble!" He stomped outside, slamming the door. Everyone else froze. Ramon paced the length of the porch, occasionally kicking a box.

Rosa glared at Hector and Jem. They avoided her eyes.

Outside, Ramon paused and stared at the Backpacker. Then he burst back into the house. "We need your vehicle. I need to get out of this state." He slapped the box on the table. "Those supplies—they'll come in handy." He whipped a knife out of the sheath on his belt and pointed it at Rob. "Sit down."

Rob sat.

Ramon slit open the box and took out a can of stew. "Hector, let's warm this up."

Rob didn't take his eyes off Ramon's knife. Rosa didn't take her eyes off Rob. Hector carried the stew into the kitchen, dumped it into a pan, and turned on the stove.

Rob said, "If I don't get home soon, my father will be looking for me."

"Then we need to act fast. Jem, help me with these boxes." They carried everything into the house. Hector set two bowls on the table. Ramon shoved one at Rob. "Bon appetite."

Rosa's stomach was too knotted to eat. She stared at Rob, hungrily attacking the stew. *How can he possibly have an appetite?*

Rob paused and looked at Rosa. "I went to your house looking for you."

"I wasn't there."

"I know. Do you know about your parents?"

She bit her lip and nodded.

"I, uh, I hired a funeral home. To take care of the bodies. They cremated them. They'll hold the ashes until you claim them."

Hector blurted, "That's the biggest pile of bullshit...."

"Hush," Rosa said. "Somebody really did. Rob? That was you?"

He shrugged. "It was the least I could do."

Tears slide down Rosa's cheeks. She reached across the table and grasped his hand. "Thank you."

The front door flew open. Everyone but Rob sprang to their feet.

"Oh, Greta!" Rosa cried. "You scared me."

Greta set down a bag of groceries. "I went to three stores. This is all I could get."

Hector kissed her. "That's okay. Food came to us. I'll get you some stew."

Greta glared at Rob. "What's this?"

Rob stood and extended his hand. "Rob Hardman."

Greta ignored him. "What's he doing here?"

Ramon said, "Mr. Hardman has graciously offered to take us to Georgia."

"What makes you think so?"

"Well, we didn't give him much of a choice."

Rob sat down.

Greta shook her head. "Are you insane?"

Hector took her hand. "It's okay. You and Rosa aren't involved. You can follow us in Rosa's car."

Rosa spoke up. "You're wrong. If you guys get caught, Greta and I go to jail, too."

Rob said, "I don't want anybody to go to jail. I just want to go home."

Ramon gritted his teeth. "We need to get across the state line."

"Okay. You can have the Backpacker. Just let me go."

"Just like that?" Ramon said. "How far do you think we'll get before you have the police after us?"

"Just drop me off somewhere. I'll give you time to get across the border before I call my family to come get me."

"We need *you*."

"What for?"

Ramon huffed. "To get us across the border. I've never seen it so heavily guarded. You'd have no trouble getting across. After that, we'll let you go."

Rob turned to Rosa. "How'd you get mixed up in this? Why do you want to go to Georgia, anyway? I thought you were teaching."

She lowered her head. "I was. Everything's changed. I've run out of options. I have no home anymore. No family. Nothing."

"What about your brother?"

She looked at Ramon.

"Don't tell me that's your brother? A…a car thief?"

Rosa shook her head. "He's no criminal."

Ramon snorted. "I am now. A few days ago, I was a respected, productive Citizen." He snarled at Rob, "A pudiente like you changed that. And I'm helpless to defend myself."

Rosa laid a hand on his arm. "Ramon, let's not get into that now. If we're leaving, we have things to do."

Ramon nodded. They sorted through the cases of food and debated what to take with them. They settled on what could be easily prepared on the road and stashed it in the storage compartments.

Rosa took Rob into the living room. "Why did you go to my house?"

Briefly, he told about his excursion to the resort. "I knew your neighborhood was flooded and I wanted to find you."

"Why?"

"Because I was worried."

"You didn't have to take care of my parents' bodies."

"I know. But they were just being left there to rot. I wouldn't want my parents treated that way. I didn't know what you'd want done, but cremation seemed best, under the circumstances. Hell, I didn't even know if you were alive or dead."

"Thank you, Rob. It was very kind. More than kind. I'm sorry you got mixed up in our mess."

He gave her a wry smile. "Well, I'm glad I found you alive. Rosa, why are you doing this? This isn't like you."

"I know. I have no choice. Things happened beyond our control. Ramon needs to leave the state and I have to go with him. Someday I'll explain it to you." She turned away. "I need to get my things."

The others loaded their belongings. Hector, Greta, and Jem had backpacks. Rosa brought out her box of books.

"You're going to have to leave them here," Ramon said.

"I already put the fiction in the attic. These histories go with me."

Ramon looked around. "Who's watching the kid?"

"He's in the living room. And he's not a kid. He's my age."

Ramon grunted.

* * *

Rob watched through the window. The men bolted a rack onto the roof of the Backpacker, behind the solar panel. He cringed. He'd hoped to take the vehicle home in one piece. He thought about running away while they weren't watching but didn't know where he was or where to go. He doubted Ramon would shoot him, but could he outrun Ramon's long legs?

Rosa carried out a suitcase. She was the last person he'd suspect of doing something nefarious. Could he have been so wrong about her?

Rosa returned and sat beside him.

"Rob, I could probably convince Ramon to let you go, but we really need your help. We aren't bad people. There isn't time to tell you everything right now, but I need you to help us get across the state line. I need you to do this willingly, not be forced at gunpoint."

Rob thought about how deep in trouble he already was. He wouldn't willingly expose Rosa, but his father could force the truth out of him. He knew Rosa could be trying to manipulate him, but he desperately wanted to believe in her. He had a choice: help Rosa or betray her. Either way, his father was going to make his life miserable.

He drew a deep breath and said, "I'll help you."

"Oh, thank you." Rosa squeezed his hand.

Rob couldn't account for the feeling that came over him—the thrill of promised adventure. Consequences be damned!

The gang had secured tents and sleeping bags to the luggage rack and covered them with a tarp. Rob said, "What's our cover story? We're a group of friends going camping?"

Rosa almost smiled.

Ramon walked in. "Well, we're ready. Last minute bathroom visits. Rob, how is that thing on solar? How far can we get?"

"It's been in the sun all day, so the batteries should be fully charged. After dark, it can go several hours." They said they wanted to get into Georgia. How much farther did they plan to go? He followed Ramon outside.

"You'd better drive," Ramon said. "And we better be able to trust you. If we can't..." He seemed to search for a believable threat. "If we're caught...well, Rosa would be in a heap of trouble."

"I understand." Rob checked his Nebula. There was a message from Father, "Where the hell are you!!!" Another from Andreu, "Rob, what's wrong? Your father is beside himself and your mother is worried. Please contact us." His mother. He'd been snatched from her side at breakfast. He didn't even have time to say goodbye. But if he disappeared for a few days, would his father be happy to see him again?

Ramon grabbed his arm. "I can't believe we didn't take this away from you."

"I was just checking messages."

"Take it off."

Rob handed it to him.

"This probably has a tracking function."

"So does the car," Rob said. "And a separate device."

"I hadn't thought of that."

"The computer can be reprogrammed to disable the tracking function. I have no idea where the bug is."

Jem said, "I do." He grabbed a tool and crawled under the Backpacker. After a few minutes, he stood up holding a tiny device.

Ramon nodded. "We'll throw both of these in the first creek we come to."

Rob reached for his Nebula. "Not that. We may need it. We can disable the tracking function."

"You expect me to trust you?"

Rosa spoke up. "You can trust me." She opened a screen and studied it for a moment, then touched an icon. Another screen opened. Rosa entered a few commands and handed it to Rob. "It's ready for your thumbprint." He pressed his thumb to it. "I also disabled the telephone mode so you can't make calls or send messages." She pocketed the Nebula. "Now let's reprogram the car."

Once on their way, Ramon directed Rob down a series of back roads.

"Wait," Hector said. "We're going the wrong way."

"Only temporarily." They came to a raging creek. Ramon said, "Stop on the bridge." He lowered his window and tossed the tracking device into the stream. "With any luck, they'll track you to the Atlantic Ocean. Now, turn around and go the other way."

They discussed which route to take. "The turnpike's faster," Rob said.

"No," Hector said. "What if we get stopped?"

"They're not likely to stop this car," Rob said. "Besides it'd save power. I just engage the radar pilot, and we cruise right along."

"Wait a minute," Ramon said. "That would identify the vehicle."

"Uh, I guess so."

"What's the likelihood your father's reported you missing?"

"I don't know. Probably a matter of time. So, not the turnpike?"

When they reached Lake City, Ramon told him where to turn. "Don't go too fast, or too slow. Maybe a little over the speed limit. We don't want to attract attention."

The tension in the Backpacker was palpable. At a traffic light, a police car pulled beside them. Rob half expected Ramon to reach for the gun, wherever he'd hidden it. Instead, Ramon clenched his jaw and gripped the armrests as though holding on to dear life. Rob noticed Ramon wore a Citizenship ring. *Not your typical thug. What's he running from?* When the policeman turned off, Ramon relaxed.

At the state line was a sign: "Agricultural Inspection Station. All vehicles must stop." Rob stopped and lowered his window. The officer didn't leave his air conditioned booth, only stood up, peered at the Backpacker, and opened the gate. Simultaneously, everyone let out their breath.

"Wow! That was easy," Jem said. "If it was my old man's truck, they'd of torn it apart searching for contraband."

Rob looked in the rearview mirror. "Hey, if we're supposed to be friends, how come I don't know everyone's name?"

Rosa said, "This is my cousin Hector and his girlfriend Greta. And this is their friend Jem."

After a series of "Pleased to meet yous," Ramon said, "Cut the crap."

Rob glanced at Greta. He had a feeling he'd seen her before.

* * *

Rosa sat beside Jem, staring at the back of Rob's head. What errant twist of fate had thrown them together? And why at the lowest point in her life? She couldn't believe the guys would carjack someone. Ramon must be more desperate than she thought. But why did Hector and Jem go along with it? She didn't know Jem well, but Hector had always been level-headed. And now she was complicit. She hoped she could keep Rob on their side.

She had mailed the necklace to Salli's mother, because it was the right thing to do. Although it was probably futile, she'd included a note that she found it in her things but had no idea how it got there. Her conscience was clear on that matter, but what were they to do about Rob?

He broke the silence. "Well, we're in Georgia now. What next?"

Rosa looked at her companions. Some criminals! Their goal had been to get out of Florida. Beyond that, they had no clear plans. While at Jem's farm, they'd discussed possibilities. Greta's aunt worked at a resort in the mountains. She thought she could get hired there for the summer, perhaps Hector and Jem as well. But neither Ramon nor Rosa dared reveal their identities. They would be limited to manual labor, paid in cash, and not paid well. The loss of Hector and Greta's car had been a major setback. How were they to reach the mountains?

Then fortune had smiled—or smirked—bringing transportation and food. By a cruel twist, it also brought Rob, not a rapacious rich guy they could unscrupulously take advantage of, but Rob Hardman, a fairly decent fellow, one who triggered feelings Rosa wished she didn't have. What were they going to do about Rob?

Apparently he was impatient for an answer. "Well? What's the plan?"

"Just keep driving," Ramon said. "We'll tell you when you need to know."

Rosa looked out the window. She'd never been outside Florida before. The land here was low and flat, mostly pine trees. She saw little wind damage from the hurricane, but it must have rained heavily. The water in the ditches came up to the pavement. Creeks were flooded.

Rob stopped before a bridge covered by flowing water. "Do you think it's safe?"

Ramon got out, removed his shoes, and waded across the bridge. "It's okay. Come on."

An hour or so later, they came to a small town, Homerville.

Rob said, "My family came from here over a hundred years ago. I wonder if any of them are still around?" Near the center of town was a sign, "Hardman Building Supply."

"Don't you want to stop in and say hello?" Greta said.

Rob didn't respond.

Miles down the road, Greta said, "I need to stop soon."

Ramon consulted his map and said to Rob, "Take the next right. It should be a dirt road."

A sign by the road read, Hebron Baptist Church. Ramon directed Rob to park in the church yard. "Wait." He got out and walked around the building. "No one's here. Y'all can get out."

Rob didn't move. Hector said, "Weren't you told to get out?"

"I wasn't sure."

Rosa and Greta walked around behind the church. Greta said, "Keep a look out for me and I'll do the same for you."

"Greta, what are we going to do? Rob's not just any rich boy."

"I know. His father's vindictive."

"I don't see a clear way out of this."

"Neither do I. Let's hope something turns in our favor."

When they returned, the men leaned on the Backpacker, talking quietly. Rosa watched Rob walk about the church yard, then disappear behind an azalea bush. "Aren't you afraid he'll run off?"

Ramon looked Rob's way and said, "We should be so lucky."

"Well, we're out of Florida. Do we have a plan?"

"The mountains. Apex Resort where Greta's aunt works. At least we have transportation."

Rosa shook her head. "We can't keep a stolen car. And what about Rob?"

"When we get there, give him the car and let him go. And hope he doesn't rat on us." Ramon looked at the ground. The sand was covered with footprints. He shuffled a foot back and forth as though to erase them. "Well, if we're done, let's go."

Rob rejoined them.

Hector said, "I'll drive now."

When Rob started to take Hector's place, Greta said, "Jem, switch places with me. I don't want to sit with the likes of him."

Rosa watched Rob's face. If Greta's remark offended him, he didn't show it. If anything, he looked resigned. Greta slipped in beside her. Rob gave Rosa a half smile.

In Douglas, Georgia, they passed a hotel. Rob said, "I wish I could put us up somewhere for the night, but they won't take cash and they could track my payment."

Ramon said, "We don't want your money."

Rob slumped in his seat. He was close enough for Rosa to catch his scent. He didn't smell like Rob, the college boy. He smelled of fear. His Nebula vibrated in her pocket. She looked at the message: "Robert, you need to call me right away or suffer the consequences." She decided not to show it to him. Something besides this abduction was not right in his life.

She explored the Nebula. Small enough to be worn on the wrist, it had almost as much capacity as a full size computer terminal. Flipping up the watch face opened a virtual screen made of light beams. She played with it, touching icons that opened additional screens. It was fed information through satellites, but censorship filters prevented it from receiving material banned by the government. One icon led to Rob's personal files. A thrill tripped down Rosa's backbone. What would she find there? Girlfriends? No, only a directory of their graduating class, with a few friends added, a few personal photographs, and a video of hurricane damage taken from the air.

A tone sounded. The battery was low. She shouldn't look at his private information, anyway. The Nebula could be charged by its solar cell or a slot in the Backpacker. "Ramon, will you plug this in?" She handed it to Jem who passed it to Ramon. "By the way, Rob, why were you on Jem's road?"

He took a deep breath and lowered his eyes. "I'd sent supplies to Olustee Academy, and my father didn't like it. He sent me back for them. While I was there, a tree fell across the road. I tried to find a different way home, and got lost."

"Why did he want the supplies back?"

Another deep breath. "Because it wasn't designated a disaster zone and he wouldn't get reimbursed for them."

Ramon turned around. "Why did you send the supplies in the first place?"

"Because the people had been hit hard and needed help." He lowered his head. "I think I just made things worse for them. The headmistress will probably lose her job over this."

Rosa couldn't help herself. She leaned forward and patted Rob's shoulder. "At least you tried."

He laid his hand on hers and smiled sadly. "In my father's world, no good deed goes unpunished."

Hector hit a pothole. "Sorry." The jolt dislodged their hands.

Ramon harrumphed. "I don't understand why they don't maintain these roads like they should."

"Because," Greta said, "the pudientes don't use these roads. So nobody cares."

On their approach to the Ocmulgee River, a sign said, "Bridge Out." Ramon told Hector to drive forward to the barricade where a man was fishing. Ramon got out and asked, "What happened here?"

"Oh, the state inspectors were saying for years this bridge needed work, but there was never any money. Last year we had so much rain, the river swolled up and tore out the middle of the bridge. They keep saying they'll fix it, but there's no money."

"How can I cross the river?"

"The bridge at Lumber City is still there."

The detour took more than an hour. After they were back on track, they passed a sign for Little Ocmulgee State Park. "There's a place to camp for the night," Rob said. "Unless you want to keep going…"

"We'll stop when I say stop."

CHAPTER 11

Rob shielded his eyes from the sun, which was settling into the tree-tops. They passed a bean plantation. Across the road was a row of small houses, quarters for farm workers. Ramon had Hector stop. He walked up to an old man sitting in front of a house, returned shortly, and said, "He told me where we could camp." Ramon directed Hector down a dirt track through the fields to a line of trees. They found a small clearing by a stream swollen from rain. Ramon looked pleased. "Let's set up camp."

While the gang unloaded what they needed from the Backpacker, Rob stood idly by, slapping mosquitoes. Was this his opportunity to escape? While everyone else appeared occupied, he slipped into the driver's seat, but the SUV wouldn't start. He checked for the antitheft mechanism, a little device that, if removed, prevented the vehicle from operating. Ramon, or more likely Jem, had apparently taken it out. Rob got out of the Backpacker, trying to act innocent.

Ramon hollered, "Hey! Make yourself useful. Gather some fire-wood."

There were plenty of downed branches in the clearing. Rob gathered an armload and broke them into usable pieces.

Rosa and Greta pitched a pup tent and the men set up a larger one. Then the girls walked down to the creek. When they returned, Ramon asked, "Is the water fit to drink?"

"It looks clean enough. Boiling would kill any germs."

Jem said, "We need to worry about runoff from fertilizer and pesti-cides. I'll go ask that man what he knows."

While he was gone, Ramon asked, "Who knows how to start a fire?"

Hector said, "Jem does."

"So do I," said Rob. "Where do you want it?"

"Over here."

Rob stacked kindling and gathered dry leaves and Spanish moss for tinder.

Hector squatted beside him. "Where'd you learn to build a fire?"

"Scouts. Do you have matches? Rubbing two sticks together takes time."

"You can do that?"

"Yeah. I've done it before."

"Just a minute." Hector went to the Backpacker and returned with a lighter.

Jem brought back two jugs of water. "The old man said he wouldn't drink the water or cook with it, but it's okay to bathe in. He gave us these, just wants his jugs back."

Ramon stripped off his shirt. "I need a bath." Then he looked at his sister. "Do you girls want to go first?"

"Only if you guys do the cooking."

"Sure. We'll warm up some soup. Hector, where'd you stash that soup pot?"

The girls grabbed fresh clothes and left.

Ramon opened a gallon can of soup and poured it into the pot. "Hurry up with that fire."

Soon Rob had a blaze. He found a broken cement block and nestled it close to the fire to set the pot on. The mosquitoes were getting worse. *Maybe the smoke will discourage them.*

Jem said, "I know something that'll dress up this soup." He disappeared into the bean field and returned carrying an armload of bean plants. "Rob, help me wash these and break them up."

Rob helped him pull the green beans off the vines, wash them with drinking water, and add them to the pot. "I assume that's not an organic farm, if we can't drink the water."

Jem shook his head. "When the big guys buy up the little farms, most of 'em can't be bothered."

Jem washed the leaves. When he started to put them in the soup, Rob asked, "Aren't those poisonous?"

"Naw. You're thinking of tomato vines."

By now, the girls had returned. Greta said, "What do you think we common people live on after you pudientes get the good parts?"

"Yes, Rob," Rosa added. "Commercial farms don't bother with a lot of things that are edible."

As much as he thought he knew about agriculture, this was new to Rob. Did the servants at Hardman Hall eat the plant parts his family didn't?

Rosa said, "We need something to hang our wet clothes on."

Ramon laughed. "What—you swam in your clothes?"

"We washed them."

Ramon and Hector took the rope from the luggage rack and strung it between two trees.

"Now it's our turn," Ramon said. He rummaged through his bag. "Hey, rich kid!" He tossed Rob a shirt and pair of shorts. "I don't want to smell your stinky self all the way to the mountains. But I'm not loaning you my underwear."

"Uh, thanks."

The creek wasn't deep enough for swimming, but they stripped and splashed in the water to get clean. Rob rinsed out his clothes and put on what Ramon had loaned him. Ramon was taller, but they were the same girth. When he put on his shoes, Rob wished he had clean socks. They draped their wet clothes over the makeshift clothesline.

Rosa and Greta spread sleeping bags by the fire to sit on.

"Is the soup ready?" Ramon asked.

Rosa stirred the pot. "Almost. The beans aren't quite done." She resumed her seat.

Rob ignored Ramon's scowl and sat beside her. "So, why aren't you teaching?"

Rosa sighed. "I got fired."

"What?"

She looked at him, as though debating what to say. "I was assigned to a school Salli's father owns. When he found out about Ramon's arrest, he fired me."

"But you didn't do anything wrong!"

"He didn't want his daughter associating with trash."

"I don't understand. What did Ramon do?"

Ramon grunted. "My *crime* was falling in love with a pudiente."

"What's wrong with that?"

Rosa looked into the fire. "Her father had Ramon arrested for rape."

"Huh?"

Ramon's eyes bored into Rob's. "You heard her. Love outside one's 'caste' is a crime. Depending on which 'caste' you belong to, that is."

"But why are you on the run? No way could they convict you if it was consensual."

"You don't live in the real world, do you? I was convicted before I was charged. That's how it works for us."

Hector spoke up. "I have an uncle rotting in prison. He's a book-keeper. Somebody higher up got caught embezzling and rigged it so he got blamed. Now he's a bookkeeper for the prison, with no pay. Every time his parole comes up, a guard picks a fight with him, he gets charged with assault, and they tack on more time. They'll probably let him go when he gets too old to work."

"But that's not right!"

"No, it's not right," said Ramon. "But that's the way it is."

Rosa said, "That's not what they teach us in school, Rob. They tell us our country has the greatest justice system in the world. Maybe for some people, like you, but not for the rest of us. There's no way Ramon could get a fair trial. He'd spend the rest of his life in prison."

"Yeah. And it came close to being a short life."

Everyone looked at him.

Ramon poked a stick in the fire. "Before the hurricane, the warden went home. The worse the weather got, more staff went home. Then the next shift didn't come in. We were locked in there with no food, no nothing, for two days. We were left in there to die." He threw the stick into the fire.

"No!"

"Yes."

"Who owns that detention center?"

"Guy named Morton Cooper."

Rob sputtered. "He'll have a fit when he hears about that!"

Ramon said, "Relax. He already knows."

"What?"

"After the storm, the assistant warden came in. He called Cooper, asked him what to do, and you know what that asshole said? Leave us locked in 'til the staff came back! It could have been a week. But that assistant warden's a decent fellow. He opened the doors and let us go. I don't know what kind of trouble he's in now. Probably worse than me."

"I don't understand. I know Mort. We played golf together last week. His son and I are friends. I went to his hurricane party. I can't see him doing that."

"Believe."

Rosa asked, "Where was this hurricane party?"

"Same neighborhood as the Stubens."

"Humph. Salli was invited to that party, but we couldn't go."

Rob hoped the dim light hid how red his face got. He wasn't proud of his behavior at the party and was glad Rosa hadn't been there to see it.

"Tell him why you couldn't go," Greta said.

"Because, when Salli's father found out about Ramon, he threw me out. In the middle of the hurricane."

"Threw you out in the middle of the hurricane?"

"Yeah. Their groundskeeper took me in."

Rob reeled. This blow hurt worse than anything his father ever dished out.

"In the morning, I had to leave before the Stubens caught me there." She began to sob. "I called home first. They were still alive. I told them I was safe. I didn't know they weren't."

Rob started to put an arm around her.

"Leave me alone!" She threw off his arm.

"But you've done nothing wrong, why are you on the run?"

"Because I've been branded a thief."

"What?"

"There was a necklace in my overnight bag. It belonged to Salli's mother. Her father planted it there to have something to hold over me. So I can't go home, even if I had a home to go to." She ran to the other side of the Backpacker. Greta followed.

Rob could hear her crying. Everyone else remained silent.

Jem stirred the soup and cleared his throat. "It's ready." Hector ladled it into bowls.

Greta returned for two bowls of soup and took one to Rosa. No one spoke while they ate.

Rob spooned food into his mouth but barely tasted it. *They threw Rosa out during the hurricane? She could have died! And Mort didn't care that human beings were locked in jail and abandoned?* He wasn't sure how much he trusted Ramon's word, but he believed Rosa.

After supper, Rob followed Ramon to the creek to wash their dishes. "Hey, when this is over, I'll see about hiring a lawyer for you and Rosa. It isn't right..."

"Forget it. Maybe Rosa could be helped, but all the lawyers in the country aren't likely to help me. Besides, it's not your problem." He shook his head. "Let's get some sleep. The tent's going to be crowded with four of us. Sorry, Mr. Hardman, we don't have an extra sleeping bag. You can sleep on the tarp. It's warm, you don't need a blanket."

Rob shook out the tarp and folded it to make a not very comfortable mattress. He glanced at the campfire. Rosa was reading a book by the light of his Nebula. He longed to sit beside her, but he knew Ramon wouldn't let him, even if Rosa did.

It was hot in the tent. Mosquitoes buzzed in Rob's ears. The folded tarp provided little cushioning from the hard ground and it stuck to his sweaty skin. A few times, he heard someone whimper—Ramon, probably having bad dreams.

Rob woke feeling as grimy as he had before his bath. There was no coffee. Breakfast was a few slices of bread with bean paste. After tents were taken down and gear loaded, he waded into the water to rinse off. While he stood on the bank letting the breeze dry him, a dove's cry reminded him of cool mornings at home. Was he homesick? He wasn't sure.

He returned to the middle of a discussion. Apparently, the plan was to find a mountain resort where Greta, Hector, and Jem hoped to get jobs.

"I don't know about housing," Greta said. "Rent is so expensive in those places."

"We have tents," Jem said.

Rob interrupted, "Why are you three on the run? You don't have criminal charges, do you?"

"No, but we don't have jobs, either. No work, no eat."

Ramon took the wheel. "I'll drive as long as we have a good road. When we run into a detour, someone else will have to take over so I can navigate."

Rosa sat beside her brother, and Rob took the middle seat with Jem. He'd ridden through Georgia before, on the turnpike. The backroads gave him a more intimate view of the countryside. They drove through an agricultural area, large tracts of land with clusters of farm buildings and small houses. Occasionally, they passed a school or church. Rob knew that not everyone attended the Sanctuary of the Loving Spirit, but he wasn't aware there were so many different denominations. Many of the churches were small. Their neighborhoods were so poor, he wondered how they could support a church. Now and then, he spotted an estate house on a distant hill.

Rob was used to the contrast between wealth and poverty in Florida. It seemed more pronounced here. He was familiar enough with farming to observe that many fields which should be under production were fallow. Some, overgrown with weeds and tree seedlings, had not been used for several seasons.

By habit, Rob checked his wrist, but the Nebula wasn't there. Rosa still had it. He wanted to check for messages, even if he couldn't answer them. He thought about home. Eventually he'd have to go back. When he did, how was he going to deal with his father?

Rob leaned forward. "Rosa, do you still have my Nebula?"

She took it out of her pocket and looked at it. "The battery's down." She pushed it into the charging slot.

"You're not calling anyone," Ramon said.

"No. I just want to know what's going on in the world." The more time and distance between him and Florida, the more Rob's anxiety grew. He saw no good way out of this situation.

North of Dublin, the road was well maintained. When they passed through Milledgeville, Rob said, "You might want to bypass Lake Sinclair."

"Why?" Ramon asked.

"I know people who have vacation homes there. They might recognize the car."

"Aren't there a hundred cars like this?" Yet Ramon pulled over. "You can drive, just in case."

Rob happily took the driver's seat, but to his disappointment, Rosa yielded the passenger's seat to her brother.

Ramon navigated down a series of backroads through the Oconee Forest. After they bypassed the lake, he tried to take them back to the highway, but they encountered another bridge out. The resulting detour took an additional hour. When they finally crossed the river, they stopped at the boat ramp for lunch—bread and bean paste again.

"I don't understand why so many bridges are out," Rob said.

"Because they don't fix them, unless they're on an important transport route," Ramon said. "I'd lay money down, the bridge over Lake Sinclair is in good condition because of who uses it. Nobody cares about these little communities. The powers that be would like nothing better than for these people to stay isolated. And starve."

Rob noticed Greta glaring at him again. "I know you from somewhere," he said. "I just can't place you."

"Oh, you've forgotten me, have you? I thought you were just being rude. I guess playthings are forgettable, when you have so many."

"Playthings?"

"I was your brother's. If I'd stayed around long enough, I'm sure you'd of had your way with me, too."

Like a thunderclap on a clear day! When Rob was about eight, they had a cook with a teenage daughter. He remembered Doug chasing her through the house, both of them laughing. Then one summer when he came home from the mountains, she and her mother were gone. He was told they found other employment.

"Don't you want to know what became of me?"

"Your mother got a job somewhere else."

Greta barked a mirthless laugh. "Yeah, we did! Begging on the streets."

"Why?"

She looked hard at him. "You don't know?"

"Of course not."

"For standing up to your father."

Most servants knew better than to cross Gregory Hardman.

Greta turned to Hector. "Rob here finally recognizes me. He claims not to know what his family did to me and my mother."

"What did they do, other than fire you?"

Hector looked at Rob, then back to Greta. "Tell him."

"Everything?"

"Yes. I think you should."

She sighed. "I was Doug's plaything. You know what I mean, don't you?"

"Yes." Rob thought of Cisli and blushed.

"Well, he didn't always use protection. I was very young and naïve. He told me he loved me. I believed him. I thought he would marry a girl he loved. Besides, the pudientes like blue-eyed blondes like me. When my mother tried to keep us apart, Doug told your father we weren't doing our jobs." She paused. "Mama didn't realize *that* was part of the job."

"What happened?"

"What do you think? I got pregnant."

"Is that why he fired you?"

"Oh, no. Not yet. He had to take care of *that* first. He made me get an abortion."

"What? My father's against abortion!"

"Not when a pregnancy's inconvenient. He couldn't have your pudiente seed mixing with the likes of mine."

"I…I'm sorry."

Hector interrupted. "That's not all. Tell him."

Greta swallowed. "Well, the abortion was botched. I ended up with a hysterectomy."

"Oh."

Hector looked at him. "Not just 'Oh.' It was deliberate."

"Deliberate? How? Why?"

"So Greta could continue to be your brother's plaything, or maybe your father's, without producing any inconvenient bastard offspring."

Rob shook his head. "I don't believe it."

Greta said, "Believe it. While I was recuperating, your father would comfort me. In a paternal way, at first. He gave me a gift, a bracelet, and held me while I opened the box. Then his hands began to wander. I screamed at him, threw the bracelet at him, tried to get away, but he had the door locked. He told me he could give me a good life, I wouldn't have to work hard."

"Who did this? Really—who are you talking about?"

"Your father!" she screamed.

Rob felt like she'd slapped him. "I had no idea. That's when he fired you?"

"No, it was after I told my mother and she threatened to call the police. He told her to go ahead. Then he put us out with nothing but the clothes on our backs. He didn't even pay her. But he let me keep that friggin' bracelet. So he could accuse us of stealing, I guess. I only kept it so I could sell it."

Despite the warm day, Rob felt cold. "What about my brother? Did he know anything about this?"

"I don't know how much he knew. But he knew about the hysterectomy. He acted real nice to me, real loving, but he said it was unfortunate, that he couldn't marry me, because now I couldn't give him children."

Rob went numb. He looked at his half-finished sandwich. If he ate another bite, he'd vomit. He glanced up. Rosa avoided his eyes. He couldn't read her expression and didn't want to. How could he convince her he wasn't like that? He thought about Cisli. He'd used her as a plaything, with no intention of marriage. But he'd always been careful to use a sheath, even though she said she had an implant. How willing had she been? She always acted like she enjoyed his attentions.

Distant thunder rumbled. Ramon cleared his throat. "Let's get back on the road. Hector, you take the wheel."

Rob sat in the back with Jem, who soon fell asleep. Rob wrapped himself in a cocoon of misery. Yes, he knew his father was mean and vindictive, but was he the beast Greta pictured? A botched abortion? A deliberate hysterectomy? Could Father actually have done these things?

He looked at the back of Hector's head. Hector loved Greta, even though she couldn't give him children. Was Hector a better man than Doug? And what of himself? He came from the same stock as Doug. Did he harbor seeds of malevolence waiting to develop? These people, with all their flaws, regarded him with contempt. Could they be right? Rosa hadn't spoken to him since Greta's disclosure.

Despite his despair, Rob's sleepless night caught up with him. He nodded off.

Another pothole jarred him awake. Hector had to drive slowly, steering around the worst places. Sometimes the useable pavement was so narrow he had to stop and wait for oncoming vehicles.

They went into another forested area. Rob hadn't realized there was so much undeveloped land left in the country. He was concerned about the shaded roads. The Backpacker was using energy faster than the solar cells could recharge, yet Hector had the radio and air conditioning on. To make matters worse, the sky clouded over and they drove into a thunderstorm. During the rain, they were bombarded with hail. Visibility was so poor, Hector pulled off the road. The music continued to play, even though the pounding hail threatened to drown it out.

"Hector, why don't you turn it off?" Rob said. "We should save the battery."

Hector complied.

The hailstorm was brief, and soon they were on their way. As they approached Athens, Ramon turned to Rob. "I think we're as safe going through town as trying to get around it. But why don't you drive, just in case."

When Rob got out to change seats, he noticed one of the solar panels was cracked. "Ramon, look at this."

Ramon examined the entire solar array. "Must have been the hailstorm. The other panels are okay, but this one isn't going to give us any charge."

Rob nodded. "Maybe we should stop at a boosting station."

"No. That would give away our location. Let's drive with the windows open and not use A/C. Hopefully we have enough power to get to a camping place."

Rosa spoke up. "If we had the batteries they have in Europe and Asia, we wouldn't need a boosting station."

"Why don't we?" Hector asked.

"Because in the mid twenty-first century, companies that produced batteries resisted innovation. They were making money and that's all they cared about. Our battery technology went abroad, and we were left with the obsolete stuff."

Rob had heard rumors like this, but he'd never given them much credence. Now that Rosa said it, he wondered if it were true after all.

It was hot and humid. Riding through the countryside with open windows gave them a cooling breeze, but in town they felt every discomfort. Otherwise, the drive through Athens went without incident.

The terrain became increasingly hilly, almost mountainous. They came to a section of recently-paved road that was lined with well-maintained stone fences. On top of a hill sat a mansion, like a castle from a fairy tale. They passed an arched gate. A wrought-iron sign proclaimed, "Mandeville Manor."

Without thinking, Rob said, "Mandeville—he's a friend of Father's. I forgot he had a summer home here."

"Summer home?" Hector said. "Humph. I'd consider one of his sheds a luxury."

"Well, Mr. Hardman," Greta said, "why don't you just drive up to your friend's front door and ask him to give us a good meal and a soft bed for the night?"

Rob looked into the rearview mirror at her hard blue eyes and pressed the accelerator.

They approached a turnpike with a boosting station. Rob glanced at his power indicator, but he said nothing. After the turnpike, the smooth road gave way again to broken pavement.

The sun was going down. Rob resisted using the headlights. As they passed a dirt road, Ramon craned his neck and said, "Stop and turn around. Go down that road we just passed."

When he turned around, Rob smelled food and saw a small fire.

"Pull up there and stop."

A handful of people scattered as they drove up. Ramon got out and shouted, "It's okay. We're not cops. We won't harm you." He opened the back door. "Everybody out." The firelight reflected off shelters made of scraps of metal and wood. A pig roasted over the fire.

A man crept out of the shadows. "Who are you?"

"We're refugees from Florida," Ramon said. "We're tired. We only want someplace to camp."

The man looked at the Backpacker, then at its sweaty, disheveled occupants. "Where'd you get the car?"

Rob stepped forward. "It belongs to my father. These are my friends."

Rosa produced two gallon cans of fancy vegetables. "We have food we can share with you."

The man looked hungrily at the vegetables. "Well, then, come join us. My name's Joe."

Other people crept out of hiding. They took the cans from Rosa and soon had the contents warming on the fire.

Rob helped pitch the tents. A few at a time, they went down to a nearby brook to wash, but it wasn't deep enough to bathe. Rob cleaned himself as well as he could, rinsed out the clothes Ramon had loaned him, and changed back into his clothes.

Their hosts were two families of migrants who traveled by foot, looking for work, sheltering where they could. One woman had a baby at her breast. She hardly looked robust enough to produce milk.

Joe sliced off pieces of pork and passed them around. He said they wintered in Florida when possible and followed the harvests north during summer. "It's hard," he said. "None of us is legit. Some of us had IDs once, but they was taken away when we got arrested for one thing or another." He pointed his knife at the remains of the pig. "These wild pigs are a nuisance. They tear up crops. We do the landowners a favor by killin' them, but if we get caught, they throw us in jail and make us work for nothing. Until the work's done, or we get too sick to work, then they throw us out on the street to starve."

He pointed at the baby. "They won't give the women any help to not have babies, but they won't feed 'em either. If Effie here went to jail, that baby'd go to an orphanage. And those pudientes live in big houses with all they want to eat. They cook big meals and what do they do with the leftovers? Chuck 'em in the trash, then arrest the likes of us if we pick through their garbage for somethin' to eat."

Rob couldn't listen anymore. He went to the tent to lie down. It wasn't long before the others joined him, but he couldn't sleep. He kept turning over.

Ramon said, "Settle down and let me sleep."

Instead, he went outside and paced. If he were home, he could have a glass of wine, or a shot of whiskey, or something to help him sleep. Here, he had nothing.

He had less than nothing. He'd lost his family and his self-respect. He'd taken up with outlaws, going from hostage to accomplice. And for what? They looked down on him. Greta branded him a rapist and hypocrite. Rosa would have nothing to do with him.

An owl hooted. Rob jumped. Then he noticed how quiet it was. Everyone was asleep. He opened the door of the Backpacker and checked the antitheft device. They had forgotten to remove it.

Quietly, Rob opened the rear, took out the food, water, and his companions' possessions, and set them on the ground. Then Rosa's books. He hated to leave Rosa, but there was no future for them. Their worlds were too far apart. He took the cash from his pocket and tucked it into a book. Very gently, he pulled the tarp he'd been sleeping on out of the tent and covered the books. By starlight, he found the path he had driven in on. He slipped into the driver's seat and started the Backpacker. The motor silently hummed. He didn't turn on the headlights until he had pulled away from the tents. Then he drove down the lane and out to the road, hoping he could find his way to the freeway.

CHAPTER 12

By some miracle, Rob was able to retrace his route. When he reached the freeway, he pulled up to the boosting station, pressed his thumb to the reader, and keyed in his code. He didn't mind being found now. He was going home. But instead of turning on, the indicator flashed red: "Invalid." He tried again with the same result. Maybe his thumb was dirty. He washed it with drinking water, but that didn't help. He drove to the boosting station across the road but was rejected there as well.

He looked for his Nebula. It was no longer in the charging slot. Rosa must have taken it out. Did the car have enough power to reach the Mandevilles? Surely they'd help him. He pulled out onto the road and drove until the battery died. He had no idea where he was. There were no lights to be seen, no one around to help. He steered to the side of the road, leaned back, and fell asleep.

Intense flashing lights woke him. He got out and approached the police car. "Officer, I'm so glad to see you…" but was rudely shoved to the ground and handcuffed. "Wait! I'm Robert Hardman. My father is Gregory Hardman of Hardman Aquatics."

The officer laughed and called to his partner, "Get a load of this! He claims he's a rich boy. Next thing, he'll say this is his car."

"It is my car." Rob was jerked to his feet and searched.

"He don't smell like no rich boy, does he."

Rob had no deodorant with him when he was kidnapped. He also hadn't been able to shave since he left home, and his hair was dirty. He repeated his name and his father's. "We had an argument the other day and I ran away. I'm all over it now, and was going home. If you don't believe me, call my father."

The first officer said, "Check the runaway bulletin."

"I'm too old to be listed as a runaway."

The other came back with, "He ain't listed as a missing person, either, but the car has been reported stolen."

They searched the Backpacker. "Well, lookee here! Not just a stolen car, but illegal weapons."

He'd wondered where Ramon hid the guns. "Those aren't illegal. My family owns them, legally."

Both officers laughed. "Come on, boy. We'll take you home, all right."

When they reached the police station, Rob renewed his plea to call his father.

"We ain't gonna wake that man up in the middle of the night."

Rob flashed his Citizenship rings. "Look, I'm who I said I am."

The officers looked at the rings and each other. "Probably stolen, too. Or fake."

They turned him over to a jailer who took fingerprints. "That'll tell you who I am," Rob said.

After a few minutes, the jailer said, "You're not legit."

"What?"

"No record. You don't exist."

Rob was stripped of his rings and his belt and thrown into a cell with several other men as dirty and smelly as he. They looked at him curiously but showed no hostility. *They think I'm one of them.* He told them no different. The other men dozed off, leaving Rob alone to think about his situation. Somehow, he'd been wiped off the database. How did that happen? Father? His heart sank.

* * *

Rosa woke at dawn. Ramon was banging and cursing, stomping about camp, kicking everything in sight.

"What's wrong?"

"That sonofabitch is gone! He took the f—damn car and left!"

"What?" The Backpacker was missing.

Ramon beat himself in the head. "I forgot to take out the antitheft device."

By now, everyone was awake.

"Well, at least we don't have to put up with his shit anymore," Greta said.

"But what are we going to do?" Hector said. "How are we going to get to the mountains?"

Jem cocked his head. "Looks like we gotta walk."

Rosa went to where the Backpacker had been. "Did you see this?"

"What?"

"It looks like he left the food, and other things." She lifted the tarp. "And my books." *How can I carry them to the mountains?*

A soft murmuring drew her attention. The migrants were grouped together, kneeling on the ground, praying.

"What day is it?" Hector whispered.

"Sunday."

Ramon sat down with his chin on his fist. "We better get away from here as soon as possible. Before the police come."

"I don't think Rob will turn us in."

"Why not?"

"Don't you see what he did? Left the food and water. He even left my books, and put the tarp over them to keep them dry. I think he was trying to help us as much as he could. He just wanted to go home."

"I hope you're right."

"He left my tools, too," Jem said. "Good thing. I can't afford to replace 'em."

They shared breakfast with the migrants. Joe said, "You can take up with us. Today we rest, but tomorrow we'll be in the fields. When the harvest is done here, we travel north."

After breakfast, they discussed what to do next. Their goal remained Apex Resort where Greta's aunt worked. Ramon had his parents' cash and Greta had money in the bank, so they didn't need to work yet. Rosa twisted her Citizenship ring. They could sell it, and Ramon's, if need be. Fugitives had no need of status symbols.

"I'm glad I took my atlas out of the car last night," Ramon said. "It's not as up to date for Georgia as it is for Florida, but it's something."

Rosa took out Rob's Nebula and opened it to news. She wasn't sure what to look for, but there was no mention of anything that could pertain to them, except rain in the weather forecast. She looked at Rob's messages. Two more threats from his father and a plea from someone named Andreu, "Rob, please reply if you get this. Your father has reported the Backpacker stolen."

For the first time since they left Florida, Rosa got that cold feeling in her stomach. She had become complacent, riding in Rob's comfortable car, worrying less about consequences when he seemed cooperative. Consequences for carjacking and abduction, in addition to the unjustified crimes they were fleeing from. Reality stared her in the face —car theft!

"Ramon, his father has reported the car stolen."

"Sanctuary! Maybe it's a good thing he took off with it. If we'd been caught, it'd all be over."

What must Rob think about her now? In college, he seemed to like her, but now she was a criminal. She hated losing his respect. She didn't think he would betray them, but his father could force the truth out of him. And they were now without transportation. Plus, there were her books.

"I don't know what we were thinking, bringing all this stuff," Greta said. "We knew we'd have to give up the car at some point. I suppose Joe's people would be happy to get some of the food."

"What about our tents and clothes?" Ramon asked.

Hector, Greta, and Jem had had the foresight to bring backpacks. Ramon's clothes were in Rosa's overnight bag, and she had a suitcase. Those would be difficult to carry. The sleeping bags and tents could be rolled up compactly enough to be strapped to backpacks. "What about my books?" Rosa said.

Ramon said, "You'll have to leave them."

"I'm not going anywhere without my books."

When Ramon offered Joe some of the food, his eyes lit up. "Thank you. You ain't outfitted to go on foot, are you?"

"No. We thought we had a car."

Joe went into his shelter and brought out two backpacks. They were old and ragged but basically sound. "Sometimes people give us things, and we never refuse them. These are spares."

"Thank you."

Without a word, Rosa snatched the larger one and gave Ramon a look that said, "Don't cross me!"

* * *

Rob sat with his back against the wall. He must have fallen asleep. It was morning when someone opened the cell door and kicked him. "Hey, rich boy, you're free to go."

"Really?"

"Yeah. The owner of the car doesn't want to file charges."

"Can I call him?"

"Hell, no."

"But he's my father!"

The jailer laughed. "Tell it to the movies."

"Can I at least have my rings back?"

"What rings?"

"They took them away from me last night."

The jailer turned to the officer at the desk. "Did this joker come in with any possessions?"

The other laid Rob's belt on the desk. "Naw. Nothing but this and the stolen car."

Rob puffed himself up. "When I get back home, I'm going to get my lawyer to look into this. I *will* get my rings back!"

The men looked at each other and laughed.

Once outside, Rob deflated. He looked up and down the street, wondering what to do. His cell mates filed out of the building. "Why'd they let us go?" he asked.

"It's Sunday. Guess they didn't want to work us today. Or feed us, either."

Too numb to be dejected, Rob sat on the curb, his eyes filling with water. He felt a hand on his shoulder.

"Son, you can't stay here. You should go home."

Through his tears, Rob could see the man only as a shimmer of color. "I have no home to go to, it seems. I don't understand. Yesterday, I was the son of a wealthy man. Now I can't contact my family, and they tell me I'm not legit." As his eyes cleared, Rob was surprised to see a policeman standing before him.

The officer shook his head. "If I were allowed to, I'd let you call him, but the information we got was clear. The car's owner wanted no contact." He cleared his throat. "We get these cases from time to time, a parent who for one reason or another wants to cut off a child. Sometimes it's because they have too many to provide for, and other times, well, there's no reason I can figure out."

"I don't know what to do."

"I can give you some water and a sandwich. Do you have any friends?"

Rob nodded. "Unless they plan to cut me off, too."

The man handed him a small bag.

"Thank you." Rob walked towards the Mandeville estate. Maybe they would take him in. While he walked, he drank the water and ate the sandwich. He couldn't identify the filling, probably some kind of bean. He wondered if this had been the policeman's lunch.

Rob's shoes were not designed for walking. Sweat rolled down his legs and dampened his socks, which rubbed against his tender skin. When he thought he could go no further, a farm truck slowed and the driver offered him a ride. He fell asleep and woke when the truck stopped.

"This is my turn," the driver said.

Rob looked up. They were in front of the Mandeville estate. "This is where I was going."

"You looking for work?"

Rob looked down at his clothes. Did the grime and sweat mask how expensive they were? "Yes."

"I don't think they're hiring, but you look young and strong. I'd advise you to wash up first."

The driver drove to a back gate, showed Rob to a lavatory, and said, "I might could loan you a clean shirt."

"Thanks." Rob used his dirty shirt to wash away sweat and odor. He stuck his head under the faucet and doused his hair. After he was ready, a foreman walked up.

"There ain't no work now," he said.

Rob held out his hand and said, "I'm Rob Hardman. My father is a friend of Mr. Mandeville. I've fallen into some difficulty and I need to talk to him."

The men stepped back as though to compare his appearance with his manner of speaking. The foreman said, "Mr. Mandeville isn't home right now."

"Can I use the phone? Maybe we could call him. I'd like to call my father. See, I ran away and now I'm trying to get back home. The police picked me up but they wouldn't believe me. They wouldn't let me call. They told me to walk home."

"Where's home?"

"Florida."

Both men laughed. "That's a long walk!"

The foreman said, "What did you say your name was? And your father's?"

Rob told him.

The man nodded and left. After what seemed like an hour, he returned. "Sorry. I called Mr. Mandeville and told him what you said. He said he'd call your father. Then he called me back and said Mr. Hardman told him you're an imposter. Mr. Mandeville wants you off the property before he gets home."

Rob stared at him, trying to decipher what he'd said. Then he tried to take off the borrowed shirt, but his hands shook so hard he could barely grip the fabric.

"What're you doin'?" the truck driver asked.

"Giving back your shirt."

"Don't worry about it. I'll trade it for yours."

When he tried to walk, Rob stumbled over his feet.

The foreman said, "Why don't you drive him out."

At the gate, the driver asked where he wanted to go.

"Back the way I came. I don't know what else to do."

He took Rob several miles past the police station and said, "This is as far as I dare take you."

"Thank you," Rob said. "Thanks for trying to help me."

"Wish I could 'a done more."

Rob suspected the man believed him. That was some comfort.

He hoped he could remember the way back to camp. Fortunately, he caught a few rides. He marveled at the willingness of strangers to pick him up. Riding with Andreu in the past, he'd seen men and women walking the roads, holding up a hand to request a ride. He'd been told those people were trouble, to be avoided. And now he was one of "those people," yet others were not avoiding him.

* * *

Rosa went through her books. The ones she absolutely could not part with, she put in her backpack. When it was full, she tried it on for weight. It was heavy, but with enough determination, she could carry it.

"What about clothes?" Greta asked.

Rosa opened her suitcase. First, she took out Grandmother's doily, which Ramon had salvaged from their ruined house, and tucked it into a pocket of the backpack. Then she crammed in some underwear. "The rest I can do without."

Greta pursed her lips and stuffed a few of Rosa's garments into her own backpack.

When Rosa started to put the rest of the books in the suitcase, she noticed something sticking out of one—ten twenty-dollar bills.

Greta said, "What's that?"

"Money. Rob must have put it there. He said he had some cash. Maybe he thought he wouldn't need it."

"Well, I'll be damned. Are you sure he's a Hardman?"

"I think he likes us, despite what we did to him." Rosa pocketed the money and finished packing her books and what clothes would fit in the suitcase, then wrapped the tarp around it.

"We may need that tarp," Ramon said.

"No, *I* need it." She hunted for a safe place to hide the suitcase, somewhere Ramon wouldn't find it.

The men tried to see how much water and food they could carry. Jem also had the weight of his tool belt. They divided the most necessary items among them. The sky clouded over. Thunder boomed. Hector dropped his bag and groaned. "We can't walk through a thunderstorm. I say we stay here today. After all, it is Sunday. Tomorrow, we head out on foot. Rain or shine."

Rosa dragged the suitcase into her tent. She took out her notebook and, for the rest of the day, went through books, taking notes. When she ran out of paper, she made notes on Rob's Nebula.

* * *

Night was falling. Rob peered out the truck window. He didn't want to miss the campsite. Rosa and her friends had likely moved on, but where else could he go? Maybe the migrants would take him in. A lane branched off and dipped into a forested area. Through the trees he saw the glimmer of a campfire. He asked the driver to let him out. When he set his feet on the ground, pain shot up his legs.

As he stumbled out of the darkness, several people jumped to attention. Greta said, "Well, get a load of this!"

They're still here! Rob sat down on the wet ground and took off his shoes.

No one spoke, until Hector said, "Where's the car?"

"I don't have it anymore." Then words tumbled out of his mouth: his arrest; no one believing who he was; his father "not pressing charges," telling the Mandevilles he was an imposter; discovering he was no longer on the database, that he was not legit. "I didn't know what to do except come back here." He scanned their faces. He read anger, disgust, frustration, resignation, and—pity?

He put his hands beside his head and shook it. "I don't understand. It's got to be a mistake. Father probably thought the car was stolen, but why wouldn't he talk to me? Why did he tell Mr. Mandeville I was a fraud without at least talking to me? To see if it was really me? Even if he thought I was dead, wouldn't he want to know?" He slumped forward and hung his head, his arms dangling between his knees. "How the hell did I get wiped off the database?"

Greta said, "Your dear daddy. He's showing what a son of a bitch he really is. This doesn't surprise me. You're expendable, and now that you're an embarrassment to him, he's expending you."

"There's got to be a mistake. Just because I did something stupid, why would he turn his back on me?"

Ramon said, "Because that's the way he is."

Something was cooking. It smelled good. Rosa handed him a dish, but he couldn't swallow food. He set it down. When he tried to stand up, he winced with pain.

"Sit down," Rosa said. By firelight, she examined his blistered feet. She left and returned with a wet rag. Even her gentle touch hurt as she washed his feet, but her attention was a balm for his soul. She patted his feet dry and slipped on dry socks. Ramon's?

"Thank you," he said.

Rob didn't remember being put in a tent and falling asleep on a blanket one of the migrants loaned him.

* * *

Rosa said, "He can't walk with his feet like that."

"So?" Greta said. "He can stay here with Joe and them until they're ready to move on."

Ramon shook his head. "No. We're responsible for him."

"What?" Greta said.

"We're the reason he's here. If we hadn't hijacked him, he'd be home with his family."

"Some family," Rosa said.

"Don't you think his daddy will have a change of heart in a day or so and come looking for him?" Hector asked.

"Actually, no," Greta said. "Greg Hardman's not the type to admit he's wrong. It'd be just like that mean bastard to throw him to the wolves."

"So what do we do?" Jem asked.

"Let's see what kind of shape he's in in the morning," Ramon said.

Rosa went to bed but couldn't sleep. Earlier, she'd been relieved that Rob was out of her life again, this time for good. She could concentrate on survival, hers and Ramon's. Then Rob came back. How could she explain the glimmer of joy in her heart when she saw him? *It's impossible. There can be nothing between us.* The lament of a mourning dove in the distance reflected her mood.

CHAPTER 13

By morning light, Rosa examined Rob's shoes. They weren't fancy dress shoes, nor were they suitable for outdoor walking. Why would someone with Rob's money wear shoes like these?

Before the migrants left for work, she asked Joe's wife what to do about Rob's feet. The woman walked over to the roadside and pointed at a low-growing plant that had sent up green flower spikes. "This is plantago. Mash up the leaves and make a poultice. Put it on his sores and change it every few hours till they start to heal." She reached into her shelter for a rag. "Tear this up into strips to keep the poultice on."

Rosa thanked her. She prepared a poultice and called Rob to wake up.

When he crawled out of his tent, Rosa said, "Let me see your feet." The only thing that had changed overnight was that the light was better. She turned to Ramon. "He shouldn't be walking."

Ramon stomped away.

Rob lowered his head. "I'm sorry. I know you have to get going. I'll stay with these folks until my feet heal."

"Then what?"

"I'll think of something. Maybe Father will have a change of heart."

How can he have a change of something he doesn't have? "No, Rob, you don't get shut of us that easily. Go down to the creek and wash up. I'll help you. I have some medicine for your feet."

"Okay. I wish I had clean clothes."

She went into Ramon's tent for the clothes he'd previously loaned Rob. "By the way, that's not the shirt you left in."

"No." He told her how he got it.

She helped him to his feet and wedged her shoulder under his arm. "You can lean on me." With her support, he hobbled down to the creek. She lowered him to the bank.

"What did everyone say when I was gone?"

"You don't really want to know."

"I was surprised to see you still here."

"It was raining. After you bathe, wash out your dirty clothes. I don't mind playing nursemaid, but damned if I'll be your washerwoman. Call me when you're decent."

Am I being too hard on him? Conflicting feelings about Rob waged war in her heart. When he called out, Rosa helped him back to camp and dressed his feet. "We'll change the poultice every two hours." She took the money out of her pocket and handed it to him.

"What's this?"

"Your money."

"No. You keep it. I'd only lose it." He held out his hands. "They took my rings and didn't give them back. If I'd had cash, they'd have taken that, too."

Rosa pocketed the bills and found a comfortable place to read. She tried to ignore Rob. He didn't question her use of his Nebula.

* * *

Rob watched the rest of the group try to devise ways to carry canned food. Being idle and useless chafed him.

Jem found a discarded bicycle wheel. "If we had another of these, we could make a cart."

Rob said, "Bring it to me. And those staves and some twine. I'll see what I can do."

"What makes you think you can make a cart?" Hector asked.

Rob said nothing, only studied the materials available. He asked to use Ramon's knife and Jem's tools to shape pieces of wood and fit them together with twine and rusty nails. Soon he had a frame for a makeshift wheelbarrow. "We need something to make a bottom and fill in the sides."

Jem took the cart. "I can do that."

He and Hector finished the wheelbarrow. They filled it with cans of food and bottles of water and rolled it up and down the lane. It worked. The next time Rosa changed his dressings, Rob asked, "What are you studying?"

"History."

"Why?"

She took a deep breath. "I can't carry all those books, but there's too much knowledge in them to leave. I'm taking notes so I can keep the information."

"Can't you find that stuff online?"

"No. They rewrite history."

"What do you mean?"

"What do you know about the partitioning of the United States?"

"Partitioning?"

"Dividing the country into regions."

"It's always been that way."

Rosa shook her head. "No, it hasn't. In 2047, Texas seceded from the Union and declared itself an autonomous state. Then others followed. Do you know why?"

Rob shook his head.

"Because during the early part of the twenty-first century, the central government was weakened, bit by bit, until it was nearly dysfunctional."

"But a weak central government is a good thing. Local rule is best. National defense is still strong, isn't it?"

"Yes, but partitioning crippled us in other ways."

"Such as?"

"Quality control, for one. There used to be national standards for things such as health and safety, and education. Now regions like

Northeast and Pacific have tighter regulations than Texas or Deep South. Northeast won't import meat from Texas because of poor quality. That hurts both areas. Southern regions charge tariffs on goods from Northeast, so people here can't always get what they need. Haven't you noticed it's hard to get parts when things break down?"

He thought about Syntat switches.

"And education—our college degrees from Florida don't hold the same weight as those from other regions. If we wanted to get a job in New York, we'd have to take additional courses and pass the licensing exams."

Rob nodded.

"Do you see the weakness in the present system? At one time, there were federal agencies that regulated such things. The whole country was better off, but some people didn't like it. Bad for business, they said. In the end, it has weakened us as a nation. We used to be the greatest country in the world."

"We still are," Rob said.

"You don't believe me?" She shoved the book at him. "Read this. And this isn't the only source of information. There are others, all in print. The truth has been censored, nearly wiped out. That's why these books are important."

Rob took the book and began to read. He was tempted to dismiss this as subversive propaganda, but as he read, things began to fall into place. Stories the servants had told him, handed down from their grandparents. Also, little things that never added up. His world view began to fall apart.

When he looked up, Rosa asked, "Aren't you the least bit curious as to why I've commandeered your Nebula?"

"You didn't want me to contact my family. Now, it seems, I have no family to contact."

"It's good for more than that. Don't you want to know what's going on out there in the world?"

He shrugged. "What's happening that I'd want to know about?"

Rosa huffed, shook her head, and went back to her studies.

* * *

When the migrants returned that evening, Rosa thanked Joe's wife for the plantago. "It worked. Fast, too." Rob's feet had healed enough for him to walk with minimal discomfort.

"Keep putting poultices on until he's completely healed and it won't get infected." She gave Rosa a rough pair of moccasins. "We make these out of pig skin. Not as good as tanned leather, but it's the best we can do."

"Thank you." After Rosa dressed his feet again, Rob slipped them on. They fit well enough.

After supper, Ramon called a conference. "We set out as soon as it's light. I have a route planned. I'd like to cover twenty miles a day. This wheelbarrow will come in handy. Rob, you don't have a backpack. Do you think you can handle the cart?"

"I'll try."

"Good. If you get so you can't, tell me right away. I'd rather relieve you than have you crippled up again."

Rob nodded.

"Rosa, what'd you do with that tarp?"

"Put it to good use."

"Where is it?"

She put her hands on her hips. "In a safe place. I wrapped it around the suitcase so the books I'm leaving won't get wet."

"Why?"

"If we come back here under better circumstances, I want them back."

"What good is all this stuff anyway? Do you think you'll be a teacher again?"

"You never know." That she would teach again was doubtful, unless it was at some underground school, with little to no pay. But the knowledge in these books was too precious to waste. Even if she couldn't retrieve them herself, perhaps they would fall into the hands of someone who would appreciate them.

That night, she stayed up late, reading by the light of the Nebula.

In the morning, Ramon said, "We really need that tarp."

Rosa ignored him.

Joe approached with the young mother. "Effie here likes to read."

Effie said, "I can keep your books safe, if you let me read them."

"They're history books, not stories. They may be boring."

"That's okay. I'll read anything. I'll keep them in my shelter, out of the rain."

"But what about when you leave?"

Effie grinned. "I know where you hid them. I can put them back there, and I'll wrap the suitcase in cellophane so they won't get wet."

"Effie, I'd be honored for you to read them. I'd like you to tell people what you learn from them, too."

"Yes, ma'am," Effie said. "I'd like to do that. And the books will be waiting for you when you come back."

"Thank you."

* * *

With fresh poultice, clean socks, and moccasins, Rob could walk, although his feet were still tender. He put his shoes in the wheelbarrow, picked up the handles, and they set off up the road. He didn't get past the first mile before he had to stop. "It's too heavy," he confessed. "My feet can't handle it."

Ramon didn't look entirely pleased. "We'll take turns pushing it. I'll take the first turn." He gave Rob his backpack.

It was heavy, but at least Rob could stand straight and distribute his weight less painfully when he walked.

They passed a small store where Greta bought bread and fruit for a late breakfast. Whenever someone took the wheelbarrow, Rob carried their backpack. When it was Rosa's turn, he was surprised how heavy hers was, yet he hadn't heard her complain.

The next time they came to a ruined bridge, instead of looking for a detour, they hiked down to cross the river. The banks were steep. Ramon and Hector carried the wheelbarrow. The descent was hard on Rob's feet. By the time he reached bottom, he was exhausted. The water was low and the streambed rocky. Rob crossed barefoot but slipped on the rocks and nearly fell. With dismay, he looked at the bank he now had to climb. He was the last one to reach the top.

That afternoon, Rosa said, "You're getting sunburned. You need a hat."

The other men appeared accustomed to outdoor work and all wore caps. Fair-skinned Greta had a hat that shaded her face. Rosa's skin was darker, but her forehead was turning pink, too.

She asked Jem, whose skin was darkest, to lend his hat to Rob. "Maybe we can buy him one at the next store."

Ramon said, "You need one too, Sis," and gave his to Rosa.

They didn't get beyond ten miles that day and passed no store. When they stopped for the night, Rob said, "I'm slowing you down too much. Why don't you all go on without me?"

"Nah. We stick together," Hector said.

Rob slept twelve hours and felt better in the morning. The gallon of soup they'd consumed for supper and the water they drank lightened the wheelbarrow, so he was able to push it further before switching with someone. Gripping the rough handles took a toll on his hands and they began to blister. When they stopped to rest, he wrapped the rags from his feet around his hands as gloves. The roadway was in such poor shape, he was constantly veering around potholes and tree roots. He began to doubt the practicality of the wheelbarrow.

They walked in the shade as much as possible because the sun burned everyone's exposed skin. Late that morning, Jem left the roadside and fished for something in the ditch. "Here you go." He held up a battered cap, beat it against his thigh, shook off dirt, and tossed it to Rob.

"Thanks." It was better than nothing.

They met other groups of walkers, coming and going, including families with children, carrying their few worldly goods. Sometimes they stopped to talk, exchanging information about what lay ahead or behind. Occasionally motorcycles or bike riders passed by, all carrying packs. Rob marveled at the number of people wandering the countryside in search of work, shelter, and sustenance. All his life, he'd heard rumors of this but hadn't realized how widespread the problem was. He mentioned it to Ramon.

Ramon laughed. "You've led a sheltered life, haven't you? Things have been like this since I can remember. My grandmother used to tell me about her childhood. Things weren't so hard then. A working class couple could provide for a family as long as they both worked. Her grandmother told her that when she was growing up, every family had a car, maybe two, and most people owned their own homes. Working class families, like ours, had a good life. And her mother, my great-great grandmother, had told her about the days when women stayed home to tend to the family while the husband worked."

"But things cost more then," Rob said.

"That was before the dollar was revalued." Ramon's face hardened with anger. "It backfired for everyone except the rich. Ask Rosa. She can tell you how it worked for us. My family needed three incomes to get by. My grandmother couldn't retire before I finished school and went to work. I knew people who had jobs but couldn't afford a place to live. They lived on the streets. Somehow they managed to clean up and go to work every day, then spent the night in a tent, if they were lucky to have one. But the first morning they went to work dirty, they got fired."

Rob didn't know what to say. He'd been taught that people with a good work ethic were rewarded with a good life. Now he was finding otherwise. In school, currency revaluation had been taught as a good thing for the economy. Ramon thought differently.

He looked at Rosa, struggling with her load of books. Why was she doing that? What future did she have? And Ramon, was he to be a fugitive the rest of his days? A thought struck him—he, too, was a homeless, penniless wanderer. Unless Father changed his mind, his fate was little better than theirs. But if Father did change his mind, and he went back to his old way of life... He shuddered.

CHAPTER 14

When evening approached, Rosa caught a whiff of roasting pork. *Dare I hope?* They followed the aroma to a campfire. She said to Ramon, "Do you think they'll share?"

Four men sat by the fire. Ramon approached them. "Greetings. Would you exchange a can of haricot verts for a taste of meat?"

"Gladly."

Rosa unburdened herself of her backpack and sat down. Hector took the stewpot and vegetables out of the wheelbarrow.

This band hailed from Florida. After the hurricane, they'd hiked through the woods, climbed a fence at the border, and come this far on foot. They brought with them rumors of insurrection. Rosa unfastened the Nebula from her backpack where she carried it to charge the solar battery and opened it to news. She found trouble behind them in Florida, ahead in the mountains, and nationwide. What was being reported was probably only a modicum of what was happening.

Ramon stared at the man with red hair. Finally, he said, "Don't I know you?"

A bald man sitting next to the redhead said, "You look familiar, too." He squinted. "Weren't you in Carraway Correctional?"

From a yard away, Rosa could feel Ramon's hackles rise.

"Yeah! I thought so." The bald man slapped the shoulder of the redhead and said, "This is our guardian angel. He's the one that let us out."

The man extended his hand to Ramon. "My name's Ned."

Ramon shook his hand. "You're on the run?"

"'Fraid so. What do you think they'd have done to me if I stayed?"

Rob spoke up. "You let those prisoners out?"

Ned nodded. "What else could I do? Nobody'd fed them for two days. There was no running water. Sewage was building up in the toilets. I couldn't get staff to come in, and I couldn't do it all myself."

"Were any of them dangerous?"

"Maybe. But they're still human beings. And there are plenty worse ones out there going free." He shook his head. "Some of them are pudientes."

Rosa glanced at Rob. He looked at the ground. When the green beans were warm, she dished up a generous helping for Ned. "I'm in your debt. My brother would have rotted in there if you hadn't let him out."

Ned said, "It was the only decent thing to do."

Ramon cleared his throat. "So, where are you headed?"

"As far from Florida as possible. Someplace where I can be anonymous, live out my life." He frowned. "Left a house half paid for, and friends. But I'd do it again under the circumstances."

They talked about many things over supper, but Ramon didn't mention why he was in jail, and Ned didn't ask.

After supper, Rosa took out a book and began to read, using the Nebula as a lamp.

Ned looked at her curiously. "What are you reading?"

"*Chronicles of the Twenty-First Century* by W.L. and Edith Barnes."

"I didn't know there was such a thing."

"Not many were printed. My high school history teacher gave me this one. I think she had two copies, otherwise she wouldn't have parted with it."

"Why was it in print form? Why not digital?"

Rosa marked her place and set the book on her lap. "Because it tells the true history of the century, not the official version. It was published in 2093, after the economic collapse. The digital version was censored, wiped off the database, so the Barnes printed and distributed as many copies as they could before they were stopped. They were arrested on trumped up charges and died in prison."

"That's too bad." Ned hung his head. "There seem to be a lot of people in prison that don't belong there. My mother didn't approve of my career, but I had to work. At least I could show a little kindness to the prisoners."

The bald man nodded. "Guys like you made it more tolerable."

Rosa picked up the book. "The authorities destroyed as many of these as they could, but they didn't find them all. My teacher told me that some of the police who were supposed to confiscate the books actually saved a few and sold them on the black market. That's how she got her copies."

Rob spoke up. "What does it say about currency reform? Ramon said I should ask you."

"Well, towards mid-century, inflation was so out of control the economy was about to collapse. Somebody came up with the hare-brained scheme of devaluing money, so Washington passed the Currency Reform Act in 2051. They also stopped printing money. By then, transactions were almost exclusively electronic, anyway. People with cash money hoarded it, and eventually it became the basis for the underground economy." She paused.

"Rob, I don't know how much you know, but a lot of people earn a living through cottage industries, making or repairing things, and selling them for cash. Almost nothing gets wasted. Second hand goods are cheaper than new ones. The cash economy helps working people."

Rob nodded. "I went to a money changer a few times for cash."

"Why?"

"Well, I didn't want my father to find out what I did for your parents, so I got cash. The other time, Father fined our cook for no good reason. She had a family to support. I got cash to replace what he took from her."

Rosa looked at him. Here was a side of Rob she hadn't suspected. "That was kind of you."

"No. It was only right."

She sighed. "Back to currency reform. Money was revalued at half its former value. That meant people earned half as much, but prices were cut in half. You were probably taught that this saved the economy."

He nodded.

"It did for some. The other side of the story is, outstanding loans were not revalued. They remained the same, which essentially doubled those debts. People had the right to petition to have their loans adjusted, but most couldn't afford the legal fees. That meant a lot of people lost their homes and businesses and Currency Reform didn't prevent the total collapse in 2089."

She brandished the book. "I knew some of this already, and the book confirmed it. I used to ask Grandmother what she remembered of the old times. When she was a child, she remembered her parents talking about Currency Reform. Her family was fortunate because her mother received a small inheritance, enough to cover the legal fees to have their mortgage adjusted, but their neighbors weren't so lucky. The houses were heavily mortgaged and, even with two or three incomes, most families couldn't afford the payments, or the legal expenses to have them lowered." She shook her head.

"Banks foreclosed on mortgages. Pudientes bought the houses and paid the fees to have the loans adjusted. Most of those houses became rentals. Sometimes they were leased to the former owners. Their credit had been destroyed and they had no other choice. Grandmother remembered her best friend having to move away."

She paused. "When I was a child, I knew my family used cash to buy things on the black market. My parents always cautioned me not to mention it to anyone outside the family."

Rob appeared to be deep in thought, but he didn't say anything.

In the morning, Rosa prepared more poultice for Rob's feet. They were healing. "You need to learn to do this for yourself."

"Okay."

What happened to the Rob she knew in college? This one acted like a whipped puppy. Upon reflection, he was. She was sorry they'd messed up his life, except it seemed his life was messed up to begin with. She wondered how he'd turned out to be so nice with a father like his.

A little plantago paste remained after his feet were dressed. "I wonder if this will work for sunburn?" She rubbed some on her face and arms. It was soothing. She made more and shared it with her companions.

When she hoisted her backpack onto her shoulders, she winced.

Ned asked, "What's wrong?"

"It's killing my back."

He walked around her and said, "That's because you're carrying it wrong."

"How else should I carry it?"

He fished in his bag and brought out a coil of heavy cord. "You need a sort of belt so the weight is carried on your hips instead of your back. Ramon, may I borrow your knife?"

Ramon handed it to him and watched skeptically as Ned passed the end of the cord through the bottom of the straps on Rosa's backpack.

Ned stepped back and said, "Tie this in front, comfortably tight. Use a square knot." After Rosa did so, Ned cut off the excess rope. "How does that feel?"

She straightened her back. "Better. Where did you get this idea?"

"I was in the Army in my younger days."

"Thank you."

They all set out together, but Rob still couldn't keep pace.

"Go on without us," Ramon said to Ned. "Smaller numbers are less likely to attract attention, anyway."

"Watch out for the Highway Patrol," Ned said. "They've been rounding up people for work crews."

This section of the road was in better repair. Soon they encountered the first Patrol, a small, fast car followed by a large van. Hector spotted them first and cried out, "Hide!" He grabbed the wheelbarrow from Rob and heaved it into the ditch. They scrambled into the bushes.

Rosa's heart pounded. She whispered. "Do you think they saw us?"

"Hard to say," said Ramon. "We need to be more careful."

They waited and listened. Jem crept out to the edge of the vegetation and said, "They seem to be gone."

They righted the wheelbarrow and reloaded it. "Good thing they didn't notice our stuff," Hector said.

After this, they were alert to every sound on the road. Car motors were silent, but they could hear the air displacement and the hum of tires. They jumped into the bushes every time one approached. Most were innocent private vehicles, but later that day, as they rounded a curve, Greta, who was in front, held up her hand and stepped back. "Highway Patrol. They're stopped ahead. I think they got somebody."

Hector, who had the wheelbarrow, pulled it off the road, and the band melted into the undergrowth. Then Hector made his way through the woods toward the police. He returned and reported, "They got those guys from camp last night."

"Ned? The prison guard?" Rosa asked.

Hector nodded.

"I sure hope they don't figure out who he is. It won't go well for him."

They waited until the police had moved on before returning to the road. That night, they left the wheelbarrow in the brush and carried what they needed well off the road. They built no fire, fearful that any light could alert the Highway Patrol.

Ramon said, "We need a plan in case any of us gets caught. From here to North Carolina, Old 441 was replaced by a turnpike some time ago, so I think it's a safe route to travel. It'll take us to Rabun. Greta's aunt works near there at a resort called Apex. That's our goal. Some churches have soup kitchens and aid stations. If one of us gets caught, the rest of us will wait outside the next town for two days. If whoever's caught doesn't show up, we'll move on, but we'll leave a note at the next friendly church. We'll keep moving, but always leave a note at a church, especially if we have to change the route."

Rob spoke up. "Can those churches be trusted? I'd always heard…"

"Heard what?"

He shrugged his shoulders.

"Do you have a better idea?"

"No."

The next morning, Rosa let Rob tend to his own feet. As the day wore on, she began to regret it. He walked awkwardly and seemed to be in pain. *Why is he so incompetent?*

When they stopped for a late breakfast, Rob took off his moccasins and put his hand through the bottom of one. "I guess these are done for."

"My goodness! No wonder you're walking funny." Rosa fished out his shoes and dressed his feet for him before he put them on. "Do you need to stop for the day?"

"No. I'll be all right."

That afternoon, they walked along a stretch of road with no over-hanging trees. The sun beat on the pavement, reflecting heat into Rosa's eyes. She nearly fell asleep on her feet.

She saw the car before she heard it. "Highway Patrol!" A small car, silent but swift. Rob had the wheelbarrow. Rosa grabbed it and tried to pull Rob along with it into the brush. She only succeeded in upsetting the cart. Rob sprawled on the roadside. She reached for him.

He looked into her eyes, and shouted, "Run!"

Rosa ran. Down a bank, across a stream, up a timbered hillside. Her companions filtered into the woods. She stood behind a tree and peeked out. Two men dragged Rob to a van that stopped behind the police car, threw him in, and slammed the door. That's when she noticed two other men following her.

Rosa flitted from tree to tree, to the top of the hill and over it.

"Rosa!" It was Ramon. She ran to him. He grabbed her hand and they ran to their right, hoping to get out of the path of the policemen. They came to an overhanging rock. Underneath was a hollow filled with leaves. They burrowed under the leaves and tried not to breathe.

Gunshots in the distance. Rosa stifled a scream. "They don't shoot people, do they?"

"I hope not," Ramon whispered. After forever, they heard someone shuffling through the woods.

"Ramon? Rosa?" Greta called softly. "It's safe now. They're gone."

"Where are the others?"

"Hector and Jem are going back to the road. I haven't seen Rob."

"They got him." Rosa finally let herself cry.

* * *

When Rob saw Rosa fade into the woods, a burden lifted from his heart. *She'll be safe.* He didn't resist the policemen.

One demanded, "Your name and your business."

Rob decided that the truth, or near truth, was the best course. "My name is Robert Hardman. I ran away from Florida and when I tried to go home, my father didn't want me back."

They threw him into the armored van. At least he could sit down, but there was no air conditioning, and the van was hot. He wiped his forehead. His hat had been knocked off in the scuffle. He heard cans rattle and knew they were plundering the wheelbarrow. Then he heard gunshots. His heart jumped at each report. Would they shoot fugitives?

A policemen opened the door and tossed in his cap.

Rob gulped. "What were you shooting at?"

The man looked at Rob's face and began to laugh. "Relax. Just target practice. Do you want to revise your story, starting with your name?"

Rob breathed deeply. "No, sir, I told you the truth." He hoped his friends were safe. He also hoped his father hadn't changed his mind about dropping the auto theft charges. He didn't want to spend the rest of his life in prison, although at the moment he was almost too tired to care.

The door closed, and when the van began to move, some wind wafted through vents near the roof. Several miles later, they stopped. Rob heard the officers questioning people. Some were told they could go, but a man and woman, both middle age, were unceremoniously thrown in. They stared at Rob but didn't speak for many miles. Finally, the woman asked, "Why did they pick you up, son?"

Rob shook his head. "They didn't say. I told them who I am, but they didn't believe me."

She nodded. "Vagrancy. Us, too. We had IDs once, but the police took them away and never gave them back. Don't worry. They must need a work crew somewhere. When the work's done, they'll let us go. Until then, at least we'll get fed. Where were you heading?"

"To the mountains. I was with friends, but they hid. I don't think they got caught." He wiped sweat from his face. "Tell me—I heard gunshots. Do they shoot people who run away?"

The woman frowned. "They're mean as sin, but I don't think so." She laid her hand on Rob's. "Do you have any family?"

Rob wished she hadn't said that. He fought tears. "I used to, but they don't want me anymore."

"Mm hum. That happens. When there's one mouth too many to feed, one has to go. Usually the one best able to take care of himself. That's better than sacrificing the least able."

Rob started to tell her that was not the case with his family, but stopped himself. His true situation was not believable.

When they reached the police station, he and the man were taken to a cell and the woman was sent in a different direction. To Rob's surprise, among the other men in the cell was Ned, the former prison guard.

He smiled at Rob. "It sure feels strange to be on this side of the bars."

"Are you going to be okay?" Rob asked. "Do they know...?"

Ned shook his head. "I'm just another nameless vagrant."

Rob was relieved. "Is this the first time you've been arrested?"

"Sure is." He grinned.

"My second," said Rob. "They didn't believe who I am the first time, either, so I'm just another nameless vagrant, too."

"Well, who are you? You talk like an educated person."

Rob repeated his story but kept to the narrative that he'd run away, not that he'd been kidnapped. He'd told this version so many times he almost believed it. When he mentioned his father's name, Ned whistled and said, "I had no idea I was sharing poached game with a prince of industry."

"I was. Not anymore." Rob noticed Ned's companions weren't in the cell. "Where are your friends?"

"They let one go, said he wasn't fit to work. The others, I don't know."

* * *

When Rosa, Ramon, and Greta reached the roadside, Hector and Jem were sorting through the remains of the wheelbarrow. Rosa examined the pavement for evidence of blood. None, thank God!

"Look at this mess," Hector said. "They didn't need to do this." The wheelbarrow was a total wreck. Hector held up the stewpot, which had several holes in its bottom. "Why'd they do this?"

Rosa said, "So, that's what they were shooting at."

Jem picked up a can of beef stew. The broth dripped out holes in its side.

Greta picked up another can which had been ripped open. "You'd think they'd want the food. Why spoil it?"

"Let's see what we can salvage," Ramon said. Nothing was intact.

Rosa began to examine the cans. She set a few aside. "If we eat these right away, they won't be a total loss." She picked up another. "This one has holes near the bottom, but if we take the bottom off, we might be able to use it to cook in. Good thing the other dishes weren't in the wheelbarrow."

They carried what they could to a shade tree and opened cans. A family heading south walked by. "Care to join us for a picnic?" Ramon called.

As they stepped into the shade, the man looked at the mess and asked. "What happened?"

Ramon told him.

Greta heaped a plate with stew meat and handed it to the woman. "Thank you," she said. "We haven't had much to eat the past two days." She set the food between the children and said, "Share this." Greta handed her another plate, which the couple shared.

"Where you headed?" Ramon asked.

"We got family near Macon," the man said. "We hope they'll take us in."

Rosa wondered what they were leaving behind. Part of her wanted to ask, but another part didn't want to know. She looked at the children, a girl and a boy, about eight and ten. They were grimy, and the girl's long hair hadn't been combed in some time. At their age, she had a stable home. The whole family walked barefoot, carrying their shoes.

The children cleaned their plate and asked for more. "No," said their mother. "You don't want to get a belly ache." She accepted a damaged can of stew for later.

"Watch out for Highway Patrols," Ramon said when they were ready to leave.

"Yes," the man said. "We know."

After they'd eaten, Ramon said, "We still got the tents and sleeping bags. Good thing we only put the heavy stuff in the wheelbarrow."

"What about Rob?" Rosa asked.

"We'll follow the plan we agreed on. We'll wait for him two days at the next town. I hope they have a soup kitchen or store. I'll be hungry by then."

* * *

A few hours later, one of Rob's cellmates was called out and didn't return. Then another, then Ned. When it came Rob's turn, he asked the guard what was happening, but the only answer he got was, "This way." He was conducted into a small room where a man in a business suit sat at a desk with papers in front of him.

"I'm your lawyer," the man said without looking at Rob. "It says here you're charged with vagrancy and public nuisance."

"Well, what happened is…"

The man put up a hand. "I don't need your bullshit. You have no address and no ID."

"I have an address. My thumbprint is my ID. Or used to be."

The lawyer ignored him. "No ID. You could be facing six months for public nuisance, but I can cut you a deal that'll get you only thirty days for vagrancy."

"But I haven't done anything wrong!"

"I said I don't want the bullshit." He looked up at the guard and nodded.

The guard said, "Come on," and took Rob into a courtroom where the other men sat on a bench. Rob was told to sit beside them. A few women occupied another bench.

Rob leaned around and asked Ned, "What's happening?" Ned shrugged his shoulders. A guard said, "No talking."

A few minutes later, the man beside Rob whispered, "This your first time?"

Rob nodded.

"The judge will come in and ask how we plea. The lawyer will tell him. Then the judge will sentence us to thirty days hard labor."

"But…"

The guard shouted, "Quiet!"

Once the bench was full, the lawyer and another man, similarly dressed, entered the room. The guard said, "All rise." Everyone stood.

A man in a black robe took a seat on the dais. The guard announced, "The Honorable John H. Stafford of the Fourth Judicial District. You may be seated."

The judge spoke to them as though they were a single nameless entity, reading the charges of vagrancy and public nuisance. He said, "Do you understand these charges?"

Rob raised his hand but no one acknowledged him.

The judge continued, "How do you plead?"

The lawyer said, "These men and women wish to plead guilty to vagrancy and ask the court to show mercy and rule them not guilty of public nuisance."

The judge nodded and addressed the other lawyer, whom Rob assumed was the prosecutor. "Does the State concur with this plea?"

"Yes, your honor."

Rob stood up. "Your honor…"

The judge glared at him.

"I don't have an ID, because my thumbprint is my ID, but I do have an address and a family."

"Do you wish to be charged with contempt of court in addition to the other charges?"

"No, sir."

"Then don't waste my time."

Rob looked at his lawyer, who only studied the floor. He turned his head and glanced at the men beside him. Ned shook his head ever so slightly. Rob sat down.

The judge continued, "The court will show mercy and accept the plea of vagrancy, which carries a sentence of thirty days, hard labor. Court is adjourned."

Rob remained silent until they were back in the cell. "That's no kind of justice!"

Someone laughed, "Where'd you grow up?"

Ned said. "I've had many people tell me about this. I didn't quite believe them, but now I do. Rob, you weren't about to get justice by speaking up, only a longer sentence. You were wise to shut up and sit down."

A few hours later, they were crowded into vans and driven to an-other, larger facility where they were stripped of everything, hosed down, and given coveralls. Then they had a supper of beans and rice and were taken to cells that were so dark there was little to do but sleep.

CHAPTER 15

Exhausted and foot weary, Rosa and her friends walked to the next town, a hamlet with two small churches and a store, all closed by the time they arrived. Here and there, people sat on their porches, taking advantage of the relatively cool evening.

"Anyplace we can camp for the night?" Ramon asked.

"Yeah, about a half mile ahead, there's a copse of trees where folks stay. Are you looking for work?"

"Is there any?"

"They's a squash field that needs pickers. Be downtown at sunrise."

"Thanks."

"What are you thinking?" Hector asked.

"If we're gonna to be here two days, why sit around? Squash—even if they don't pay much, I bet we can eat."

They were the only ones camping in the grove, yet firewood was hard to find, probably because everyone who camped there built a fire. What Rosa missed more than fire was a bath. Whenever they'd found water, they didn't have time to do more than wash hands and refill water bottles. She had changed her underwear but couldn't see putting clean clothes onto a dirty body. A nearby building, which looked abandoned, had an exterior faucet that worked. She washed off some of the day's dirt.

Before turning in, they discussed what to do in the morning. "I think someone should stay here just in case Rob comes," said Rosa. "And to keep an eye on our stuff."

Everyone saw the wisdom of that, but who should stay? Hector said, "Jem and I are used to this kind of work."

"I can work, too," said Greta.

"Ramon and I aren't exactly pansies," Rosa said.

"Why don't we take turns?" Ramon said. "We'll leave the girls here tomorrow, and if we work again the next day, I'll stay here and plan our next itinerary."

Rosa woke in the middle of the night with intense itching under her clothes. "Damn! Chiggers!" She heard someone moving around outside the tent and peeked out. Ramon was stomping about, scratching. "Try not to scratch," she told him. "The bites could get infected."

"Those leaves we hid in must have had a nest of red bugs."

"Well, it was that or get caught. Maybe the store will have something for them."

* * *

Rob woke in the dark. While trying to remember where he was and why, the lights came on, blinding him with their harshness. Men around him stirred. Someone banged on the metal doors, shouting, "Get up! Get up!"

A line of men marched by. A guard opened the door and ordered them to follow. In the mess hall they were fed beans and rice and issued work boots and hats before being herded into the back of a cattle truck. Through the slats in the side, Rob watched the countryside roll by. They rode to the turnpike and south several miles before turning off. The truck stopped in a peach orchard.

Before they were allowed to leave the truck, two guards brandished automatic weapons and one growled, "Don't even think about escaping."

Rob thought he knew how to pick peaches. At Hardman Hall, Josei had taught him to pick at perfect ripeness. But none of these were ripe. A foreman demonstrated how to harvest and handle the fruit.

"Why pick them so green?" Rob asked.

"Because if we wait till they're ripe, they won't ship well."

Still, it was pleasant to be outdoors. The ground was soft and the trees offered a little shade. The peaches were too green to eat, but occasionally Rob came across a nearly ripe one. He glanced to see if the foreman was watching and hastily ate it.

Rob was used to physical activity—sports, but not to this kind of labor. By the midmorning water break, his feet hurt so badly he could barely stand. *How am I going to last a month of this?* He took off the poorly-fitting work boots. Lunch was a large tortilla wrapped around a clutch of half-cooked vegetables. By the end of the day, he could barely move. When he boarded the truck, one of the guards ordered him to put his boots back on. He could barely squeeze his swollen feet into them.

On the way back to the prison, he asked Ned. "Think we'll last thirty days?"

Ned laughed. "You're younger than I am!"

"Would they shoot us if we tried to escape?"

"I've been listening to the seasoned convicts, and they think it's too dangerous to try. We wouldn't get far, anyway. They might not shoot, but they'd make us wish they had. If we got away, we'd likely get picked up again. They purposely keep prisoners tired, feed us just enough to get the work done, no energy left over for running. Then at the end of our sentence, if they still need workers, they find a way to add charges so they can keep us longer. Escape charges could add another month."

Rob groaned.

Supper was more beans and rice. Hungry though he was, Rob had to force himself to eat. He fell asleep as soon as he lay down.

* * *

Rosa and Greta walked through the little town and visited the churches. The pastor of the Baptist church was working on his sermon. He gave

Rosa a piece of paper and showed her a bulletin board where she could leave a message for Rob. At the Holiness church, a few ladies were cleaning up for tomorrow's service. They had a small room of donated clothing and household items and invited the girls to help themselves. Greta spotted a battered frying pan and Rosa found a ragged straw hat and a waterproof canvas bag that would fit inside her backpack. "This will help protect my books," she said.

When the women offered them clothes, Greta said, "What we really need is a way to wash them."

A lady loaned them a bucket and soap. "Just bring it back tomorrow when you come to the service. It starts at ten."

"Thank you."

On their way back to camp, Greta said, "Well, I guess we know what we're doing tomorrow."

"What surprises me is, no one turned their noses up at us. They must be used to dirty people."

At the store, they used Greta's money to buy a few groceries and salve for the chigger bites. They washed the dirty clothes and draped them over the line.

"I wish we had clothes pins," Rosa said. "They'd dry better. I saw some in the store, but I can't justify the expense."

"Jem knows how to whittle. I'll ask him to make some."

After laundry was done, they dragged bucket loads of water behind the building to bathe and wash their hair. "I wonder if I'll ever get all the grime out of my skin," Rosa said.

Supper was ready by the time the men returned from work, carrying as much squash as they could. "Let's fry some up." Hector said. "There'll be plenty for breakfast, too."

"There's no work tomorrow," Jem said. "They're pretty strict about observing the Sabbath."

"Are you guys going to church with us tomorrow?"

"Church?"

"Some ladies gave us the frying pan and soap, and loaned us that bucket. They expect us to return it tomorrow," Greta said. "We need to keep people's good will."

Ramon groaned. "I don't want to listen to some Holy Roller if I don't have to. Besides, it's supposed to be a day of rest. You girls can keep the good will."

After supper, Rosa opened her book.

"What are you reading now?" Ramon asked.

"The history of religious expression in the last century. Did you know the First Amendment of the US Constitution says, 'Congress shall make no law respecting an establishment of religion, or prohibiting the free exercise thereof...?'"

"I thought the Third Covenant *was* the state religion," Hector said.

"Not officially. It's just that most pudientes are members and you pretty much have to belong to it in order to advance in business or politics. Besides, they do all they can to squelch other denominations."

"How?"

"By taxing them, for one thing. At one time, churches were tax exempt. The Third Covenant influenced the government to change the law, arguing that it was being abused. Any evangelist could form a church and avoid taxes. Now there's an expensive process to go through to become tax exempt, and most churches can't afford it. Of course, the Third Covenant can. They hope to starve out other denominations by taxing them. And they've done a good job of it.

"In the past, most ministers were supported by their congregations and didn't have to work other jobs. Their job was to minister to their flock. As the economy got worse, things changed. The preachers in this town have to work for a living because their congregants don't have much money to give them."

"That's all Catholic priests do," said Hector. "They don't work other jobs."

"Yes, but they take a vow of poverty, and the Catholic Church is tax exempt. Besides, it's a global organization that supports its priests. The Jewish and Muslim congregations also get support from abroad."

"You know," Greta said, "I don't think I've ever met a Muslim or a Jew."

"We don't have many in Florida. Most of them are in the more liberal parts of the country, in the larger cities. The Third Covenant tolerates Jews but they persecute Muslims."

"How did the Third Covenant get to be so powerful?" Jem asked.

"Charisma. The so-called Prophet Joachim could charm the scales off a snake. It started out as a small movement." She glanced at her book. "'In 2028, Joachim Stretcher claimed God appeared to him and established a new covenant.' You see, the First Covenant was between Yahweh and the Hebrew people. Then Jesus came along, and at the Last Supper he said, 'This cup is the new covenant in My blood, which is poured out for you.' Stretcher called his revelation the Third Covenant and said it supersedes the previous ones. What appeals to the pudientes is his message that money is not evil, that God rewards the righteous with wealth."

Greta nodded. "I can see how that would appeal to them."

Hector laughed. "Yeah, I guess they got tired of Jesus telling them a camel can fit through the eye of a needle easier than they can get into Heaven."

"Right," Rosa said. "And they're no longer asked to support the poor, because poverty is punishment for sin. Ironically, Joachim's first followers were working class people who wanted to get ahead in the world and didn't want to wait for Heaven for their reward. The churches they went to were pretty conservative. They prohibited alcohol, recreational drugs, secular music, and 'immoral' sexual behavior." She grinned. "Basically, anything that felt good. 'Prophet' Joachim promised a more pleasant life. He took a clue from the old Baptists that if you were 'saved' you would never lose God's favor, and he expanded it to mean you could no longer sin. That meant they could drink and screw around and still go to Heaven.

"But the 'unsaved' have to be protected from themselves. The Third Covenant couldn't outlaw every vice, but they did their best to restrict them, or at least tax them. For instance, working class people pay more for alcohol, because the rich can get a license to buy it tax free. The old fundamentalist churches didn't fight this sort of thing very hard, because they agreed with the prohibitions. Joachim was behind the censorship of the internet and other media on the premise they contained too much pornography and other 'immoral' material."

She closed her book. "The Third Covenant filled a void in many lives, and it grew like wildfire. By the middle of the twenty-first century, the Third Covenant unofficially became the state religion."

Sunday morning, Rosa and Greta washed yesterday's clothes before they went to church. Jem tried whittling clothes pins. He broke several before he got the hang of it.

As they walked down the street, Rosa said, "It can't be as bad as a Third Covenant service. I had to go to them when I was in college, unless I went home on the weekend."

"Yeah, you won't get me into one of *them* again," Greta said. "I had enough of that when Mama worked for the Hardmans."

It was a long service. Rosa liked the woman minister, even though she didn't entirely agree with her message. She noticed that many of the parishioners were shabbily dressed but had cleaned up for church. Afterwards, they were invited to refreshments, which consisted of unsweetened mint tea and squash casserole.

One of the ladies said, "We don't always have food, it all depends. Sometimes we don't have anything to spare, but squash is in season and the mint grows wild. In my grandma's day, they'd have a feast at least once a month, but times are hard now."

"It was kind of you to invite us," Rosa said. "Especially when we weren't able to contribute anything."

"It's quite all right. We see so many travelers, we try to make their journey easier. The Bible tells us to. If I may inquire, are you young ladies traveling alone? It's dangerous out there."

"No, ma'am. We're well protected. My brother is with us, and my cousin and his friend. They didn't come today because they worked yesterday and needed to rest."

She nodded. "I'll pray for you."

"Thanks. By the way, we got separated from one of our friends. Is there someplace we could leave a message for him if he comes this way?"

"The post office would be the best place. There's a board inside where people write messages."

"Post office? I didn't know they existed anymore."

"What's a post office?" Greta asked.

Rosa said, "At one time it was a service run by the federal government where you could send letters anywhere for under a dollar. It was discontinued in the twenty-first century."

"I don't know about that," the lady said, "but our post office has been a community center as long as I can remember. We had a city hall once, but it burned down. Some towns use a church, but our churches do double duty as schools. The post office comes in handy when you want to leave messages for someone, or announce something, like a new baby. And if somebody official comes to town, like the tax collector, they use the little office space in the back."

They stopped by the post office on the way back to camp. It was a small cement block building over a hundred years old. "This is a piece of history," Rosa said. What had once been a large plate glass window was boarded over. They went inside and turned on the light. Across from the door were tiers of small cubbies. "That's where they got their mail, and this…" She pointed to a slot under a sign "Local mail." "That's where they'd put mail they wanted to send."

The sheet of plywood covering the window had been painted black. Written in white was an announcement about the need for squash pickers. A tin can was nailed to the bottom of the board. Greta asked "What's that?"

"It must be chalk." Rosa picked up a piece and made a mark. "I wonder where they got it?"

When they returned to camp, Hector had a pan of fried squash ready for them.

"Thanks, but we ate at church." Greta said.

"What did you have?"

"Squash."

Everyone laughed.

They spent the rest of the day preparing to resume their journey. When Rosa had completed her tasks, she opened her book to the chapter on the Postal Service.

"Wow!" she said. "The Postal Service goes back to the Revolutionary War. Ben Franklin was the first Postmaster General. This chapter doesn't have everything. It makes reference to other books. I wonder if they still exist."

Greta sat down beside her.

"Just think, Greta, at one time ordinary people like us could afford to send letters and packages anywhere in the world. Just like the rich people do now."

"So, why'd they stop using it?"

"Electronic messages took the place of paper letters. That was before you had to have a license to use the internet. Then they privatized the Postal Service. There were already package delivery companies, and they took over its functions. But they were in it for profit, so they charged more. After the economic collapse, the companies that were still in business stopped delivering to non-profitable areas, like inner cities and little towns like this."

Greta grunted. "That fits right into the master plan. Keep people isolated. Forget they exist. Until it's time to collect taxes, that is."

Later, Ramon asked, "Rosa, are we going to leave a message for Rob?"

"Yes. I left one at the Baptist Church, and I'll leave another at the post office."

"You can write it on that chalkboard," Greta said.

"But what if somebody erases it before he sees it?" She slapped her head. "Paper! I don't have paper. I didn't think to buy any at the store. They're closed today."

"What about your notebook?"

"It's full."

"Tear a page out of one of your books."

"No!"

Greta said, "Rosa, there are blank pages in the books, at the beginning and the end."

"Of course. I'd forgotten." Rosa hesitated to disfigure a precious book, but she carefully tore out a blank page. She dated the note and wrote, "Rob, we waited two days and are moving on tomorrow." In a way, she wanted to write something more personal, but he might not even find it. She looked at Ramon. "So where are we going?"

Ramon dictated the list. "Tell him we'll leave a message in every town."

I hope I can buy paper somewhere. I don't have that many blank pages.

At the post office, she looked for a place to put the note. The boxes were numbered and some had names. When Rosa looked closely, a few contained folded papers. She chose one that looked unused and wrote on the chalkboard, "Rob, look in box 109 for your note. Rosa."

CHAPTER 16

The second day, Rob and Ned were taken to a different peach orchard. Rob removed his work boots and let the soft ground massage his feet. He ate any ripe peach he found and noticed other prisoners furtively doing the same. Halfway through the morning, he remembered it was Sunday. "I'm surprised they have us working today," he said to a cellmate.

The man laughed. "Probably the owner of this orchard ain't a Covenanter. Somebody that don't care about the Sabbath."

The next two days, they returned to the first orchard and worked until the crop was harvested. Wednesday, they were trucked to a large estate where they cleared brush. Rob tried to work barefoot but the stubble hurt his feet and he had wear boots. A few of the inmates, Rob included, returned the next day to work on landscaping. His father often used prison labor at Hardman Hall. Rob always wondered what crimes they'd committed. Now he wondered if they'd committed any at all.

* * *

It was slow going for Rosa and the gang. This part of the old highway was more mountainous and they had to dodge occasional Highway Patrols. Most of the people they encountered were penniless. They didn't let on that they were better off. Not knowing what lay ahead, they were miserly with the money they had left.

Some towns had stores. On Monday, Rosa bought a paper notebook and inquired where she could leave a message. The store had a bulletin board where notices were posted. Rosa hoped Rob would look there. At the next town, there was no store or post office and the only church was closed. Rosa found a loose nail on one of its door posts and attached her note, praying it would stay there until Rob found it. Not every hamlet had a public building, only ruins of what once had been businesses. She wondered where people bought what they needed.

Tuesday, they found work and were rewarded with a few vegetables in addition to their meager pay. Wednesday, they were able to glean a few discarded zucchini from a field that had been harvested. After that, they walked through a forested area with no stores or crops.

Thursday, the wind carried the scent of roast pork. They followed it through the woods until they found a hunting party. Three men sprang to their feet, one aiming a crossbow at them.

Ramon took a step back and held up empty hands. "It's okay, we mean you no harm. We're just hungry."

The man lowered his bow.

"We don't have much to offer," Ramon said. "Only some rather aged zucchini, but if you could spare a few bites of meat, we'd be forever in your debt."

"How did you find us?"

"We smelled your meat cooking."

The men looked at one another. "Told you we should have camped on the other side of the hill," one said. Then he turned to Ramon. "Of course, you're welcome to what we have."

They roasted zucchini on the fire. The hunters were glad to have something besides pork.

After supper, Rosa resumed reading. A half hour later she said, "This is interesting. Something I never thought about. Seems they did do a few things right in the twenty-first century, besides converting to solar. Agricultural production wasn't keeping up with population, despite chemical fertilizers and hormones to make animals grow faster. The rising levels of carbon dioxide in the atmosphere actually made rice less nutritious. They tried breeding new strains of crops, but production and nutritional value continued to decline. Meanwhile, the organic movement gained popularity. Finally, the Department of Agriculture noticed that the organic farms were more productive, acre for acre."

Jem said, "That's true."

"Until the latter half of the twentieth century, moderately sized family farms had been the norm. Then the trend was bigger farms, mega farms, owned by companies that ran them like factories. As the climate destabilized, farming became riskier. Extreme weather events destroyed crops, and farms of all sizes were going out of business." She turned the page.

"Then the principals of regenerative agriculture, to sequester carbon in the soil, became more accepted. In the 2040's, Jerriann Kidwell, the Commissioner of Agriculture, started breaking up bankrupt factory farms and sponsoring planters who would live on their homesteads and use recommended practices. Her idea was that a more intimate relationship with their land would produce better results, and she was right. Soil conditions improved, production increased, the atmosphere began to stabilize, and for a while people's health improved."

"Then why are so many people starving today?" Ramon asked.

"It's as much a problem of distribution as production. The powers-that-be don't believe in giving food to people who can't afford to buy it." She held up the book. "The Barnes suspected that surplus food was being exported instead of distributed at home. That may be one reason they were persecuted. And of course, as the economy got worse, many small farmers could no longer make it, and the big guys took over again."

That night, Rosa woke when rain began to drum on the tent. It was still raining at daylight. She peeked out. The fire was extinguished and the hunters were gone. She had to relieve herself and ran to the questionable shelter of a large tree. She returned to find Ramon cutting cold meat from the hog carcass.

He offered her some. "It looks like those hunters took as much meat as they could, but it was a big hog."

"Well, do we travel today or wait it out?"

"Let's go in my tent for a powwow if everyone's awake."

Rosa consulted the Nebula. "According to this, it's a low pressure system that's expected to dump rain on this area for the next three or four days."

"Well, I don't want to sit in this tent that long," Jem said. "I say we pack up and go on. We're gonna get wet anyway."

Rosa checked the waterproof bag inside her backpack to ensure her books would remain dry. Ramon wrapped the sleeping bags in the tarp and strapped them to his back. They rolled up the wet tents and secured them outside Greta and Jem's backpacks. Hector removed all the meat he could from the pig and carried it in his makeshift soup pot. By then, everyone was soaked to the skin.

Before nightfall, they found a house in a small clearing that was overgrown with weeds. The house was dark and looked abandoned. They huddled together on the porch while Ramon tried the door. It was unlocked. "Hello? Anyone home?" There was no answer. He reached in and touched the light switch. Lights in the front room came on. They stepped inside. There was no furniture.

Hector and Ramon searched the house. Ramon said, "It's empty but clean. There's even running water. Whoever lived here must not have left very long ago. Why don't we spend the night?"

"How long do you think the solar batteries will last in this rain?" Greta asked.

"The indicator said they're almost at full charge. Let's not be extravagant, and maybe they'll last as long as we need them."

The kitchen had a stove. Hector made a stew with the rest of the meat.

There was hot water. They took turns bathing and washed their dirty clothes. Rosa and Greta strung the clothesline in front of the open oven door and turned it on. "I don't consider this extravagant," Rosa said.

With full bellies and dry clothes, they turned out the lights and settled down to sleep. The rain continued all night.

In the morning, they discussed whether to go on or stay longer. The decision was made when Jem found the remains of a vegetable garden in the back yard. They foraged for everything edible that could be baked or boiled. "I wish we had some salt," Hector said.

"I'll buy some at the next store," Greta replied.

Jem, rummaging through a shed behind the house, found a roll of thick cellophane. "Hey, I think we can make rain ponchos with this stuff. Then we won't get so wet."

"What does the weather report say?" Ramon asked.

Rosa shook her head. "I haven't been able to charge the Nebula. Not enough solar, and there's no charging station here. Last time I looked, this was expected to last all week."

"Well, we can't stay here that long. We should head out tomorrow," Ramon said.

Greta found a way to make hooded ponchos that at least sheltered their heads and upper bodies. In the morning before they set out, they breakfasted on leftover vegetables.

* * *

Working barefoot allowed Rob's feet to heal. Friday it rained and they stayed in their cells. Rob kept his boots off. Rain continued all night and into Saturday. Just before lunch, they were given the clothing they'd arrived in and told to change. Ned was handed his backpack, and they were set free.

Before they left the overhang in front of the building, Ned paused and opened his backpack. "My blanket's missing."

Rob indignantly turned as though to rush back inside.

Ned grabbed his arm. "Let it go. They'd only deny it and we don't need to give them an excuse to detain us again. At least they washed what we were wearing."

"And now they'll get an extra rinsing. If it's any consolation, I had nothing but the clothes on my back, so they kept my belt." Rob laughed. "I guess they didn't want my hat." They walked out into the rain. "I wonder why they let us go?"

"Probably don't want to feed us if we can't work."

"That's right," said another released prisoner. "If I had any money, I'd wager there's rain in the forecast for the next several days. By the time the weather clears, they'll have picked up another crew."

For the first hour, Rob was completely miserable. His cap did little to keep off the rain. He took off his shoes because they rubbed his nearly-healed blisters. As much as possible, he walked on the grassy roadside. Eventually he learned to ignore the rain. Before long, his empty stomach gave up complaining. With his sore feet, he couldn't walk as fast as the others, who went on ahead.

Ned lagged behind. "Don't worry, brother. I'll stay with you."

As it grew dark, they looked for shelter. A tumbledown house sat close to the road. They peeked in. All Rob could think about was roaches and spiders.

Ned stepped inside and tested the floor. "Eat up with termites. It could collapse any time."

Rob looked up at the porch roof, which was hanging on one post, and pushed at the drooping corner. It creaked but didn't fall. "Out here at least there's less to fall on us."

The porch floor was more solid than the house. "This doesn't make sense," Ned said. "Usually the porch goes first."

Rob looked closely at the wood. "It looks like it was replaced at some time."

Ned gingerly walked through the house and came back dragging a tattered mattress. "Doesn't smell as good as the ones in the jail, but I bet it's softer. If you want a pillow, I'll share my backpack with you."

They positioned the mattress on the most solid part of the porch, out of the rain, and slapped mosquitoes until they fell asleep.

Rain continued through the night and into morning. As they approached a small town, they heard music.

"What day is it?" Rob asked.

"Must be Sunday."

Service at the Pentecostal Church was in full swing. Ned tried to squeeze water out of his clothes. "We can't go in like this." They sat on the floor of the portico. "At least we're out of the rain."

"Ned, are you a church goer?"

He shook his head. "When I was a boy, but not since then. What about you?"

Rob smiled. "Not anymore, thank God! My family's Third Covenant."

"I'm not surprised."

"Ramon said if we got separated, they'd leave messages at churches. I'd like to check for one when the service is over."

"Maybe we'll get lucky and they'll feed us."

Rob fell asleep. He half woke when the church grew quiet. No one disturbed them. He slept again until the door banged against his knee. Ned was already on his feet, apologizing.

A couple stood in the doorway. "You don't need to stay out here," the lady said. "Everybody else is in the back having a little snack."

"We're all wet…"

"So is everyone else."

Rob stood up. "I only wanted to check to see if there's a message for me. My friends were ahead of me…"

"Check at the post office," the man said. "Meanwhile, go back and have something to eat." He chuckled. "We're only leaving 'cause we're sick of squash."

"Post office?"

"Yeah, it's out on the main road, a little block building. You won't miss it."

The man opened an umbrella and the couple huddled together and went out into the rain.

"What are we waiting for?" Ned said. "Aren't you hungry?"

They walked through the sanctuary and hesitated at the door to the social hall. A lady glanced up. Ned said, "A gentleman at the front door invited us…"

"Then, come in. Sit over there. I'll get you something." She returned with two plates of squash casserole.

Another woman brought two cups of hot tea. It smelled minty. "It's unsweetened, I'm afraid. Sweetening is expensive."

As the warmth of the tea spread through him, Rob said, "Thank you. It's good."

She smiled. "Where are you fellows going?"

"North," Rob said. "We're trying to catch up with our friends. They probably came through about a week ago."

"Two young ladies?"

"Yes, there were two girls. Did they leave a message for us?"

"We told them to leave it at the post office."

"Pardon me, but what do you mean by 'post office?'"

Ned laughed. "It was an old way to send letters. I'll explain it later." To the woman, he said, "Thanks. We'll check there. And we appreciate your hospitality."

Rob tried to identify what was in the casserole. He forked a leaf and held it up. "I wonder what this is?"

A man at their table said, "Squash leaf."

Ned stared at his plate. "I don't want to appear ungrateful, but are they edible?"

"Haven't killed anybody yet."

Rob said, "Rosa told me bean leaves are edible, so why not squash?"

"You must be city boys," the man said. "But be careful what you eat. Some things, like potato plants, are poisonous."

After they ate, they took their dishes to the kitchen and offered to wash them. "That's okay," a woman said. "We have plenty of help."

She scraped leftovers from a baking pan into a cellophane bag. "Here, take this with you."

"Thank you," Rob said.

"You're welcome. God bless you."

Ned took her hand. "And may God bless you, too. You've been so kind." After they left, Ned said, "My faith in humanity has been restored."

On the way to the post office, Ned gave Rob a short history lesson. "How do you know all this?"

"Where I grew up, there was a building that my grandfather said used to be a post office." Ned pointed ahead. "I'll be! It looks just like the one back home."

The door was not locked. They went in and looked around. Rob's heart leaped. In a corner of the blackboard, he recognized Rosa's handwriting. "109—where'd that be?"

Ned pointed at the boxes.

Rob found Box 109 and opened the little door. It held a piece of paper. At the top was printed, *Chronicles of the Twenty First Century.* "She tore a page from one of her books to write this." He unfolded the note. Rosa's voice sprang out. His hands shook. "Ned, we're on the right track." Rob folded the letter and started to pocket it. "I don't have a dry place to carry it."

Ned opened his backpack. "I have a little pocket here. Unless we fall in a river, it should stay dry."

They looked outside. The rain seemed to be coming down harder, if possible. "I wonder if anyone would object to us staying here tonight?" Ned asked.

"Probably not, but we'd lose a day's journey. We're a week behind them, and we're wet anyway. I'd like to catch up, if we can." So out into the rain they went.

* * *

Rosa looked at the ruined bridge with dismay. The ravine it once spanned, fed by days of rain, was a rushing torrent too treacherous to cross. Once again they had to go miles out of their way, this time on foot.

In the evening, they approached a small town with a church full of bright lights and music. "It's Sunday, isn't it?" Jem asked.

"Yes. They must have an evening service," Rosa said.

They laid their belongings on the porch, took off their ponchos, and tentatively opened the door. A man in the back beckoned them in. Then he motioned for people in a few pews to slide over to make room for them. Rosa sank to her seat and slipped off her wet shoes. It was such a blessing to be out of the rain and off her feet. Without being aware of it, she fell asleep.

When Greta stood for a hymn, Rosa jolted awake and joined her. After the benediction, the minister walked down the aisle to shake their hands. "Are ye traveling?" he asked.

"Yes, sir," Ramon said.

"Do ye need a dry place to spend the night?"

Rosa spoke up. "That would be wonderful."

"You're welcome to bunk in the sanctuary. But first, let's get some food in you. You must be hungry." He led them to the social hall. "Our custom is to bring our leftovers from Sunday dinner, if there are any, to the evening service and share them. Sometimes it's only a mouthful apiece, but other times it's like the loaves and fishes. Either way, the Lord provides spiritual nourishment."

"Tell me something," Rosa said. "All the churches are so hospitable. It doesn't matter what denomination. There are so many people on the road, don't you get overwhelmed helping everybody?"

"We do what little we can. A kind word goes a long way. But not all come to us. Some have been wounded by their religions and don't trust us. Many are so downtrodden they don't believe anyone would help them. And, I'm sorry to say, there are a few who exaggerate their need—they try to take advantage of us. We try to send that kind on their way as soon as possible. I'm not always right, but I can usually spot sincerity. And you would do well to be cautious. Not all wanderers are honest."

Ramon nodded. "I know. We try not to put ourselves at risk."

They were given more than a mouthful apiece. Before the pastor left, Rosa said, "We want to leave a message for a friend who'll be following us in a few days, maybe a few weeks. Where's the best place to put it?"

"Where will your friend look for a message?"

"At a church or post office, or any place people post notes."

"You can leave it with me. We don't have a post office, or anything like that."

Rosa wrote a more personal note than usual. *I wonder if he'll get these? Is he even following us?*

CHAPTER 17

By now, Rob was accustomed to walking through rain. The soles of his feet had toughened. Occasionally he'd stop in a little rivulet to enjoy the sensation of water running between his toes. At the next town, they found no church or post office, only a little store. "Let's check with them," Rob said.

Ned sighed. "I wish I had access to my money."

"Me, too."

A little bell rang when they opened the door. A woman stood behind the counter. "May I help you?"

"I'm looking for word from friends who traveled through here. They were going to leave a note…"

"A couple of girls?"

"Yes."

She pointed at a bulletin board. "They left one there."

Rob scanned the notices. On a piece of lined paper, he saw his name. There was little to the message other than the date and next destination, but after reading it, he closed his eyes and pressed it to his chest. Then he turned to the clerk. "Weren't they traveling with some men?"

"I don't know. Only the girls came in the store."

Ned stuck his hands in his pockets and turned to the clerk. "We don't have any money…"

Rob saw a flash of fear in her eyes and spoke quickly. "We're willing to work for something to eat."

She seemed to relax. "Up the road they're harvesting squash. Nothing around here, though."

"Thank you." They turned to leave.

"Wait. My roof leaks over the storage room. If you can patch it for me, I'll give you some food."

Ned grinned. "Where's your ladder?"

She led them to the back room and pointed to the ceiling. Water dripped into a nearly full bucket. Ned emptied the pail for her.

The ladder hung on nails by the back door. She showed them a heap of empty tin cans. "You can use those for patches. I'll get my hammer and nails. Be careful of the solar panels."

When she went inside, Rob asked, "Do you know anything about roofs?"

"Not much. You?"

"A little."

Cautiously, they climbed up to survey the damage. The metal roof was slippery, but not very steep. A tree branch had fallen and dented it at a seam. "Good thing it didn't hit the solar panels." Rob cleared debris out of the hole. "I know what to do. We'll flatten a few cans and use them as shingles."

The clerk stood by the ladder with hammer and nails and tin snips.

"Do you have any caulking, or tar, or such?" Rob asked.

"Fraid not. Stuff like that's hard to get."

"We'll do our best."

Ned held makeshift shingles in place while Rob puzzled out places to drive nails. He said, "If we had proper materials, we wouldn't need such a big patch."

"How do you know this?"

"Once I helped our yard man patch a shed roof. Had to hide it from my father, of course. He thought such work was beneath me." After they finished, the leak was substantially reduced. "We did our best," he said. "There may be some water under the roofing that's still drizzling in."

"Thank you. I can't spare much, but here's some bread and bean paste. You're welcome to stay back here out of the rain and eat before you go."

They ate half. The clerk gave them a cellophane bag to keep the rest dry.

* * *

Rosa stopped to catch her breath. The road was getting steeper and the pavement was slippery. Ramon said, "We're getting close. We should reach the resort tomorrow."

Near midday, they came to a little store with a table and chairs under the overhang in front. "Must be a hangout for the locals," Hector said.

Jem circled the building. "The back door's not locked."

"That doesn't help," Greta said. "We're not going to just take things."

"We have cash," Rosa said.

"Then let's go shopping!"

"Not all of us," Ramon said. "In case anyone comes by. Just me and Rosa."

There was no produce, only dry goods. They chose a small container of salt, three loaves of bread, four small cans of bean paste, and five of vegetables, "We'll have to eat them cold," Rosa said. "We can't start a fire in the rain."

They left cash on a shelf under the counter. Ramon locked the door on the way out.

Rosa wrote a note to Rob and wedged it in a window where the caulking was loose. Although she didn't write down her thoughts, they were: I sure hope you get this, Rob. If you've come this far, you're almost there.

They spent a leisurely half hour at the table eating lunch. The rain let up temporarily. Rosa looked out at the bluish-white clouds drifting across the blue-green mountains, leaving tendrils of cotton candy. She sighed. Surrounded by all this beauty, between rain and fatigue, she hadn't been able to appreciate it.

They finished eating. As they stashed the remaining food in their backpacks, a party of walkers came down the hill, two couples and two children. Rosa surmised one couple was the grandparents. Both children had stringy hair and were barefoot. They looked up at her with anxious eyes.

"The store's closed," Ramon said. "Where'd y'all come from?"

The older man said, "Mountain City. And you?"

"We're headed for Apex Resort."

The man rubbed his chin. "Ain't heard about no trouble there. Not yet, anyway."

"Trouble?"

"Haven't you heard any news?"

"No. What's happening?"

The man shook his head. "The world's falling apart. Uprisings everywhere. Riots. That's why we're heading south. Haven't heard about so many problems there."

"Why are people rioting?" Greta asked.

"Because they sick and tired of being hungry. Working hard, and nothing to show for it. The weather's part of the problem. It's so damn hot. Then we get these downpours and floods. Me and my wife got fired because we were flooded in and couldn't get to work." He indicated the younger couple. "The kids been living with us because they can't get steady work. What's it like south of here?"

"Not much better," Ramon said. "People are poor and it's even hotter. You need to watch out for Highway Patrols. They arrest people and put them to work."

"Yeah, that's why there's so little paid work."

"Probably."

So, Rosa thought, those news reports are true.

The younger woman peered through the store window. "Too bad it's closed. I was hopin' to buy somethin' for the children."

"When did you last eat?" Greta asked.

"Yesterday."

Greta opened her backpack and pulled out a loaf of bread. Ramon glared at her. She glared back. "Hector, get them a can of bean paste, and carrots."

The woman looked hungrily at the offerings, but her husband said, "We can't take your food."

"We ate today. And we don't have kids."

"At least let us pay you," the grandmother said.

"No. You'll need your money," Ramon said. "We need to be on our way,"

"Thank you," the grandfather said. "Have a safe journey."

"Thanks. You, too."

Later that day, their road intersected with a turnpike. Despite the rain, there was an unusual amount of vehicular and foot traffic, as well as check points at the entrance ramps to the highway. They stopped a distance away and studied the scene.

"I don't like it," Ramon said.

"Neither do I," said Rosa. "The rest of you might be okay. You have IDs."

"No, we'll stick with you."

They looked for a way around, but the highway was fortified by a high fence. They saw a man walking towards them with an almost defiant air. "I think we can trust him," Ramon said. "Sir, is there another route to take?"

"You don't want to chance the check points?"

"We'd rather not."

"Go back a mile or so. There's a county road that runs under the highway. No check points. Then if you take the second right after the highway, you'll run back into Old 441."

"Thank you."

Rosa said, "We need to leave word for Rob. He'll want to avoid checkpoints." They went back two miles before they found a tiny old post office with a message board. "I wonder how we missed this."

Greta said, "The rain."

Rosa secured her note with a tack. "I sure hope he finds this." She wished she could hear from Rob, where he was, if he was safe, whether he still followed them. So much could happen on the road. He could still be in jail, have gone home, or joined a different group. Why did she care? *If he follows us, if he shows up, I'll know it's the right thing.* It might take a miracle.

Towards evening, another highway crossed over Old 441 but there was no intersection. Under the overpass was a crowd of travelers camping out of the rain. Someone had built a fire. The light provided comfort. One woman had children, a teenage girl and a younger boy and girl. All three were as wet and grimy as Rosa herself. The teenager was skinny, arms and legs coming out of her clothes. The younger ones' garments were too large.

When Greta saw them, she said, "Children shouldn't have to live under a bridge. There is enough wealth in this country, children, at least, should be provided for."

Rosa talked with them. "Where did you come from?"

The older girl said, "Tennessee."

"Where are you going?"

She didn't know.

"Do you go to school?"

"No, ma'am. But I used to go to school. I liked it. I taught my brother and sister how to read."

"Really? Do you like to read?"

"Yes, ma'am. But I don't have any books."

"I do." Rosa opened her backpack and took out one of her history books.

The children's eyes grew wide. "Is this really a book?" the girl asked.

"Yes. It's the old fashioned kind."

The children touched the book almost reverently.

"If it wasn't so dark, I'd read to you."

Their mother came over. "Time to sleep."

"I'm hungry," the youngest whined.

"Maybe we'll find something to eat tomorrow."

"Wait," Greta said. "We have food."

Ramon objected.

"Ramon," Rosa said, "we'll be at Apex tomorrow. We can eat then. Tonight, we can share."

The food they had left wasn't adequate for the five of them plus three hungry children and their mother, but Greta made sure the youngsters had enough. While they ate, Rosa sorted through her books. After they finished, the children thanked them. Rosa handed the oldest girl a book. "This is for you. I already read it. Take good care of it, and when you finish reading it, give it to someone else who likes to read."

Her eyes shone. "Thank you. I will."

Rosa spread her sleeping bag on the hard roadside and tried to sleep despite the rumble of cars passing over them. During the night the weather cleared.

* * *

Towards evening, Rob and Ned reached a small town with only one church, which was closed and locked. Rob looked for a note from Rosa but didn't find one.

Ned took off his backpack. "Why don't we camp here for the night?"

"I wish I had dry clothes."

"We're about the same size." Ned opened his backpack and handed Rob a shirt and pants.

"Thanks." They both changed and held their dirty clothes under the pouring eaves to rinse them, then wrung them out and laid them on a dry part of the floor. "They won't dry," Rob said, "but at least we have a bag to carry them in." They finished their bread and bean paste and lay down for the night.

By morning, the rain had stopped. As they left the churchyard, Ned bent down and picked up a wet scrap of paper. He handed it to Rob.

It was the same kind of paper Rosa used for her last note. Rob unfolded it but found only a smear of ink. "I think this was from Rosa. It's not readable, but it's something."

They stopped at every church they came across, as well as anything that looked like a post office, store, or public building, but there was no more word from Rosa. "I'm sorry, Ned, I know this is slowing us down, but I don't want to miss anything."

"It's okay. I know how important it is to you."

Two meals of bread and bean paste had awakened, rather than satisfied, their appetites. Now Rob's stomach complained more than his feet. During the afternoon, they passed a house where a woman sat on the front porch. Rob approached her. "Please, ma'am, we're hungry. Do you know where we can get something to eat?"

The woman rushed into her house and slammed the door.

Ned said, "You should have offered to work for her."

"I know." He ran his hand through his hair and rubbed his chin. He looked down at his clothes. They'd been clean last night but now were soaked with sweat and caked with road dirt. "I don't blame her. I probably would have slammed the door in my face, too." He sighed. "I never thought I'd stoop to begging."

A few miles later, they met a family with two children. "Up ahead," the man said, "in the next town, there's a church that'll give you a meal and dry clothes. It's a few blocks off the main road. A Methodist church. You'll have to watch for the sign."

Rob looked at the sky. How long would clothes stay dry? At least they'd be clean. His thoughts flashed back to a young man with expensive clothes, who was clean shaven, hair styled. That workman back at the Mandevilles was willing to trade shirts because he recognized the quality of Rob's. What was his story?

They found the Methodist Church close to supper time, but there was no note from Rosa. The man and woman in charge shared vegetable soup and bread with them. They also shared their story.

The man said, "I used to be a nurse, and my wife was a teacher. Our children were grown and our house almost paid off when things went sour. I'd worked twenty years, with a good record. Then I started getting poor evaluations. For no reason. Then medications began to disappear from the supply cabinet, and they blamed me. Then the worst thing—a patient got the wrong medication and died." He paused and swallowed. "They charged me with murder."

His wife said, "He was set up. He was getting too expensive to keep. They could hire two young nurses fresh out of school for what they were paying him."

"I know they wanted to get rid of me, but I don't think they deliberately killed that woman. Someone made a mistake, and when she died, they had to blame somebody."

"Wasn't that patient terminal? Facing a long period of expensive treatment? How convenient!" His wife looked at them. "He was in jail for months. The jail was required to have a nurse, and a prisoner would do, so they kept him. But he was too much trouble. He was healing patients instead of letting them die. When another nurse got arrested, they released him on bail but we had to put up our house."

"Then what?" Ned asked.

"I was facing a life sentence, so we skipped bail. That was four years ago. If they looked for us, they didn't try very hard. Why should they? They got our house."

"The bank?" Rob asked.

"No. The bail bond company. Same outfit that owned the jail."

Ned shook his head in disgust. "So how did you get this church?"

"It's not our church. We're volunteers. We get room and board in exchange for using our skills to help people."

"What about your children?" Rob asked.

"We don't dare let them know where we are. It'd be too dangerous. They could get arrested."

After they ate, the man showed them the clothes closet. "You can take a new outfit, but we ask that you leave an old one. That way we don't run out."

"I borrowed what I'm wearing from Ned. My clothes are wet and dirty."

"That's okay. We wash everything." The woman gave them each a sheet of cellophane to wear when it rained. "We'll give you a blanket, too, but we can only spare one."

The mission had showers and cots for wayfarers. For the first time in weeks, Rob slept in a somewhat proper bed, with sheets. As he drifted off to sleep, he thought about how he'd lost everything he'd left Florida with except his underwear, socks with holes, and shoes he couldn't wear. He'd lost family and friends. Then he thought about people he'd met on the road. Many had less than he, and some had children they couldn't provide for. At least tonight, he had a full belly and a friend, Ned, who was loyal to him. And somewhere up the road, Rosa was leaving notes for him.

CHAPTER 18

It was already June. One month ago, Rosa had graduated from college and started a job. Now she was homeless, unemployed, wet, dirty, tired, and facing a doubtful future. How much longer could this to go on? Surely not the rest of her life! Something had to change.

They passed a small country church. "Let me leave another message." It was locked, and no one was about, but by the entrance was a glass-covered bulletin board with removable letters announcing the service time and sermon topic. Rosa wrote a quick note for Rob, opened the glass door, and stuck it inside.

The road climbed steeply up the mountain, with sharp hairpin turns, hazardous when vehicles whipped around, incognizant of pedestrians. The pavement was narrow, with almost no shoulder to walk on.

"If a Highway Patrol came, we'd have to jump off the cliff," Hector muttered.

Finally, the road intersected with a landscaped boulevard. A sign announced, "Apex Resort One Mile."

Ramon said, "This road comes from the turnpike. I'd rather not walk that way. We might get picked up. Greta, how do we find your aunt?"

"Ask for her at the back gate."

"Do you know how to find it?"

"I hope so. I haven't been here in years. There's a service road that connects with the turnpike."

Ramon took out his maps. The hologram projection was dim. "My battery's almost dead." He flipped pages and studied them. "Okay. It looks like the service road is up ahead."

There was more traffic there, and the back gate was guarded. Greta approached the security shack while everyone else stood well back, holding their breaths.

She came back looking disappointed. "Her shift is over. She's gone home and won't be back till Thursday. He wouldn't tell me where she lives or how to get in touch with her."

Ramon beat his thigh with his fist.

"Hey! You knew I had no way to call ahead when we set out," Greta said.

"I know. I'm sorry. Let's find somewhere to camp tonight. At least it's not raining." He picked up his backpack and slung it over his shoulder.

"Hey," a woman walked up to them. "I heard you ask about Mabel. How do you know her?"

"She's my aunt," Greta said. "Do you know where she lives?"

"Yes, but it's fifteen miles away. Why are you here?"

"I was hoping to get work."

The woman eyed them. "Been walking long?"

"We came from Florida."

"We're short of help. People keep quitting and going—I'm not sure where they go, or why. Tomorrow's the first day Mabel's had off in weeks. How many of you are looking for work?"

"Well, me and Hector and Jem are the only ones who are legit." She pointed to Rosa and Ramon. "They'd like to work, too, but they don't have IDs."

The woman nodded. "I might be able to help the three of you. I'm not a supervisor, but Mabel is, and our boss is pretty reasonable." She took in their appearance. "You can't ask for a job looking like that. Come with me." She led them past the back gate to a dirt lane that wound down into the woods. "These cabins are for summer help, and most of 'em are empty right now." They went to the last one in the row. "Why don't you stay here tonight and get cleaned up. I'm two doors down. Come to my place a little before five AM and I'll see what I can do."

"Thanks," Greta said. "Do you know where we can buy food?"

"You have money?"

"A little bit."

"There's a store back by the Turnpike. Pretty expensive, though."

The cabin had one room with a kitchenette, bathroom, and loft. Downstairs were two threadbare couches and a table with four kitchen chairs, one with a broken leg. Upstairs were two sets of camp-style bunkbeds. The place was disordered and in need of cleaning. The kitchen cupboards yielded a handful of mismatched items. "Not fancy," Greta said, "but it's better than a tent."

Ramon said, "Greta, why don't you and Hector go to the store and we'll clean the place?"

Hector groaned. "Oh, I was looking forward to putting my feet up."

Greta elbowed him. "You can do that when we get back."

They found a closet on the back deck that held a broom, mop, and pail. A tattered rag hung over the railing. Jem shook out the dirt. "We're in business."

"I'm going to do something about those sleeping bags," Rosa said. "I wish we had a way to wash and dry them."

After a cursory cleaning of the cabin, Rosa dug in her backpack for her grandmother's doily and set it on the only end table in the place.

Jem smiled at her. "Home sweet home."

Greta and Hector returned with a bag of groceries and another of toilet paper, soap, and towels. Rosa threw her arms around Greta. "Thank you! I'm so tired of dripping dry. But could we afford it?"

"It took almost all my money," Greta said. "Keep your fingers crossed that I get a job tomorrow. By the way, the store takes cash, but their prices are larcenous."

Supper was chicken soup. "I need a microscope to find the chicken," Hector said. "But at least it's not squash or bean paste. No produce at that store. It probably all goes to the resort."

Rosa and Greta slept on the couches and the men slept in the loft. Rosa let Greta use the Nebula as an alarm clock. It rang well before dawn. Rosa sat up.

"Go back to sleep," Greta whispered and went upstairs to call Hector and Jem.

Ramon came down with them. No more sleep for me, Rosa thought.

After the rest had left for work, Rosa and Ramon breakfasted on bread and bean paste. "Well, now what should we do?" Rosa asked.

"I'd like to look for work, but let's wait and see what they find out."

As soon as the sun was up, Rosa set the Nebula out on the deck to charge.

An hour later, Jem came back. "They were hired, but they didn't have anything for me. I was told about an outfit that hires day labor to work on the grounds. You and I can probably get on with them," he said to Ramon.

"What about me?"

"It's not women's work."

Rosa grabbed Jem's arm and twisted it. "Do I need to show you how strong I am?"

"Ow! I didn't mean anything..."

She let him go.

Ramon said, "Rosa, let me and Jem scope it out. If there's work for you, I'll tell you."

Rosa burst into tears. "I had work. Work I was educated for."

Ramon put his arms around her. "I'm sorry, Rosa. So sorry. It's all my fault."

She shook her head. "No. It's not your fault. It's the fault of that stupid, crooked system." She tore loose and stomped outside, slamming the door. She sat on the porch steps and cried. A bird trilled. She took a deep breath, wiped her face on the hem of her shirt, and went back inside.

'You guys go on. There's plenty here to keep me busy."

And there was. The perfunctory housework they'd done the evening before hadn't been enough. Rosa draped the sleeping bags over the railings and strung up the clothesline. There was no laundry machine, so she washed dirty clothes in the bathtub. As she hung them out, she looked at the sky. *I should check the weather.*

By now the Nebula was charged. The meteorologists predicted a sunny day with possible thunderstorms in the afternoon. Time enough to dry clothes, but not sleeping bags. She beat them with the broom to knock out as much dirt as she could. Then she attacked the house.

At lunchtime, Rosa realized it had been some time since she'd been alone. She was always surrounded by people. She took her sandwich to the front porch and settled into the silence. Somewhere in the woods, a dove cried. She remembered sitting on the front porch at home, hearing that mournful sound. Sitting beside Grandmother. Rosa laid down her sandwich, covered her face with her hands, and cried. In the past weeks, with one crisis after another, she'd had no time to grieve. Now she gave into it.

When she was done, she finished her sandwich and went for a walk. A path led into the woods. She heard a creek gurgling before she saw it. Beside it lay a grassy area. She sat down, took off her shoes, and dangled her feet in the water. How nice to enjoy the water and not to have to depend on it for bathing and laundry. She was thankful for the little cabin, even though their stay might be short. Where would they go from here?

Her thoughts meandered down roads she'd walked. Unbidden, Rob came to mind. Where was he and what was he doing? Was he out of jail yet? Would he find the notes she'd left? Was he following them or had he taken another path? She worried about him. He was ill equipped to deal with the world on his own. Maybe he'd reconciled with his family. She hoped not, even though that might be for the best. If he had, she wouldn't see him again. Why did that sadden her?

She returned to the cabin, did more cleaning, then thought it would be nice to sit down and read. She wished she had a novel. Rob's

Nebula had books. What sort of thing did Rob read? She found the usual "guy" stuff— mystery, adventure, science fiction, few classics, and thankfully, nothing smutty. To her surprise, there was also nonfiction, including books on farming practices and architecture. She chose a mystery.

Her legs grew restless. She wasn't used to sitting. She got up and walked to the paved road and back. On the way, she noticed plantago growing in the middle of the dirt road. It made a good poultice, all right. What else was it good for? She used the Nebula to look it up. In addition to medicinal properties, it was edible as a salad or potherb. *That'd be a change from squash.*

Rosa walked back down the road and gathered a good handful. After she washed it, she tasted a leaf. Rather tough to eat raw, she decided to cook it. "I wish I had some pork drippings, or something." With salt, the plantago was palatable.

Greta and Hector came in from work, each with a small bag of food. "They let the employees take the leavings," Greta said.

"What 'er you cooking?" asked Hector.

"Not squash! If you like it, I'll pick some more."

Ramon and Jem were dirty and tired when they came in. They bathed and changed while Rosa set out a nutritious supper. When Ramon emerged from the bathroom, Rosa noticed his hands were red. She grasped one and examined his palms. They were covered with blisters. "Do these hurt?"

"Only when I grab a shovel. I wish I had gloves."

"Maybe the store does."

"They'd be too expensive. My hands will toughen up."

Rosa looked at Jem's hands. They weren't as bad as Ramon's.

"I'm used to physical labor," Jem said.

Rosa wished she hadn't cooked all the plantago. Then she remembered discarding a few leaves that were old and chewed by insects. She retrieved them and mashed them into paste. "Smear this on your blisters," she told Ramon. "That's what I put on Rob's feet."

They discussed their day. Greta said, "Hector and I can have employment as long as the resort is open for summer, but after that… we'll have to come up with something else. At least we can stay in this cottage rent-free till then. Nobody checks on who else stays here, so you all will be safe."

"Jem and I can probably get day work through the season, too," Ramon said.

"What about me?" Rosa asked.

"I don't want you where we're working. And it's not because I think the work's too hard. It's a rough group. There are a few women there, and… well, if they treated you like they treat them…" He shook his head. "You don't want me back in jail. If you can keep house for us and search for options on that Nebula… We've got to make plans before winter. Planning the next step—that'll be your job."

"I agree," Greta said. "You're more qualified than the rest of us for that kind of work. By the way, these greens are good."

* * *

Rob's underwear was still in his bag, damp and starting to smell. When they came to a swiftly flowing stream, he tried to rinse it out. The rushing water tore the garment from his hands and carried it away. He followed it downstream and found it snagged on a blackberry bramble. Carefully, he tried to untangle it, bloodying his hands on the thorns. When he finally worked it free, it was torn in several places, beyond repair. *Now I'll just have to go commando.*

Ned took off his shoes and stuffed them in his backpack. "They're starting to wear out. Have you noticed the places that give away clothes don't have shoes? I'll save mine for later, when I really need them."

That afternoon, they found a soup kitchen run by a church. While a woman dished up their plates, she asked if they were a couple.

Rob gave her a puzzled look.

Ned blurted out, "No. Just friends."

Rob couldn't concentrate on eating. Some things suddenly made sense. Nights sleeping huddled together, at times Ned's arm crept around him the way his mother's used to when he was a child. He shuddered. His father's religion loomed like a phantom pronouncing justice.

Afterwards, on a quiet stretch of road, Rob ventured, "Ned, are you …." He cleared his throat.

"Gay? You can say it."

Rob instinctively drew away from him.

"Don't worry, Rob. I know you're not, and I respect that. I don't want to be your lover, but I've come to think of you as a brother. I never had one." Ned sighed. "Didn't you wonder why I never married? I've had lovers, but it's a dangerous way to live. My family accepts me, but I had to leave them, to protect them from persecution."

Rob studied his face. They looked more alike than he and Doug. Ned's hair was red, Rob's sandy brown, but their eyes were a similar shade of hazel, and they spoke with the same North Florida accent. He thought about Doug. When they were children, Rob always looked up to Doug, even though he was somewhat of a bully. He examined his feelings and found a degree of warmth toward Ned—certainly not romantic, but he trusted Ned in a way he never trusted Doug. "Brothers. That's what we'll be—brothers. Let's tell people that. We look enough alike."

Ned smiled. "Thank you, Rob."

They spotted a Highway Patrol and faded into the roadside brush. "They weren't patrolling in the rain," Rob whispered.

"Yeah. Didn't need workers then."

Later, they encountered a group of people carrying squash. "Where'd you get it?" Rob asked.

A woman pointed up the road. "There's a field they're done harvesting. You can pick what you want for free. Turn left on the next dirt road. It's down there a ways."

The field was full of over-mature zucchini. "Back home, we'd feed this to the pigs," Rob said. "But I'm hungry enough to eat it raw."

"We'll have to. We don't have any way to cook it."

Rob bit into one. The rind was tough but the flesh was soft. Not very tasty, but it began to fill his belly. They gathered as much as they could carry and joined a group of families dining on raw squash in the shade of trees lining the field. One woman had salt which she shared. It improved the flavor.

Rob overheard conversations. The travelers traded rumors of civil uprisings in various parts of the country.

A woman with stringy hair and wild eyes claimed to have been part of one. "I come from Atlanta," she said. "Last winter, there was a new ailment. We called it the 'bloody shit.' We think it came from the drinking water. It was bad. Worse for kids. They had this new medicine, and the public clinics started givin' it out. It stopped the shitting, all right, but then you'd come down with fever and a rash. Most people got better in a few days, but not old people, or children." Her countenance froze as though she faced an unspeakable horror.

"My little girl suffered for five weeks before she died. There was nothin' I could do. The hospital wouldn't take her. They said it was a bad batch of medicine. They were sorry. Reparations would be made." Her voice rose an octave. "How can you make 'reparations' for a dead child? Can you bring her back to life? How much money is a child's life worth?"

Another woman spoke up. "She's telling the truth. After the funerals, there were riots. People stormed the clinics and beat some of them doctors and nurses to death. The Guard was called in. They shot into the crowds and killed people."

The grieving woman said, "They killed my husband. When they started shooting, he got in front of me. He saved my life." She laughed mirthlessly. "I wish they'd killed me!"

A man nodded. "It was only the public clinics, none of the pudientes died. Then it leaked it out—the drug hadn't been tested. They were using us poor people as guinea pigs. I think they were deliberately culling the poor. Just like that hurricane in Florida, leaving all those people to drown. It's happenin' all over the country. These cullings are getting more and more common."

Rob couldn't leave soon enough. When he and Ned were alone, he said, "The hurricane wasn't planned. It was a natural disaster."

"But what about the people who didn't get evacuation warnings? At first I thought the prison disaster was an oversight, a mistake, but as I think back, it was a convenient way to cull the undesirables. Except, I thwarted their plan."

"It's mass paranoia," Rob said. "People are suffering, so they have to blame someone." Was Ned, the stalwart, the rational, starting to succumb to paranoia? That night, trying to sleep, Rob gave it more thought. Such events were accidental, of course, but they did effectively reduce the numbers of marginal people.

The closer they got to the mountains, the more Rob thought about his brother. He said, "I'm not exactly sure where we are, but Doug has a summer home in North Carolina. If things don't work out where Rosa is, I wonder if he'd be willing to help us."

"Is that a possibility?"

"I don't know. My father may have turned him against me."

Though Rob checked everywhere Rosa could have left a note, they'd found nothing since the unreadable one two days ago. "I hope we haven't missed something," Rob said. "I hope we're on the right track."

"If they're going to that resort, we should be able to find them."

"But what if they changed their minds? What if something happened to them?"

"Rob, some things are beyond your control. Fretting only makes it worse. Besides, isn't your Plan B to find your brother?"

Rob nodded. "If he hasn't disowned me, too." They walked in silence. "I'm sorry, Ned, I shouldn't complain so much. I may be a nobody, but you're a fugitive."

The jeans Rob had received at the church mission were old and worn. The man had warned them that men's clothes in good repair were hard to come by. They stopped to rest. When Rob sat down, he heard a ripping sound and felt the seat of his pants give way. *Wonderful. Now what?* He had no spare and hated to borrow from Ned, who had few clothes himself.

When he stood up, his fears were realized. One buttock was exposed. He took off his shirt and tied it around his waist to cover his backside.

The next house they came to had a clothesline full of laundry. "I wonder if they'd loan me a needle and thread?"

"Do you know how to sew?"

"I think so. I've never done it. How hard can it be?"

Ned smiled. "It's okay. I can sew."

Rob knocked on the door. Then he shouted, "Anyone home?" The house was quiet. They tried the back door. No one answered.

Rob eyed the clothesline. This was not a wealthy family, but some man had five pairs of pants and he had none.

"Rob, I'll share with you."

"I know, but... This guy has more clothes than you and I together." He removed a worn-out pair of shorts from the line, folded his torn pants, and laid them under the clothesline. "Let's go."

Ned shook his head but said nothing.

The pilfered shorts were big in the waist and threatened to slip off. Rob picked up a piece of twine from the roadside, threaded it through the belt loops, and tied the ends.

The miles weighed heavily on Rob's conscience. He was tempted to retrace his steps and take the shorts back, but by then the people might be home. How could he explain himself? "Ned, I've sunken as low as I can. Are you sure you want to stay with me? A rich man's son who steals from peasants?"

"I'm just glad it's you and not me." Ned shrugged. "But our journey's not over yet."

That afternoon, a thunderstorm caught them. The wind was so intense, their cellophane sheets couldn't keep them dry. They spotted an abandoned Victorian era house. The front door and many of the windows were missing. Although there were solar panels on the roof, they couldn't get the electricity to work. But they were soaked to the bone and the house was dry.

Ned said, "When I was a boy, my aunt worked as a housekeeper in a place like this. I always wanted to own one when I grew up. But I never had enough money."

"Well," said Rob, "this one looks like a haunted house from a movie. If it's haunted, I'm too tired to care." He collapsed on the floor and let Ned explore the rest of the building.

Rob encountered no ghosts, but he developed a fever. By morning, he shook with chills. He ached all over and was too dizzy to stand up.

Ned wrapped the blanket around him. "I'll go see if I can find help."

By the time Ned returned with drinking water, Rob was delirious. "We gotta get going," he said, struggling to get up.

Ned pushed him down. "You're not going anywhere. Someone told me about a church that'll help, but it's on the other side of town. If you promise to drink water and rest, I'll go see what they can do for us."

"See if you can...look...for a note...from Rosa."

"I will."

Rob drank and fell back to sleep. When he woke, Ned hadn't returned. What time was it? Through the broken window, all he could see were large shade trees and no hint of the sun's direction. He drank more water and slept again.

Still no Ned. Would Ned abandon him? How could he blame him? He'd been nothing but a hindrance. What if Ned had been arrested? He might not return for days, or weeks, if ever. Rob began to cry. He'd been crying a lot since he left home. He couldn't help it. He thought about his family, of the father he didn't really know. Of his mother—he missed her. What was his absence doing to her?

Doug—how would he react if Rob showed up on his doorstep? What had Father told him? Had Doug disowned him, too? Then there was this new "family" he'd acquired on his journey. That is, if he ever found them again. Would Doug be willing to help Ned? Or would he throw him to the wolves? How would Doug and his wife react to Greta? Would he have to choose between his new "family" and his old one? He was never going to get his old life back. What new life, if any, could he look forward to? His fevered brain spun into unconsciousness.

When he woke again, Ned was there with a man who seemed to have some medical knowledge. He had pills for Rob. "What are they?"

"Aspirin." He gave Rob a fruity-tasting liquid.

"What is it?"

"Peach juice."

He also had a sleeping bag. Ned helped him roll Rob into it and wrap him like a cocoon. "I'll need this back before you leave town."

"Certainly. I appreciate all you've done for us."

Rob drifted off again.

The voices faded to another room, but Rob caught snatches of conversation. "Bad all over," the man said.

"Any work?"

"Only if you're lucky. That's why there're so many on the roads. They're starving. Some are trying to find relatives. But the relatives are in bad shape, too. And people are sick. Your brother's lucky. He has something he'll recover from. People pick up diseases none of us can treat. The lack of sanitation on the roadsides is part of the problem. They come in puking and shitting their lives away. We've buried more babies... I've never seen anything like this before."

They returned from time to time to tend to Rob and encourage him to take nourishment. Then they'd leave. Rob wanted Ned to stay with him. He felt jealous of Ned's new friend.

Finally, his fever broke. Ned's friend was gone. Rob managed to sit up and eat the stewed vegetables Ned offered him. "I'm better now. Why don't we go?"

"Not yet. Let's see how you feel tomorrow."

"What day is it?"

"Sunday."

Rob scrambled to his feet. "We're falling behind." He tottered and almost fell.

"Put your behind back down on that bed and we'll see if you're fit to travel in the morning."

"Yes, mother."

"By the way, here's a note for you. From Rosa."

Rob nearly tore the paper in his haste to open it.

"Dear Rob, We're continuing up Old 441. If we take another road, I'll leave word in more than one place so you won't miss it. Rosa"

It was the best medicine Ned could have given him. "Wait, it's dated May 30th. What's today?"

"June 6th."

"We're a week behind them."

"Rob, we're not going to catch up until they stop somewhere."

"Where'd you find this?"

"Rosa left it at our friend's church."

CHAPTER 19

The next day after everyone left for work, Rosa soon had the cabin clean and tidy. What more should she do? They said they liked the plantago. They were probably so starved for nutrients they'd eat mineral-rich mud if she served it. What else besides plantago grew here? On the internet, she found a book, *Edible Plants of the Appalachians*. She paged through the pictures. One caught her eye, a plant that grew out by the deck. She'd thought it was a flower that hadn't bloomed yet, but it was a potherb called lambs quarters. She took the Nebula out to compare the picture with the plant. Yes, that was it. The recipe sounded simple enough. Greta had brought some onions back from the resort. All she needed was butter or oil.

How much would that cost? Probably twice what it should. Rosa walked to the store. Along the way, she looked at whatever grew beside the road. She was surprised at the number of edible plants but decided to stick with lambs quarters today. She found more plantago and picked a few leaves for Ramon's hands.

Back at the cabin, she cooked a small mess of greens for lunch. Why was this considered a weed? It tasted better than many vegetables. The afternoon dragged on. She wished Ramon would let her work. Then she remembered he had given her a job, to figure out where to go next. She hardly knew where to begin.

At supper, Hector asked, "Where'd you get the spinach?"

"It's not spinach. It's a weed that grows outside the kitchen door."

"Really?" Ramon looked at his plate skeptically. "Are you sure it's okay to eat?"

"I had some for lunch and I'm not dead yet. Silly, do you think I'd feed you something without researching it first?"

* * *

In the morning, Rob and Ned crossed town to return the borrowed sleeping bag. Their benefactor wasn't there but had left sandwiches for them.

Rob was still weak, so they had to stop frequently and made poor time. "I don't understand why you didn't just leave me," he said.

"How could I leave my little brother? Besides, I don't have a clear idea where I'm going, and you seem to."

That afternoon, an elderly woman sitting on a front porch called to them, "You boys looking for work?"

"Yes, ma'am!"

"I'll trade you a meal for a few odd jobs."

They followed her inside.

"If one of you will sweep the house—it's too hard on my back anymore." She handed Ned a broom. "What do you know about plumbing?" she asked Rob.

"Not much. What do you need?"

"I got a leaky pipe in the basement. It's not hard to fix, but my hands aren't as strong as they used to be."

Ned grinned at Rob. "Want to switch?"

"Let me give it a try. I need to learn a few manual skills if I'm to survive."

"Come with me." The woman led Rob outside and through a low doorway into the basement. The ceiling was so low he couldn't stand up straight. She turned on the light and handed him a tool tray. Rob recognized most of the tools from watching servants make repairs, but he'd never used some of them.

"Let me show you." She turned a valve and water gushed from an elbow in a pipe leading to the water heater. "I haven't had hot water since that broke. Good thing it's summer." She closed the valve.

"What you need to do is cut the pipe here, and here, then we'll replace it."

Rob picked up the saw. "I've never done this before."

"What are you, some kind of city boy?" She took the saw from him and cut into the pipe. "Just keep sawing until it's through."

Rob grasped the pipe with his left hand and sawed with his right. When he finished, the cut was not clean. A small piece of the composite material jutted out.

"You need to take that off."

This required more subtle handling and Rob cut a finger. He watched blood ooze out and wondered how to stop the bleeding.

The woman wrapped a piece of rag around the wound. "We'll tend to that when we're finished."

Rob did better with the second cut. The woman took out a new piece of pipe and fittings. She had Rob cut the pipe the lengths she needed and glue them to an elbow. "If you'll give these a little twist … That's right." Then she used sleeves to attach the new part to the existing pipes.

Rob mostly watched, somewhat ashamed that this little old lady had skills he lacked. But now he had an understanding of how to make such a repair.

"Good, now let's see if it works." She turned on the valve and felt around the joints. "Yes! No leaks." She flipped an electrical switch. "I'll have hot water again in a few hours. Now let's doctor your finger."

After a few hours' work, she fed them a hearty meal of beans and rice. There was even meat in the dish. Sitting at her kitchen table, Rob asked, "Aren't you afraid to let strangers in your house?"

She smiled and said, "I'm eighty years old. What is the worst they can do? Rape and kill me? I'm a survivor, and I'll die someday anyway. Besides, most of you guys are decent fellows. And I have a sixth sense about people."

After supper, she rummaged through a closet for clothes from her late husband. "You boys look about his size. And here's a better bag to carry them in."

At last, Rob had a change of clothes and a hat to replace his old cap. There were even shoes that fit Ned, but none for Rob. "That's okay," he said. "I'm used to going barefoot."

"Where you boys stayin' tonight?"

"Anyplace we can find shelter."

"Well, I don't let anyone stay in my house, but if you want to sleep in the old barn out back, that'd be okay with me. And I'll fix a little food you can carry with you in the morning."

"We will forever be indebted to you," Ned said.

"Well, it's cheaper to feed you than to pay you by the hour, 'specially since I don't have any money."

* * *

While her companions worked, Rosa continued her study of edible plants. She tried each one before serving it to the others. A few she found disappointing by themselves, but they blended well with other foods in soups and casseroles. Although it didn't sound appetizing at first, she read about the virtues of pine needle tea and brewed a batch. It was surprisingly tasty, even without sweetening. When she served it at supper, she received mixed reactions.

"It could use a little sugar, but it's very good for you."

The next day, Greta smuggled home a small bag of sugar. "I bet the guys will drink it now." They did.

Part of each day Rosa spent reading and taking notes from her history books. She began to put together a timeline of forgotten history. Why, she wasn't sure, but she had a feeling it would come in handy one day.

The more difficult task was to look for jobs and housing over the internet. The net listed possibilities for people who had a license to use it, but not for her or her friends, even Hector, Greta, and Jem, who were legitimate and had skills. Ramon had to stay under the radar, and her options were limited. In order to teach outside Florida, she might have to take additional classes. And she owed Florida five years.

Which direction should they go? North, east, west? Her inquiry found reports from around the country, many of them alarming. One article read:

> Norman, OK. An Interstate Consolidated plant was infiltrated by a group of anarchists that calls itself DISSENT. They had organized a strike among employees, who stopped work and shut down the assembly lines. When management instructed the striking workers to leave the plant, they refused and staged a sit in. Security teams arrived to drag the strikers outside the gates, and police arrested the ring leaders. When newly hired workers arrived to resume production, the strikers attacked them. Riot squads were brought in to enforce order.
>
> A spokesman for the management said the strikers were demanding better working conditions and pay. "This was not the workers' idea. Our company pays above standard wages and we have an award-winning record of safety and cleanliness. This was caused by a group of troublemakers who prey on the ignorance and gullibility of the working class. Now those workers will no longer be employed. Let this be a lesson for others not to be misled by troublemakers."

She found more such reports. Production stoppages had a ripple effect throughout the economy. When a component became unavailable, other factories that depended on it were shut down, generating more unemployment and unrest.

There was a growing paranoia among the pudientes. Starving people were storming the homes of oligarchs, who employed security forces to contain them. When they were ineffective, District Guards were activated. She debated whether to tell her companions about these events. She decided to wait. They had enough to worry about.

Some of her searches ran into barriers. It seemed even Nebula owners were restricted from certain sites.

Ramon and Jem were paid every day in scrip, redeemable at the store. Greta's and Hector's wages were deposited into their bank accounts. On Sunday, the men were off work and wanted to rest, but Rosa booted them into action. "I made a list of minor repairs this place needs. Jem, you can start with this chair. Ramon and Hector, the tents need to be cleaned and aired out. I'd have done that, but it's easier with two sets of hands."

Greta's day off was Monday. She and Rosa walked to the store and looked at household items that would make life easier, but they were hesitant to spend money. "Besides," Greta said, "when we leave here, we don't want more than we can carry. I sure wish we had a car."

Rosa thought about her parents' car back at Jem's farm. Sometimes she regretted leaving it, even if was too small. She thought about going back for it, but it was too far to walk. Besides, if the authorities had somehow found it, going back could be dangerous. "By the way, how are the bank accounts doing?"

"We may be able to save enough to rent a place, but unless we find employment after the resort closes, I don't know how we're going to eat."

"Greta, do you regret coming with us?"

"Do you?"

"Other than wishing I could turn back time and bring my parents back... I really had no choice. I had no job. Ramon couldn't stay in Florida, and he's all the family I have left. But you had a home and job."

"To be honest, the adventure sounded better at first. Then our car broke down. Yeah, we should have made do with yours. I didn't know the guys were going to carjack somebody, and then lose the car! Hector and I still have options. So does Jem. You and Ramon don't. We've been through so much together... Hector and I talked about it. We're not leaving you and Ramon as long as you need our help."

Rosa hugged Greta.

CHAPTER 20

Rob and Ned entered a forested area with few houses and no towns. The old woman had provided them with a few baked sweet potatoes and bean-filled tortillas, enough for several meals if they rationed them. They met a pedestrian heading south.

"What's ahead?" Rob asked.

"Well, last night I stayed at a campground where they roasted a hog. If you like pork, they'll feed you. The forest rangers kill the wild hogs and take them to the campers. There's plenty of meat for everyone."

"Seem to be a lot of wild hogs around," Ned said.

"Yeah. They're a problem, have been for years. They have no predators any more, except humans, and they breed like rabbits. Some people blame them for the decline in other wildlife populations, but I'm not so sure. Deer and other animals are susceptible to pollution and diseases that don't seem to affect the hogs so much. Or maybe the hogs have evolved to adapt to changes more quickly than game animals."

"How do you know all this?"

"My father used to be a game manager."

When they reached the campground, Rob was surprised at the number of people living there. Many had tents, a few had cars and camping trailers, and there was one motorhome. Some of the campsites had flowers, yard art, and other paraphernalia that indicated they were permanent residents. Rob wondered how many of the vehicles still worked. The aroma of roasting pork permeated the air.

A man stepped out of the motor home and said, "Can I help you gentlemen?"

"We'd like to camp for the night," Ned said.

"No gear?"

"No. Just what you see."

"Choose a spot not too close to anyone else. Folks here like their privacy. There's a restroom in the middle of the campground, and it has showers. We're roasting a pig. You're welcome to join us for supper. If you have food to share, bring it with you."

The fire pit was surrounded by a circle of benches and picnic tables. Two people were turning a spit with a nearly-roasted hog. Not far away, they found a shelter with a table which no one seemed to have claimed.

"What do you think, Ned? If it rains, we might stay dry."

They set their belongings on the table.

"Should we share what's left of our victuals?" Ned asked.

"It would be neighborly, but what would we eat tomorrow?"

"We've been blessed with the kindness of strangers. Let's at least take our sweet potatoes. If these folks have been subsisting on pork, they could use a few vegetables."

* * *

Rosa found an announcement on the Nebula:

> A total eclipse of the Moon occurs tonight, with maximum at 05:02 UT. This dramatic eclipse will plunge the full moon into deep darkness as it passes through the center of the Earth's umbral shadow. The Moon may be stained a deep orange or red color at maximum eclipse. This will be a great spectacle for everyone who sees it. The penumbral eclipse lasts for six hours and fourteen minutes. The partial eclipse lasts for three hours and fifty six minutes. The total eclipse lasts for one hour and forty six minutes.

She did a quick calculation. UT 5:02 was two minutes after midnight Eastern Time. The weather was predicted to be clear. She couldn't wait for the others to get home so she could tell them.

When Greta and Hector came in from work, Greta said, "I hear there's a lunar eclipse tonight."

"That's right. Around midnight. If we take naps, we can stay up and watch it."

"They're having an eclipse party at the resort," Greta said. "But I don't think we're invited. I'm just glad they didn't ask me to work."

"We can have our own party. I still have lemons you brought home —I'll make lemonade. We don't have much sugar left, so it won't be very sweet."

Greta unloaded her bag. "I have strawberries and apples. Bruised, of course, but they'll help sweeten the lemonade."

* * *

Rob knew it was time to eat when the campers began to gather at the picnic tables. The cooks sliced meat off the pig and set it on platters. Most people brought food to share. A few men came out of the woods with jugs of moonshine. One passed a jug to Ned.

Rob asked, "Where did this come from?"

The man grinned. "A few of us have stills. The rangers look the other way, especially if we give them some. That's about the only way to make a living around here."

Ned took a swig and passed the jug to Rob. The liquor was strong but smooth. "Good quality stuff," Rob said.

"The best. We just took it off today."

After they ate their fill of meat, they retired to their campsite. Since the weather was clear with no hint of rain, they spread their blanket on the ground under the trees.

The full moon rose. Rob lay on his back and stared at it. When had he last enjoyed the moon? These last few weeks, when it hadn't rained, he'd slept under one roof or another. Life had been too taxing for him to notice the beauty of the natural world. Tonight, he had a full belly and someone at the campfire serenaded them with a harmonica. Rob settled into a peaceful reverie, watching the moonlight paint the leaves on the trees above him silver.

A guitar joined the harmonica. Someone began to sing. Before long, the tempo increased. Sounds of feet on the hard ground were accompanied by joyful shouting.

"I think they're dancing!" Ned said. "When was the last time you went to a party?"

"Hurricane night."

"It's been longer for me. Let's go."

* * *

Rosa served a light supper. Afterward, they lay down for naps. She woke before everyone else and went outside. The moon was shining through the trees. She walked up the dirt road to an open area where she could get a better look. A few neighbors were also out moongazing. She could hear music from the party inside the resort. The woman who had helped them get jobs came out and glanced at the moon. "They need me to work tonight. Maybe I can bring some party food back for you."

"Thanks," Rosa said.

A screen door shut and Ramon cried out, "Rosa? Where are you?"

She laughed. "He watches over me like a mother hen." She turned toward the cabin. "I'm over here, watching the moon."

Ramon joined her.

"Are the others up?" she asked.

"Not yet."

Rosa and Ramon roused their companions after 11:00 p.m. when the Earth's shadow crept across the edge of the moon. They watched for an hour, sipping Rosa's fruit concoction.

"Some vodka or rum would go nice in this," Hector said.

"Yeah," Greta said. "Some of the employees pilfer booze from the resort, but I'm afraid of getting caught." She sipped her drink. "They have wine and spirits at the store, but they cost too much."

When the full eclipse began, they could hear increasing sounds of merriment from the resort. Suddenly, there were explosions. Ramon grabbed Rosa. "Gunshots?"

"Relax," said Jem. "Firecrackers." A few minutes later, they heard the whistle of fireworks and flashes in the sky accompanied by booms. The crowd cheered.

"How long do these eclipses last?" Greta asked. "I have to work tomorrow."

"According to the internet, this one's unusually long. The whole thing is six hours long. Maximum eclipse is almost two hours."

"Well, I've seen enough. I'm going to bed." Greta turned toward the cabin. "Whoa!" She stumbled.

Rosa felt the ground tilt. The men beside her swayed. "What was that?"

Shouts of alarm rose from the resort. The music and merriment abruptly ceased.

"If I didn't know better," Ramon said, "I'd think it was an earthquake."

"I think it was," said Hector.

"Do they have them here?" Ramon asked.

"Yes," Rosa said. "They can. Seems strange to have one at the same time as an eclipse."

"If I was superstitious," Jem said, "I'd think it was a bad omen."

* * *

The campers and moonshiners were different from friends Rob was used to partying with. They seemed to enjoy themselves more. A banjo player joined the other musicians. While Rob watched the dancers, someone passed him a jug, but he couldn't drink much. The brew was too strong and he hadn't touched alcohol since he'd left Florida.

An hour later, the mood changed. The jubilation ceased and people pointed at the sky. Rob looked up. A shadow fell across the edge of the moon. "Ned, look! We're having a lunar eclipse."

Voices rose in alarm. Ned said, "They're too drunk to understand what's happening."

Rob got up and stood next to the silent musicians. "It's okay, everybody. It's only a lunar eclipse. We're lucky we have clear weather to enjoy it."

A man spoke up. "Yeah, that's all it is. I've seen them before."

Rob resumed, "They happen all the time, but sometimes they're on the other side of the world. And they happen so late at night, most people are asleep."

"What causes it?"

"The sun and Earth and moon are lined up just right. The sun's on the opposite side of the Earth right now. What you see is the Earth's shadow on the moon. Just like…" He stood in front of the fire. "See my shadow on that bench? It's like the fire is the sun, I'm the Earth, and the moon is the bench."

"How do you know so much?"

"I read a lot."

Parents woke their children to show them the eclipse. After watching for a while, everyone resumed eating, drinking, and playing music, but there was less singing and dancing. As the eclipse progressed, the moon turned deep red. A woman screamed, "Aaiiee! Blood on the moon!"

"It's nothing to be afraid of," Rob said.

"Why's it doin' that?"

"Probably the atmospheric conditions. Like the sun will look red at sunrise or sunset."

The red shadow showed no sign of leaving the moon. Jugs were drained. The anxiety was palpable.

"Mr. Smarty-pants, how long does this last?"

"Oh, I don't know," Rob said. "An hour or so."

"Will it turn silver again?"

"Of course."

Rob felt a momentary disorientation, as though the moonshine had suddenly rushed to his head. Several drinkers lost their footing and fell. The skewer holding the hog collapsed into the fire and flames leaped up. A woman yelled, "What was that?"

Ned looked at Rob. "Was that what I think it was?"

"An earthquake?" Rob said softly. "I think so."

"Did it have anything to do with the eclipse?"

"I doubt it. Just a coincidence, I'm sure."

Pandemonium broke out. A man shouted, "It's like the Prophet said, 'The moon will turn red and the Earth will falter.' Armageddon is upon us!"

"Wait!" Rob raised his arms but couldn't make himself heard over the uproar. Fights broke out. Women grabbed their children and dragged them away.

Ned seized Rob's arm. "Let's get away before they turn on you." He pulled him into the brush on the other side of their campsite. "What prophet was he talking about?"

"Prophet Joachim. Third Covenant. He said a lot of nonsense. There must be a Covenanter here, or somebody who worked for them. You'd expect people with money and education to have better sense, but they don't."

"The alcohol wasn't such a good idea tonight."

"I agree."

No one pursued them. In caution, they moved their things into the bushes and tried to sleep. "That sure is a long eclipse," Rob said. Eventually, the Earth's shadow moved on, and the commotion in the campground subsided.

In the morning, Rob and Ned set out as soon as they could. The campground was still quiet. A few people were up but no one mentioned the previous night's events.

* * *

Rosa felt anxiety in the air for days after the eclipse. That night, after the earthquake, the jubilation at the resort had remained subdued. Rosa imagined she heard vehicles leave and drive down the road, and at least one copter took off.

Greta verified this. "Guests are leaving faster than new ones arrive. The management's afraid they may have to shut down early. Usually they stay open until the roads are closed by snow."

"What's going on?"

"Lots of rumors. Some say people were spooked by the earthquake."

It's more than that, Rosa thought. Exploring the possibilities on Rob's Nebula, she managed to worm her way into hidden communications. She found a growing paranoia on the part of the ruling class, that the lower classes were conspiring to overthrow them. *Pitchforks and torches.* She bit her lip. *Could it really come to that?* If it did, those on top would not fall gracefully. It would get ugly. What could she do to protect herself and her friends?

CHAPTER 21

One extreme or another, Rob thought as he trudged along. Days of rain, then it stops, the mud dries, and now the glare of Georgia's sun rivals that of Florida.

The red dirt turned to powder which blew into his eyes, ears, and nose. Perspiration dripped down his chest, soaking his clothes, and the dust on him turned to mud. Creeks, which had been rushing a few days earlier, dried to a trickle. Drinking water became hard to find.

In each small town, they checked likely places but found no word from Rosa. Had Ramon changed their route? Had he missed Rosa's notes? Had the band fallen afoul of the law? Was Rosa doing hard labor on a road crew? Or on some rich man's estate? His stomach knotted. He shouldn't think about such things. *Just put one foot ahead of the other and keep going.*

On the second day, they entered a town where churches were locked. Instead of finding welcome, they were gruffly told to leave.

Finally, a man, either very old or so burdened with life he had aged beyond his years, was willing to talk. "Them Berkshires raided the travelers' shelter and arrested ever'body there."

Rob and Ned looked at each other. "Who?"

"I guess you ain't from these parts."

"No, sir."

He licked his toothless gums. "Waal, the Berkshires own almost all the land here 'bouts. They has this castle up on a hill outside town. They has they own police force. Couple o' days ago, they sends their police into town and raids the AME Church where folks feed anybody who's hungry. They took old Pastor Robert out in the road in front of the church and hit him with their rifles and kicked him with them heavy boots o' theirs. They 'bout killed him."

The man sobbed. "Maybe they did kill 'im. They took 'im away an' we ain't seen him since. They also took his wife and children, the ones that didn't run away, that is." Tears ran down the old man's cheeks. "There warn't no call to do that. He was a kind old man what never hurt nobody. They also took the good people who was helpin' at the church, and any travelers they could catch. They brought out dogs and chased people down. I don't know how many they got."

Rob shivered. "Why did they do that?"

"Nobody knows. Them policemen didn't say nothin' about why."

"Has anything like this happened before?"

"Not in my recollection, and I recollect many a year."

Rob and Ned moved on. Rob reassured himself that all this happened after Rosa and her friends passed through. The next town had heard about the Berkshires, and rumors circulated that it was happening in other places as well. "It's like they're declaring war on the poor people," an old woman said. The traveler's shelter was not serving food. "We don't want to be next."

Occasionally he and Ned nabbed fruit that had fallen from trees or vegetables from unattended gardens. With each theft, Rob's guilt increased. But he was hungry. His thighs ached from climbing the increasingly steep hills. Walking down precipitous slopes was just as difficult.

They came to a small store with tables in front. A man sat at one, shelling and grinding acorns.

"What are you doing?" Rob asked.

The man shook his head. "Folks got to eat something."

Inside the store, the shelves were nearly bare. Ned asked the man behind the counter, "Is there any work we can do for food?"

"I don't have anything. Barely getting by myself. The only jobs I've heard about are security units, but…" he regarded their appearance. "I don't suppose that's what you boys have in mind."

"No, sir!" Ned said. "Why are they hiring?"

"Riots and uprisings everywhere. The pudientes are getting scared."

Rob said, "We heard that. I wonder what's going on."

"I suppose people are getting tired of working their fingers to the bone, when they're lucky enough to find work, but still getting farther and farther behind. I know I am. And they're tired of being called lazy when they can't get work, or poor money managers when they can, and being blamed for the economy being bad, while the rich get richer off the sweat of our backs." He lowered his voice. "It's not always safe to say such things. Sometimes I just need to vent."

"I understand," Ned said.

Rob looked around the store but saw no message board. "We're trying to catch up with some friends. Sometimes they leave notes for us. Has anyone left one with you?"

The clerk reached under his counter. "Good thing you asked. I found this tucked into a window one day. Thought somebody might come along."

"Thanks." Rob stepped outside to read it. "Dear Rob, We should get to Apex Resort tomorrow. Greta's not sure where her aunt lives, so ask for Mabel Green at the back gate. She'll be able to tell you how to find us." Weariness and tension drained from Rob's shoulders. He smiled at Ned. "We should get there tomorrow."

When they stopped to rest, Rob said, "I'm starting to worry about my family."

"Your mother?"

"Yes, but also my brother. I thought he'd be safe in the mountains, but now… Doug has two children. Good kids. I feel responsible for them."

"But what can you do for them?"

"I have no idea."

That afternoon, they passed a little building under a shade tree. Rob's attention was on his feet. Ned said, "Isn't that an old post office?"

Rob stopped abruptly. "I think so. Let's check." Inside was a message board with a note that bore his name. "Good thing you noticed this." Silently, he read, "A few miles ahead is an intersection with the turnpike. There are checkpoints, so we didn't chance it. A local told us about a county road, about a mile ahead, that runs under the highway. He said the second right after the highway leads back to Old 441. If this doesn't work, we'll find another way and I'll do my best to notify you. Rosa." Rob clasped the note to his chest.

"Well?"

He showed it to Ned. "To think I almost missed this!"

Ned nodded. "That must have been the way they went. If they had to double back, she'd have changed the note, wouldn't she?"

Rob frowned. *Unless something happened and they couldn't get back. No—got to stay positive.* On the side of the building was a faucet with running water. They drank deeply and filled their water bottles.

After they turned back onto 441, Ned said, "What do you want me to do when we find your friends?"

"Stay with us. You're my brother, remember?"

"Will they want another mouth to feed?"

"We're all in it together. If we can get work, you'll contribute the same as everyone else. If Greta got a job at the resort, maybe we can, too."

As it grew dark, they came to another highway that crossed over Old 441. Under the bridge, people were camping. One was building a fire. "Looks like as good a place as any to spend the night," Ned said. "If it rains, we'll stay dry."

A man approached. "Do you have any food?"

Ned shook his head. "Sorry. We haven't eaten since yesterday."

"Well, you're welcome to join us."

A woman laid a small blanket on the ground and several travelers contributed peaches, zucchini, and an assortment of greens. One set out a loaf of bread. The woman counted heads and divided the items. Rob and Ned each received a peach, a slice of bread, a handful of unidentified greens, and one zucchini to share.

The woman pointed at the fire. "You can roast your squash if you like."

While waiting for it to cook, they ate the peaches and wrapped bread around their greens. Rob took a generous swig of water and burped. "Haven't eaten this well in…I don't remember when."

"Go easy," Ned said. "Our stomachs aren't used to it. We should save the squash for tomorrow."

"Let's get it off the fire before it gets too mushy."

Later, Rob said, "Before we reach the others, there's something I need to tell you. You might change your mind about staying with them."

"What is it?"

"I didn't really run away. I've only been saying that to simplify matters. Ramon and them carjacked me and made me drive them across the state line." He told the whole story, about how he had come to be friends with them, about losing his car and discovering he'd been disowned by his father. "At that point, I had no option but to throw my lot in with theirs. And they waited for me. Even though I took off with the car and came back without it, they waited for me. And you see how they've been leaving messages so I could find them. I can't help thinking about the risk they took—if those notes fell into the wrong hands—if the authorities here are looking for Ramon."

Ned nodded. "We've all done things we shouldn't have. They seemed like good people when I met them. I'll accept them if they'll have me."

Sunday afternoon, they stopped at a small rural church to check for a message. Rob tried the door, but it was locked and no one was around. If Rosa had left a note, where would it be?

"What's that?" Ned pointed at a glass-covered bulletin board. In a lower corner, among cobwebs, was a folded piece of paper.

Rob opened the glass door and took it out. "It's from Rosa!" The paper was wrinkled and the ink smeared, but it was readable. "We're on the right track. But it was written June first. We're still almost two weeks behind them. It's a miracle no one threw this away." Hope buoyed his spirit as they labored up the steep mountain road.

They paused to rest at an overlook, standing by the rock wall to admire the vista. Below stretched a wide valley, mountains beyond, more blue than green. Tendrils of clouds drifted in the air.

Ned smiled. "Beautiful, isn't it?" He drew a deep breath. "No wonder I'm so tired. Look how high up we are."

Rob remained silent. He, too, breathed deeply. *We're so close. I'll see Rosa soon. That is, if they're still there. If not…He looked up the road. If not, I'll follow them until I find them.* He turned his attention to the view.

Ned sat on the wall. Rob did the same. A sense of peace enveloped him. "You know, Ned, even though I have nothing, never in my life have I felt so free." He looked down at his bare feet. "It would be nice to have some money in my pocket, enough to eat, decent clothes, a comfortable place to spend the night… But if my father showed up at this moment and apologized, and offered to give me back my fortune, I wouldn't take it. I'd go on walking up this road until I found Rosa. Then I'd find some way to support us. Tell me, does this sound crazy? I think I'll ask her to marry me."

Ned smiled. "There are worse things you could do."

"All I want is enough money to get by, a simple place to live, raise a family, a chance to be happy." He sighed. "You know, we've suffered a lot these past few weeks, but in my old life, I suffered, too, in a different way. Right now, I feel good about myself. Back then, whenever I did anything I should have felt good about, something happened to ruin it." He watched a cloud drift by, obscuring a distant mountain.

Ned broke his reverie. "Are you ready to move on?"

Near sundown, they came to a wide, well maintained road that bent up toward the summit where a building gleamed in the sun.

"We need to stay off this road, especially in daylight. It'll be heavily patrolled," Ned said.

They hid until nightfall, then returned to the road, diving into the forest whenever headlights approached. Finally, they saw a sign for Apex Resort. "Now how do we find them?" Rob asked. The back gate was locked and unmanned. "We'll try in the morning." They followed the road until they came across a dirt lane.

Ned said, "Let's hide down here until morning."

They found a row of cottages, evidently housing for workers. Most were dark. All were silent. Rob yearned to knock on a door and inquire for Mabel Green.

Ned whispered, "We've come this far without mishap. Let's wait until morning." They slept in the woods the rest of the night.

CHAPTER 22

Around dawn, Rob heard someone on the road. Creeping from his hiding place, he saw a man and woman walk uphill past them. Rob scrambled up the bank. The couple turned toward him, and when Rob burst from among the trees, they jumped and assumed defensive postures.

"Hector! Greta! It's me."

They stared at him. Then they rushed forward, Hector grabbed his hand, and Greta acted like she was ready to hug him. "Man, we thought you were lost forever," Hector said. "Rosa was so persistent, leaving all those notes—we thought she was crazy. She kept saying you'd find us…"

Greta interrupted. "We have to get to work."

"Yeah," said Hector. "But I want to hear all about it when we get home."

"Where are you staying?"

"The cottage on the end. Go on, the others are awake."

Rob approached the cabin hesitantly. He was dirty, smelly, and anxious to see Rosa. He was also a different person. No longer the suave young aristocrat, he was a vagrant, a beggar, a thief. How would she react to this new Rob Hardman?

His tentative knock was answered by whispers. A curtain moved. The door opened a crack, and Ramon peeked out.

Rob stroked his chin. "Don't you recognize me?"

"Well, I'll be damned!"

He heard a shriek. Rosa threw open the door and rushed into his arms. "I don't believe it!" She began to cry.

He pressed her to him. "I know I smell bad, but are you really so sad to see me?"

"Oh, you stupid man—I thought I'd never see you again!" She pulled him through the doorway.

Ned cleared his throat. "Do you remember me?"

Ramon grasped his shoulder. "Yes, of course! Come in."

Once Rosa released him from her grip, Rob said, "Ned and I've been traveling together since we got out of jail. He saved my ass more times than I deserve. I couldn't have made it without him. I told him he could stay with us."

"We don't have much," Jem ventured.

"We never did." Ramon glanced about the cabin. "But we've got better accommodations than the last time you saw us."

"You sure do. I'd say you've come up in the world." Ned sniffed. "Don't tell me that's coffee."

"Usually we can't afford such luxury, but we got lucky," Rosa said. "Someone in the resort kitchen spilled a bag of beans and Greta swept them up and saved them for us. We picked out the dirt and figured the heat would kill any germs."

Breakfast was black coffee and dry toast. Rob raised his cup. "Here's to fine dining. Best I've had in weeks."

Ramon said, "Jem and I have to go to work. We'll ask if they can use you tomorrow. Today, I suppose you'd like some rest."

"And a bath."

Rob felt he was in the lap of luxury. No dip in a cold mountain stream, not even a crude shower. The cabin had a real bath tub and hot water. He thought about asking for shaving gel, but his beard was growing on him. He borrowed a comb and untangled his hair. After changing into clean clothes, he emerged from the bathroom a new man. "Your turn," he told Ned.

"Where are your shoes?" Rosa asked.

"They fell apart and I couldn't find any to fit me. It's okay. I'm used to going barefoot. Is there anything I can do to help you?"

"Yes. Crawl up in the loft and take a nap. Maybe I can scare up some lunch."

* * *

Rosa washed and hung out their dirty clothes. Then she rummaged through the pantry. She wanted to serve Rob something special, but her choices were limited. They couldn't afford meat. She cooked a pot of rice with onions and carrots discarded from the resort's kitchen. To this she added several handfuls of lambs quarters. It was probably better than Rob had been eating, and at least it wasn't squash or beans.

At lunch, he said, "I don't think I've dined this well since I left home."

Ned agreed.

They exchanged accounts of the past few weeks. "I couldn't believe you took such pains to stay in touch with me," Rob said. "But I'm so glad you did."

"I had a feeling you were following and would eventually catch up with us." She smiled. "And I was right." Rosa sensed a sadness in Rob and suspected he was holding something back. He had changed. No longer the cocky gallant she'd known in college, nor was he the whipped puppy they'd kidnapped. Being disowned by his father and losing everything had affected him, but it was more than that.

Rosa and Ramon had lost everything, too, but for them and their friends, life had always been a struggle. They never had as much to lose as Rob, and they were survivors. She studied him. He seemed haunted by something he chose not to share. It had wounded, but not destroyed, him. Underneath the hurt, the confusion, the indecision, something had hardened, like tempered steel.

After lunch, Rosa said, "Let's go for a walk."

"I'll just stay here and rest," Ned said.

They walked up the road. Without thinking, they caught each other's hands. Rosa sighed. Hadn't she always fantasized that if Rob weren't a member of the upper class, there might be a possibility…?

She led him to her little bower by the stream. In the distance, a dove cried. She closed her eyes and breathed in the perfect day. They sat on the grassy bank. Water bubbled among the rocks. "Ramon won't let me work. He's afraid somebody will try to take advantage of me." She shook her head. "Like I can't protect myself."

Rob's hand tightened around hers. "Does Greta have any problems?"

She laughed. "Can you imagine anybody trying to take advantage of Greta? Besides, she's legit, and so is Hector. Since Ramon's not legit, he's afraid he can't protect me."

"I'm afraid I'm not much protection, either. I'm not only not legit, I don't even exist."

She leaned against him and he put his arms around her. She turned her face up to him and they kissed. Slowly, they lay back on the grass. He caressed her head, her back, her hips. She melted into him.

Then he whispered, "I wish I had a sheath."

"It's okay." She whispered back. "I have an implant."

He hesitated.

"I said, I have an implant. I won't get pregnant."

He didn't respond.

She sat up and drew away. "Why do you need a sheath? Do you think you need protection from me? Just because I didn't grow up rich?" She slapped his face. "I'm not that kind of girl!" She sprang to her feet and ran back to the cabin, sobbing.

Ned looked up when she entered. "Rosa, what's wrong?"

She fell into his arms and cried. "Why is Rob such an asshole?"

"Dear heart, guys are like that. Do you want to talk about it?"

"No."

* * *

237

Rob pounded his fists on his knees. *What was I thinking?* His father's voice resounded in his head. When he'd first shown Rob the supply of sheaths, Father had said, "You have to be careful with those girls. They can carry disease."

What's wrong with me? He knew Rosa wasn't that kind of girl. *Why did I hesitate?* He'd yearned for her for so long, but their class differences had kept them apart. Now that was no longer an issue, so why did he let his father ruin his chances?

He paused a moment to consider his own behavior. Despite being fond of Rosa, he'd slept with other girls. And not always with a sheath. Indeed, Rosa might need protection from him! How could he mend this?

He returned to the cottage and cautiously opened the door. Rosa was in Ned's arms.

Ned said, "I'm trying to explain to little sister what scum men can be."

Rob fell to his knees. "I am scum. I'm not worthy of you."

"That's a hell of an apology," Ned replied.

* * *

Disappointment hung in Rosa's chest like a stone. Maybe Rob hadn't changed after all. Her schoolgirl fantasies withered like discarded weeds. She stayed in the kitchen worrying about what to fix for supper. When home alone, she often skipped meals. Today, she had used for lunch what she'd planned to serve for supper. *A lot of good that did!* She stomped to the front door. "I need to go to the store."

"Want me to go with you?" Rob asked.

"No."

Ned said, "I need to stretch my legs. Mind if I go?"

"Okay."

To her relief, Ned didn't pry into her troubles, but on the way back from the store, he said, "I've been through thick and thin with Rob. I never saw him as someone who would take advantage of a woman."

"He didn't." She couldn't help herself. The tears started again.

They sat on a fallen tree beside the road and Ned held her hand. When she didn't speak, he said, "Rob is fond of you."

She could no longer hold it in. "I'm fond of him, too. Or thought I was. I hoped there could be something for us. I thought he was different than the rest of those bastards. But he's not."

"What do you mean?"

"Ned, I *wanted* him to make love to me. But he wouldn't. Because he didn't have a damn sheath! I've never been so insulted in my life." When Ned didn't respond, she went on. "Those pudientes—they think working class girls are full of disease. I know how they think. I went to school with them. I thought Rob was different."

Ned's voice was soft. "Maybe there's another reason. Why don't you ask him?"

"No. I don't want to talk to him." She stood up. "We need to get home."

She banged around the kitchen until Greta arrived and unloaded her day's gleanings.

"The resort will be closing soon. I don't know how much longer I'll be able to work, so we need to make plans what to do next."

Rosa shook her head. "I've searched all over the internet, but they don't list anything for working class. And when I read the news, it sounds like mayhem all over, too many people unemployed, homeless, rioting. I suppose there are jobs for policemen."

Greta chuckled. "Only one of us is qualified for that—Ned. And I don't think he's interested." She put a hunk of moldy cheese in the refrigerator. "Why not have Rob work on it? It's his Nebula. He should be better at navigating it than you are."

"Yeah, you're right."

"By the way, Hector and I are going to move into the house next door."

"Why?"

"This one's getting crowded, and we'd like a little privacy. We'll still share our earnings and eat here."

Rosa retrieved the Nebula from the back porch where it had been charging in the sun. Rob and Ned were on the front steps. "Hey. If I can interrupt your important meeting, I need Rob to earn his keep." She handed him the Nebula.

"You still have it!"

"Of course I still have it. I don't lose things, like some people."

"What do you want me to do?"

"We have to leave here when the resort closes. We need to know where to go. The only jobs I see listed are for college graduates. None of us qualifies for those anymore."

Rob tightened his lips and nodded. He expanded the screen and started tapping icons.

Rosa watched over his shoulder. "I've already tried there." That was her answer to every avenue he attempted. Finally, she said, "I need to see about supper."

"I'll keep trying. And no, I won't try to contact my family." Under his breath, he muttered. "Not that they'd acknowledge me, anyway."

* * *

Rob was impressed with Rosa's understanding of the Nebula, but he knew how to access pathways she couldn't. He looked for communications between users asking for advice on where to find workers. *I could do more if my identity was restored.* To his surprise, he stumbled across numerous discussions of civil unrest. The pudientes were indeed frightened. He took the Nebula into the kitchen and laid on the table. "Rosa, let me show you something I found."

It was open to a message: "Two of my security guards have quit. Said they were going home to their families. Right now, there's a mob by the front gate, and one of the guards is out there, front and center, shaking his fist and yelling."

She looked at the screen. "Yeah. I've seen stuff like that. What about jobs?"

"Haven't found any yet. Aren't you worried about what's going on? I don't have a clue where these people live, but we don't want to stumble into a neighborhood like that."

"No shit! But we've got to go somewhere."

Rob grabbed her hand. "Rosa, I am truly sorry. You don't know what was going through my head."

She pulled her hand away. "Not much goes through your head, Robert Hardman."

"Please hear me out."

"I'll hear you out when you find jobs and housing. Somewhere safe. By the way, your clean clothes are on the couch."

Supper was ready by the time the others got home. Ramon announced, "Good news, Rob and Ned, you can work tomorrow. But don't expect a fair wage. They pay with company scrip and we can only redeem it at the store."

Hector said, "Not so good news—I'm working this week to help prepare the resort to shut down. And that's it. I don't suppose they'll want day labor much longer, either."

"Rosa, how's the job search coming?" Ramon asked.

"I've handed it over to Rob."

"No luck yet," Rob said, "but I'm working on it."

After supper, Hector and Greta retired next door. Ramon said, "Ned and Rob, you can sleep in the loft. I'll sleep downstairs on Greta's couch."

In the morning, Rob found Rosa up early packing lunches. He gave her the Nebula and showed her what progress he'd made. "I haven't found any jobs for us yet, but I've identified places we want to stay away from."

The day laborers looked no more prosperous than people Rob had seen on the road. Some were outfitted for manual work, but others, like Rob, were ragged and barefoot. They were not allowed inside the resort but were given tasks on the grounds outside.

Rob was assigned to remove Lygodium from a section of the woods. He was familiar with this climbing fern. Both the Hardman's forester and their farm manager had instructed staff and family alike to report any they found. Left unchecked, it would engulf trees and other vegetation, choking them out and killing them. Rob was surprised to find it growing so far north, especially in the mountains.

Another worker, who seemed glad to be relieved of the task, gave him instructions. "Pull it out of the trees and get every bit you can find. If you leave any spores, they'll make new vines. Stuff everything in bags and close them tight. Pull up all the roots, too. It ain't easy." He gave Rob a few tools and said, "Also, watch out for poison ivy. Tomorrow, bring gloves."

He found out why. The vines were tough and wiry and had tiny thorns that tore his skin. He used leaves to protect his palms.

At lunch, the workers gathered under a shade tree to talk. Some had drifted here from other parts of the country. They told of trouble in every quarter. It was mostly rumors, but a few had seen news stories and one claimed to have witnessed an incident.

"I was workin' over in the Smokies," he said. "We was buildin' this rock wall at a resort something like this 'un. They'd cut a road in the side of the mountain and wanted to pretty-up the bank, so we was stackin' stones and cementin' them together." He shook his head. "Not a man among us had any experience layin' stone. What happened is, that wall, it started to topple, all them rocks comin' down like an avalanche. I was lucky. I got outta the way."

By now he had the attention of the whole crew. "Was anybody hurt?" someone asked.

"Yeah. A couple guys ended up with broken bones, and one a' them got buried."

"Buried? Under the rocks?"

He nodded. "They took the injured men to get medical care. At least, they said they did. Then they told the rest of to rebuild that wall."

"What about the man who got buried?"

He shook his head. "Never found 'im."

Rob gasped.

Several men cursed. "Why not?"

"This engineer comes along and says we didn't put a wide 'nough foundation under the wall. So he starts tellin us what to do. We told him they was a man buried under there an' we had to git 'im out first. The engineer says, 'What man?' We called him Lester, but nobody knew the poor soul's last name. The boss an' the engineer, they talked together, then said everybody was 'counted for, an' we was to get on with the work."

His eyes flashed with anger. "Well, we seen that man go under, an' he never come back up! We tried to tell them, but they wouldn't listen. I know that guy was probably dead, but still, it just wasn't right to leave his body under there an' not even give him a decent burial."

The crowd grumbled.

"So what did you do?" someone said.

"Most us refused ta work till they got him out. The boss got mad and started hittin' men with this stick he always carries. That's when we started fightin' back. The engineer run off an' comes back with security. An' they had guns. Some a' the workers started throwin' rocks. I saw one security guard go down, an' then somebody started shootin'. That's when I got the hell outta there. I got a wife and kids back home. I couldn't let myself get kilt, so I left. Without my pay. Then I come here."

Another worker said, "Yeah, I heard that story from somebody else who was there."

A man who'd been listening quietly said, "I watched a news video about it, but they said a gang of thugs were trying to rob the resort, and the security guards broke it up."

243

Several began muttering. "They twist everything around."

"Yeah. They always blame it on us little people."

Rob recalled what he had seen on the Nebula. *It's worse than I thought.*

The boss announced, "Lunchtime's over."

Rob had become hardened to long hours of walking with occasional stints of physical labor, but a day of reaching, pulling, and bending wore him out. At the end of the day, they received their scrip and went home. On the way, Rob asked, "Does that store sell work gloves?"

Ramon shook his head. "Mostly they sell groceries and things the tourists want. You'd have to go into the next town to find stuff for workers."

* * *

Rosa busied herself around the house but couldn't stop thinking about Rob and how he'd disappointed her. She mixed up a batch of bread to go with the vegetable soup she planned for supper. As she kneaded the dough, she thought about yesterday's encounter. Had she misunderstood his intensions? Afterward, he'd reverted to his "whipped puppy" mode. Maybe she'd been too harsh. Still, she wasn't ready to let him back into her heart.

When the others came in from work, Rob said, "Wow, it sure smells good here. What are you cooking?"

Rosa ignored him.

After supper, she handed Rob the Nebula. He sat down at the kitchen table and studied it intently while she cleaned up. He lifted his arms to let her wipe the table. *Why doesn't he go somewhere else?* She rinsed out the rag and said, "I don't think we're going to find any useful job information. We need to find someplace relatively safe, free from violence, then hope for the best."

He nodded. "The violence seems to be everywhere. Do the others know?"

"I've told them a little. I didn't want to alarm them prematurely, but it looks like they need to be told."

"Yeah." He looked up at her. "Rosa, I really am sorry for hurting you. It wasn't you. It was me."

You can't leave it alone, can you? She started to leave the room.

"Please. Give me a minute. That's all."

Reluctantly, she sat down.

"Rosa, I haven't exactly been celibate."

"No kidding. Your reputation is legend."

He blushed. "I was only trying to protect you. You see, I wasn't always careful."

"So you start being careful with me?"

"Rosa, I love you. I think I've always loved you, but our worlds were so far apart. I didn't think I could fit in yours, and you wouldn't have been happy in mine."

"You're right about that."

"And now everything's changed. I've seen so much, been through so much—even if my father wanted me back, I couldn't go back to that way of life." He set down the Nebula and sighed. "I don't know why I'm going on about this. I have nothing to offer you, anyway."

"What do you mean?"

"Since we left Florida, I'd been hoping we could be together. When you kept leaving me notes, I thought you wanted me, that we could be together. But right now, well, there's no way I can give you the life you deserve. All I own are the clothes on my back." He looked at his feet. "Not even a pair of shoes."

Her heart went out to him. What was it like to be so incredibly rich only to be reduced to nothing? "You forget. I'm in the same boat. Worse. I've skipped out on scholarship obligations, helped a fugitive escape, been complicit in kidnapping and car theft…" She shook her head. "I just didn't have as far to fall as you did."

He seized her hand and she didn't immediately pull away. "Please don't give up on me. I can't see the future, but who knows? Maybe something will work out." He released her hand.

"Yeah. Well, we've thrown our lot in together. We need to see it through." She looked down. Bloodstains on her fingers! She grabbed Rob's hands and looked at his palms. "Why didn't you tell me your hands were all torn up?" She opened the refrigerator and took out a small jar. "I made this for Ramon and he didn't use all of it. Rub it on as often as you can until it heals. I'll make more tomorrow."

That night, Rosa had trouble getting to sleep. She lay on the couch and listened to Ramon's soft snoring across the room. Upstairs, a cot occasionally creaked. Hadn't she told herself not to let Rob back into her heart? So why was she yearning for him? And why was he holding back? Because he thought he had nothing to offer her? What century did he live in! She was no helpless maiden who needed a man's support. The pudientes pampered their wives, but they didn't respect them.

On the other hand, what did she have to offer? A few weeks ago, both were on the cusp of bright futures. Now all they had to look forward to was poverty and uncertainty. Nothing to build a future, or family, on.

Family. Memories of her parents and grandmother rose in her mind. Turning her face into the pillow so Ramon wouldn't hear, she let herself cry. Although he didn't show it, she knew Ramon grieved, too. He'd taken on the responsibility for their entire group. She feared the burden was too much for him. That's why she'd stopped arguing with him and tried to make their home life as comfortable as possible. But she was stagnating. They all were. Get up, work all day, bring home a paltry pay. Something had to change.

CHAPTER 23

Rosa woke with new resolve. There was little they could do to secure their future, so they must plan for insecurity. After everyone left for work, she set herself to that task. When it came time to hit the road, what would they need? Moreover, what could they carry?

Their company scrip could be spent only at the little store. She made lists of foods and other necessities, focusing on what would bring the most benefit while being the most portable. Next she inspected the tents and sleeping bags, mending any rents. Then she sorted through clothes, washing and mending them.

Last of all, her books. She'd continued to devote a portion of each day to studying and taking notes. She wrapped her notebook and Barnes' *Chronicles* in cellophane and put them in her backpack. Almost reverently, she hid the others in the back of a closet. Maybe someday she could come back for them. Or perhaps someone would read them, love them as much as she did, and spread the word.

* * *

Rob noticed not many workers showed up for work. The bosses didn't smile or joke among themselves and any sudden movement startled them. One worker walked by Rob muttering. "All I did was ask a simple question. Didn't need to bite my ass off."

Despite the heat, the bosses wore jackets. Ned whispered, "They're wearing guns and body armor under their coats."

No sounds of merriment came from inside the resort walls. A copter rose into the sky and sped away. Every so often a car left the front gate.

When they got home, Greta said, "Tomorrow is my last day." Workers in neighboring cabins moved out.

Rosa said, "Neither Rob nor I have been able to get any employment information on the Nebula. However, we've found places we need to avoid—too much violence. I've been making plans for when we leave. We'll need to travel light." She told them what she'd accomplished so far.

Jem spoke up. "If we have no job prospects anywhere, why leave? At least we have a roof over our heads."

"He has a point," Greta said. "We can starve here the same as in a tent, and more comfortably. The resort won't care."

Ramon shrugged. "Well, that's an option."

After supper, Rob offered to help Rosa clean up. When they were done, they sat on the porch. A soft rain was falling.

"I'm not looking forward to being on the road in the rain again," she said.

"I hope it stops before tomorrow so we can work."

"Yes. We need all the scrip we can get."

Hesitantly, he put his arm around her. "Are you ready to forgive me?"

"What's to forgive? We've got bigger problems than hurt feelings."

"If I try to kiss you, will you hit me?"

"Why don't you find out?"

She didn't hit him, but the kiss was brief.

"Rosa, I love you so much. I wish I was worthy of you."

"Why do you keep saying that?"

"Because I want to marry you. That is, someday, when things improve for us. When Hector and Greta moved next door, I thought about the other empty cabins. Wouldn't it'd be nice…."

She shook her head. "We're not ready for that. We need to clear up a few things between us first."

"I know. Besides, it wouldn't fly with Ramon."

"I'm not worried about Ramon."

Well, I worry about Ramon. He looked back at the cabin and hoped no one had been watching them.

The next day, the bosses were even jumpier. Once again, they wore coats and constantly wiped sweat from their faces. Around noon, a security guard approached the head boss. They carried on a heated discussion, then called the workers together. "The resort is closed," the boss announced. "Turn in your tools and go home."

The men began to acquiesce, grumbling, until someone shouted, "What about our pay?"

"You'll get paid in due time."

"Oh, yeah? When?"

"Turn in your tools and go home. You'll be notified when your pay is available."

"I'll be damned if I give you my tools if I'm not getting my scrip!" This was followed by a chorus of assent, and workers began to leave with their shovels, rakes, and hoes.

"Put down those tools or you'll be arrested for theft!"

"You gonna arrest all of us?"

The bosses took out their guns.

Ned grabbed Rob's elbow. "We're outta here." They faded to the back of the crowd and into the woods. As they scurried toward the cabin, they heard shots, followed by shouting and the clang of metal striking metal. Rob realized he was empty handed. Ned carried a hoe, Jem a shovel, and Ramon a pickax.

"Why do you want the tools?" Rob asked.

"We didn't get paid and they're worth a little money. Besides, if it comes down to it, they're better weapons than bare hands."

Hector, Greta, and Rosa waited nervously in front of the cabin. "We heard shots," Hector said. "What's going on?"

"Trouble," Ramon said. "We got fired but they wouldn't pay us. Some of the guys didn't like it."

"Now what?" Greta asked.

"We should hide these tools in the woods," Jem said. "If they find them, we can play dumb and say we didn't know anything about them."

Shouting and more shots echoed from the direction of the resort. "We don't want to be out on the road with all that going on," Ramon said.

"I'm not sure we want to be here, either," said Ned. "After that riot is settled, one way or another, they're going to search every building within fifty miles."

"You're right. We got to go."

Rosa produced the backpacks. "I've already put food and dishes in each one and divided up the cash and scrip. Get your clothes and sleeping bags. Rob and Ned, you carry the tents."

Ramon said, "And bring your tools. We'll hide in the woods." He looked at Rob. "Where's yours?"

"I dropped it."

Ramon shook his head and handed Rob a mop. Rosa was armed with a broom and Greta with a butcher knife. Ramon gave Hector his pickax. "I have my knife."

"Follow me," Ned said.

They ran down to the creek and waded upstream for some distance before climbing the hill on the other side. They skirted an open field and hid behind a screen of tangled brush surrounding a stand of trees.

"This is good," Ned said. "We can see anyone coming before they can see us."

"How do you know so much?" Hector asked.

"Army. Ranger training."

Portions of the road were visible from their hideaway. By late afternoon, military-type vehicles had moved in. Armed men herded civilians with their hands on their heads. Dogs barked in the distance.

"Can they track us here?" Greta asked.

"Hopefully they'll lose our scent at the creek."

Soundlessly, a shadow crept across the field.

"Copter!" Ned whispered. "Stay under the trees."

* * *

Despite Rosa's offer to fix something to eat, no one was interested. They didn't build a fire or pitch tents. They slept under the trees and took turns standing guard, grateful it didn't rain.

The next morning was quiet. Jem offered to scout the area. When he returned, he said, "I didn't see anyone. The resort looks deserted. They ransacked the cottages, including ours."

Rosa's heart jumped. *My books?*

They kept careful watch until late afternoon. When nothing else happened, they quietly returned to the cottage. Rosa ran to the closet where she'd hidden her books. They'd been disturbed but not damaged. The food and belongings they'd left were disordered but nothing was missing.

"I'm going to the store to see what they know," Rosa said. "And use up more scrip while I still can."

Ramon stopped her. "No. It's too dangerous."

"Then let someone come with me."

"I'll go," Rob said.

Ramon scowled. "Let Ned. At least he knows self-defense."

Rob bit his lip.

"Man up," Rosa whispered as she brushed past him. "Your day will come."

They encountered no one on the way to the store. The door was locked, but the clerk let them in when she saw Rosa. "You survived the melee?"

"We hid in the woods," Rosa said. "What about you?"

She gestured at the almost empty shelves. "I just gave them whatever they wanted, and they left me alone."

"What happened?" Ned asked. "We heard gunshots."

"All I know is what I was told. The workers had yard tools, but the security guards had guns. Still, they got the best of the guards, at first, until the Regional Guard showed up. They arrested as many of the workers as they could find. I heard they executed some." She shook her head. "I don't know how true that is. Most folks stayed locked in their houses, but it didn't stop the Guard from searching their homes and looting."

She looked at her shelves. Nearly all the drinks and snacks were gone. Only a few canned and dry goods remained. "I'm responsible for the inventory. All the losses come out of my pocket. I never thought I'd see the day when I had to kowtow to bullies in uniform. I thought things like this happened in lawless countries. This is supposed to be America."

"We'll buy what we can. That should help you. We can't use this scrip anywhere else."

When they returned to the cabin, Hector had supper ready. "We might as well eat what we can't take with us."

"Do we know where we're going?" Rosa asked.

"Not yet."

Rob was on his Nebula. "I think I've found something."

"What?" everyone asked at once.

He cleared his throat. "A farming community needs workers. The farm workers are on strike."

"Any violence?" Ramon asked.

"None reported."

"Wait," Rosa said. "I've looked for weeks for jobs like that and they weren't listed. How did you find one?"

"By accident. I wasn't looking for it."

"Where is it?"

"Near where my brother lives."

"And?"

"I was trying to check on him, to see if there was any trouble where he is, and I found a communication. I don't know who sent it or who it was intended for, but they mentioned the town, Summer Valley, and the strike, and the need for workers."

Greta crossed her arms. "Rob, is this a ruse so you can go to your brother?"

"No! I've been worried about him, sure, and his family. That's why I was trying to check on him. I've found no unrest in his area, only the strike. A farming community—at least there'd be food. Something to think about."

"We'll discuss it in the morning," Ramon said.

That night, wary of attracting attention, they didn't turn on any lights. Instead of spending the night next door, Greta and Hector dragged a mattress over and slept in the living room.

* * *

Rosa got up when she heard the others stirring. They held a council over breakfast. Hector said, "I don't like the idea of taking jobs from people on strike."

No one did. "But we need to work if we're going to eat," Greta said.

Rob said, "Maybe when we get there, my brother will help us."

Everyone stared at him. "I thought your family disowned you," Rosa said.

"My father did. I don't know about my brother."

Ramon frowned. "Why would he help a bunch of fugitives?"

"Because you're my friends. I don't mean we should ask for a hand-out. I mean jobs, even day labor."

"What if he turns his back on you like your father did?"

Rob threw up his hands. "I have no idea what he'll do. He might turn me away. Hell, he might have me arrested. It's something to try. At least we'll be where there's no violence and food is being grown. Unless someone has a better idea."

No one did. The choices seemed to be: stay and starve, hit the road and face danger, or take their chances at Summer Valley. Ramon consulted his maps. "It's a two or three day walk from here, unless we have to detour around trouble."

Rosa took their remaining scrip to the store. "We're leaving today," she told the clerk. "I've bought as much as we can carry, but we still have more scrip. What we need is cash. Are you willing to trade?"

The clerk winced. "Not dollar for dollar."

"Okay, what can you do?" They settled on two for one, scrip for dollar. "Thanks," Rosa said. "We both come out ahead."

They finished packing, lunched on the food they were unable to carry, and set out, armed with their yard tools.

CHAPTER 24

The pavement burned Rob's bare feet, so he stayed on the grassy roadside. Ever alert, they hid whenever a vehicle approached. On back roads, they encountered collapsed bridges and seemed to be forever climbing in and out of gullies. As before, they met wanderers who carried news, none hopeful. After hearing stories of further crackdowns on relief missions, they bypassed towns large enough to have them. At night, they camped in the wilderness.

Rob tried to walk with Rosa. There was no opportunity for intimate conversation, so they chatted about less personal things, sharing details of their separate journeys and discussing Rosa's studies. Rob learned more about Rosa's life but he was hesitant to talk about his. He longed to be alone with her and ached to hold her hand. The most he could do was assist her when the climbing was hard, but in truth, Rosa required little assistance.

On the third day, they passed a small post office with the sign, Otto, North Carolina.

Rosa said, "I almost feel compelled to leave a note."

Rob laughed. "I nearly went in to look for one!"

Later, they found a man sitting beside the road talking on a phone. Rob stared at him. He looked as down on his luck as everyone else, yet he had a phone. When he saw them, he glanced at their weapons and ended his conversation.

"What's going on in the world," Ramon asked. "Any trouble ahead?"

"The mountains have been pretty peaceful all summer, but trouble is finally catching up with us. It's real bad in the resort areas near Cherokee. Around here, not so bad. No resorts. Not so many pudientes."

"Is there any work to be had?"

"Not really. Not even day labor."

Rob eyed the phone. Finally he asked, "Is there any way I can call my brother? He lives over near Summer Valley."

"Sure," the man handed the phone to Rob. "Just don't talk too long. It's an old phone and the battery is weak."

Rob dialed Doug's number and waited with trepidation.

"Hello?"

"Doug, it's me, Rob. It's good to hear your voice."

"Who?"

"Rob, your brother."

"Oh, hello, Rob. Where are you?"

"Up here, not far from Franklin."

"Franklin?"

"North Carolina."

"What are you doing there?"

"Trying to get to your house. I've walked nearly all the way from Florida."

"Why are you walking?"

"Have you talked to Father? Did he tell you anything?"

"Not anything I care to discuss over the phone."

"Are you okay?"

"Sure, I'm fine. What about you?"

"I'm all right. What about Wannis and the kids?"

"They're okay."

"Doug, is there any violence near you?"

"Business is bad. Ever since that hurricane..."

The non-sequitur puzzled Rob. "Um, I'm coming to your house."

"You are?"

"Yes, and I'm traveling with a few friends. I hope you'll welcome them."

"Oh, I don't know, Rob. Things are a little dicey around here. I don't think it's safe."

The phone began to pulse. "What do you mean dicey?"

There was no reply. Rob was talking to a dead phone. He handed it back to the man. "I'm sorry. I guess I ran it down all the way."

"That's okay. I was done talking."

The rest of the group had their eyes on Rob. Ramon said, "We planned to go to Summer Valley to find work. I have no intention of hobnobbing with your family."

"I know. Something's wrong. At first Doug acted like he didn't know who I was. He seemed distracted. He wouldn't tell me what Father said about me."

"What was that about it not being safe?"

"He said things were dicey there and he didn't think it was safe."

"Safe? For you? Or him?"

"I don't know. I'm worried. If bad things are happening there, Doug won't know how to handle it." *Like I know how to handle it?*

That afternoon, on the crest of a ridge, Rob looked out at a vista of mountains and valleys. On top of the closest mountain sat a walled city, bright against the dark green of the mountains beyond. Solar paneled roofs glinted in the sun. "There's Summer Heights," Rob said.

Jem whistled. "That's your brother's summer place?"

"It's not all his. About a dozen other families have houses there. Summer Heights is the name of the community." Rob looked at Rosa. "It's similar to where the Stubens live." To think that he had once been part of such opulence....

Ramon pointed to the village in the valley. "That's our destination?"

Modest houses snuggled among agricultural fields. "Yes. It's called Summer Valley." Some of the fields had been harvested, others looked untouched. A few had been planted to hot weather crops, but others lay fallow. In Rob's estimation, it looked like a thriving plantation where work had abruptly halted, presumably by the strike.

The company started to follow the road to the valley. "Wait," Rob said. "Let's go to Doug's first."

Greta grunted. "No thank you!"

Ramon said, "If there's trouble anywhere, I'll take my chances with the people in town. We should go there first, find out what's going on." The others concurred.

"But Doug is expecting me."

"Are you sure?"

"I want to try. Maybe we could spend the night there."

"You go right ahead," Rosa said. "I want no part of those people."

Ramon pondered a moment. "I'd like us to stick together, but people might feel threatened if seven strangers show up at one time. Rob, what are the chances your brother would have us arrested?"

"I don't know."

"Take Hector and Jem with you. They don't have any legal issues. The rest of us will go into town and find a place to camp. Whatever reception you get from Doug, let us know what the situation is there."

* * *

The road wound down to the valley. Rosa keenly felt Rob's absence. Over the past few days, she'd been aware of his yearning for more familiarity, but she still had mixed feelings. One worry was Rob's intentions regarding his family. If he were to reconcile with them—did he think he could have both her and his money? No. That life was not for her. She looked up the hill and saw three figures walking toward Summer Heights. *I'd hate to lose him. Still, I hope things don't get ugly with his brother.*

The few townspeople they met looked at them with suspicion. "I wonder what's wrong?" Rosa asked

Ramon said, "Don't forget, they're looking for farmhands to break a strike. We look like strike-breakers."

The road led to a park in the center of town where a crowd had gathered. As they approached, a man dressed like a farmer, with a tricolor ribbon on his shoulder, demanded, "Who are you and what do you want?"

"We're travelers looking for work," Ramon said.

"There's no work here."

Ramon shrugged. "Then, can we camp somewhere for the night? We'll move on tomorrow."

The man scowled. "You need to talk to the mayor."

"Okay. Where do I find him?"

The man pointed to a log building. "You'll find *her* in there."

"Thank you." They headed toward the building. The farmer and several others with tricolor badges closed in behind them. At the door, the farmer said, "You need to leave your implements here."

Ned laid down his hoe and Rosa her broom.

"What's that?" The farmer pointed to the butcher knife tucked in Greta's belt.

"A woman can't be too careful." She handed it to him. Without a word, Ramon surrendered his knife.

"Leave your bags here, too."

They entered a large, dimly-lit meeting room. Rosa wondered why they didn't turn on the lights. A woman sat at a table in front of a stone fireplace, beside her, a man with a notebook.

The woman stood up. "What is it, Darryl?"

"These people just wandered into town."

"I'm Margaret Stokes, the mayor of Summer Valley. May I ask who you are and why you're here?"

"We're from Florida," Ramon said. "We left after the hurricane and walked most of the way. We're looking for work. We were working at Apex Resort until it closed."

"Your names?"

"Ramon Ortiz, my sister Rosa, our friends Greta and Ned."

The mayor looked irritated. "Do your friends have tongues? Let them speak. Tell me your full names and exactly where in Florida you're from."

Rosa said, "Rosa Ortiz. Ramon and I are from Palm Rise."

"I'm Greta Robinson, from Middleburg."

"Edward Smith. From Carraway." The man jotted this down.

Ramon crossed his arms. "Do you mind my asking what's going on here?"

"There's no work for you, and we're not running a charity."

"Ma'am," said Ramon, "we aren't looking for trouble. Or charity. We're simple people just trying to survive."

"You look like manual laborers, but you talk like you're well-educated."

Rosa spoke softly. "Even educated people can fall on hard times."

Suddenly, the room lit up. Outside, the crowd cheered. The mayor gestured at a row of chairs. "Sit down and tell me about yourselves. The truth."

Rosa began, "Our home was destroyed in the hurricane and our parents died. We have no other close family. We also lost our jobs." She shrugged. "We had to go somewhere. Greta's aunt works at Apex and we went there to get work."

"What kind of work did you do before the hurricane?"

Rosa swallowed. "I was a teacher. Ramon worked for the road department."

"I'm sure there are still schools and roads in Florida."

"You can't imagine the extent of the destruction."

A woman came in and whispered to the mayor. She stood up. "Is it just the four of you or are there others?"

Ramon sighed. "We have three friends. They took a detour."

"You need to wait here." She left the building.

Greta whispered, "This is the kind of reception I'd expect from those assholes on the hill."

* * *

Rob fretted over Rosa's comment that she wanted "no part" of his family. He was prepared for Doug's possible rejection, but what if his brother welcomed him and they reconciled? Would he have to choose between his family and Rosa? His choice would be easy. That is, if she'd have him.

When they reached Summer Heights, they searched the wall looking for Doug's gate. In Rob's recollection, it faced the valley, but none of the gates had numbers or names, and every yard had vicious dogs. He tried ringing buzzers and shouting. No one answered. *This is strange. Where is the staff?* He paused in front of the gate he thought was Doug's. He considered climbing over it, but the dogs deterred him. "I wouldn't expect Doug to keep dogs like these."

"Why not?" Jem asked.

"We had a little sister who was killed by dogs. My family hasn't kept dogs since. Let's go down to the town."

The road descended through a series of switchbacks. It was growing dark. As they rounded a turn, Hector said, "I wonder why there are no lights in town." As he spoke, the town lit up, and cheering rose from the valley.

"Something must have interrupted the power," Jem said. "I wonder it what could have been." He pointed at the hill. "Look."

Summer Heights, which had been well lit moments ago, was now dark. A chill ran up Rob's spine.

They reached the valley and walked through town. When he had been here before, Rob had found the pastoral setting pleasant, the people going about their daily business in apparent harmony. Tonight, faces looked tight, anxious, suspicious. No one greeted them, only stared.

A half-dozen men and women marched up to them. Each had a tricolor ribbon attached to their shoulder. "What's your business here?" one demanded. "What were you doing up on the mountain?"

"Looking for work," Rob said.

"There's no work here. Put down your weapons and step back."

Although the squad appeared unarmed, Hector laid down his pickax and Jem his shovel. One pointed to his tool belt and made him take it off. Rob looked at the mop he carried and set it down.

"Step back, please."

They complied. The townspeople gathered the implements. "Come with us." Three ahead, three behind, they were escorted to a park where a group of farmers had gathered. A woman stepped forward and said, "I'm Mayor Stokes. Who are you, where are you from, and what brought you here?"

"We're just looking for work," Rob said.

"What were you doing up on the mountain."

"Looking for work."

"Follow me." She led them to a large building at the edge of the park. Their escorts followed. "Set your bags down." Rob recognized his companions' backpacks by the door and laid his beside Rosa's. They entered a large meeting room. Rosa sat with the rest of the gang in a row of chairs.

The mayor took her seat behind a table and directed them to stand in front of her. When Ramon started to get up, she waved at him to remain seated. "Once again, who are you, where are you from, and why are you here? Full names, please."

"I'm Hector Ortiz from Middleburg, Florida."

"Jeremiah Green. Same place."

"I'm Robert Smith from Orange Park, Florida."

"Oh? Another Smith?"

Ned spoke up. "We're brothers. We just lived different places."

Mayor Stokes shook her head. "And what do you gentlemen do for a living?"

Jem said, "Hector and me, we just do whatever we can find."

"What about you Smith brothers?"

Ned stood up and drew a deep breath. "I worked at a prison. When I went to work the day after the hurricane, there was no staff on duty, and all the prisoners were locked in. I couldn't get anyone else to come in to work." He lowered his voice. "The hurricane damage was just too much, I guess. Communications were down. Roads blocked." He looked at the mayor. "All those people locked in their cells, no food or water, sewage building up—I had to do something. There was still electricity, otherwise I wouldn't have been able to open the doors." He shrugged. "I let them out. After that, well, I had to leave Florida."

"You released all the prisoners?"

"Yes, ma'am."

"Were any of them dangerous?"

"Maybe. But they were still human beings. What would you have done?"

She turned to Rob. "And you?"

What could he say? "I was unemployed."

Several people filtered into the room. One man stepped forward and looked closely at Rob. "Say, don't I know you?"

Rob recognized him—one of Doug's employees.

"Yeah, I know who you are—you're the brother of that asshole Doug Hardman!"

The occupants of the room muttered. The mayor said, "Are you sure?"

"Damn straight I'm sure!"

The crowd in the room surged forward. Before Rob could think, two men grabbed his arms and started to drag him toward the door. The mayor's voice was lost in the din.

CHAPTER 25

Rosa watched in alarm as the farmers turned on Rob. She sprang to her feet and was only vaguely cognizant of Ramon and Ned doing the same. When two men seized Rob and started to drag him off, she rushed forward but was cut off by the press of humanity. She turned to the mayor, who was gesturing to the squad that had brought Rob in, and shouted, "Do something!"

Hector and Jem attacked Rob's handlers and all five men fell to the floor. Ramon and Ned forced their way through the pack. The mayor's security force held the mob back. "That's enough!" she shouted.

Ned was on one knee with a would-be attacker in a headlock. Ramon stood with his foot on another's throat. Hector and Jem struggled to their feet, pulling Rob up with them. Ned hissed through his teeth to the man he held, "You want me to break your neck?"

"No!" the man grunted. Ned let him go and stood up. Ramon released the man he held.

The mayor stepped forward and faced the crowd. "You should be ashamed of yourselves. This is not how we conduct business here!" Her deputies expelled the troublemakers from the room.

Rosa approached Rob. "Are you okay?"

He grinned at her. "I've been through worse."

Doug's employee remained in the room. "I'm sorry, Mr. Rob. You just don't know how things have gone down around here."

"I'm trying to remember your name..."

"Henry. Is you all right?"

"Yes, Henry. I'm okay."

Mayor Stokes resumed her seat. "Everyone please sit down. Let's sort this out like civilized people."

Rosa sat by Rob.

The mayor continued. "Now, Mr. Rob-whoever-you-are, it's time for you to come clean."

"I'm Robert Hardman, and Doug is my older brother."

"So why are you traveling barefoot and dressed like a common vagabond?"

"Because that's what I am. I displeased my father and he disowned me. I ended up on the street with nothing but the clothes on my back. That's when I took up with these folks." He smiled at Rosa. "Rosa and I went to school together."

"What were you doing up on the mountain?"

"I was hoping my brother would give us work."

"And? What did he say?"

"Nothing. No one answered the gate."

The mayor rested her chin on her fist and looked at each of them. Then she turned her attention to Rob. "What about this other 'brother?' The prison guard?"

"In our travels, I got separated from my friends. Then I met Ned and he helped me find them. We've been through a lot together. We're brothers in spirit, not blood." He shifted in his chair. "Can you tell me what's happened here?"

"We've had a serious labor dispute. I won't bore you with the details, but my people went on strike, stopped harvesting. Those people up on the mountain are shareholders in the corporation that owns most of the farmland here..."

Angry voices rose outside and the door burst open. The deputies were unable to contain the mob that poured into the room. Rob stood and turned to face them.

The mayor came around the table and stood in front of Rob. Rosa stood up beside him and held his hand. The rest of their friends joined them.

Rosa felt Rob tremble and forced herself to remain calm.

"Where's that sombitch?" a man yelled.

"Horace!" The mayor put her hands on her hips. "You are out of order."

Horace backed off, but several others came forward. A bald man said, "Ms. Stokes, we don't mean you no disrespect, but that asshole Hardman needs to answer for what he's done."

"*This* Hardman has done nothing to you."

Rosa watched the crowd. Their eyes darted from one to another of her companions. *They don't know which one is Rob.*

Then Rob took a deep breath, released her hand, and stepped forward. Standing beside the mayor, he shouted, "I'm the sombitch Hardman. What is your problem with my brother?"

The bald man answered, "You rich bastards been robbin' us blind for years. We're tired of it and ain't gonna take no more!"

There was a chorus of, "Yeah! You got that right!"

The mayor held up a hand. "Give me a minute. I was trying to explain the problem to these good people when you all interrupted."

"Good people?" a woman shouted. "Why, I'll…" Someone shushed her.

The mayor faced Rob but spoke loudly enough for all to hear. "We began as sharecroppers, but over the years, the corporation has taken more and more of the share. My people are tired of it. It came to a head this year when we started harvesting the spring crops."

She frowned. "For as long as I can remember, the produce has gone to packing sheds and we've seen none of it, except the seconds that were discarded. Oh, they pay us for a portion of the harvest, then sell the processed goods back to us at retail, so they profit twice."

A few voices in the room muttered agreement.

"Our people always took the leavings for their own use. Last year, we didn't even get that. The corporation had everything plowed under after each field was harvested. This year, when they started to do that, my people rebelled. They disabled the machinery and confiscated what produce hadn't been shipped off. At first, we kept it for bargaining power, until the corporation sent in their police. They trucked off the produce and tried to force people to work, but we refused. So the corporation brought in inmate labor. My people resisted. Then they called in the Guard."

She bit her lip. "We got lucky. Trouble erupted somewhere else and the Guard left, but not before they cut off our electricity. Up on the mountain, many of the employees were so fed up, they joined us. Tonight, we figured out how to switch the power back on."

"Yeah! An' we turned it off to them sombitches up on the hill," a short man yelled. "An' we got them blocked in so they cain't leave. Let 'em starve up there and see what it's like."

Rob shook his head. "They won't starve. Every family up there has a store of food that would probably last a year."

"He's right," Henry said. "They've got food, water, medicine, booze, guns, anything you can think of, stored away."

The crowd erupted into unintelligible grumbling. Even the mayor couldn't silence them. The room got quiet when Rob held up his hand.

Rosa watched the "whipped puppy" transform into the Rob she'd known in school. "Hear me out! I know you've suffered and been cheated and that needs to change. I know the Guard left before you got in a battle with them, but they'll be back."

"How do you know?"

"We know where they went. A few days ago, my friends and I were working at a resort in Georgia. We worked half a day and they closed the resort and told us to go home. When we asked for our pay, they threatened to shoot us." He paused.

"My friends and I hid in the woods until it was over. They brought in the Guard and rounded up everyone they could find. We heard they executed a few of them, all because they'd done honest work and wanted what was coming to them."

The bald man yelled, "Bunch a horseshit. No pudiente's gonna work like that."

Rob held up both hands. "Look at my hands. See my blisters? Look at my feet. I've walked barefoot halfway through Georgia and all the way here because my shoes fell apart and I couldn't get another pair. Do I look like a pudiente to you?"

"You're a Hardman, ain't you?" Horace asked.

"I was born a Hardman, but I've been disinherited. I'm not legit."

"You cain't believe a word he's sayin'," said the short man.

Rob took another step forward and stood taller. "I was once a rich man. Now I'm a poor man." He paused. "I am also a beggar. I've known hunger. I've served time in jail for vagrancy and public nuisance. And I'm a thief. I've done what I had to do, to survive."

He scanned the crowd. "I'm willing to bet that not one among you is guilty of more sins than I am, but as God is my witness, I speak the truth."

Rob made eye contact with those who'd been most vocal. "They *will* bring the Guard back here. They can't let something like this go unpunished. And no matter how brave you are—doesn't matter that you're in the right—you can't fight an army."

Someone in the back shouted, "He's tellin' the truth. I heard about that trouble in Georgia."

"My friends and I came here because we are jobless and hungry, and I hoped my brother could help us, but it looks like he can't."

"Bah!" the short man shouted. "He's still a Hardman."

Ramon stepped up beside Rob. "No. Rob is one of us."

The mayor motioned to her secretary. "Bring a BATI." He brought her a portable transaction device. She opened it and held it toward Rob. "Your thumbprint. Let's see who it says you are."

Rob complied.

Mayor Stokes studied the screen and reset the device. "Try again."

Rob did.

"Nothing. You're not legit."

Rosa studied Rob's face. Mixed with vindication was sadness, resignation.

"A Hardman not legit?" echoed through the crowd.

"I told you," Rob said. "Even so, maybe I can help you."

"How?"

Rob said, "We need to negotiate with the pudientes."

"Negotiate! Are you insane?"

The Mayor raised her voice. "We can't fight them. We need a different strategy."

"Yeah, go back to work like nice boys and girls and starve to death."

"No, that's not what I mean." She paused. "Do you trust me? Have I lied to you or cheated you? Haven't I always stood up for you? Didn't you elect me mayor for that reason?"

"Yes," someone shouted.

Another added, "You always done right by us."

"Then trust me in this. Let me and my staff talk to these folks. We'll come up with a plan. Let's meet here in the morning to discuss it."

Rosa watched the crowd disperse, muttering among themselves. The mayor asked Henry to stay. Then she turned to Rosa and her friends. "Let's sit down. Have you had supper?"

"No, ma'am."

She sent two of her deputies to fetch food. The others set chairs around the table. Rosa sat down. Rob collapsed into a chair beside her. He was shaking again. She took his hand. He gave hers a little squeeze and relaxed. She glanced at Ramon. If he noticed their hand-holding, he gave no indication, only slapped Rob on the back and said, "That was a pretty impressive speech. I didn't know you had it in you."

"Thanks. You guys didn't do so bad yourselves."

Henry sat across from Rob. "You wondering why I turned against my boss?"

"Yes."

"I been a loyal employee for a lot of years, but I seen too many things I don't approve of. Your brother ain't what I was raised to believe is a good Christian."

Rob nodded.

"When he told me to shoot what I know to be honest, hard-workin' people, then we were done."

"What? He told you to shoot people? Who? Were they armed?"

"These farm workers. No, they weren't armed. Except with their mouths."

Rob swallowed. "Tell me, is Doug alive?"

"Oh, yes. Nobody done nothin' to hurt him. Or his wife or children. I wouldn't let that happen. Not to Ms. Wannis and the children, anyway."

The mayor asked, "Henry, how many families are staying at Summer Heights right now?"

"Seven others besides the Hardmans. Some of them took off when the trouble started. And a few servants are still up there."

"Who would you say is the most influential?"

"They already left. Of the ones who stayed, I guess Mr. Doug carries as much weight as anybody."

The food arrived. Besides an array of vegetables, there was beef. "This is so good!" Rosa dug in. "It's been so long since I've had meat."

The mayor let them take the edge off their hunger. Then she asked Rob, "How did a Hardman come to be not legit?"

He and Ramon exchanged glances.

Rosa said, "I think we can trust her."

The mayor frowned. "The truth needs to be on the table."

Rob looked at Ramon. "You've got the most to lose."

Ramon nodded. "Let's tell her everything."

And so they told her the whole story.

"We're really not bad people," Rosa said.

"I know. You're the victims of circumstance. You're also young and susceptible to poor judgement. But you have a different perspective on our situation than we in the valley. How much do you know about what's going on other places?"

Rosa said, "Mostly rumors, and what we witnessed back in Georgia. We've had limited access to news videos."

Mayor Stokes sighed and leaned back. "The videos skew the truth, but there seem to be uprisings everywhere. It may have started in Florida after that hurricane, but then insurrections started popping up all over, and escalating in numbers. People are tired. The pudientes keep putting the squeeze on the rest of us to the point that even those with good jobs can't make ends meet."

She leaned in. "The people have the numbers but the pudientes have the upper hand. And they have the guns. But I think it's only a matter of time before even the police and the Guard get tired of it and turn on their bosses. Maybe they have it coming, but a lot of innocent people are going to get hurt. I hate to see it end in a blood bath."

Rosa felt Rob shudder. Some of those who "had it coming" were his family.

A few people trickled in. The mayor introduced them as her advisors. Once they were seated, she said, "I have no control over what happens in other places. I just want peace here, and safety for my people."

Rob said, "You need a truce that will keep the Guard from coming back. I'm hoping Doug can help with that."

"How?"

"I won't know until I talk to him. How can I get into his compound? He wouldn't answer the gate."

Henry said, "I can let you in."

"What about the dogs?"

Henry grinned. "They're my dogs. I raised them from puppies."

"When should we do it? I hate to wait, but I'm pretty tired. I'd like to get some rest."

Mayor Stokes said, "I'm sure they're all asleep up there. We turned off the power, so that's about all they can do."

"How did you turn it off? It's solar."

"Yes, but the electricity is looped through a central battery bank. They designed it that way so they could control what goes where. If they run short, they tap ours. But it works both ways. For the moment, we have control."

Rob laughed. "Well then, let them cool their heels. I'll go up in the morning and see if I can talk sense into Doug."

"We need a plan first."

"A plan?"

The mayor nodded at her secretary. "Take notes."

Then she looked at Rob. "First, safety for both sides. My people are angry enough to do violence. I can restrain them if they know there won't be further retaliation. I concede we broke our deal with them regarding the harvest, but they've broken deals with us for years. We didn't have the power to fight back."

They went around the table. The advisors, deputies, and even Henry gave input. Finally, they had a list of what the townspeople could agree to.

The farmers' first demand was the cessation of violence. Of nearly equal importance was making amends for the many years of broken deals. The farmers demanded that an independent accountant, agreed upon by both parties, would review the books for the past twenty two years and determine the amount and schedule of reparations to be made. A third demand was that "rent to own" agreements be honored, allowing the farmers to purchase the properties they'd been working. Part of this was a review of foreclosures to determine if any had been illegal, and if so, reparations should be made.

The mayor beckoned to her deputies. "Inform the people that we have a plan." To the advisors, she said, "Meet me here first thing in the morning." She turned to Rob. "I'll have this put together for you by morning."

"For me?"

"You have the best standing to negotiate. Those pudientes won't listen to us. Not even to me. You're one of them, or you were. They've got to listen to you."

Rob straightened his back and nodded. Rosa squeezed his hand. *I hope he's up to this.*

The mayor said, "Where do you plan to sleep?"

"We have tents."

"We have a bachelors' barracks. And you ladies can come to my place."

* * *

Henry took the men to the bunkhouse. "We have beds made up for you. Doc'll want to see you first."

"Who?"

"She checks out everybody who comes here, for disease and the like. If you're sick, she'll do what she can for you."

While he waited for the doctor, Rob asked, "Henry, you're staying here? Don't you have a family?"

Henry hung his head. "I used to. But they're all dead."

"Oh! What happened?"

"My wife had asthma real bad. So did the children. That's why we moved to the mountains. The heat and humidity in Florida was killin' them."

"But you worked for my family. Didn't we give you medical care?"

"Yeah, but we couldn't afford air conditioning, and they suffered real bad. When we came to the mountains, we worked for someone else. That was before Mr. Doug got his summer home here."

Henry wiped his eyes. "We didn't have medical, and they got sick. We lost our babies, and my poor wife, she died of a broken heart."

"Oh…Henry! I…I'm so sorry. I wish…I wish I could have helped."

"How could you help, Mr. Rob? You were just a kid."

Yes, Rob thought. *And I'm still just a kid. Yet I'm supposed to save these people from retaliation by the class I grew up in? Dear God! I hope I don't screw it up.*

Ramon came in. "Rob, Doc's ready for you."

Rob held nothing back. Doc was both thorough and reassuring. Afterward, he showered and put on clean clothes. The bunkhouse had proper beds. Rob snuggled between the sheets. "If I don't wake up in the morning, leave me be. At least I'll die happy."

Ned said, "If you don't wake up in the morning, who's going to conduct those brilliant negotiations?"

"Truthfully, I'm not sure how the hell I'm going to do it!"

Ramon said, "Rob, you've done a lot of growing up since I first met you. I think if any of us can pull this off, it's you."

Had he earned Ramon's respect? Now if only he could earn Rosa's.

* * *

Mayor Stokes lived in a modest but comfortable house. The room she gave Rosa and Greta had a private bath. Rosa washed off three days' road dirt and put on clean clothes. While Greta was bathing, the mayor knocked on the door. She had another woman with her.

"This is Doc," the mayor said. "We like to give everyone who stays in town a medical screening. It's good for our visitors, and it keeps us safe."

Doc asked several questions as she examined Rosa. One was, "How long since you've had good food on a regular basis?"

"Almost two months."

"You and the others don't seem to be as malnourished as I'd expect."

"I was supplementing our meals with wild foods."

"Good. I wish more people would do that."

"You've examined the men?"

"Yes."

"I need some advice. Rob wants to marry me. Is that a good idea?"

"Why—I can't advise you—that's your decision. Do you *want* to marry him?"

Rosa blushed. "Yes, but... Um, Rob's been, well, somewhat of a playboy. We haven't had relations yet. Medically, would it be safe?"

Doc laughed. "I can't give you confidential information about another patient. But…" She whispered, "Go ahead and marry him."

Rosa's heart soared.

Greta emerged from the bathroom. Rosa introduced Doc and her purpose. "I'll give you some privacy." She left and found the mayor in the kitchen.

"Rosa, would you like some milk and cookies before you go to bed?"

"Milk? Real milk? I'd love some."

"We *are* farmers. The corporation doesn't own everything. Some of us were able to hold onto a few acres. We make the most of what we have."

Soon Greta joined them. After a few cookies, she said, "Mayor Stokes, I had some ugly thoughts about your people at first, about how you treated us. Now I take it all back. I don't know when I've had such hospitality."

"Please call me Margaret. Greta, I don't think I got your full story."

"You got most of it. My job in Florida wasn't enough to cover the rent and buy food, and Hector couldn't get work. When he decided to leave, I went with him" She was silent a while. "What you don't know is, my mother once worked for the Hardmans. I have no use for them. Doug and his father aren't worth shooting."

"What about Rob?"

"Well, he was just a boy when Mama worked there. And now, well, he doesn't seem as bad as the others."

"Is he a decent person?"

"I suppose so. For a Hardman."

Rosa laughed.

Greta glanced at her. "He seems to have become a better person since his father disowned him."

CHAPTER 26

Maybe it was the soft bed. Rob dreamed he was at home. Morning light nudged him. He went down to breakfast. His smiling mother sat at the table beside a little girl with a round face and big blue eyes—Michaela. She said, "Gud monin', Robbie."

He woke and found himself in unfamiliar surroundings, lying on something soft and clean. Before the dream faded beyond memory, he thought about Michaela. He used to dream about her often but hadn't in quite some time.

He rolled over and was seized by trepidation. Today, he faced a challenge that was likely beyond him. After a wave of helplessness, he said aloud, "Whatever I do, I'm not likely to make things any worse than they are now." He looked around to see if anyone heard him, but he was alone.

The others were in the kitchen. "We thought you were going to sleep all day," Ramon said. "We're invited to breakfast at the lodge."

"Lodge?"

"Where we were last night."

They hurried over. Rosa and Greta were already there, helping Mayor Stokes lay out a breakfast of eggs, toast, and—was that sausage? "Wow! You eat well here," Rob said.

"That's the advantage of a farm. That is, when the corporation doesn't take the hog's share."

Townspeople arrived, including the advisors and deputies. The mayor went over the plan with the farmers and gave Rob a copy. "We turned their power back on. Didn't want them to get too angry. Come with me, I'll drive us up the mountain."

Greta crossed her arms. "I'll stay here. I don't want to see Doug."

Rob said, "Rosa, why don't you stay with her? There could be violence."

"If there is, I want to be there."

Rob threw up his hands. "I know better than to argue with you."

The mayor's truck seated only five. "I'll ride in the bed," Rob said.

"I'll ride with you." Rosa climbed into the back before he could object.

They sat close together. Rob put his arm around her. "I hope we can have some time together later," he said. "There are some things I want to talk about."

"Let's see how everything plays out."

A row of poles climbed up the side of the mountain. Rosa said, "See the platforms suspended from those cables? It's an old ski lift. They use it now to haul goods up the mountain. Margaret told me this used to be a ski resort—back when it still snowed on a consistent basis. The pudientes built that fortress when they started spending more of their summers in the mountains. With farming on the decline in the lowlands, growing crops here became more profitable than skiing."

Rob saw people riding the platforms up the incline. "Always looking into the history of things."

"When you know where you've been, you can better plan where to go."

The truck climbed slowly around the switchbacks. Rosa leaned against him, soft and warm under his arm. This feels right, Rob thought. We belong together. For a moment he forgot the daunting task that lay before him. Insects sang in the trees. Cattle lowed in the distance. A dove cried.

"I've always loved that sound," Rob said. Then he grunted. "Father and his friends hunt doves. They shoot them just to kill something."

The truck stopped. He leaned over and kissed Rosa. She kissed him back. "Wish me luck," he said.

"Just be yourself." She slipped his Nebula onto his wrist. "In case you need it."

Henry waited for them in front of a gate. *So, I did have the right one last night.*

Henry said, "Stay back," opened the gate, and stepped among the snarling dogs. They sniffed him and calmed immediately. "Poor babies, hasn't anybody fed you?" He led them away and returned within minutes. "It's okay. I penned them up."

At the interior gate, Rob pressed the intercom button. "Doug, it's me, Rob. It's safe to come to the door." He listened for an answer. None came.

Henry unlocked the gate and the front door. As they walked through the rooms, Rob said, "Things aren't right. Doug always demands a spotless house. It looks like no one's been cleaning lately."

Henry said, "The maid took off when trouble started. The only one still here is the cook, and she's gettin' old."

"I bet they're holed up in the safe room. Henry, do you have access to that?"

"Sure nuff."

The safe room was hidden in the basement. Rob said, "Just Henry and the mayor and I'll go down. The rest of you wait here. A crowd might frighten Doug. I don't want him to start shooting." Rob noticed Rosa behind him. "Wait..."

"No," she said.

He shook his head.

No one answered the intercom at the safe room. Henry opened the door. Doug stood inside, pointing a rifle at them.

Rob was startled, yet relieved to see him alive. He stepped in front of Rosa. "Doug, it's me."

"No closer," Doug said.

"Uncle Robbie!" A little girl ran around Doug and hugged Rob.

Rob stared at his brother, who finally lowered the rifle. "Doug, let's talk."

"I don't know you," Doug said.

"No, but your kids do." A boy a few years older than the girl appeared in the doorway, followed by their mother.

Rob nodded to her. "Hello, Wannis."

"Get back," Doug growled at her. Wannis grabbed the children and pulled them into the safe room.

Henry quietly took the rifle from Doug.

Rob said, "Why don't we leave the children here and go somewhere to talk."

Doug nodded, but when Wannis started to accompany him, he barked, "Stay with the kids."

They convened in the family room. Rob removed dirty dishes and articles of clothing from the furniture so they could sit. "Doug, I'm concerned about the safety of you and your family. I promised the people in the valley we'd find a peaceful solution to this stalemate."

Doug's face darkened. "So, you've become one of them. Father warned me. What is it you want? My inheritance?"

"Of course not. Only everyone's safety."

Spittle flew out with Doug's words. "You're a bunch of outlaws. You deserve everything you get. Ms. Stokes, call off your dogs and send our produce where you were paid to send it."

"Mr. Hardman, that's something we can talk about later. Right now I have a valley full of people who are ready to tar and feather everyone on this hill, and I'm doing all I can to hold them back."

"All I need to do is make one phone call and I'll have an army here to take care of your mob."

"That's true," she said softly. "But can they get here in time? Before the 'mob' reaches you?"

Doug's eyes widened.

Deer in the headlights, Rob thought.

The mayor continued. "We have a plan that will ensure the safety of you and your family, as well as your neighbors. Let's sit down and…"

"I want no part of your plan!"

"Doug," Rob said, "we need to avoid violence…"

Doug turned on him. Rob found himself staring into his father's eyes. He began to quail. Rosa beside him squeezed his hand. Rob took a deep breath and set fear aside.

Doug spit out, "You! You are a disgrace to the name Hardman. You always *were* soft. Like a woman. Let emotions rule you. Father tried to make you into a man, and look at you. Long hair like a woman. Can't stick up for yourself. Thugs to back you up." Doug's mouth jerked, but no sound came out.

Rob gritted his teeth. "Are you finished?"

"Hell, no, I'm not finished!" Doug's face turned purple, then his eyes rolled up in their sockets, and he collapsed.

Rob rushed to his brother.

The mayor said, "Henry, go get his wife."

Rob felt for Doug's pulse. It was irregular, but he had one. Wannis flew into the room. "Doug!" She slapped his face. "Doug, snap out of it!"

"What's wrong with him?" Rob asked.

She gestured. "In the safe room. There's a cabinet with medicine. Bring me the bottle of green liquid."

Rob ran to the safe room where Henry sat with the children.

"Doug's sick. Where's the medicine?" He fumbled around for the green liquid.

Back in the family room, Doug lay on the couch, Wannis beside him. Rob handed her the bottle. "What's wrong with him?"

Wannis poured a dropper-full into his mouth. "He was up all night. Sometimes he gets these fits."

The mayor said, "I just called Doc and asked her to come up. Rob, let's go talk with the neighbors. We weren't getting anywhere with him, anyway."

Rosa nudged Rob. "If you're representing the Hardmans, don't you think you should dress the part?"

Rob looked down at his tattered apparel. "You're right. I'll borrow some of Doug's clothes. Wish I had time to shave."

Rosa followed him into Doug's room and helped him find an outfit —casual, a shirt and shorts. He recalled how Leonard used to choose his clothing. It seemed like forever ago. He hadn't thought about Leonard since he left Florida. How was he? Was he still working at Hardman Hall?

"Let's find some shoes," Rosa said.

"No, Doug and I wear different sizes."

"Well, don't forget to comb your hair." She left the room.

The shirt was tight in the shoulders and he couldn't fasten the upper buttons. That couldn't be helped. Doug was more pear shaped than he. The shorts were too big in the waist, but he found a belt. He used Doug's comb and looked in the mirror. The man staring back at him was hardly recognizable. The old Rob Hardman was gone. This one had weathered into maturity.

Rosa waited in the hallway. She smiled and said, "You look almost dangerous."

A small crowd of Summer Valley residents waited in front of the gate. "Let's get representatives of the pudiente families into the clubhouse," Rob said to the deputies. "If they balk, tell them the Hardmans called the meeting."

He led the farmers to the clubhouse in the center of the golf course. Leaving them in the large social hall, Rob climbed into the cupola where he could get a view of the surrounding area. The countryside looked peaceful, no sign of invading armies. Two copters were parked at the port. *Why didn't they take those and leave?* He looked down at the green. A few Summer Heights residents straggled from their back gates toward the clubhouse. *Might as well go down and face the music.*

Rosa hadn't followed him. *Why?* She sat with their companions in the back of the social hall. This isn't her fight, he thought. On second thought, it's everyone's fight. He felt weighed down, as though the destiny of the world lay on his shoulders.

The farmers congregated on one side of the room, the landowners on the other. Rob stood in the middle, agreement in hand. "Why don't we sit closer together so we can talk?"

No one moved, but Summer Heights people began shouting their grievances. On the other side of the room, the townspeople geared up for a counter attack. Helplessly, Rob looked at his friends. Ramon gave him a thumbs up.

Rob turned to the landowners and said, "Let me meet with you all in a quieter place. Just one representative from each family, please."

Heads of households balked. "Who's going to protect our families if we leave?"

Mayor Stokes stepped up. "You have security officers here, and I have my deputies. If they can cooperate with each other, we can keep the peace."

One man looked Rob up and down, frowning at his bare feet. "Who do you think you are to tell us what to do?"

"You know who I am. Robert Hardman, Doug's brother."

"Where's Doug?"

"He's sick. Wannis is taking care of him. I'm here to represent them."

With that, they filed into an office.

Rob opened his Nebula to the notetaking mode. "I'm familiar with the situation in the valley, and the people there have entrusted me to help find a solution." He read the farmers' proposed agreement. "Now, tell me what you want to see happen."

They wanted things to go back to the way they'd been.

"That's not going to happen. The world has changed, and you know it."

After several minutes of grumbling, their foremost issue came forth —they were frightened and wanted to go home.

"The farmers want the same thing, for the violence to cease. That'll be part of the agreement."

The pudientes agreed not to call out security forces if the farmers ceased hostilities. They wanted the harvest to be shipped out but balked at any idea of reparations.

Rob met with representatives of Summer Valley. "I think I can get them to make a few concessions, but you'll need to as well."

They agreed to give the landowners half the harvest. "That's what sharecropping means," one farmer said.

The corporate representatives agreed to this, after the cost of seeds, fertilizer, and equipment supplied to the farmers was deducted. The farmers insisted the cost be shared. "We did the work for them. They're benefitting from that."

The issue of reparations was tabled, but the pudientes agreed to a review of the "rent to own" agreements. Rob was glad he'd eaten a hearty breakfast. By midday, he was exhausted. "Let's break for lunch. One hour, then we'll meet back here." Both groups must have been as tired as he. No one objected.

Many of the valley people went home. After the Summer Heights residents left, Rob said to the mayor's delegation, "Let's go to Doug's house for lunch."

Rob found Doug's family in the safe room. "How is he?"

Wannis said, "No different. That quack the mayor sent said she couldn't do anything for him. He needs to go to a hospital. I wanted to call a copter but the quack told me not to."

"Why? Let me talk to the mayor."

Mayor Stokes said, "A copter would be seen as a threat and might get shot down. I'll alert my people that it's a medical copter. Go ahead and let her call."

Rob returned to the safe room. "You don't have to stay in here. You're in no danger."

Wannis glowered at him. "My house is no longer my own."

While she called the hospital, Rob checked his brother. Doug lay on a cot, motionless, yet breathing. *I'm sorry I didn't get here sooner. Maybe I could have prevented this.* He headed to the kitchen for something to eat.

Rosa said, "Go sit down in the dining room. Lunch is almost ready."

He joined Ramon, Ned, and Jem at the table. "You guys have got to help me. I have no idea what I'm doing. I feel like I'm holding the fate of the world in my hands and I don't want to screw up."

Ned chuckled. "From what I've seen of the state of the world, I don't think you can take credit for screwing it up."

"But what should I do?"

"If I had the answer, I'd be leading this, not you."

"Just keep them talking," Ramon said. "Both sides. Give them a chance to work it out."

Hector brought in a large pot of soup and began ladling it onto bowls. He set one in front of Rob. Doug's cook followed with a platter of sandwiches, and the mayor's deputies brought in drinks. *Good thing Doug has a large dining room.*

The mayor turned on the screen. "Let's see what's happening elsewhere."

Locally, there were no reports of violence, but that couldn't be said for the rest of the country.

The mayor said, "They're finally calling it class warfare. Before, they were downplaying the people's grievances and blaming it on a few troublemakers."

Some sources showed war machines mowing down protestors armed, at most, with hand tools. Ramon snorted. "I knew those shovels and hoes would come in handy."

"They're no match for tanks," Ned said.

"I'm surprised they're showing this," said Rob. "They usually whitewash everything to make the pudientes look like the good guys. Have the news people joined the revolt?"

After lunch, Rob convinced leaders from both sides to meet together. The landowners finally agreed that if there had been any illegal transactions, they would authorize reparations. But they refused to go back twenty two years. "Half that time is more than enough." The farmers agreed, only if the auditors found no criminal intent. If they did, review and reparations would go back fifty years. To Rob's surprise, the pudientes agreed.

After an hour or so, Henry interrupted him. "Mr. Rob, that copter never came. Ms. Hardman is worried to death."

"Let's take a break," Rob announced. "Wannis needs me. I'll be back as soon as I can."

He rushed from the room. Rosa followed him.

Wannis sat in the backyard gazebo, wringing her hands. The children were playing. They ran up to Rob and hugged him. The boy eyed Rosa suspiciously and the girl said, "Who's that?"

"This is Rosa, my girlfriend. Rosa, this is Edwina and Little Greg."

Rosa smiled and put out her hand. "Pleased to meet you."

Little Greg shook her hand, but Edwina clung to Rob and said, "I thought I was your girlfriend."

He laughed and picked her up. "You're still my little girlfriend. Go play. I need to talk to your mama."

"They're fond of you," Rosa said.

"Yeah. They're good kids. I hate to see them corrupted."

As they drew near, Wannis broke into tears. "I called the hospital again. They're not sending the copter. They said it's too risky."

"What about your neighbors' copters?"

"I already asked. They're planning to leave as soon as they can. They said they don't have room for Doug."

Rob shook his head and turned to Henry. "Will you drive Doug to the hospital?"

"Yes, sir."

"I'm going, too," said Wannis. "And I'm taking the children."

"That's a good idea," Rob said. "I'd like to stay in touch, but the phone function's been disabled on my Nebula."

"I'll give you Doug's."

"Ms. Hardman," Henry said. "I'll bring the car around."

Rob transferred his notes to Doug's Nebula and gave his back to Rosa before he returned to the negotiations.

Progress had been made in his absence.

Mayor Stokes said, "Rob, not everything can be settled today. Those folks want to get out of here and go home. They agreed not to call the Guard. They'll release my people from criminal charges, and we won't harass them when they leave. There'll have to be further negotiations at a later date. We need to put things in writing and get them signed."

"Aren't you afraid their lawyers will rip apart the agreements?"

"That's a chance we have to take. Although, the way things are going, we may not have to worry about the lawyers. A lot of them are going on strike."

"What?"

Rosa said, "Pudientes don't study law. Most lawyers went to school on scholarship. They may side with the common people."

The mayor nodded. "If they do, we'll soon see a different world."

Agreements were drawn up in both electronic and paper form, the latter signed in ink and the former by thumbprint. Rob stored them on Doug's Nebula. He evaded requests for his signature and thumbprint, saying, "I'm only the mediator, not a party to this."

One of the farmers said, "Aren't you acting on behalf of your brother? If no Hardman signs, what's to stop your family from reneging on the agreement?"

Mayor Stokes intervened. "Rob has given his word that Doug will sign when he's able to. We can trust him."

After the meeting broke up, Rob said to the mayor, "Thanks for covering for me. If the pudientes found out I'm not legit, this whole thing would have fallen apart."

"Actually, a mediator *is* supposed to sign. Thankfully, no one had the presence of mind to question it."

They returned to Doug's house.

CHAPTER 27

Now what? Rosa wondered. The immediate crisis was over, but their personal problems remained. They still had neither jobs nor a place to live. And what were Rob's plans?

Over the past twenty four hours, she'd witnessed an unexpected metamorphosis. He'd handled not only the farmers, but the pudientes. They must have been desperate to allow someone so young and inexperienced to wield influence over them. Watching his performance from the back of the room, her schoolgirl admiration for him had rekindled. But this was not the college boy she'd been infatuated with. This new Rob looked and acted like a leader of men.

And he looked good, even unshaven and wearing his brother's ill-fitting clothes. The burgundy shirt enhanced the highlights in his hair, bleached by the sun. Nicely-tanned biceps strained at the sleeves. The half-open front hinted at a well-muscled torso. He looked exotic, a beach boy on a mountain top. Rosa sighed. *Please don't disappoint me, Rob.*

"We should think about supper," Rob said.

"Here?" Ramon asked.

"Why not?"

Hector said, "I want to go back to town, to Greta."

Rob said, "I feel obligated to stay here until all the families leave, just in case there's trouble. But you all are free to go."

"I'll stay here in case it's more than you can handle," Ned said.

Ramon said, "Me, too."

Rosa relaxed. That meant she wasn't expected to go back to town.

The cook came in and asked, "Will you be wanting supper?"

"Yes, thank you," Rosa said. "Can I help you with it?"

"No, ma'am. I can handle it."

Henry returned from the hospital. "Mr. Doug is still unconscious. They haven't told Ms. Hardman what's wrong with him. She told me to come home and get some things for her, and she'll call when she wants me to come back."

"Do you plan to go back to work for them?" Rob asked.

"Well, I always got along okay with them. They treated me right, 'til Mr. Doug went crazy and told me to shoot people. Maybe what's wrong with him now is what made him say that. By the way, Mr. Rob …"

"Henry, please don't call me 'Mr.' Just Rob. I'm no longer a Mr."

"Um, Rob, I'm sorry about the things I said to you last night. I was pretty upset."

"That's okay. I can't even remember what you said."

"I'll go find the things Ms. Hardman wants."

He came back shortly. "I can't find Mr. Doug's medicine."

"What medicine?"

"It's in a green bottle."

"This morning I brought Wannis a bottle of green liquid from the safe room. Did you look there?"

Henry left and returned with it.

Rob examined the bottle. "This is cathine! Henry, how often did Doug use it?"

"I don't know. What's it for?"

"It's a recreational drug, a stimulant. That's why he's been having trouble sleeping. It's addictive. I can't believe Doug would use it. It's against his religion. Wannis gave him some this morning. Did she tell the hospital?"

"I'm not sure."

Rob tried to call her using Doug's Nebula. "She's not answering." He called the hospital and asked for the doctor who was treating Doug.

Rosa was close enough to hear, "We can't discuss patients over the phone."

"I'm not asking you to discuss anything. I want you to know my brother was using cathine. Did his wife tell the doctor about that?"

"We cannot give out that information."

"Then just tell the doctor about the cathine. It might be important."

"I'll relay the information. Thank you for calling."

"Shit!" Rob ripped the Nebula off his arm as though he were ready to throw it. "I wonder how long that's been going on."

Rosa laid a hand on his arm. "Rob, you've done what you can. It's out of your hands."

"I know."

Jem said, "I wonder how that old ski lift works? I've done enough walking for a lifetime."

Henry said, "I'll show you."

Rob said, "I'm going to check on the neighbors." Ramon and Ned went with him.

Rosa stayed at the house. It wasn't as big as Salli's, but it was similar enough to make her uncomfortable. She wondered about Salli, what she was doing, how the chaos was affecting her.

When the men returned, Rob said, "About half of them are leaving. Some plan to go in the morning, so I'll need to stay here tonight. The pudientes are afraid the farmers will assault them, despite the agreement. Humph! They're even afraid of their own servants, the ones who haven't abandoned them. Ramon and Ned said they'll stay with me. What would you like to do?"

Rosa said, "I'll go down to the valley with Greta." Was that disappointment on his face?

Rob insisted that Henry and the cook eat supper with them. Afterward, Rosa was ready to leave. "Rob, come with me and operate the lift."

As they approached it, a copter rose above the compound and headed south. Rob grumbled, "They couldn't be bothered to take Doug to the hospital."

A car left a gate and stopped by them. The driver asked, "You're sure it's safe to leave?"

Rob said, "The valley people won't bother you. I can't guarantee what you'll find out on the road." After they left, he said, "I'll be glad when this is over. Then we can make some decisions about what to do next."

"What do you want to do?"

"Get some kind of employment so I can support a family."

"What family?"

He stopped walking, held both of her hands, and looked into her eyes. "Rosa, I love you. I'm serious. I want to be with you forever. You don't have to give me an answer now, but I do want to marry you."

She looked down. "I love you, too. I'm not worried about you not having a job. Something will work out for us. But there's one thing—I refuse to become a pudiente. I've had a taste of that life, and I didn't like it. They're not all bad, but as a class, they're selfish and dishonest and insincere. They value money over love." She looked up at him. "I know you're not like that, but I cannot live among them. They're your people, so if you go back to them, I'll understand, but I won't go with you."

He threw his arms around her. "Oh, thank you, Rosa. You've given me hope. I don't want that life, either. I don't know how things are going to work out, but together, we'll make it work."

They kissed until they heard another gate open.

* * *

Rob's heart descended with Rosa as she rode the lift to the valley. What did the future hold? As non-legits, they would roam together, finding work and food and shelter where they could, like others on the road. But that was no way to rear children. It was also no way to spend one's old age. Rosa deserved better.

Lost in thought, he almost failed to stop the lift when it reached bottom. Did Rosa notice the hard landing? She waved, stepped off, and walked toward town. He watched until she disappeared among the buildings. Then he made his way back to Doug's house and what promised to be a lonely evening.

His companions sat in the family room with Henry, watching TV. This house didn't have a lavish theater like Hardman Hall, only a modest hologram stage. Rob smiled. It was quite a treat for these guys. However, he was in no mood for entertainment. He looked for somewhere to spend the night and chose the guest room where he'd stayed when he used to visit.

His friends were watching the news when he returned. A clip showed soldiers taking the side of a group of protestors. One covered his face with his hat and tried to disguise his voice. "This just isn't right," he said. "I pledged to defend my country, not fight against it. These are my countrymen. The ones making the decisions—who are they? Americans don't go to war on other Americans."

After that story concluded, Rob said, "You guys are welcome to sleep in the guest rooms."

Ned said, "I wish I had a clean change of clothes. Mine are still at the bunkhouse."

"My brother has more clothes than ten men can wear. Let's borrow some of his."

Afterward, he showed them their rooms and checked for toiletries in the bathrooms. "Feel free to use anything." He stroked his chin. "Should I shave?"

Ramon said, "Your beard makes you look older."

"Yeah," said Ned. "That may be an advantage when you're trying to handle people."

Once they had bathed and changed, Rob took their dirty clothes to the laundry room.

The cook caught him loading the washer. "Mr. Rob, let me do that."

"Just call me Rob. Not 'Mr.' And I can wash clothes. You've done enough for us. Why don't you go to bed?"

She looked at him uncertainly. "Uh, Rob. Are you sure?"

"Yes I am. And thank you for everything you've done for us today."

"I'm glad to help. Goodnight."

* * *

Rosa felt Rob's eyes on her as the lift carried her down to the valley. She longed to spend the night with him. But not yet. There was Ramon to consider. Rob had finally earned his friendship and she didn't want to undo that. Not that Ramon should object to what she did, but he had lost so much. She was all he had left.

As for Rob, he'd lost everything, too, and now she was asking him to sacrifice more— to choose her over his family. *Dear God, there has got to be a solution!*

Hector and Jem were at the mayor's house with Greta, all three grinning from ear to ear.

"What is it?" Rosa asked.

Greta nodded toward the mayor. "Margaret may have jobs for us."

"Really?"

The mayor motioned for Rosa to sit down. "It all depends on how things go in the next few weeks. Of course, the workers from Summer Heights who've already joined us come first, but once everything settles down, we may need more workers. Pay won't be great, but as long as the farms are productive, and the pudientes don't rob us blind, no one will go hungry. Also, we have a school, and we always need teachers."

"That would be wonderful!" Rosa thought about her books, strung out between here and Florida. Maybe someday she could retrieve them. Meanwhile, she had her notes. "What about Ramon and Rob? Oh, and Ned?"

"As long as they're willing to do farm work."

"I'm sure they will. They'd be safe here, wouldn't they?"

"As safe as anywhere. I won't report them."

Rosa wanted to run up the mountain to tell them, but it could wait till tomorrow.

* * *

Rob rose early to oversee the exodus of the remaining families. He visited each compound. Most employed servants who, like Doug's cook, lived here permanently. Many had deserted their bosses, but a few remained.

He found one man yelling at his housekeeper and yard man. "You'll get your pay, all right, but when I come back here, I expect to find this place in tip-top shape, and nothing missing. That trash in the valley is not allowed inside my house. If I learn otherwise, you're gone. Now, bring my car around and start packing it."

Rob accompanied the yard man to the car park. "Is he always so mistrustful?"

"He's not usually this bad."

"Why do you tolerate it?"

"Well, the pay's good, we get housing and meals, and he's not around all the time, so we just put up with him when he is."

When the last family left, Rob allowed himself to relax. "I should call and check on Doug." He tried Wannis' phone but got no answer. "We don't need to stay here," he told his companions. "Let's go down to the valley."

Before they reached the lift, Doug's Nebula rang.

"You've got to do something," Wannis' voice was shaking. "They want to discharge Doug."

"Is he better?"

"No!" she shouted. "He's still unconscious and they don't know what's wrong! They say they can't do anything for him and he's taking up a bed someone else needs."

"Okay. I'll get there as soon as I can."

"You're going to the hospital?" Ramon asked.

"Yeah. They want to discharge Doug."

Ned said, "We'll go with you."

"Let's take the Travelor. It's big enough to hold everybody, especially if we need to bring him back. Where's Henry?"

"I'll get him," Ned said.

Ramon said, "We should tell Rosa where we're going."

"It'll take too long to drive down to the valley. I'll call the mayor."

Margaret Stokes answered on the first ring. "She's right here."

Rosa came on the phone. "Rob?"

"Rosa, something's come up. I have to go to the hospital to see about Doug."

"Okay. I'll go with you."

"I'm sorry, I don't have time to drive down to get you. I need to leave right away."

There was a pause. "Well, let me know when you get back."

"I will. I love you."

"I love you, too."

When Rob looked up, Ramon was staring at him. "What is it?"

Ramon shook his head. "Nothing."

* * *

That morning, Rosa had awakened with more hope than she'd experienced since her world had crashed around her. She could barely keep herself from rushing up the mountain to tell Rob the good news, that they may have jobs and could plan for their future. Then Rob called. He wasn't coming to see her. He was going to rescue his brother. After she handed the phone back to Margaret, she crumbled into tears. Anxiety dogged her all day.

CHAPTER 28

Rob parked the RV illegally in front of the hospital. Wannis and the children were sitting on a bench near the front door. Across her lap lay a blanketed figure. When Wannis jumped up and rushed toward Rob, Doug rolled to the ground. Little Greg tried to pick him up. Edwina cried. When Rob touched Doug, his skin was hot and dry. "My God! What happened?"

Wannis collapsed into Rob's arms, sobbing. He was unable to learn much more than he already knew. "Stay with him. I'll go in and see about this."

The hospital was a scene of chaos. Patients occupied every seat and much of the floor in the lobby and hallways. Rob had difficulty finding a staff member and was told there was no doctor available. "Where can I find the administrator?" He was directed to an office on the second floor. Rob burst in without knocking and startled a man who slunk behind his desk. "My brother is sitting out beside the street, unconscious, burning up with fever. He needs treatment and I won't take no for an answer!"

"There's nothing I can do! I'm not a doctor. Half my staff is gone and we're running out of supplies. You see all those people downstairs? They need treatment, too, and we can't help most of them."

The door slammed open and two burly guards stormed in. "You need to leave," one said.

"All right." Rob turned back to the administrator. "I want you to know who you're messing with—the Hardmans. You'll regret this." He shook with rage all the way downstairs.

Wannis was waiting in the lobby. "What happened?"

"Nothing. Where's another hospital?"

"I've called everywhere. No place will take him. We've got to get him back to Florida to Dr. Robertson."

A nurse approached them. "My name is Betsy Farrell. I have family in Florida. I'll take care of him if you'll give me a ride there."

Rob looked at Wannis, who said, "Sure."

To Betsy, "Do you need to go home for anything first?"

"Wait just a minute." Betsy ducked into the nursing station and brought out a bag. "I've been waiting for such an opportunity."

They laid Doug on the bed in the Travelor. Henry took the wheel. "Do you know what's wrong with him?" Rob asked Betsy.

"Let me use your Nebula." She pulled up Doug's chart. "There's nothing useful here. They didn't even do lab tests."

"What?"

Betsy shook her head. "The whole system has fallen into dysfunction."

Rob looked at Wannis. "Why didn't you insist?"

Wannis squeezed her children to her. "I couldn't be there the whole time."

"Where were you?"

"At a hotel. There was no place for us at the hospital."

"So you just left him?"

Ned put a hand on his shoulder. "Rob, you saw what it was like there. She has children to worry about."

After Rob calmed down, he asked Wannis, "How do you plan to get him back to Florida?"

She threw up her hands. "I don't know."

"Have you called my father yet?"

"No."

"Then call him."

Rob thought about options. The fastest way would be flying, but that probably wasn't safe. The second choice was the Travelor, but he worried Henry wouldn't be able to manage Wannis in her present state.

After a while, Wannis said. "He's going to send Andreu for him."

"Good."

"But he won't get here until tomorrow. I don't want to wait so long."

"What choice do you have?"

"Why can't you take us? We could leave today."

"Wannis, my father has disowned me. I don't want to see him, and besides, I can't legally get across the Florida border."

At Doug's house, they carried him inside and put him to bed.

"Betsy," Rob asked, "what do you think is wrong with him?"

"I don't know yet. Wannis can't give me a good history. That was probably part of the problem at the hospital. Do you know if he was taking any medication?"

"What did Wannis say?"

"She claimed not to know."

"Come with me." He led her to the safe room. "This cabinet is where I found the cathine, and there's a lot of other stuff, too."

Betsy carefully checked each container. "Most of this is pretty innocuous, but these…" She picked up three bottles. "These are usually prescribed for anxiety, sleep, and pain. Was he drinking alcohol with them?"

"I don't know."

Wannis' answer was, "Doug likes wine with dinner. You know that, Rob. And a little nightcap. Nothing wrong with that, is there?"

"Not a good sign," Betsy said after Wannis left. "The sooner we can get him to his regular doctor, the better."

* * *

Rosa didn't hear from Rob until after lunch.

"Rosa, I'm back. Doug is still unconscious, but Father is sending our driver for him. I'll be down to see you in a little bit."

Hours dragged. Ramon and Ned came without him. "He's dealing with a problem," Ramon said. "Most of the pudientes took their dogs with them, or left staff to tend to them, but a couple of them didn't, and Rob's trying to find someone who will. Henry can't because he's going back to Florida with Doug and Wannis."

Finally, Rob called. "Henry knows someone who might take care of the dogs. He used to work for my family. I'm coming down to talk to him."

Rosa met him at the foot of the lift, brimming with optimism, but Rob only kissed her perfunctorily and gave her no time to tell him the good news. "I need to talk to this guy. About more than dogs." She tried to keep up with him as he rushed down the street. He knocked at a door. A man answered. "I'm looking for Kevin Drury."

The man smiled and extended his hand. "Good to see you, Mr. Rob. Come in."

"Please, just Rob. Did Henry call you?"

"Yes, and I told him I'll look after the animals as long as I don't have to buy dog food."

"I'll make sure there's plenty stocked up. There's something else. Henry said you used to work for my family?"

"That's right. When you were a wee tyke."

"You were the groundskeeper before Jamis?"

"That's right."

Rob swallowed. "You were there when Michaela died?"

Kevin's eyes narrowed. "I had nothin' to do with that."

"With what?"

"Killin' that little girl."

"I...I didn't say you did. Why did you say kill? You know something about it?"

Kevin nodded. "Do you really want to know?"

"Why, yes. Of course. Nobody will tell me.... Some say the dogs .... All I know is my mother found her body and it nearly destroyed her."

"Please sit down." They sat. "What did you know about your sister?"

"Not much."

"Have you seen pictures of her?"

"No. We don't have any. Father said they upset Mother too much."

"Your father was ashamed of her. She was retarded. Downs Syndrome. Your father wanted to put her in an institution, but your mother wouldn't let him. She was a sweet little girl, but he was always cross with her."

"Yeah. It wouldn't do for a Hardman to be less than perfect. Did the dogs actually get her?"

"I'm not sure. Somebody let the dogs out. But there were rumors she had injuries besides dog bites," He looked Rob in the eye. "Some said she was already dead, that it was a cover-up."

Rosa gasped.

"I was blamed for it—negligence. I wasn't negligent. I didn't let those dogs out." He clenched his jaw.

"Why a cover-up?"

Kevin counted on his fingers. "One, your father didn't want the child. Two, your mother wouldn't let him put her in a home. Three, he had the means of opening gates. Can you add?"

Rob turned pale. "I...can't believe that. My father?"

Kevin nodded. "I didn't give them time to fire me. There was no way I was gonna work for that man another day."

Rosa said softly, "Maybe it wasn't just finding her child dead that made your mother go insane. Maybe it was finding out what kind of monster she was married to."

After they left Kevin, they walked in silence, aimlessly, out of the village. It was a beautiful, sunny day, a few puffy white clouds, warm, with a cool mountain breeze, but Rosa knew Rob wasn't paying attention to these things.

At the edge of a field was a copse of trees. They sat under them. Rosa took Rob's hand.

Rob said, "He's mean and controlling. But is he really a monster?"

Rosa didn't know what to say. She threaded her arm around him.

"I thought I wanted to know the truth. Why? Why couldn't I leave well enough alone?"

"Because you care."

"Maybe Kevin's wrong. Maybe it was an accident."

Rosa tightened her embrace.

"But if it's true…If my father was behind it…" He buried his face in his hands. "Rosa, I'm his seed. What kind of atrocity am I capable of? Do you really want anything to do with the likes of me?"

She leaned her head against his chest. "Rob, you are not your father. You're nothing like him."

Rob draped his arms over her shoulders, laid his head against hers, and began to cry. Rosa's grief for her own parents and grandmother escaped from the small corner of her heart where she'd kept it buried. Her losses were great, but in a way Rob's were greater. She let her tears mingle with his.

How long did they grieve? Rob finally said, "I'm sorry, Rosa. That's not very manly of me."

"Don't be silly."

They wiped their eyes. Rob cleared his throat. "Um, earlier, you wanted to tell me something. I'm sorry I didn't listen. It was rude of me."

"Yes, it was."

"Do you still want to tell me?"

She wiggled around to face him and took his hands. "It's good news. Margaret might have jobs for us."

"Jobs?"

"Yes. Work." She chuckled. "That is, if you're willing to work for a living."

"Of course I am! Farm work?"

"Right. Now, it depends on how things play out here, with the pudientes and all, and if there's work available. As for me, their school needs teachers. Won't pay what I was supposed to make in Florida, but better than nothing."

Rob squeezed her hands. "Rosa, that's wonderful! I don't mind farm work. I always liked our farm back at Hardman Hall. Sometimes I wished I could be a farmer, not a businessman." He jumped up and paced. "Rosa, that means we could get married, that is, if you still want to."

"You know I do."

He got down on his knees. "Rosa, will you be my wife?"

"Don't be so melodramatic. I already told you I would."

"You deserve a church wedding, with a beautiful dress…"

"Maybe, but I don't want to wait until we can afford it."

* * *

Rob jumped when Doug's Nebula sounded. It was Henry. "Mr., I mean, Rob, can you come up here? Ms. Wannis doesn't want to wait for Andreu. She wants to head out in the Travelor."

"Okay. I'll be there as soon as I can." He hung up. "Henry needs me."

As the lift ascended, Rob gazed out at the valley. Today's perfect weather belied the storms raging inside him. Until a few months ago, he'd led what passed for a perfect life, marred only by conflicts with his father. He had wealth and privilege, an education, a future. Then the world had come apart. His personal world as well as the larger one. His youth had been stripped away, and people were now relying on him for their very lives.

And if that weren't enough, the family myth, a tragic loss, was now exposed as a sinister plot. He'd always known his father was cold and calculating, but this? *Am I the son of a murderer?* How could he go through life with this? How could he face innocent people with that shadow hanging over him? He was tempted to walk away from it all, return to the roads, the life of a hobo, a beggar, a nobody, blending into the background.

But beside him stood Rosa, who believed in him, who agreed to join her life to his, come what may. She put her arm around his waist. He set his across her shoulders and pulled her closer. "Rosa, I won't let you down."

"You better not."

Wannis was packing the Travelor. She looked at Rob. "I want you to go with me. I'll feel safer with an extra man along."

"I'm sorry, Wannis. I can't get across the border. Besides, I don't want anything to do with my father."

"Fine!" She threw down the bag of clothes she held. "You Hardmans are all alike. You don't give a damn about anybody. Well, we're going anyway. I can't waste any more time. I've got to get Doug to a competent doctor."

Betsy was in the bedroom with Doug. "Any change?" Rob asked.

"A little. He was dehydrated. I've been giving him sips of herb tea and it's brought the fever down. Otherwise, I'm just keeping him comfortable and diapered."

Rob wrinkled his nose. "Let's get him into the Travelor."

Once Doug's family had left, with Henry at the wheel, Rob breathed a sigh of relief. "I suppose I should lock up."

"Everyone's gone?" Rosa asked.

"Yes. The cook went back to her cottage. It's just us." He looked at Rosa. She was grinning. "Just us!" He grinned back and encircled her with his arms. She melted against him. "Let's go inside." They landed on the nearest couch.

When they came up for air, Rob whispered, "Are you sure?"

"Of course I am. I love you."

"I love you, too. Let's find someplace more comfortable." They went to his guest room. In their lovemaking, Rob found the joy he always knew he'd experience with Rosa.

* * *

Rosa wanted the moment to last forever.

Rob broke her reverie. "Are you hungry?"

"No. Let's stay like this." They did, until they heard someone at the front door. "Didn't you lock it?"

Rob sat up. "I guess not."

Ramon called, "Anybody here?"

Rob shot out of bed and tried to put on his clothes. "He's gonna kill me."

Rosa lay back and smiled. "At least you'll die happy." But Rob looked worried, so she dressed and combed her fingers through her hair. Rob straightened his shoulders and stepped out of the room as if he were going to his execution. She couldn't help laughing.

"It's not funny!"

Ramon came down the hall. "When you didn't come back, I was worried…." He glared at Rob, whose shirt was inside out.

Rosa giggled.

Rob shot her a pained glance, then squared himself before her brother. "Ramon, I want to marry your sister."

Ramon scowled. Rosa stepped up beside Rob, took his arm, and smiled. Ramon's anger deflated. "She's a grown woman," he muttered and turned away. Then he spun back around. "But so help me, if you hurt her, I'll kill you."

"I expect no less." Rob extended his hand and Ramon accepted it. Then Ramon embraced him.

Rosa hugged her brother. "Thank you."

"For what?"

"Your blessing."

Ramon patted her back. "I hope you know what you're doing."

"I do."

When they reached the valley, they sought Mayor Stokes. "We want to get married," Rosa said. "How do we go about it?"

"We have a minister, but I also perform ceremonies."

Rosa beamed. "I'd like you to do it."

"When?"

Rob said, "As soon as possible."

"Tomorrow?"

They looked at each other. Rosa said, "Why wait?"

"Can we do it tonight?" Rob asked.

The mayor smiled. "Give me an hour to finish a few things, then meet me at the lodge. Do you have vows in mind or do you want the standard ones?"

"Gee, I hadn't thought of that," Rob said.

"The standard ones will be fine," said Rosa. "But let me make a few modifications."

They had time to bathe, get ready, and gather their friends. Greta was disapproving, but not surprised. "Where are you going to live?"

"In Doug's house, I guess, unless we can find somewhere else. I don't really want to live there."

"Margaret gave me and Hector a cottage that needs repair. It has two bedrooms. You could have one."

"That would be perfect. Why don't you and Hector get married?"

"We're good the way we are." She pulled a dress out of her backpack. "This is something you tried to leave behind, but I saved it for you."

It was the one Sally had bought her, powder blue, sprinkled with forget-me-nots. "Thank you, Greta. You're such a good friend."

"If you'd wait, we could put on a proper wedding. We could have the cottage ready, and maybe I could make you a new dress."

Rosa sighed. "I see no point in waiting. I love Rob and I want to be with him."

"At least let me pick some flowers."

Ramon waited at the lodge. "Mama and Papa would have wanted you to get married by a priest."

"I know. Those were better times. But there's no priest around here. Margaret will get the job done." She choked back a sob. "I'm sure they'd understand."

Rob came in, smiling sheepishly. He wore a clean shirt he'd borrowed from Ned and a battered pair of jeans. To Rosa, he'd never looked more handsome.

"You are so beautiful!" he said.

She pulled up a screen on his Nebula. "Here. You'll read the first verse and I'll read the second. As for the vows, I was tempted to leave off the 'for richer' part, but I don't think it's going to be an issue."

"Let me see what I'm swearing to." After he read it, he said, "Rosa, this poem is beautiful. Did you write it?"

"No, silly. If you'd paid attention in English Lit, you'd know it was Sir Christopher Marlowe."

"Oh, Rosa, I'm not worthy of you."

"Then try harder."

Margaret laid a colorful certificate on the table. "Rosa and Rob, read this and sign it. Since Rob's not legit, I can't register the marriage on the internet, but you'll have this, and it'll be registered in our village records."

Greta handed Rosa a bouquet of wildflowers. "I always wanted to be a bridesmaid."

Ned stood as best man, and Ramon gave away the bride.

After the mayor's opening words, Rob read:

> Come live with me and be my love,
> And we will all the pleasures prove,
> That Valleys, groves, hills, and fields,
> Woods, or steepy mountain yields.

Rosa continued:

> And we will sit upon the Rocks,
> Seeing the Shepherds feed their flocks,
> By shallow Rivers to whose falls
> Melodious birds sing Madrigals.

Then Rob:

> And I will make thee beds of Roses
> And a thousand fragrant posies,
> And if these pleasures may thee move,
> Come live with me, and be my love.

Rosa was so filled with joy she could barely choke out the words:

> The Shepherds' Swains shall dance and sing
> For our delight each May-morning:
> If these delights thy mind may move,
> Then live with me, and be my love.

When they said their vows, Rosa noticed Rob was as overcome with emotion as she was. Their kiss, both passionate and chaste, told Rosa she'd made the right choice.

After a celebratory supper, the couple ascended the lift.

"Lock the door this time," Rosa said.

CHAPTER 29

Rob's sleep was disturbed by someone who knew the door codes. He crawled out of bed and pulled on his pants. "Stay here," he whispered. "I'll go see who it is."

Wannis and Henry entered the foyer. Wannis said, "Go to the valley and find Rob."

"What's wrong?" Rob asked.

Wannis shrieked. "Oh, you're here!"

"What's going on? Has something happened to Doug? Why'd you come back?"

Henry said, "We had to. The road wasn't safe."

"Not safe?" By now Rosa had joined him.

"What's she doing in my house?"

"She's my wife."

"Since when?"

"We got married tonight. Now, tell me what happened."

"Outlaws! They took over the turnpike. We were stopped. And searched. They said to go back where we came from. I told them we were from Florida. They said the border's closed."

"Then you need to wait until Andreu gets here."

"But he's not coming!"

"What?"

Henry said, "We tried calling Mr. Hardman, but he wouldn't talk to us. Ms. Amaline said Andreu quit."

"Quit?" Why would Andreu quit? "Wannis, get Amaline on the phone."

"It's the middle of the night."

"So?"

Wannis managed to rouse Amaline. She handed Rob her Nebula. "Here. You talk to her."

He'd never seen Amaline look so frazzled. "Amaline, it's Rob."

She stared at her screen. "Rob! You're alive!"

"Didn't anyone tell you I was here?"

"No! Your father won't even speak your name. Your mother's so distraught. If she wasn't asleep, I'd have you talk to her."

"No, don't disturb her." His mother. How he missed her! "Tell me what's going on. You know about Doug, don't you? Why isn't Andreu coming for him?"

"Andreu quit." She grimaced. "They caught a man trying to steal avocados, and your father ordered Andreu to beat him. Andreu refused. Your father threatened to fire him, so he quit."

"Beat a man for stealing fruit? Why not just turn him over to the police."

"Because…" she stifled a sob. "There are no police."

"What?"

"It's total chaos here, Robbie. No law and order. We're like prisoners in Hardman Hall. The only servants we still have are the ones who live here, and a few loyal security guards. You should stay where you are, where you're safe. Doesn't Doug have a nurse?"

"Yes, but she can't do anything for him. He needs to see Dr. Robertson. He needs to be in a hospital. The ones here won't take him."

Amaline's tears flowed. "I haven't told your mother about him. It'll break her heart."

"Don't tell her. But tell her I'm alive and well. Does Father have any other plans?"

"Your father won't talk to anyone. Even me. Ever since Andreu left. There's no one we can send for Doug. I don't know what to do."

Rob drew a deep breath and looked at Rosa. Promise of wedded bliss in a cottage in Summer Valley slipped away.

He read disappointment in her face and avoided her eyes. "Amaline, does anyone there have access to legal records?"

"Only your father."

"Shit."

"I know his codes. What do you need?"

"I'll call you back on Doug's Nebula."

"Okay."

Rob handed Wannis her Nebula. She left the room, weeping.

Rosa stepped into his arms. "I know. You want to take Doug home."

"What choice do I have?"

"I'll go get ready."

Rob called Amaline. "Run a records check on me. See if there are any warrants, or any reason I shouldn't return to Florida."

He searched on Doug's Nebula for information on the state of the world. What news he could find was sketchy, but it appeared the entire southeast was embroiled in lawless rebellion. He looked down at his tattered jeans and bare feet. *At least I fit in. If outlaws are in charge, I look like one of them.*

Amaline called back. "Your father wiped you off the system. You don't legally exist."

"Good. See if you find anything on Ramon Ortiz or Edward Smith."

"Hold on." A minute later, she said, "I don't find anything, but I need their full names and birthdates to be sure."

"I'll get them." He turned to Henry. "Will you go down to the bunkhouse and ask Ramon and Ned to come up?"

Rosa came in with a satchel of clothes. "How soon do you plan to leave?"

He stood up and grasped her shoulders. "Rosa, you're staying here. I can't take you into danger."

"If you're going into danger, I'm going with you."

"Not this time. I need you here."

Rosa's face reddened with anger.

"Listen. Wannis will go with us, but I want to leave the children here. Will you take care of them for me?"

"You think your sister-in-law is going to trust me with her children?"

"If she wants me to take her husband home, she'll have to. I'm going to ask Ramon and Ned to go with me."

"Ramon and Ned can't go back to Florida."

"I'm trying to find out. What's Ramon's middle name and birth-date?"

She told him.

He called Amaline. "Ramon Gabriel Ortiz, date of birth January 6, 2094."

"He's clean and legit, no warrants. Let me know when you get Edward's information."

Rosa looked surprised. "I thought there'd be an arrest warrant for Ramon."

Rob shrugged his shoulders. "Apparently, there's no functioning law enforcement." When his friends arrived, without explaining why, Rob relayed Ned's information to Amaline.

"He's legit, nothing negative. No warrants or anything."

"Are you sure? Both are clean?"

"Yes, Rob. I know how to do a records check."

"Thanks." He spoke to Ramon and Ned. "I just had my...my mother's secretary do records checks. She found nothing on either of you. No arrests or warrants, and you're both legit."

"Really?" Ramon looked at Ned. "I wonder how that happened."

Ned cocked his head. "Beats me."

Rob said, "I need to take my brother back to Florida. There's trouble on the roads. I'm hoping you guys will go with me. I think you'll be safe. Legally, anyway."

Ned nodded. "I'll go."

Ramon glowered. "You marry my sister, and then you want to take off? Damn right I'll go with you. You're not getting away that easy."

By now, Hector and Jem had arrived. "What's going on?" Hector asked.

Rob explained. "I'm not asking either of you to accompany us. I need someone to stay here and look out for Rosa and the kids. Besides, Hector, I don't want to take you away from Greta. Rosa, will you get Wannis?"

Ned turned to Ramon. "If we're traveling, we need to get our things."

When Wannis appeared, Rob said, "I'll take Doug home. I assume you're going, too."

"Certainly."

"Okay. The children will stay here with Rosa." He didn't give her time to object. "If the roads are as dangerous as you say, you don't want them out there. Besides, Rosa's a certified teacher. She's trained to deal with children."

"Do I have a choice?"

"No. Are the children awake?"

"I'll get them."

With Wannis frowning in the background, Rob explained to Little Greg and Edwina, "You're going to stay here with Aunt Rosa while we take your daddy to the hospital in Florida."

The children, half awake, whined in opposition.

"Do you trust me?"

They nodded.

"Then you can trust Aunt Rosa. She'll be good to you."

Under her breath, Wannis muttered, "God help you if anything happens to them, Robert Hardman."

"They're my blood, too. They'll be safe here."

* * *

Rosa helped the children get their belongings out of the Travelor. She was amazed at the efficiency of this small palace on wheels. It could sleep six or seat twice that many and provided all the comforts of home. Doug was lying on the main bed, Betsy at his side. "How is he?" Rosa asked.

"The same."

Rosa fed the children and their mother breakfast. Wannis didn't lift a finger to help. Rosa thought, I'm not your servant. But she decided this was not the time to ruffle feathers.

Wannis took a few bites, then left the room. She looked pale when she came back.

"What's wrong?" Rosa asked.

"Nothing. Just morning sickness."

After they'd eaten, Rosa told the children, "Tell your mama good-night, and you can go back to sleep. Wannis, why don't you get some rest until it's time to go?" Wannis retired to her room. Rosa tucked the children in their beds and kissed them goodnight.

She removed her things from the satchel and gave it to Rob. "I'll be waiting for you. You better come back."

"Rosa, I don't want to leave, but this is something I have to do."

"I know. It's your family."

"No, Rosa, *you* are my family. But I can't just let my brother die. Listen. I had Amaline run a check on you, Hector and Greta, and Jem. All of you are legit and clean. Your bank accounts are intact and, somehow, your scholarship debt is gone. I had her activate my Nebula under your identity, so now it's yours. I'll keep Doug's so we can stay in touch."

My scholarship debt has been wiped away? She hadn't been aware how much that weighed on her. *I'm free!* She closed her eyes and let out her breath.

"What's wrong?"

"Nothing. How did that happen?"

"What?"

"My scholarship debt."

"It seems somebody's been hacking into systems and changing things. Amaline called it 'restoring justice.'"

"How soon do you leave?"

"Henry's charging the Travelor. When that's done and the others come back, we'll go."

"Do we have a few minutes for each other?"

"We sure do." He set down the satchel and followed her to their room.

She put her arms around his neck and kissed him. "I want you to remember what you're going to be missing."

"Ah, Rosa, you temptress! Already I don't want to leave!"

It was Greta who knocked on their door sooner than they wished. When Rosa came out, Greta asked, "Do you want me to help with the children?"

"Yes. Thank you."

Wannis woke the children to say goodbye. "I'll come back for you soon."

They cried after her. Rosa was grateful for Greta's help. "They trained us to teach, not to comfort children."

"Apparently, they don't think that's important."

"How'd you learn to handle kids?"

"Babysitting. Cousins mostly. So their parents could work." Greta kept gazing at the youngsters. "Those children could have been mine."

"But would you want to be married to their father?"

"Hell, no!" She was silent for a while. "But why did they have to…?" She shook her head. "I was so naïve. I thought I had a chance with Doug." She grunted. "Rob always was the black sheep of the family. He didn't breed true in his father's eyes. Maybe there's hope for him. For your sake." She wiped an eye. "Hector loves kids. That's why I won't marry him. It'll be easier to let go if someday he wants a woman who can give him children."

"Oh, Greta!"

"Don't worry about me. I'm a survivor."

* * *

They were on the road by sunrise. When they reached the turnpike, Rob asked Henry why he wasn't using the radar pilot.

"It ain't working." Henry pointed at a signal pole. Wires and components dangled from it. "Somebody used them for target practice."

Wannis called Dr. Robertson and asked him to meet them at Hardman Hall.

Rob overheard him say, "I don't dare leave the house. There are mobs everywhere."

"You've got to—he's in a coma! The hospital up here wouldn't treat him." She began to cry.

"I'll do the best I can. Call me when you get to Florida."

Rob went back to check on Doug. Betsy was stretched out beside him, asleep. *She had a long night.* Doug's breath was shallow.

They hadn't been on the road much over two hours before they encountered the first roadblock, manned by Highway Patrol. Rob let Henry and Wannis handle it.

An officer talked to Henry, and others peered through the windows. One demanded, "Who's traveling with you?"

Wannis opened her window. "Look, I don't have time to waste. I have my sick husband and his nurse, plus my security detail and servants."

Rob tucked his feet under the seat and wished he'd dressed better, if that was to be their cover story.

"Mind if I search the vehicle?"

"Yes, I do mind. My husband is Douglas Hardman. You've heard the name? Hardman Aquatics? He's critically ill and I need to get him to his physician in Florida. The longer you hold me up, the sicker he's going to be."

The officer stepped back and waved an arm. "Let them go."

Henry drove on. Rob breathed a sigh of relief. He tried to call Rosa but couldn't get through. When he looked at the Nebula, the display said, "No Signal." The widespread unrest probably interfered with communications. In spite of himself, he nodded off. He woke when the vehicle stopped again.

Henry said, "Rob, we got a problem." Chunks of concrete barricaded the highway. Rob and Ned got out. The overpass ahead had collapsed onto the road below.

Ned said, "It looks like it was dynamited."

"Yeah. I don't see a way around it." He climbed into the Travelor and nudged Ramon awake. "Hey, bro, did you bring your maps?"

Ramon fished in his backpack for his atlas. "Never travel without them."

Wannis fumed. "Why are we stopped?"

"The road's out. We have to take a detour."

Rob tried again to call Rosa, without success. Betsy walked through the Travelor to stretch her legs. "How is he?" Rob asked.

"Seems like he's trying to wake up."

They made sandwiches for lunch. Wannis bit into hers, threw it down, and rushed into the head.

Rob could hear her retching. "Oh, no, we don't need another sick person!"

"Relax," Betsy said. "It's only morning sickness."

"What?"

"She's pregnant."

"Oh. I forgot."

That afternoon, Ned was driving. He slowed to a stop and said, "Rob, you're needed for this one."

The roadblock was staffed by civilians with hard faces.

Ned whispered, "We're outnumbered."

Rob got out and smiled at the man who appeared to be in charge. "What can I do for you?"

The man looked him over. "Who are you and where are you going?"

Rob extended his hand, but the man ignored it. "I'm Rob Hardman, and I'm taking my family back to Florida. My brother's sick and we need to get him to his doctor."

Another man brushed past Rob and entered the Travelor. "Rob!" Wannis shouted. "Do something!"

"Take it easy, Wannis." To the leader, he said, "What do you want from us?"

The man crossed his arms. "Your disguise doesn't fool us. We ain't letting no pudientes get through here."

Rob spread his hands. "We're not pudientes. We borrowed this vehicle. We have a very sick man here…"

A woman who had been standing behind the barrier stepped forward. "What did you say your name is?"

Rob grimaced. *I hope my family hasn't offended these people!* "Rob Hardman."

"From Summer Valley?"

"Yes, ma'am."

"Jason, this is the guy they told us about. He stood up to those pudientes. He stopped the Guard from attacking the farmers!"

Jason's demeanor changed. "Are you really the one?"

"Yes, I did help the farmers, but the Guard left before I got there."

"Well, that's a horse of a different color. Come with me."

Wannis cried, "Rob, we need to go!"

The woman shouted to the man in the Travelor, "Cliff, leave those people alone."

Cliff emerged from the Travelor. "The guy in there really is sick."

"We won't hold you up," Jason said. "I just want everyone to meet you." Rob followed him to the crowd collecting by the road. "This is Rob Hardman, everyone. From Summer Valley."

A line of people shook his hand and muttered gratitudes. One couple lingered. After the man pumped Rob's hand, the woman hugged him. "Thank you so much for what you did. We got people in Summer Valley. They were afraid for their lives before you come along and settled things."

"I'm glad I could help."

Jason shouted, "Clear the road for these good folks."

The woman who had recognized Rob's name handed something to Jason. "They're gonna need safe passage."

"Right." He handed Rob a small, metal four-leaf clover painted green. "Drivin' that fancy bus is gonna get you stopped. This'll show people you're one of us. Now, if the pudientes find it on you, tell them it's just a good luck charm."

"Thank you, Jason." He climbed back into the Travelor. After Ned drove past the barricade, Rob said, "That was a close one."

Ramon slapped him on the back. "How 'bout that! Your reputation precedes you."

"So it seems."

They faced two similar roadblocks. All Rob had to do was show the token, and they were allowed to pass. At the second, he asked, "How are things at the border? Will we have any problem getting across?"

"Don't know. We get conflicting reports."

After they were waved through, Rob pocketed the token. "I wish I dared ask what's going on. It smells of a secret society, but I can't risk someone finding out we're not really part of it."

Ned said, "It appears to be pretty extensive. I wonder how long it's been in existence."

"Yeah. And what do they have in mind?"

* * *

The cook wouldn't let Rosa or Greta help in the kitchen, insisting on doing her duty. She was grateful, however, for their offer to clean house. "I'm not up to that work like I used to be."

Rosa was not surprised at the children's foot-dragging when she asked them to pick up their rooms. *I can't change them in a day.* When they got tired of playing outdoors, she tried to get them to read, but they wanted to play holo games.

"Too much of that isn't good for them," Greta said.

"I know. What else can we do?"

"I, for one, am getting tired of this place. Why don't we go down to the valley?"

"Good idea."

"Hey, kids," Greta said, "have you ridden the lift yet?"

They hadn't been to the valley at all. Edwina was delighted by the lift. Little Greg said, "Can't it go faster?" They explored the town. When they saw other children at the playground, Greg said, "We're not supposed to play with them."

"Really?" Greta said. "That's too bad. They look like they're having a good time."

"I'm getting too big for that stuff anyway."

The stream that flowed through the valley had been dammed to make a pond. A boy about Greg's age stood on the bank with a fishing pole.

"What's he doing?"

"Fishing," Rosa said. "Do you like to fish?"

"I've never done it."

"Let's go watch him."

The boy said, "Hello," and baited his hook.

"Eeew!" said Edwina, but Greg was fascinated.

"You have to be quiet," Rosa whispered. "You don't want to scare the fish."

After several minutes, the fishing pole bent and the boy jerked it and brought in his line. They watched the fish emerge from the water, twisting and flapping. Little Greg moved closer. The boy wet his hands, grasped the fish, and removed the hook. Then he threw the fish back into the water.

"Why'd you do that?" Greg asked.

"Because it's too small. I'll wait for a bigger one."

"Does the hook hurt the fish?"

"Probably, but its mouth will heal in a few days."

"Can you teach me to fish?"

"Sure. I have another pole at home. If you come back tomorrow, I'll let you use it."

"Aunt Rosa, can I?"

"Why, sure."

Edwina whined. "I don't want to do this. I want to go to the playground."

Greta said, "Rosa, I'll stay here with the boys if you want to take her to the playground."

By suppertime, both children were tired and dirty but excited about their new experiences. "Their mother probably won't appreciate us corrupting her kids," Greta whispered.

Rosa laughed. "I think it's the best thing we could do for them." She checked Rob's Nebula for the hundredth time. She wanted to call him, but was afraid to interrupt in case he was in a critical situation.

CHAPTER 30

There was little traffic on the turnpike. Most of it was local people who, Rob knew, would have been restricted from the highway two months ago. Occasionally, they saw caravans accompanied by armored vehicles. *I wonder what happens when they're stopped by civilian patrols?*

As they approached the Florida border, they found out. A farm truck heading north crossed the median ahead of them and stopped. A man jumped out and flagged them down. Rob produced the token.

"Are you trying to cross the border?" the man asked.

"Yes, why?"

"Better find another way. We were in control, but a bunch of armed pudientes attacked us."

Rob heard what might be gunfire in the distance. "Can you suggest another route?"

"'Fraid not. But if you have any weapons and can help us out..."

Rob shook his head. "Sorry. We're not armed, and we have a sick man we need to get to a hospital."

"Well, good luck. I'm heading back for reinforcements."

Rob turned the Travelor around. "Ramon, get out your maps."

The next road they tried was secured by Florida Guard officers. "You'll have to turn around and go back. The border is closed."

"I'm Wannis Hardman." When the man gave no indication of recognizing the name, she said, "Mrs. Douglas Gregory Hardman. Of Hardman Aquatics. My husband is very sick and I need to get him to his physician in Orange Park. We are Florida Citizens."

"I'm sorry, ma'am, but the border is closed."

Wannis got out and stormed up to him. "This is a life and death situation. I'll not take no for an answer."

A superior officer stepped up. "The border is closed. To everyone. No exceptions. Unless you want to spend a night in jail."

"Wannis," Rob said. "We'll find another way. Get in."

"I got your badge number," she shouted at the officer. "You will regret this!"

Ramon said, "There's a dirt road through the woods. Last month it was fenced off, but unguarded. Henry, do you have any tools that will cut fencing?"

"Sure do."

They found the road. It hadn't been repaired since the hurricane, and the Travelor got stuck. While the men dug and maneuvered the bus out, Wannis fussed. "Hurry up!"

"I don't know what we're gonna do if we can't get across the border," Rob said.

"Let me drive," said Ramon. "I've had experience driving in sand."

At the border, the fencing had been removed but several sturdy posts blocked the road. They saw no lookouts. The men jumped out. As they began to remove the fence posts, Wannis screamed.

Rob looked up. A man stood beside the Travelor with a rifle trained on them. Another joined him. Rob took his hands off the fence post and raised them. "We're just trying to get home." Heart pounding, he started to reach into his pocket.

"Don't try it."

Rob raised his hands higher. "I have something to show you. My left pocket." He nodded to the second man. "Go ahead, take it out."

The first man pointed his gun at Rob's head while the second cautiously pulled the token from his pocket. The first lowered the weapon and pointed at the Travelor. "Why are you driving somethin' like that?"

"We have a sick man we're trying to get to his doctor in Florida."

The second man went into the Travelor. When he came out, he said, "There is a sick man in there, and two women."

"What's your name?"

"Rob Hardman."

The men looked at each other. "Do you have any identification?"

"No. I'm not legit."

"Where'd you come from?"

"North Carolina."

The man leaned his rifle against a tree. "We heard you was comin' this way."

"What? How?"

"The less you know, the better. We'll let you through. Where are you headed?"

"The Orange Park area."

"Who's your contact?"

"Contact? I'm just trying to get my brother to his doctor. Is there someone I should be in touch with?"

The man shook his head. "They'll get in touch with you."

Once they were on their way, Ramon asked, "I wonder what we're getting into?"

Ned said, "It sounds like the resistance is more organized than we thought."

"How the hell do they know who I am?"

They encountered no more roadblocks, but a few bridges were out, so Ramon's navigational skills were needed. Rob drove. They passed an intersection that looked familiar. Was that where he'd tried to find a way around a fallen tree and ended up falling into Ramon's hands?

When they drove through Olustee, Rob thought about the school and wondered how the headmistress fared. *I'll get in touch when I have a chance.* It had only been months ago, but it felt like years.

Wannis called the doctor. "Good," she said. "He'll meet us at Hardman Hall with an ambulance."

Finally, Rob drove up to the perimeter gate of the estate. A guard stepped up to the window and said, "I'm sorry, Mr. Rob, but I was told not to let anyone in."

"What? I have Doug here. You need to let us in."

"I'll have to get permission…"

Wannis huffed. "Just ram the gate!"

"Okay." Rob backed up a few yards and revved the motor.

"Wait!" The gate opened.

They met no challenge at the gate to the compound. An ambulance waited by the front door. While Doug was being loaded, Betsy briefed Dr. Robertson. Then Wannis and the doctor climbed in beside Doug, and they left with sirens and flashing lights.

Amaline rushed out and, to Rob's surprise, hugged him. "I'm so glad to see you! You need to go see your mother."

Ramon, Ned, and Betsy followed him up to his mother's suite. As they climbed the stairs, Ramon said, "I thought Doug's place was impressive. I wasn't prepared for this."

Rhea ran to Rob and embraced him. "They told me you were dead!"

"Well, I'm not. How have you been?"

"Not very good. I was so worried." She stroked his beard. "You look all grown up."

"I am. I have so much to tell you…"

Behind him, Rob heard Father's voice. "I want you and your riff raff out of here before I call security."

Rob turned around. "No, Father. I brought Doug home. The least you can do is feed us supper and let us spend the night. Then we'll leave." Ned and Ramon moved to Rob's side.

"So, you bring thugs for protection? You can't stand up to me on your own?"

"I'll stand up to you any time you like. Alone." Rob walked up to his father and found himself looking down on an old man. He didn't remember being taller than Father.

Greg seemed to shrink further. Without a word, he turned and left.

"Ned, follow him. Don't let him call anyone."

"He can't," Amaline said. "I disabled his communications. Rob, you can't leave. We need you here."

"Why?"

"I've been trying to run things, but I can't do it alone. He's irrational. The financial crisis—some of his friends committed suicide, and he's come unhinged. I changed his codes, but not before he shut down the water plants. There've been crowds at the gates demanding water, but I don't know how to start them. Most of our staff has left. The only ones that are still loyal are his security force, and they won't be for long if they don't get paid."

"But what can I do?"

"Take control. At least until Doug gets better."

"Please, Robbie," his mother said. "Don't go away again. I missed you so."

Rob took her hands. "I'll stay as long as I can."

Ramon cleared his throat. "I'll go see if Ned needs help."

"Thanks. Mother, I have good news. I got married."

"Really? Do I know her? Is she a nice girl?"

"Of course she's a nice girl, or I wouldn't have married her. You'll like her. Her name is Rosa."

Rhea laid her head on Rob's shoulder and fell asleep. Amaline said, "Why don't you come back later."

He lowered Mother to her couch. "Is my room still available?"

"Yes."

Rob thought about his comfortable feather bed. Even though he'd been sitting most of the day, he was weary from travel and his nerves were raw from confrontations. He'd been looking forward to a few quiet moments to call Rosa. He wished she were here. His stomach growled. "Let me and my friends clean up and get something to eat. Will you find a room for Betsy?"

"Sure. Then I'll see about supper."

Ramon and Ned stood outside the office door. "He hasn't called anyone. He just watches business reports and news. One of the staff told me he's harmless as long as he stays in his office."

"Good. Come with me."

When they entered his suite, Ramon said, "This is your bedroom? It's bigger than my family's house!"

"I know," Rob said. "It's more than a person needs." He looked around. Everything was as he'd left it. "All I want to do is get back to Rosa. But they need me here until Doug recovers. I'm not even one of them anymore." He collapsed into a chair. "You fellows make yourselves at home. Take a shower if you like. Help yourselves to my clothes. Then we'll go down to supper. There are guest rooms, but I'd feel better if we stayed together. One of you can take the bed tonight and the other the couch. I'll sleep on the cot in the dressing room."

After his friends had cleaned up and changed, Rob showered and put on the oldest clothes he could find. He slipped on a pair of what had once been comfortable shoes, but they were too tight. *All those months of walking barefoot.* He kicked them off.

They went down to eat. Amaline set out sandwich-makings in the dining room. "I'm sorry, I'm no cook," she said. "We have no kitchen help anymore."

"Thank you. This will be fine." After she left, Rob said, "She's never been this nice to me."

His friends stared at the portraits lining the room. "Who are all these dudes?" Ned asked.

"My imperial ancestors."

"Does Rosa know about all this?" Ramon asked.

"I don't know. I don't think it'd impress her, though. She's got more sense. I think she likes me the way I am now."

Before they finished eating, Jamis and Dertha, the groundskeepers, came in. "Welcome home, Mr. Rob."

"Good to see you. But I'm not Mr. anymore. Just Rob. And this is no longer my home."

Dertha said, "Oh, we were hoping you could help us. We want to bring our daughter and her children here to live with us, but Mr. Hardman said no. Our son-in-law works but he wants his family someplace safe."

"My father is no longer running things. Go ahead and bring them here."

"Oh, thank you… Rob."

No sooner had they left, than Steven, the groom, came in.

"I'm surprised to see you here, Steven. I thought you'd have gone home to your family."

"Well, sir, I did, but nobody was tending the horses, so I came back. I would like a favor."

"Yes?"

"My old grandparents are having it pretty hard. They can't defend themselves. They've been robbed and…"

"You want to bring them here?"

"Yes, sir."

"Only if you stop calling me 'sir.' Or 'Mr.' Where would they stay?"

"In the stable with me. It's nicer than their old house."

"By all means, Steven. Tell me, who else is still here? Other than security guards."

"Josei and his family. He couldn't leave his gardens any more than I could leave my animals. I've been watching out for all the livestock."

"Are you getting paid?"

"I hope so. At least I have a place to stay. And everyone here is getting enough to eat. I can't say as much for a lot of people."

As they picked up their plates, Betsy came in, Amaline on her heels. "Rob, I need to talk to you about your mother." She set a bag on the table and took out a pill bottle.

Amaline said, "I asked her to look at your mother, to get her opinion."

"Look at these medications. Amaline doesn't know what she's been giving her."

"The doctor never told me what they were. He said if she didn't take them, she'd be worse."

Betsy raised her voice. "These meds are her problem!" She shook the bottle. "This is Extremedy. It's a powerful sedative, something to be taken for short periods of time only." She turned to Amaline. "How long has she been on it?"

Amaline said, "Years. Ever since…the incident."

Betsy slammed the bottle on the table. "No wonder she's so depressed. This causes serious depression. Then when it starts to wear off, it causes severe agitation. Am I right?"

Amaline nodded.

"And this," she held up a liquid. "I'm not exactly sure what this is, but what have you been told to give it to her for?"

"Agitation."

Betsy held up more pills. "And this—she takes it at night—is a sleep inducer. She's probably been given stronger doses as she gets used to it. And this other she takes in the morning to wake up." Betsy looked at Rob. "Your mother has not been given a chance to live a normal life. She's been drugged to the point she can't function."

Amaline broke down crying. "I didn't know. The doctor said to give her these medicines. He said without them she'd be suicidal."

"Amaline, it's not your fault," Rob said. "Betsy, what can we do?"

"She needs to be off these drugs, but you can't just stop them. She should be hospitalized, but if it's the same people who've been treating her, that'll do no good."

"Can you help her?"

Betsy hesitated. "It's my field, but I've always had support staff, and other drugs to use while the patient's being weaned."

"Can we hire you?"

"I came to check on my family. Let me do that, and I'll think about it."

"Do what you can tonight. I'll have Henry take you to your people tomorrow."

They returned to Rob's suite. Ned said, "Well, Rob, what are you going to do? You get one thing accomplished, then somebody wants something else."

Rob collapsed into a chair and took a deep breath. "I don't know. Right now, I'm going to call Rosa."

* * *

At last! The Nebula sounded. Rosa took it into their room. Rob looked weary. "Are you okay?" The room behind him reminded her of Salli's house.

"Yes. We got here safe and sound, and Doug's at the hospital."

"Good. I've worried all day."

"I tried to call you but couldn't get a signal. Also, the roads were crazy, and this is the first quiet moment I've had. I miss you so much."

"I miss you, too. When are you heading back?"

Rob closed his eyes and took forever to answer. "I'm not sure. Things are an awful mess here..."

"Rob! You said you'd come right back. You've done what you left here to do. What's keeping you?"

"I don't want to burden you with the world's problems. I'm tired. I'll call you in the morning."

"No! Don't hang up. Let me talk to Ramon."

The screen followed Rob to a lavish bedroom. Ramon took the Nebula from Rob.

"Ramon, what's going on? You got Doug to Florida, now when are you coming back?"

"Calm down, sis. All hell has broken loose. There was gunfire at the border..."

"What! Are you okay?"

"I'm sorry. I shouldn't have mentioned it. We weren't involved. We just had to take a different route."

"Look, I'm not a child. I need to know what's going on with you and my husband. Tell me everything."

Ramon looked up, away from the screen. She overheard Rob, "Do you want me to talk to her?"

"No. I'm talking to *you*, Ramon."

Ramon winced. "There's more going on than we knew. A resistance movement. It appears to be widespread, and they're actually battling with the pudientes. We got stopped by a bunch of rebels who recognized Rob's name and knew what he did at Summer Valley. They gave us a token that got us through their roadblocks."

"What's going on?"

"I don't know, but it's big."

"Let me talk to Rob." Ramon passed the Nebula. "Tell me the truth. Are you in danger?"

"Not at the moment. Probably not at all. Listen, Rosa, on top of everything else, things are a mess here. My father shut down his water plants. People can't get drinking water and they've been storming the gates. Amaline disabled his communications so he can't do more damage, but I need to find a way to get those plants operating before it causes a health crisis. On top of all that, Betsy, the nurse, looked at my mother's medications and said she's being overmedicated. Deliberately." He put a hand to his head and drew up a fistful of hair.

"Rob, I'm coming down there..."

"No! You wouldn't be safe on the road. Give me some time to figure this out. I'll call you tomorrow and let you know what we need to do. Listen..." He moved away from Ramon, into a different room. "Rosa, I love you. I want nothing more than to be there with you. I promise I'll come back as soon as I can."

"I love you, too. Don't you do anything foolish. Keep yourself safe. For my sake."

"I will. You stay safe, too. I love you."

After the call was terminated, Rosa rushed to Greta's arms to cry.

CHAPTER 31

Rob checked on his mother the first thing in the morning. She was asleep. Betsy and Amaline looked like they'd been up all night. "I cut back on some of the sedatives," Betsy said. "It was a rough night, but she's finally resting. When can I go to my family?"

"I'll talk to Henry. Maybe I should send Ramon, too, in case there's a problem with the roads." He turned to Amaline. "I told Betsy if she would care for Mother, we'd hire her, but I don't have any authority. Could you see that she gets paid?"

She nodded.

"By the way, how did you manage to cut Father off from his communications?"

"He paid no attention to what I did. He's no longer grounded in reality. He spends his time watching videos, like he's addicted to them. He barely eats, or sleeps."

"Do you think we could put our heads together and turn the water back on?"

"Let me get him out of his office. He's been up all night, so he should be ready for a nap. By the way, if you want breakfast, you'll have to fix it yourself. I did make coffee."

They ate in the kitchen. Rob was embarrassed that Ned had to show him how to cook an egg. When Henry joined them, they talked about getting Betsy to her family.

"Where do they live?" Henry asked.

"Clermont. It's south of here."

Ramon said, "That's high and dry. Ordinarily, it'd be a three hour drive, but I don't know what we'll run into. You have to cross rivers, so it depends on the condition of the bridges. If I could look at satellite data, I could get an idea what to expect."

Once his father was out of the office, Rob pulled up satellite images. "These are a week old."

"That's okay," Ramon said. "It's more current than my atlas." He updated his Florida roadmap.

"Take the Backpacker. And this." Rob handed him the token. "In case you need it."

Amaline unlocked access to water plants and Rob studied the operating system. "Father never schooled me in this. Doug was to inherit the plants."

"I picked up a few things, watching him," said Amaline. "Let me try."

Finally, they got in. They were unable to boot up the first plant's system, but to their surprise, the second was already operating. Rob called the plant manager. At first, he claimed not to know how or why.

"Listen," Rob said. "I need to get more plants online so people can have water. My father is no longer in charge. We need any help you can give us."

"What about Mr. Doug?"

"He's in the hospital, seriously ill. Amaline and I are running things."

"You can trust Rob," Amaline said.

"Okay. I'll show you how I did it."

Rob took notes. "If we three-way you with another plant, can you explain it to them?"

"I'd rather not. If people know what I've done, I could be in jeopardy."

Some plants had no staff on duty and they had to call them in. A few more were already running. "It looks like these managers took matters into their own hands," Rob said.

"You realize you're probably not going to be paid for the water," Amaline said. "Until Doug takes over, or your father comes to his senses."

Rob laughed. "I'm not getting paid anyway. Have you forgotten? I've been disinherited."

"I can fix that. I can restore your legitimacy, even your bank account."

"No. I'm rather enjoying my poverty."

Someone knocked on the door. Rob jumped.

It was not Father, but Andreu. "Welcome home, Rob."

It was not lost on Rob that Andreu didn't address him as Mr. Rob. He felt like hugging him. "It's so good to see you. They told me you'd quit."

"I did, but I thought you might could use my help." He took a green pen from his pocket and drew a four leaf clover on the palm of his hand.

Rob glanced at Amaline. She showed no surprise. *She's in on it, too!* "Please tell me what's going on."

"It's been building for quite some time. A bunch of us saw the writin' on the wall, so we begin to talk among ourselves. We found there were like-minded people all over the country." Andreu sat down. "We started making little changes. We thought we could do it in a quiet, orderly manner, and we thought we were making progress, but it wasn't soon enough. In Florida, that hurricane broke the camel's back. Then the Deep South collapsed, and the rest of the country started fallin' like dominoes." He looked Rob in the eye. "The oligarchy is comin' to an end. Best part, some pudientes are on our side. What we need are good people, like you, Rob, to steer us in the right direction."

"Me steer you? Andreu, I have no skills or experience. I just graduated from college with a useless degree. Besides, I just got married and my wife is in North Carolina."

Andreu smiled. "Congratulations. Is it the young lady from Palm Rise you were so smitten with?"

"Was it so obvious I was smitten?"

He nodded. "You took some risks on her behalf. We won't keep you from your bride, but the world needs your leadership."

"I'm no leader."

"That's not what I hear."

"Tell me, how did my 'fame' cross three states in a matter of days?"

"The network is extensive. Even though the pudientes try to limit our communication, there are systems they didn't know about. You see, Rob, working people 'round the country have been running things for generations. And they can keep runnin' them, given good leadership. There's no intention to take the pudientes' property or money, only to set up a fair arrangement. Do you think the Hardmans really need as much money as they have?"

"No. They have way more than they can spend."

"Rob, you've seen both sides now. How has that changed you?"

"Well, I don't want my fortune restored. I want to earn an honest living, just lead a comfortable life. With Rosa."

"That makes you the ideal leader."

Rob drew a deep breath. "What do you want from me?"

Andreu stood up and beckoned.

"Go ahead," Amaline said. "I can finish here."

Rhea was out in the hall, still in her nightgown, but at least her hair had been brushed. "Where is Amaline?"

Rob took her hand and steered her to the office. "She's in here."

"Thank you." She hugged him.

Andreu said, "Your mama seems more lucid than usual."

"A nurse took her off some of those drugs."

In the dining room, Ned sat at the table with a man and woman in security uniforms. "Rob, your reassurance is needed."

The woman spoke up. "I'm Alice Frees. I'm head of security now. When we learned you were back, we sent Kramer packing, him and a few others. We want to protect the estate from treacherous influences, but we're on the side of the working people and want to be fair to them. We also expect a fair wage. In other words, if you authorize it, we'll stay on and keep the hoards from looting, but there are a lot of hungry people out there, and we'd like to help them."

"I would, too, but I don't have any authority."

"Rob," Andreu said, "we're giving you that authority."

A shudder ran through him.

"I have a suggestion," Ned said. "If people come to the gate with a legitimate request, meet with them, hear them out, and decide what to do. On an individual basis."

A security guard came in and whispered in Alice's ear. She looked at Rob. "Dr. Robertson is here, and he asked to talk to Greg."

Rob stood up. "Excuse me. I need to keep him away from my mother."

Dr. Robertson was in Father's office. Mother was in her suite with Amaline. Rhea appeared to have lost her earlier clarity. She sat on her sofa with a blank stare, holding a remnant of fabric.

"Any news on Doug?" Rob asked.

Amaline shook her head. "The doctor told Greg there was no change."

"Keep that quack away from my mother."

"Oh, I will."

His mother said, "I'm tired, I'm going to lie down."

"Wait for me, Rob," Amaline said and accompanied Rhea to her bedroom. When she returned, she closed the door. "Rob, I want you to know, all those years that I was your father's mistress, I didn't do it willingly." Her eyes flashed with anger. "I did it to protect your mother. After what happened to Michaela, I wasn't sure what he might do to Rhea. As it is, he's done enough. I'm saying this because I know you never liked me because of what I was. I didn't like myself, either." She sighed. "Now that's all behind me, but I'll continue to protect your mother to the best of my ability."

"Thank you. Does Mother know about Doug?"

"She knows he's in the hospital, but she doesn't know how serious. None of us do."

"Tell me, was my father complicit in Michaela's death?"

"I don't know for sure, but I'm willing to bet my life on it."

* * *

After breakfast, Rosa took the children out to play in the yard. *I wonder why their mother hasn't called.* They didn't ask about her, either. While they were playing, she read *Chronicles* and took notes on the Nebula. Lately there'd been so little time for study.

Edwina ran up and threw herself onto Rosa's lap. "What are you doing?"

"Reading a book."

"That's not a book."

Rosa smiled. "Sure it is." She let Edwina hold it. "This is what people used before we had computers."

"Really?" Edwina opened the book and peered at a page. "It has real words! I can read them! Greg, come look at this book."

Little Greg tried not to look impressed, but Rosa could tell he was curious. "What's it about?"

"It's about the history of the United States before you were born. Even before I was born."

"History," said Greg. "Bor-ring."

"It doesn't have to be boring. You like stories, don't you? These are stories, but they're true stories."

"Tell us one," Edwina said.

"Okay." Rosa fished for something they could relate to. "Do you like to go to the beach?"

"Yes. Daddy takes us to Grandpa's pink castle."

"Do you go swimming there?"

"Of course. It has pools."

"But do you swim in the ocean?"

Greg said, "Unh-uh. The water's nasty."

"Well, a hundred years ago, it was different." On the Nebula she pulled up a picture of a coral reef. "This is what it used to look like. Under the water. You could swim with the fish."

"You're making it up," Greg said.

"No. My book doesn't have pictures, but it tells about it." She turned to the chapter on oceans and showed it to Greg. "The ocean used to be clean. My grandmother told me her grandmother used to go to the beach to swim and fish. Sometimes they'd sail in a boat. They'd also go to a restaurant and eat fresh oysters."

"What are oysters?"

Rosa found a picture on the Nebula.

Greg wrinkled his nose. "Those don't look good to eat."

"No, but Grandmother said they were delicious. Her grandmother once saw a whale."

"What's that?"

On the Nebula, Rosa displayed a picture of a whale.

"That's a big fish," Edwina said.

"Only it's not a fish. It's a warm blooded creature, like us. It used to live in the ocean. When I was your age, Greg, I read a book about a whale." She showed them the cover of *Moby Dick*. "When that story was written, it was in a paper book like this one, but I read it on a reader. There aren't very many of these old books still around."

"How do you know so much, Aunt Rosa?" asked Edwina.

"Because I read. Also, I went to college to be a teacher."

Little Greg kicked a dandelion. "Can I go down to the valley? That boy said he'd take me fishing."

"Why certainly. Let's make a picnic lunch to take with us."

It was midafternoon before Rosa got a call from Rob. He looked tired. "I've been holding court all day."

"Holding court?"

"Yeah, if you can imagine a barefoot king in blue jeans being petitioned by his subjects."

"What on earth are you talking about?"

"There's been a regime change. Father's confined to the dungeon, and the Pretender has taken the throne. The security guards are keeping out infidels but sending in people with legitimate needs. And I'm supposed to solve their problems."

"What do they want?"

"Food, mostly, and shelter and medical care. I'm afraid we're going to run out of food. They can forget shelter and medical care. It's really a mess, Rosa. We didn't know how good it was in the mountains." Her Nebula indicated an incoming call. "Oh, the reason I called was to tell you Wannis was going to call you. That's probably her."

Rosa slapped her hand over her mouth. "Oh, dear. The kids are fishing."

Rob laughed. "She's gonna love that! Clean them up before you call her back."

"But where has she been? This is the first time she's tried to get in touch with them."

"She claims she didn't know how to reach you. Gotta go. I'll call you tonight."

Rosa washed Edwina's face and hands with a napkin.

Greg resisted. "I can do it myself." He smeared more dirt than he wiped off.

The Nebula sounded again. Rosa took the call.

"Why aren't you answering my calls?" Wannis shrieked. "Where are my children?"

"They're right here. They're fine. How is Doug?"

"Don't ask me about Doug! I want my babies."

Rosa handed Little Greg the Nebula. The children seemed delighted to talk to their mother and excited to tell her about fishing. Rosa couldn't see the screen but imagined Wannis' expression. She questioned them about what they were eating. After they told her, she asked, "Are you going to bed on time?"

"Yes, ma'am."

"What about brushing your teeth?"

"I do," said Edwina. "But Greg doesn't always."

Rosa grimaced.

Little Greg protested, "I do, too!"

"How are they treating you?"

"Aunt Rosa's real nice."

When Wannis finished talking to them, she ended the call without so much as a thank you to Rosa.

* * *

Rob tried to relax after the last petitioner left. He'd lost count of how many had come for help. Some wanted jobs. Rob hired a cook and put him to work preparing lunch for anyone who was hungry. Most were. A few had been wandering homeless since the hurricane. From his weeks on the road, Rob knew what they needed—a meal and what food they could carry. In too many cases, Rob was stymied for a solution and wished he could ask Andreu's advice, but Andreu had left that morning and no one knew how to contact him.

Finally, there was a lull. Rob sat at the dining table and looked at the buffet, wondering if there was any coffee left, but he was too weary to get up. He asked Ned, "What do I do when we run out of things to give them?"

"Why not take inventory and see what you have?"

"I miss Rosa. I want to go back to her."

"I know. You didn't foresee this."

Rob looked out a window. The sun shone in a sky with building thunderheads. "I haven't had a breath of fresh air since we got here." Was that only yesterday? "I can't stand being inside like this."

Ned smiled. "Let's go for a walk."

It was hot. Rob breathed deeply and felt sweat oozing from his pores. "Ah, this is better. Good ole Florida humidity. Ned, let me show you around."

"I've been running back and forth between here and the front gate all day. I've seen the orchards and gardens. There's more?"

"Oh, yes. Lots more." They walked past the swimming pool and tennis courts and through the back gate of the compound. Rob pointed. "Those cottages are for employees. I wonder how many are still here? I've only seen Jamis and Steven."

"There was a fellow harvesting okra."

"Probably Josei. We have cows, sheep, goats, even emus, if you can believe it. Or did have. I guess we still have chickens. We had eggs for breakfast. Why am I saying 'we?' None of this is mine anymore." He gestured ahead. "That's the stable."

Ned whistled. "Fancier than my house!" He sighed. "I wonder about my house. I had to abandon it. But if my bank account is intact …"

"The house may still be yours, too. I'll ask Amaline to check. See that palomino? That's Cricket. He was my horse. It looks like Steven's taking good care of him." Rob walked to the paddock fence. Cricket whinnied and galloped over. Rob stroked his neck. Cricket nuzzled his shirt. "I don't have anything for you, boy, but I'll bring you something later."

"He's beautiful," Ned said.

Steven came out with an elderly couple. "Mr., I mean, Rob, these are my grandparents."

"We appreciate you lettin' us stay here," the man said. "That hurricane 'bout destroyed our house, and then people was robbin' us blind."

"I'm glad I could help. Maybe I can move you into better quarters once I see what's available."

"No need for that. We don't mind the animals, and that stable's more comfortable than our house was."

Rob and Ned walked to the top of the hill and looked over the cropland and pastures.

"All this belongs to your family?" Ned asked.

Rob nodded.

"I would have built the house here, on the hill, where you have a nice view."

"Father's not interested in a view. He wanted a fortress."

Ned shook his head. "You sure lost a lot when you went rogue. Do you think about going back?"

"Of course I do, but I've been happier since I 'went rogue,' as you put it."

When they returned to the dining room, Andreu was back. "How's it going?" he asked.

Rob shook his head. "I don't really know what I'm doing, or what good it'll do in the long run. Andreu, when I was on the road I saw poverty and suffering. Hell, I experienced it! And that was before everything fell apart. It's only going to get worse." He and Ned sat down.

Andreu straddled a chair. "Rob, there are shortages in this country, but not as much as you think. The problem is greed. We need to manage things differently, so more people get what they need. And you're doin' your part."

"We? Who is this *we*? Andreu, I need to understand what's going on and what part I'm supposed to play."

Andreu cleared his throat. "There's no organized movement, it's more of a cause. Right now I can't tell you specifically who they are because it's too dangerous. I *can* tell you, people are tired of injustice, and they're working to set things right. Rob, the pudientes have been stackin' the cards against everyone else for generations. Now it's reached a breaking point, and you see the result—a rebellion. Things could go several ways. The pudientes could quash the rebellion. A lot of people'd suffer but it wouldn't solve anything, because someday the people would rise up again and there'd be a bloodbath. After that, there'd be a dictator, then another, and eventually the revolutionaries would become the next pudientes. We don't want that. We hope to restore democracy and justice. That's where you come in."

"Me? I don't understand. I'm just a kid out of college."

"What d'ya think I am? A chauffeur! What do I have to offer? I'm just doin' what's been put before me. If each of us does their part, we can make it work."

Ned said, "You've been doing your part today, Rob. You've helped a lot of people."

"Only a handful. There are a lot more out there."

Andreu said, "Find a way to help them."

"How?"

Andreu shook his head. "That I can't tell you. You got to figure it out."

Rob slumped in his seat.

Andreu laid a hand on his shoulder. "You'll find a way. Other folks have. Other people that don't have as much going for them as you do. Behind the scenes, they've begun to restore little bits of justice. You have an advantage—you know the pudientes from the inside out."

Ned slapped his thigh. "That explains it."

Rob looked up. "What?"

"I thought there'd be warrants for my arrest. When I was picked up in Georgia—I should have guessed! They didn't find anything... My bank account should have been confiscated. But it's not. And Ramon's arrest record—somebody's been worming their way through the system, changing things. I hope they know what they're doing. Some records we may not want wiped away." He looked at Andreu. "Am I right?"

Andreu nodded. "Now, what kind of trouble did you and your friend get into?"

"I was picked up in Georgia for vagrancy. Before the hurricane, Ramon was arrested on false charges. I was assistant warden at the jail, and when the employees abandoned it, I let Ramon and the other inmates out. Didn't want them to die of neglect."

"That was you?" Andreu stood up and extended his hand. "I'm right honored to meet you, sir."

A frantic scream came from upstairs. Rob bounded up two steps at a time. Amaline leaned against his mother's door. "What is it? Is she all right?"

"Yes. That was Wannis." She glanced toward the office. "Dr. Robertson is talking to your father." She choked back a sob. "Oh, Rob, Doug is dead. I don't know how to tell your mother."

"Don't tell her yet." He barged into Father's office. "What happened?"

His father didn't look at him or speak, only left the room and went down the hall to his suite.

Dr. Robertson said, "Your brother apparently took a lethal combination of medications that shut down brain function. We tried everything, but he couldn't be revived."

Rob turned to stone.

"I'm sorry." The doctor stood up and left.

Amaline came in and led Rob to a chair. "You're the only son she has left, Robbie."

He'd set his expectations on Doug's recovery. His imagined future toppled into an abyss. "Give me a few minutes, Amaline."

"I'll wait for you in your mother's room."

Rob put his face in his hands and cried. Having no handkerchief, he wiped his nose with the back of his hand. When he noticed he was sitting in his father's chair, he wiped the snot on the seat cushion. After he composed himself, he went to his mother's suite.

"Robbie! What's wrong? No one will tell me."

Rob took Mother into his arms. "Doug has died."

She sobbed soundlessly. Then she pushed away. "I knew it. Poor Wannis."

As if on cue, Wannis' wailing was heard in the hall. Rhea went to her.

"Should I give your mother a sedative?" Amaline asked.

"No. Let her grieve for once."

Wannis resisted Rhea's attempts at comfort. "Where is Henry? I want my babies!" When she saw Rob, she screamed, "Why did you leave them back there? I need them with me. Now!"

Rob clutched her elbows. "Henry took Betsy to Clermont. He'll be back soon. Your children are safe. We'll send for them when he gets here."

His mother said, "Where are the children?"

"They're in the mountains, at Summer Heights, with my wife. They're safe."

Wannis ran to her room.

Rob whispered to Amaline. "Maybe *she* needs a sedative."

CHAPTER 32

When the Nebula sounded, Rosa's heart leaped. But it wasn't Rob. The screen displayed Wannis' face. Rosa knew something was wrong.

Wannis' breath came in short grunts. Finally, she managed to say, "My children…"

"They're playing holo games. Do you want to talk to them?"

"No. I want them to come home. Now."

"Rob said he'd call and tell me when he planned…"

"The hell with Rob! I want my children."

"Of course. Tell me, what's wrong?"

"He's dead!" She broke down and ended the call.

Rosa stared at the Nebula. *Who's dead?* She hit the button to call Rob. When he answered, she cried out, "Oh, thank God!"

"What?"

"Wannis just called and I couldn't get any sense out of her." She noticed Rob's eyes were red. "What's wrong?"

"My brother died."

"Oh, no! What happened?"

"The doctor said they couldn't revive him. He had a reaction to those drugs. It shut down his brain. For good." He wiped his face. "Wannis wants her children brought here, and I don't blame her. I'm going to ask Andreu to come for them."

She felt a surge of hope. "So, you're coming with him?"

He looked in her eyes. "I can't right now. I wish I could. I miss you so."

Rosa bit her lip. "Well, if I have a ride back to you, I'm going to take it. You asked me to look after the children. If they're going to Florida, so am I."

"Rosa, I wish you'd stay where you're safe."

"There's no way I'm going to be away from you if I don't have to be."

"Okay. Do the kids know? About Doug?"

"She wouldn't talk to them. Should I tell them?"

"No. Let her. Even if she waits until they get here. I'll call you after I talk to Andreu."

* * *

When Rob asked him to go get Wannis' children, Andreu shook his head. "I'm sorry. I don't work for the Hardmans anymore."

"I know. I guess I can send Ned and Ramon. I'd go myself, but I'd be sorely tempted to stay there."

A smile crossed Andreu's face. "Well, I don't work for the Hardmans, but maybe I could do a favor for a friend."

"Would you? I'll be forever in your debt. I'll ask Ramon to go with you. He's a good navigator."

Andreu stood up. "If I'm gonna be driving all night, I might better get some sleep. I'll be out in the garage, in my old alcove. It'd take too much time to go home."

Rob needed a diversion from grief. He decided to start taking inventory before more petitioners came to the gate. First he listed the employees that remained on the estate. Residing in the house were Amaline, the new cook, and Alice Frees. Her security guards, Jamis and Dertha's family, Steven and his grandparents, and the farm manager, Josei, lived in outbuildings. He asked each of them to catalog goods in they controlled. A substantial warehouse had been built into the side of a hill. Beyond the gates of Hardman Hall, were several other warehouses. The bursar had maintained records of their contents. *Father is such a hoarder. All this stuff sitting there, not being used. What should I do with it?*

Rob asked Ned and Amaline for advice.

Ned said, "Are you sure those warehouses haven't been looted?"

"No, I guess I should find out. But I'm in a quandary. So many people are doing without, it doesn't seem right to sit on all this stuff, but how do we distribute it fairly?"

"There's no need to rush to a decision," Amaline said.

"By the way, where is father? What's he up to?"

"He's in the holo room," Amaline said. "Watching Sanctuary videos. If we don't disturb him, he'll be there all day."

Rob realized what a burden all these goods were. *I need someone to manage them for me. For me? I want no part of it. I want to be in Summer Valley with Rosa.* But Rosa said she was coming here to join him. *Will I never get out from under this yoke?*

When Henry and Ramon returned that evening, Betsy was with them. "My family's doing okay. They don't necessarily need me and if I have a job here, I can use the money. At least now I know how to communicate with them."

Rob told his friends about Doug's death.

Henry took it hard. "I worked for him many a year. I didn't like some things he did, but I hate this. He was so young. Those poor children. Poor Ms. Wannis."

Ramon said, "I'm sorry. I never had a brother, but I don't know what I'd do if something happened to Rosa."

Betsy set her mouth in a hard line. "I'd like to see those medical records."

"Maybe Amaline can get them for you."

"By the way," Ramon asked, "have you heard from Rosa?"

"Yes," Rob said. "I've talked to her a few times today. She's doing a good job with the kids. I knew she would."

"Of course. So what's the plan now? When do we head back?"

Rob looked down. "Well, I need a favor from you."

Ramon's eyes bored into him.

"Wannis wants her children here. Andreu said he'd go get them for me."

"And?"

"I'm hoping you'll go with him."

"What about you?"

"Ramon, I'm needed here. You have your maps. You can get Andreu there and back. I'm worried the roads are in worse shape than when we came south…"

Ramon slammed his fist on the table. "What about Rosa? Your wife! Are you just going to abandon her?"

"No! She's coming back with you."

"What if she doesn't want to?"

"Ramon, hear me out. I wanted her to stay there, where it's safe. She told me in no uncertain terms she's coming back with the children. I think, like me, she doesn't care so much where we are, as long as we're together."

"Yeah," Ramon said. "I'll go. And I'll bring Rosa back. And you damn better be waiting for her when we get here."

* * *

Rosa had just put the children to bed when Rob called. "How are they doing?" he asked.

"Fine. I guess all the new experiences tired them out. They went to bed without arguing. What about you?"

"All the new experiences are tiring me out."

She laughed. "What's the plan?"

"Andreu's checking out the Travelor and charging the batteries. He and Ramon will head out soon. Henry's going, too, so there'll be three drivers. Depending on what they run into, they could be there by late morning. What about Hector and Greta? And Jem?"

"They'd rather stay here, unless you need them."

"No. I don't blame them. I'd rather be there, too. But as long as you're with me, I'll be happy."

"I miss you so much." Rosa wished she could reach through the screen and touch him. "Are you alone?" He looked away, then she saw the scene move and heard a door close.

"I am now."

"Where are you? In a closet?"

"No. It used to be my dressing room. Now it's my bedroom. Ramon and Ned have been sleeping in my bedroom and sitting room."

"What—you have your own apartment?"

"Sort of. I can kick them out when you get here, so we can have privacy."

She closed her eyes to stop the tears. "I can't wait to be with you."

"Me, too. Rosa, be careful, hear? If anything happened to you, I don't know what I'd do."

She could barely talk for the lump in her throat. Finally, "I'll be okay."

Someone knocked on his door.

"Rob..." she whispered.

She heard Henry say, "We're 'bout ready to leave."

"Rosa..."

"I know. See them off. Tell Ramon I love him. And he'd better be careful."

"I will."

* * *

To Rob's relief, most of the livestock that weathered the hurricane still survived. Apparently, the estate was too remote to suffer much poaching. Outbuildings held stores of animal feed. Father had been fearful of want. For once his paranoia paid off.

Warehouses in surrounding cities were full of supplies. Only a few had been looted. Now Rob was better prepared for the petitioners who showed up at the gate. What he wasn't prepared for was handling the logistics involved in distributing goods. He needed help. Ned and

Amaline picked up some of the slack. He hoped to recruit their old bursar or another qualified person.

The water plants were all operational, so at least the communities they served had decent water. Rob turned his attention to his father's various other businesses. Some managers had continued to operate despite having no promise of compensation, and he was able to woo others, and their employees, back.

All this kept him busy. Too busy to think about having no Doug, or anyone else, take over for him. Giving control back to Father was unthinkable.

At lunchtime, he retreated to the privacy of his dressing room and called Rosa. She had the children ready to go, but Ramon and the others hadn't arrived. "They called and said they'd run into a few obstacles, but they're on the way."

"I can't wait until you get here," he said. "But make sure Andreu gets some rest. I'd rather you be late than have something happen."

"Right. And with me, there'll be four drivers."

* * *

A few hours later, Greta called Rosa from the valley. "Ramon and them are back. They're down here. I want you to come down as soon as you can."

"Why? What's wrong?"

"Nothing's wrong, but I want you to see something."

She tore the children from their holo games. Riding the lift to the valley, Rosa could see the Travelor parked in front of City Hall. Ramon greeted her with a hug. "Greta's inside."

Greta and Hector were serving a meal to the travelers and three rather dirty children. When Rosa and the Hardman children walked in, a girl in her early teens jumped up and grabbed a book that lay beside her on the table. She held it out to Rosa.

"I read it, all of it, and I read it to my brother and sister, too. We liked it. And we took good care of it. We washed our hands before we read it."

Rosa recognized the children with whom they'd sheltered under the overpass one rainy night back in Georgia. Rosa accepted the book from her. "Thank you. Would you like another one?"

"Do you have more?"

"Yes I do. I think I can find you a reader that has lots of books." She looked questioningly at Ramon.

"On the way here, we drove by where we camped that night, remember? I thought I recognized the place, so we stopped. These kids had been on their own for weeks. Their mother died and they'd buried her near the road. We decided to bring them with us."

"I'm glad you did. Are we going to take them back to Florida?"

Greta had a big smile on her face. "No need. Hector and I will take care of them. I wish our cottage was ready to live in."

"You and Hector and the kids can stay in Doug's place until it's ready. I'm sure Rob won't mind. Bring the kids up when they've finished eating."

A large man rose from the table and extended his hand. "Ms. Hardman?

"Just call me Rosa." She shook his hand. "I don't intend to take the Hardman name."

"I don't much blame you, although Rob is an honorable person. I'm Andreu."

"Oh! I'm so happy to meet you."

"I can take you and Wannis' children up to the house. I'm done eating."

On the way, she said, "Andreu, I know you've had a long trip. Why don't you take one of the guest rooms and get some rest. Take a shower, make yourself at home."

"Thank you. I will."

Edwina asked, "Why are those children so dirty?"

"Because they have no mother or father to take care of them."

"Really? Why?"

"I don't know what happened to their father, but their mother died."

"Why?"

"Maybe she didn't get enough to eat."

"Why?"

"Because she didn't have a home or a job."

"She must have been lazy," Greg said.

"Not necessarily. Lots of people work hard but still don't have enough to eat. See if you have any clothes you don't want any more that would fit those kids."

When Greta arrived with the orphans, they had them bathe. Once they were clean and respectably dressed, Greg said, "You want to play holo games?"

"What's that?" the little boy asked.

Rosa and Greta watched from the doorway. "Part of me wants to stay here," Rosa said. "Those are some bright little minds. I would love to teach them."

"You'll be back once Rob straightens things out in Florida."

"I hope so."

* * *

After Rob had seen the last petitioner, Amaline approached him. "Your father asked to see you."

"What about?"

"I have no idea."

Before he could open the office door, Wannis flew out in tears. Rob asked, "What's wrong?"

"Why don't you ask him?" She shot Rob a hateful look, ran to her room, and slammed the door.

Father was sitting at his desk.

"What's wrong with Wannis?"

"Oh, she'll come around. I was just explaining a few facts of life to her."

"What facts?"

"She's a widow now, with two little ones, and another on the way. She needs a man's protection, someone to help her with the children. Little Greg is Doug's—and my—heir. Wannis needs someone to run his business until he comes of age. It wouldn't do if she married outside the family and her son had another man over him."

"What are you getting at?"

"I want you to marry her."

"You what?"

"I need you to marry Wannis and adopt Little Greg to preserve the family line."

"That's preposterous! For one thing, Wannis and I don't like each other, and besides, I'm already married."

"You don't need to like each other. It would be a business arrangement, a very important one." He waved dismissively. "And you think you're married? Some low class girl, not even a Sanctuary marriage. Easy to get annulled. You could still keep your little girlfriend. I'm sure we could find a suitable position for her."

Rob froze with rage and indignation. He balled his fists until they ached.

"Son, I'll restore your inheritance and your money. Here." He took a small bag out of his desk and shook out four rings.

Rob stared at them. Doug's? He picked one up. No, they were his! Stolen from him when he was arrested in Georgia for theft of his father's Backpacker. "Where did you get those?"

"That's not important. What's important is that you can have them back, and all that was once yours."

"Thanks, but no thanks." Blood roaring in his ears, he dropped the ring. He didn't recall leaving his father's office. He found himself back in his room. The Nebula sounded. He jumped. His hands trembled so badly he could barely answer it.

Rosa asked, "Rob, what's wrong?"

He sputtered. "That asshole wants me to marry Wannis."

"What?"

"And adopt Little Greg."

She laughed.

"It's not funny."

"No, it's absurd. Why would he want that?"

"To keep her from marrying outside the family. Someone else raising her children. He's afraid of the family fortune being out of his control."

"But if you married her, you'd have control."

"Except, he thinks he can control me."

"Rob, listen to yourself. You're under his control now."

She was right. He put a hand over his eyes and took several deep breaths. Why did he let his father do this to him? Well, no more. He sat down. "I'm sorry. He caught me off guard. I thought I was prepared for his manipulations, but this took me by surprise." He shook his head. "He said I could keep you as a mistress."

She laughed again. "I guess I need to get there as soon as possible to keep you out of trouble."

He sighed. "Any word from Andreu?"

"They're here. We'll head out in a few hours." She told him about the children Ramon had brought from Georgia. "Do you mind if they stay in Doug's house with Greta and Hector?"

"They're more than welcome." He chuckled. "I keep making decisions on behalf of the family that disowned me." Thinking about those orphans, a warm feeling spread through him. They had made a difference in the lives of three young people, at least.

After talking to Rosa, Rob went to Wannis' suite. "Go away!" she said.

"No, let me talk to you. I'm on your side."

She let him in. "My husband's body is barely cold and that sonofabitch is talking about my remarrying?" She glared at Rob. "To you?"

"He's trying to maintain control of Doug's fortune, now Little Greg's. No offense, but I don't want to marry you any more than you want to marry me."

"As soon as Doug's funeral is over, I'm going back to my family."

"That's a good idea. I'll help you. And I'll help you do whatever you want with Doug's money. I sure don't want it."

"Thanks, Rob." She hesitated, then hugged him. "I'm sorry I was rude to you."

He grinned. "When have you ever treated me any different?"

CHAPTER 33

Rosa had qualms about starting out so late and traveling at night, but Andreu expressed confidence, and she was anxious to get to Rob. Her misgivings turned out right. Before nightfall, they came to a destroyed bridge.

"It wasn't like this yesterday," Ramon said. "Let me find a way around it."

The "way around" took them down untested roads and further hazards. When they nearly drove over a cliff in the dark, Andreu said, "Let's park for the night. We'll have to open the windows. It'd take too much battery power to run the cooling."

The night was hot and muggy. Rosa was used to such conditions, but the children weren't. Their whining disturbed her sleep. She took them outside where it was cooler and made a pallet on the ground. Then they complained about mosquitoes. She had decided to take them back inside when she heard a noise that raised her hackles. "Shhh." Something large was creeping on the other side of the Travelor. "Go inside and wake up Uncle Ramon."

She peered into the darkness. Clouds covered the moon, but she could make out several upright shapes. Suddenly, a bright light blinded her.

Ramon, in the doorway, shouted, "What the hell?"

Andreu appeared behind him with a handgun aimed at the light. A shot rang out. Rosa froze.

"Don't try anything," a voice shouted. "Throw down your weapon."

Andreu complied. Now four lights were directed at them. Ramon pulled the green token out of his pocket and held it up. Laughter. "You think that's gonna help you? Everybody get out."

Rosa spoke up. "We have two children in here."

"Get them out, too."

Henry led Little Greg and Edwina out.

The voice said, "Get over to the other side of the road."

They obeyed. Rosa put her arm around the children.

"Kyle, search the vehicle."

Rosa got a good look at Kyle when a beam of light fell on him. *Why, he's only a boy!*

Soon Kyle said, "Nobody else in there."

The leader said, "Search them."

Four approached and patted them down. One found another gun strapped to Andreu's leg. The one who searched Rosa was a girl. *I bet not one of them is over sixteen.*

"What do you want?" Andreu asked.

"Does your vehicle run?"

"When the sun's shinin'."

"Jerome, it's like a little house!" Kyle said.

"Oh, yeah?" Jerome, carrying a shotgun, went in to see for himself. "It sure is. Nicer than any house I ever lived in." He came out and waved his shotgun. "Mark, turn this thing around."

Mark climbed into the driver's seat, started the Travelor, backed up a few feet, and tried to make a U-turn. The RV was too long. He backed it again, pulled forward, backed again. This time one of the rear wheels slid off the pavement. Mark screamed. Rosa cringed. Was the Travelor about to go over the cliff?

Like a cat, Andreu leaped through the doorway, bumped Mark aside, and took control of the vehicle. By some miracle, he coaxed it back onto the road, turned it around, and parked it. As he emerged, he said, "I don't think you boys are man enough to drive this thing."

Jerome fired another shot into the air. "Who you callin' not man enough?"

The children huddled behind Rosa, and the gang behind their leader. Rosa said a quick prayer and stepped forward, heart pounding. Andreu shifted on his feet. Rosa held up a hand toward him and approached the knot of teenagers.

"Rosa!" Ramon yelled.

She held up her index finger, then extended her right hand to the leader. "Jerome, my name is Rosa."

When he didn't shake her hand, she lowered hers and forced herself to keep her voice steady. "Can I talk to you privately? There's something I don't want the kids to hear."

"Yeah, but don't try anything."

"I won't. You have the advantage."

Jerome tossed the shotgun to one of his compatriots and stepped aside with Rosa. She whispered, "What I don't want the kids to hear is, their father died the other day, and they don't know it yet. We're trying to take them home to their mother in Florida. My brother and I came up from there last month. We walked most of the way. I won't bore you with the whole story. I just want you to know what our needs are. I'm sure you have needs, too, and that's why you're doing this. Do you want to talk about them?"

Jerome hesitated. "That's the biggest cockamamie story I ever heard. You kids, where's your daddy?"

Little Greg's voice trembled. "In the hospital. In Florida."

"Why"

"I don't know. He got sick. Mama and Uncle Robbie took him to the hospital. Aunt Rosa's taking us to Mama."

Rosa heard a stomach rumble. It wasn't hers. "Jerome, when's the last time you and your friends had anything to eat?"

Jerome didn't answer.

"We have food. How about if I cook you something?"

Kyle said, "I'm hungry."

"Don't bother," said Jerome. "We'll just take the food."

"Yes, you could," Rosa said. "But I bet I'm a better cook than you are."

The boys didn't respond. Rosa drew a steadying breath. "Andreu, do we have enough battery power to cook?"

"Probably not. We can build a fire."

"Okay. I'll see what I can cook over a fire." She turned her back on Jerome and went into the Travelor.

He followed. "Don't try anything stupid." He pointed one of Andreu's guns at her.

"I won't." She rummaged through the cupboards and fridge. She pulled a pot out of a cabinet and dropped it. The lid clattered across the floor. When she bent down for it, she dropped it again. Standing up, she looked at her hands. They were shaking.

Jerome's frown deepened. "What's wrong with you?"

Rosa closed her fists and dropped them to her sides. "Nothing's wrong with me. I'm just not used to people threatening me with guns. I'm scared, okay?"

"I'm sorry," Jerome said. Then he deepened his voice. "You should be scared. We're gonna kill you after you fix us somethin' ta eat."

Rosa didn't know whether to cry or laugh. Finally, she said, "No, I don't think you will."

Jerome said nothing.

She put together a large pot of soup from canned goods. "Will you carry this out for me? I don't want to spill it."

He pocketed the gun and picked up the pot. The men had a fire going and were sitting around talking to the youth. Everyone had laid down their weapons but kept them within reach. Henry had his arms around the Hardman children. Andreu nodded at the teenage girl. "Tell Rosa what you just told me."

The girl, almost in tears, said, "My parents kicked me out. They said they couldn't feed everybody and I could make a living on my own. You know….what I mean." She wiped her nose. "I tried it, but I didn't like it. Some of the men wouldn't even pay me. One beat me."

Rosa put an arm around her. The girl curled against her and sobbed like a baby. Rosa thought, there but for the grace of God go I. She looked at Andreu. "What can we do for these kids?"

"I don't know." Andreu looked around at their faces, lit by the fire. "Do any of you have friends or family you could go to? Work's scarce, especially if you have no skills. But roamin' the country holdin' people up is gonna get you killed."

Kyle said, "My grandpa lives near Athens. He might let me stay there." He looked at his feet. "That is, if you don't tell him about this."

"I won't tell him."

Rosa went into the Travelor for dishes and bread and took the Hardman children with her. "Are you okay?"

Little Greg nodded but Edwina appeared petrified.

"Everything's going to be all right. I promise. Why don't you stay in here and I'll bring you some soup."

They nodded.

Andreu was talking with the teenagers about their families.

Rosa stirred the soup. "It'll be ready in a few minutes."

"After we eat, we'll all get a little sleep," Andreu said. "In the morning, we'll give you kids rides to somewhere safe. One condition, though, give me your firearms. You don't need them, and they almost got you killed."

"Who was going to kill us?" Jerome sneered. "You?"

Andreu reached into his pants and pulled out another handgun. "I could have, 'cept I didn't want to make a mess that'd take me half the night to clean up." The boys blanched. Andreu grinned. "Besides, I'm not in the business of shooting kids." He replaced his weapon and held out his hands. The younger teens readily surrendered theirs. Jerome hesitated.

Andreu spoke softly. "You can't fight all of us, Jerome. Give them to me. I won't hurt you."

"Oh, Sanctuary!" Jerome threw down his guns and stalked off.

"By the way," Andreu said, loud enough for Jerome to hear. "You might think shootin' in the air shows how tough you are, but you wouldn't be so tough if that bullet came down on your head."

One of the boys said, "Could that kill you?"

"Absolutely."

Rosa dished up soup and the men passed it out. She took two bowls to the Hardmans, but she was too nervous to eat. The hungry teens finished the pot of soup and two loaves of bread. *I hope we can find a store tomorrow.* When she took the empty pot inside, the children were asleep at the table. She put them to bed.

Outside, someone was stacking dirty bowls. Andreu said, "I'll get some blankets for you. The girl can sleep inside with Rosa." He brought the dishes in and put a hand on Rosa's shoulder. "That was a brave thing you did earlier. Or foolish."

"I've never been more frightened in my life! But I know those kids —their type, I mean. I did my student teaching in a rough school. I had to learn to deal with them. They're mostly scared."

"True, but fear can make people violent. Especially youngsters with little self-control. Still, you made the right call. We weren't gonna stop them by force. Somebody would've gotten hurt. I'll sleep with one eye open, anyway." He stashed the firearms in a locked cabinet.

Before she fell asleep, Rosa thought about Rob, how her brother and Jem had carjacked him, threatening him with his own gun after he'd tried, unsuccessfully, to defend himself. Rob must have been as frightened as she was tonight.

Once she'd asked Ramon how scared he'd been when Rob held the gun on him. "I 'bout wet my pants," he'd confessed. "But I was desperate enough to take almost any risk. And I could tell Rob was a wuss." After a moment's thought, he added, "I didn't plan to steal the car, only borrow it to get to Georgia. Then he had to pull that gun on me …"

Both of the men in her life had come a long way since then. Especially Rob.

While Rosa served a light breakfast, Ramon plotted a route to Athens. Before the day heated up, they passed an elderly couple in a field, bent over their crop. "Let's stop," Rosa said. "I want to talk to those people."

When the Travelor pulled into their driveway, the couple stood up, each hefting a stick. They relaxed when they saw Rosa.

"What are you picking," she asked.

"Black-eyed peas."

"Do you need any help?"

"What do you mean?"

"We picked up a handful of homeless youth. Would you be interested in taking one in? He could work for you for room and board."

"Maybe." They followed Rosa to the Travelor.

"Kyle here has a grandfather. We're taking him there, but these other kids have nobody. I don't know what kind of workers they are, but if you're willing to take a chance…"

One of the boys said, "I'll stay, if they let me. I don't mind pickin' beans."

"What's your name, son?" the man asked.

"John."

The couple looked at one another. The woman wiped her eyes. "We had a son once, named John. He died."

John lowered his eyes and kicked the dirt. "I'm sorry."

The man studied him. "We'll take him."

On the road again, Rosa said, "I'm surprised at the number of people who have no money, yet are able to keep their homes."

"Low property taxes," Ramon said. "Unless it's land some pudiente wants, then they jack it up."

Andreu nodded. "The pudientes don't like to pay taxes. The municipal and county governments are starved for money. That's one reason they can't provide services for their people like they once did."

"I'll have to read up on that," Rosa said. She looked at the Nebula. "Ah, I have a signal!" She called Rob. "We had to stop for the night. There are more bridges out and Andreu thought it was too hazardous to drive, so we won't be there until later today. How are things?"

"Mother is doing better under Betsy's care. As for my father..." he chuckled. "I'd forgotten it was Sunday. When I went down for breakfast, I heard a bunch of racket coming from the holo room. Father was watching a church service and had the volume as high as it would go. I turned it down and he didn't seem to notice. Mother asked if I was going to the service today. I told her, 'Hell no!' Only I didn't say 'hell.' She said she guessed she wouldn't, either. Father used to make everybody attend, but I'll be surprised if anyone goes today. Steven asked if he and his grandparents could go to their church and I told him he didn't need to ask me, that was his business."

"I used to like going to Mass with my family. Maybe next Sunday, I'll go to their church, if it's still there."

"Are you going to insist I go to church, too?"

"Of course not."

"Good. I was disillusioned by religion a long time ago."

"By religion, or by your father's religion?"

"Good point."

* * *

Although it was Sunday, Rob was busy with petitioners. In between, he checked on family holdings. He wasn't surprised that few managers were observing the Sabbath. They're desperate, he thought. They need work and are gambling on getting paid. He told one, "I appreciate your dedication."

"If we don't keep things running, society will collapse completely," she said. "Besides, I have employees to look out for. Paying jobs are hard to come by."

At lunchtime, he expected his father to enter the dining room dressed to the nines for a formal dinner, but he didn't appear. Mid-afternoon, when he inquired about him, Father was still in the holo room.

Rob found him watching a recorded Third Covenant service. "Have you eaten?"

Hs father turned to him with glazed eyes. "I'm nourished by the Holy Spirit."

Rob shook his head and left. Later, he mentioned it to Betsy.

She looked concerned. "I'll check on him."

Soon after, Rosa called. "We're finally in Florida. We have a pas-senger, a seventeen year old juvenile delinquent named Jerome. We couldn't leave him to his own devices, so I told him we'd help him find work. I'll give you the full story when I see you."

"Okay." *Juvenile delinquent? What was the full story?* Surely Rosa wouldn't bring anyone dangerous with her, and certainly Andreu wouldn't.

CHAPTER 34

Rosa switched seats with Jerome, who had sat by Andreu much of the trip. They turned off the road at a fancy gate in a ten foot high fence. "Is this the place?"

"Yes, ma'am." A sentry opened the gate. Andreu drove down a tree-lined lane between orchards and vegetable fields. Rosa looked for the house, but all she saw ahead was a high stone wall. They approached a more impressive gate which opened for them. A security guard waved as they drove through. Among the trees sat a mansion larger than her friend Salli's. "Is that the house?"

Andreu nodded. "I was going to drive around back, but we can go to the front door if you want to get a good look at it."

"I guess I better," Rosa breathed. "I need to see what I married into." Andreu pulled around the front circle and stopped before the massive façade. Rosa got out and stood silently. Ramon joined her. "Ramon! Why didn't you warn me?"

"About what?"

"How…big this place is!"

"I didn't think it was important."

The front door opened and Rob rushed out.

She ran into his arms in tears.

"I thought you'd be glad to see me."

"I am, silly. But," she pulled back. "What's all this?"

"It isn't me. Come meet my mother." He led her through a foyer as large as her parents' house, up a curving staircase, and down a long hallway, where he knocked on a door.

"Come in."

A lady with the same hazel eyes as Rob laid down her book and rose to greet them.

"Mother, this is my wife, Rosa."

Rhea shook Rosa's offered hand, then hugged her. "You have made my boy so happy."

"He's made me happy, too."

After a short visit, Rob led Rosa to another door. "This is my room."

Rosa looked around at the comfortable sitting room and through the open door into the bedroom. Then she plopped onto the couch. "I don't know what to think."

He sat beside her and took her in his arms. "Don't think. I'm so glad you're here. Tell me about your adventures."

Before she could, Ramon entered without knocking, carrying a suitcase. "Oh, I'm sorry."

"It's okay," Rob said. "We're going to have to figure out sleeping arrangements."

To Rosa, Ramon said, "Where do you want your books?"

"Books?" Rob said.

"Just set them down." She turned to Rob. "You remember where we camped when you lost the Backpacker? And I couldn't take my books with me and had to leave most of them? Since we were in the neighborhood, I asked Andreu to drive by so I could get them. Thankfully, they were still there, and in good condition."

"So that's why it took you so long to get here. I was worried."

"That's not all."

Ramon said, "Jerome needs to talk to you."

"Jerome?" Rob asked.

"The teenage boy I told you about," Rosa said. "Come on, I'll explain."

Ramon led the way. Rosa told Rob about being held up by Jerome's gang.

He stopped and grabbed her shoulders. "Rosa! That's why I wanted you to stay in Summer Valley where you'd be safe."

"Look, nothing bad happened. I'm safe. Would you rather we be apart?"

"No, but...What about the other kids?"

"We found homes for them. We stopped at a church that was holding a service, and families took two of them. But nobody wanted Jerome's attitude, and he didn't want a family." They entered the dining room. Rosa's eyes got big, "How many people can you feed here?"

"About two dozen." Rob chuckled. "This is where I've been holding court."

Jerome was eating with Henry and Andreu. Rosa introduced him to Rob.

The boy looked up. Between mouthfuls, he said, "You own this place?"

"No. My family does. I'm managing it." Rob greeted Andreu and Henry and sat down facing Jerome. "So, what education and skills do you have?"

Jerome admitted to what he'd told Rosa: little formal education, living on the streets since he was fourteen. He didn't embellish or brag.

"Okay, no education, only survival skills. And thievery."

Jerome lowered his head. "Only so I could eat."

"I know. I've been there myself."

Jerome looked up. "Really?"

"Really. I'll tell you about it sometime. Can you do manual work? Lift and load things?"

Jerome nodded.

"Good. Now I just need to find you a place to sleep. You can eat here with everyone else."

Andreu said, "We did a lot of talking today. I'll take him under my wing."

"Thank you, Andreu. Any way I can persuade you to stay on and work for me? I need an advisor."

Andreu smiled. "I'll be happy to."

Rosa had been eyeing the sideboard. Not as many fresh vegetables as they'd had in Summer Valley, but there was an array of choices. All down to earth, nothing exotic.

Rob said, "I'm sorry. You must be hungry."

She filled her plate and sat at the table beside Rob. While she ate, she gazed about the room. Giorgio's cottage on the Stubens' estate could almost fit inside. And the paintings! The dining room could be an art gallery. Portraits of important-looking men reminded her of the foyer of the administration building at college. "Who are all those guys?"

"They're my illustrious ancestors. He pointed to the first one. "That's Gregory Edward Hardman, the founder of the dynasty. He emigrated from Homerville, Georgia in the 1920's and bought land on the Suwannee River, pennies per acre. I don't know why he was considered the founder of the family. I'm sure there were Hardmans before him." He laughed. "Probably scalawags."

Rosa nodded. Robber barons had acquired much of Florida's prime land in those early days, for next to nothing.

"His land had several springs, which eventually made the Hardmans wealthy, but not in his day. He ran a cattle ranch and raised tobacco. His wife gave birth to eight daughters before she had a boy. Junior is the next painting. He built a mansion on the estate. His son, Gregory Michael, tapped the springs and started a bottled water business."

Rosa shook her head. "Yeah, guys like that convinced the public that tap water wasn't fit to drink, so they made money draining the Floridan Aquifer."

"Uh huh. Next is Allen Michael, and that's where the male line died out, because he had only daughters. But his oldest, Sophia Michaela, married a man whose last name was Hardman."

"Any relation?"

"Not that we know of, but she inherited everything since she carried on the name."

"She's the only woman there."

"Yes, but her husband was the brains of the family. He's not pictured, but he patented the Hardman Process, and they started building desalination plants."

"You know, a dynasty seldom lasts beyond the fourth generation. I'd wondered why yours did. It's because of the fresh blood, or fresh brains, in this case. But your family sure didn't have much imagination when it came to naming children."

"I know."

"This was when? Twenty-first century?"

Rob nodded.

Rosa continued, "Those desalinization plants saved Florida from becoming a failed state. By then, potable water was scarce. The springs had dried up and the aquafer was mostly brackish. The tourist industry and agriculture wouldn't have survived without water."

"I know."

"Don't get a big head over it. You Hardmans didn't sell your water cheap. My family had to be very frugal. We used mostly reclaimed rainwater."

"Well, I'm making up for it now. I've been giving it away."

"That's no way to run a business."

"I know. We'll negotiate a fair price once everything settles down."

"How did you get here from Suwannee County?"

"Father sold his share of the estate to his sister. He didn't want to be a 'gentleman farmer.' Then he bought this land and built this fortress."

"He doesn't consider himself a gentleman farmer? It looks like a farm to me."

"That's because Father's paranoid. He doesn't trust other people's food, so he raises all his meat and most of his produce, even some grains. He seldom eats in restaurants, even the best ones."

"Why is his the last oil painting? The others are only photographs."

"They'll be replaced by canvas when the subject ascends the throne. I don't know what they'll do about Doug's, since he won't ascend the throne. Maybe there won't be a throne after this, who knows?"

"No picture of you." Rosa saw only an outline on the wall where a photo once hung.

"Don't forget, I'm no longer a member of the family. Also, my little sister, Michaela is missing. The one who died. When I was a kid, I asked where her picture was. Father said her death had been too traumatic for Mother to handle, so her pictures were removed. All of them." Rob snorted. "Traumatic? I think it was guilt. His."

A handsome middle age woman came in. "I heard you were here." She extended her hand to Rosa. "I'm Amaline."

"Pleased to meet you."

When Rosa finished eating, they returned to his suite.

Now that the newness of Hardman Hall had somewhat worn off, Rosa began to notice things. As she passed a side table, she swiped her forefinger across the top. It left a clean line in the dust. "The household staff has left?"

"Most of them. How'd you know?"

She showed him her dusty finger.

"Oh."

Dust bunnies had collected on the floor where it met the wall. Salli's house had always been pristine. "I guess you all aren't used to cleaning up after yourselves."

"No."

"Do you know that in other countries people have robots that clean houses?"

"Really?"

Rob's suite was no cleaner. He carried her backpack into the bedroom. The bed had not been made. He said, "I've been letting Ramon and Ned sleep here and on the sofa. I've been sleeping in my dressing room. I can put them in a guest room if you like."

Rosa surveyed the suite. The bedroom had a private bath. The dressing room was spacious enough to be a bedroom. "Why do you have a bed in your dressing room?"

"It was for Leonard, my valet."

"Valet?" She smirked. "He didn't have his own room?"

"He went home on his days off."

Rosa shook her head. "Let Ramon and Ned stay here, but we should have the bedroom. Are all those clothes yours?"

"Yes. I've been letting the guys have what they can use, and I've given some away."

Rosa put her fists on her hips. "If I'm going to stay in this apartment, I'll clean it, but not the whole house. If you're not going to hire help, everyone who stays here should do their part."

"Yes, ma'am."

"Where are the children?"

"With their mother, I assume."

"I wonder what she told them about their father."

"Let's go see."

Rob didn't need to tell her which door was Wannis'. Rosa could hear weeping from down the hallway. Wannis was doing all the crying. Little Greg was trying to console her, and Edwina stood by tearless, ashen-faced.

Rob said, "Rosa, Why don't you take the kids out? I'll do what I can here."

"Okay. Have you kids eaten?"

"No, ma'am," Greg said.

"Then let's go down to the dining room."

On their way, the face she'd seen in the last oil painting climbed the stairs toward them.

"Mr. Hardman?" Rosa offered her hand. "I'm Rosa."

"The new nanny?"

"No." Her face flamed. "Rob's wife."

Gregory Hardman gave no further acknowledgement, only passed by without even speaking to his grandchildren.

The children stared after him. "That was rude," Little Greg said.

Rosa attempted a smile. "He's just upset."

"Humph. He's always upset."

The dining room was empty. Rosa let the children choose what they wanted to eat and sat down with them. Grief didn't seem to have affected Little Greg's appetite, but Edwina just pushed food around her plate.

"Aren't you hungry?"

Edwina started to cry. Rosa took her on her lap and held her until Edwina put on a brave face and said, "I guess I better eat. In case I can't someday."

"What do you mean?"

"I don't have a daddy anymore. If something happens to Mama, who will take care of us?"

"What makes you think something will happen to your mama?"

"Those kids Uncle Ramon brought to Aunt Greta. Their mama died and nobody took care of them. They were dirty and had no clothes or food."

"Oh, Edwina!" Rosa hugged her. "First of all, your mother's going to be fine. And even if anything did happen to her, you have lots of people who would take care of you."

"Like you and Uncle Rob?"

"Why, yes. And your grandparents."

Her brother said, "Grandmother can't. She's sick. And Grandfather doesn't like us."

Rosa looked at him. Part of her wanted to reassure him otherwise, but she knew he spoke the truth. "Have you seen your grandmother since you got home?"

He shook his head.

"Finish eating, then we'll go see her."

When they entered her suite, Rhea scooped the children into her arms. "Oh, Greggie, Edwina, I'm so glad to see you. I've missed you so."

"We missed you, too," said Edwina.

When she let them go, Little Greg stood back and scrutinized her.

Rhea said, "Betsy and I were going out for a walk. Do you want to come with us?"

They did.

Rosa accompanied them. They walked out into the park in front of the house. In the middle of the circular drive, a fountain tinkled. The plaintive song of a mourning dove drifted through the air. It's beautiful here, Rosa thought.

It was growing dark under the trees. A mosquito whined in her ear.

"My goodness," said Rhea. "It wouldn't do for your mother to see you all covered with bites. Let's go out back. There aren't so many bugs." She whispered, "The bats eat them."

Rosa hadn't seen that side of the house yet. There were fewer trees. Across the lawn was a pool enclosure, with bat houses on poles. Beyond was a tennis court and a children's playground. The car park was hidden behind a tall hedge. Rhea paused and looked down at the grass. With a deep sigh, she grasped her grandchildren's hands and moved on.

Rosa studied her mother-in-law. Although the woman didn't act entirely normal, this was not the hopeless invalid she'd heard about.

Little Greg said, "Did Mama tell you about my daddy?"

Rhea audibly swallowed a sob. "Yes, she did."

Edwina buried her face in her grandmother's side and cried. Rhea knelt down to embrace her and held out an arm for Greg.

Rosa and Betsy dropped back to give them privacy. Rosa said, "Rob told me Ms. Hardman was being deliberately drugged."

Betsy frowned. "Yes. And I still worry about her safety. I can't stay here forever—she won't need me much longer. What'll happen after

I leave? Who will protect her? Poor Amaline's been trying to protect her for years, but the stakes are higher now."

"I thought Amaline was administering the drugs."

"She was, under the assumption she was helping, not hurting Ms. Hardman."

"Stakes higher? You sound like Rhea's in danger. Do you think there could be a deliberate attempt on her life?"

"I don't know. Her husband has lost control—of his business, his family, his way of life. Did Rob tell you he wanted him to marry Wannis? To keep Little Greg's business interests under family control?"

Rosa shuddered. "Yes. Bizarre."

"He spent all day in the holo room watching church services, like he was on another planet. How much do you know about the Third Covenant?"

"I was required to attend services when I was in college. I know what they're like."

"Then you can see the danger they pose. They'll do anything to bend 'reality' to suit themselves. And they consider themselves possessed by the 'Holy Spirit,' so they can do no wrong, in their eyes, or in the eyes of their God. I don't know what the man is capable of."

"Is Rob aware of all this?"

"I haven't had a chance to talk to Rob today, not since I checked on his father."

"I need to warn him. And Amaline, too." Rosa hurried ahead to tell Rhea she was going inside. As she approached, she overheard their conversation.

Little Greg said, "Grandmother, my real name is Douglas, isn't it? Like my father's?"

"Yes. You are Douglas Gregory Hardman IV."

"My grandfather's name is Greg?"

"That's his middle name. He's called Greg so no one would confuse him with his father, whose name was Douglas."

"That's why they call me Greg? So no one would confuse me with my daddy?"

"That's right."

"Well, I don't want to be Greg anymore. My daddy's dead, so now I want his name. I want to be Douglas."

"So you shall be. From now on, I'll call you Little Doug."

"I'm not little anymore. Just call me Douglas."

CHAPTER 35

Rob checked the coffee pot. Empty. He was tempted to brew more, but no one else would drink it this late. He collapsed into his chair. Ned and Ramon, sitting across from him, looked at one another. He knew what was coming.

Ramon said, "Man, you need to get some rest. You've been at it all day. You're only human."

"But there's so much to do."

"Well," said Ned, "you have to accept the fact that you can't do it all."

"You're right." Rob pushed his coffee cup away.

"Go to bed early," Ramon said.

With a devilish grin, Ned added, "Go make love to your wife. You've been away from her for what—three whole days?"

Rob slumped. *I hope I have the energy.*

Like a breath of fresh air, Rosa entered the room. "Rob, I need to talk to you."

Ramon and Ned rose as if to leave.

"You guys need to hear this, too." She told them about her conversation with Betsy and added, "I met your dad. Briefly. He thought I was the nanny. When I told him I was your wife, he ignored me. He wasn't just being rude, the man's not right."

Rob frowned. "I know. Betsy has suspicions about Doug's death, too. She looked at the medical records. Dr. Robertson had tests done. Doug did have brain damage, but it wasn't fatal. There are treatments he should have received, but didn't. She said he may never have fully recovered, he may have been like a stroke victim, but he would have lived."

"But he wouldn't be perfect," Ned said.

"No. He wouldn't have been perfect." Rob slammed his fist on the table so hard the coffee cup bounced off. "Not perfect—like Michaela. Father can't abide a child who's less than perfect."

"Did Betsy find any evidence his life was deliberately terminated?" Rosa asked.

"No. No proof." Rob drew in a deep breath and let it out. "What am I going to do about my father?"

"Have him watched," Ned said. "Night and day. And protect your mother."

Ramon asked. "Didn't Amaline cut off his communications?"

"Yes. I need to make sure he doesn't find a way to turn them back on."

Rosa spoke up. "Can you trust Amaline?"

"I hope so. She seems different now that she's not under his thumb." He'd always seen Amaline as cold, unemotional, but now... "She seems fond of Mother."

Ned said, "A woman's going to have feelings for an invalid after taking care of her so many years."

Rob nodded. "I used to think she was waiting for Mother to die so she could marry Father. But that would be beneath him." Rob toyed with a crease in the tablecloth. "My God! If something happened to Mother—would he try to marry Wannis?"

Rosa laughed. "She wouldn't have him."

"You don't know how manipulative he is." He stood up. "Wannis plans to leave after Doug's funeral. Probably the best thing. I'll miss the kids. I'm going to talk to Amaline. Ned, will you get with Alice Frees and organize a twenty-four/seven watch on my father?"

"Sure thing."

Rosa accompanied him to the office where Amaline was working. They told her their fears for Rhea and the plan to have Greg watched around the clock.

Amaline turned pale, then nodded. "I'll get with Betsy. Whenever she needs a break, I'll be with Rhea."

"Thank you," Rob said. "Now I need to get some rest." He and Rosa went to his suite. "Oh, Rosa!" Their arms twined around each other and they kissed. "Let's go into the bedroom."

They locked the door, shed their clothes, and fell onto the unmade bed. To Rob's relief, he had plenty of energy. After they made love, he fell asleep in Rosa's arms.

When he woke, he was alone. "Rosa?" He looked at the time. He'd slept only an hour, but he felt refreshed. He sat up and heard water running. Smiling, he untangled himself from the bedclothes and went into the bathroom.

Rosa shrieked when he opened the shower door, then she made room for him. She had just put shampoo on her hair. Rob massaged it into those dark curls. When she washed him, he found another surge of energy. "I never made love in the shower before," he said.

"First time for everything."

After they dried off, Rob asked, "Should I shave?"

"Why? Your beard is starting to amount to something. Just like you."

"Let's not get dressed just yet."

But before they reached the bed, someone knocked. Rosa wrapped her towel around herself.

Ramon's voice came through the door. "Rob, Amaline needs you."

Rob dashed over and cracked open the door. "What is it? Is something wrong with Mother?"

"No. It's some emergency with the business. You have time to dress."

"Okay." Rob looked around. "I need clean clothes."

By now, Rosa was dressed. "I'll get them for you." When she returned from the dressing room, she said, "We need to make some adjustments to this apartment. By the way, when we're in here with the door locked, what do Ramon and Ned do if they need the bathroom?"

"There's a privy in the servant's lounge next door. That's what Leonard used." He saw the wry look on her face. "I know, it's not very democratic. Things are going to change." He kissed her. "I'll be back as soon as I can."

Amaline was waiting for him. "Rob, are you familiar with Tomoka Estates? The neighbors have pulled together and pretty much organized their own government. They'd had a problem with roving villains, and the stores were looted, so they formed their own police. There've been shortages of food, but water's the biggest problem. It was turned off before the hurricane and not turned back on. Someone with a truck started hauling containers of water from the desalinization plant on the St. Johns Channel."

"Good. That's one of our plants. I wonder why the water wasn't turned back on? But what's the emergency?"

"I don't know the details, but someone poisoned the water."

"What?"

"No one knows who did it or why, or what they used. We don't know if it was someone at the plant or an outside person."

Rob looked toward his father's room. "When did this happen?"

"Recently. There's been sickness, and one death so far."

"What do you want me to do?"

"Go over there. We need to find out what happened and what to do about it. Andreu's coming and I'll go, too. Betsy's with your mother."

Henry was preparing the Backpacker. "Andreu asked me to put some firearms and ammo in the compartments. Just in case."

Are we going to war or something?

Ramon and Ned appeared. "We're ready."

"Wait—who's watching Father?"

Ned said, "Rosa."

"Don't worry," Ramon said. "She can handle him."

Andreu arrived, with Jerome in tow, and they drove out into the night.

* * *

Rosa looked around the room after Rob left. *How can I make this more homey?* The bedside stand was scattered with odds and ends she knew came from Ramon's pockets. She scooped them up and put them on the coffee table in the sitting room. Then she emptied her backpack and took out the cellophane package containing Grandmother's doily. It had traveled with her from Florida to Georgia, North Carolina, and back. She wiped off the night stand and spread the precious doily on top. *There. That's better.*

Next, she decided to make the bed. She found clean sheets in a cupboard in the dressing room. *Silk.* She rubbed her cheek against them. *I could get used to this, but I probably shouldn't.*

Ned knocked tentatively on the half-open bedroom door. "Rosa?"

"Yes. Come in."

"Ramon and I are going with Rob. Will you watch Mr. Hardman until we get back?"

"Sure. Do I need to keep him in his room?"

"No, just keep him away from his wife. And be sure he doesn't communicate with anyone outside the household. If he gets out of hand, ring the bell by the kitchen door. I've alerted security to come running if they hear it. Betsy's with Ms. Hardman."

"Okay." She grabbed one of her books and Rob's Nebula and followed Ned to Greg's room.

Ramon sat on a chair beside the door. "I'll ask Henry to give you a break in about an hour, but I'm not sure he can control the old fart."

"Don't worry, I can handle him. Where are you going?"

"Some self-governing neighborhood," Ramon said. "Someone poisoned the water supply and there's been trouble."

"Is there any danger?"

They looked at each other. "I don't think so. Otherwise, Andreu wouldn't let Amaline go."

Ned said, "It's a peacekeeping errand. We'll be there for Rob."

Rosa nodded. "Be careful."

She sat on the chair, but didn't immediately open her book. *However did I end up here?* She yearned for the mountains and hoped they wouldn't stay here long, but little misgivings stirred inside. They had been married...four days? And they'd been apart three of those days. No honeymoon.

Rosa mulled over her history with Rob. She'd known him three years at college. She'd yearned for him, fantasized about him, had daydreams she never expected—indeed never wished—to come true. Then, at the lowest point in her life, he had dropped out of the blue, stripped of family and fortune, a pauper like herself. *That's when I realized my feelings for him were no silly crush. I loved him.* Those weeks on the road, not knowing what had become of him, leaving notes with no real hope of seeing him again. *And he followed me. Faithfully. Told me he loved me. But he made me so mad! Said he had nothing to offer me. What did he think I wanted?*

She was so proud when Rob stood up to the farmers and pudientes. With promise of employment as a farm laborer, he committed to marriage. That was the Rob she wanted, and life in a humble cottage, a marriage like her parents', full of love and hard work. Then in the middle of the night—their wedding night!—Rob left her side to help the family that had denounced him. And here they were, in this mansion, the last place either of them wanted to be, and once again Rob was gone, this time to the service of strangers. Was that to be their life?

It was hard to believe they were actually married. It happened so quickly. She wasn't usually one to rush into things, but she'd jumped feet first into bed, then matrimony, with Rob. Somehow it felt right.

But not this. *I don't belong here. I'm no lady of the manor.* She remembered when she visited Salli, thinking how she couldn't order servants around. *And I won't.*

Behind the door, her father-in-law was stirring. *But I can order family around if I have to.* She grimaced. *Greg Hardman is not my idea of family.*

When Greg opened the door, he acted surprised to see her. *Does he know he's under surveillance?* Only a brief glance, then he walked down the hall. Rosa followed him to his office. She didn't go inside, only watched him through the window. He sat in his chair, fiddled with things on his desk, took a bag out of a drawer, and emptied it. Rings.

Rosa looked at her Citizenship ring. Could those be Rob's? The sinister reach of this man became obvious. Her backbone turned to a column of ice. *What kind of mess have I landed in?* Poor Rob, to have grown up under the claws of this monster! How did he turn out to be anything close to normal? Rhea must have been a mighty influence on him before she was rendered incapacitated.

Greg looked up. He showed no surprise at Rosa's watching him. He looked directly into her eyes with full confidence and…triumph? Rosa shuddered. *I hope I'm strong enough to resist his manipulations.*

* * *

Rob slept on the way and woke when Andreu turned into Tomoka Estates, a community of modest houses. Despite the late hour, people mobbed the streets, some standing in tight clusters, others marching and shouting. Andreu drove to the town center. In front of the grocery store, a truck was on fire, but no one tried to extinguish the flames. Men and women in yellow vests, whom Rob surmised were police, kept the crowds back.

This must have been a good place to live once, Rob thought. The greenspace was surrounded by a school and several shops. The grocery store was the only building that wasn't lit up.

After Andreu parked the Backpacker, a woman in a yellow vest approached. Andreu held out a green four-leaf clover and said, "Where can we talk?"

She pointed at the school. "We'll escort you. I'll notify the community leaders. One of my men will guard your vehicle."

"Should we be armed?" Rob whispered.

"Do you see anyone with firearms?" Andreu said. "If we show up with guns, that'll make people nervous, then they'll get theirs, and it'll go downhill from there."

Yellow vests surrounded them when they stepped out of the Backpacker. Rob noted they carried heavy staves, but no other weapons. At the school entrance, the policewoman opened the door and led them to a conference room. The other officers stayed outside. She said, "You'll be safe here."

Safe? Rob asked, "What's going on?"

"I'll let the captain fill you in."

They sat around the table. Rob said, "Andreu, they seem to know you."

"No, they only know what I stand for."

"Does your cloverleaf organization have a name?"

"It's not an organization, and names aren't important."

Rob looked at Amaline, but her stony face told him she'd be no more forthcoming.

The policewoman came in with three civilians and another officer who joined them at the table. "I'm Captain Josh Miller."

Rob held out his hand. "Rob Hardman."

The captain hesitated, then shook Rob's hand briefly. "We didn't want to ask you Hardmans for help, but we've exhausted other options."

Rob nodded.

"I don't know how much you know about us…"

"Nothing, really."

"Before the collapse, Tomoka was a comfortable community. We had a neighborhood association to supply services the county didn't offer. Including this school." His eyes bored into Rob's. "Then that hurricane blew everything to hell. You Hardmans shut off our water."

"Didn't it get turned on again afterward?"

"For a while. Then you shut it off again."

"Why?"

"What the hell do you mean—why? A few families couldn't pay their bills, so you shut off the whole community!"

Rob opened his mouth to say it wasn't him, it was Doug, or Father, but he knew that made no difference.

"People have lost their jobs. They can't pay their bills. We begged you to turn the water on, but you ignored us. People've been drinking from their cisterns."

"And FEMA was no help?"

The man leaned forward and stared hard at Rob. "Are you joking? They only bail out the factories, the big guys. Not us ordinary people. *We* pulled together, did what we could to help *ourselve*s. You saw that truck? Belonged to somebody's cousin. They let us use it to haul water. We'd go to the water plant at night and the crew looked the other way. *They* have compassion." He glowered. "Then people started getting sick. One little girl died. That's when we figured out the water was poisoned."

"Are you sure it wasn't from drinking from the cisterns?"

The captain leaned back and crossed his arms. "They boil the cistern water. The Hardman water was poisoned."

"I'm sorry."

"Sorry doesn't help. You see those people out on the streets? They can't take any more. They've turned on each other. Some are starving. They ransacked the store. They torched the truck. It was all my officers could do to keep them from torching everything else."

"What do you want me to do?"

The captain rose to his feet and slammed his hand on the table. "Something besides sit up there in your cozy little mansion, filling your belly!"

"Just a minute!" Ramon sprang to his feet. "That's not what he's been doing. You have no idea what this man has gone through. Rob, show him your hands, your feet..."

Andreu stood and commanded attention. "Gentlemen, airing our sufferings will get us nowhere, but," he nodded at Rob. "Show him your hands and feet."

Rob felt like a fool, but he complied.

Andreu went on. "See those callouses? He's been doing manual labor. His father threw him out with the clothes on his back. He walked halfway to the mountains barefoot because his shoes fell apart and he couldn't afford new ones. He only came back because he was needed here."

One of the civilians asked, "Why are you still barefoot?"

"Well, shoes just don't feel right anymore."

"Captain," Andreu said, "as I see it, you have more than one problem. The people in Tomoka Estates are suffering, *and* you have a possible murder to solve."

Captain Miller nodded.

Amaline spoke up. "I asked Rob to come here because I thought he could help you. Instead, you've done nothing but insult him. Rob's been abused by his father, just like you have. He's on your side."

Captain Miller said, "I'm sorry. I didn't know."

Rob looked at the faces around the table. *Why does this fall on me?* He took a deep breath, and said, "We need to know how much water is contaminated. Is it the water plant or just the water you trucked in? If the water at the plant is safe, I'll have yours turned back on. If it's the whole plant, we've got a bigger problem, and other people might be getting poisoned, too. Amaline, when we get back, we need to turn off that plant until we can test the water."

She nodded. "I'll notify the customers."

"Good. Captain, do you have a sample of the contaminated water?"

"Yes."

"Give it to me and I'll get it tested. How much law enforcement training have you had?"

"Not enough to solve a murder."

"Ned, can you and the captain put your heads together?"

"Yes," Ned turned to the captain. "Was an autopsy done on the child?"

Captain Miller scowled. "No. The parents can't even afford to have her buried."

"Andreu," Ned said, "do you know where we can find a medical examiner? We also need a detective, and a forensics lab."

"I'll put out my feelers."

"Thanks. Captain, we need blood and urine samples from everyone who got sick."

"Urine will be easy" he said. "I'll see if we have a phlebotomist."

"Good," Rob said. "Now, how can we defuse the situation tonight?"

"I'll get everyone in the auditorium and we can explain things to them."

After the captain and his delegation left, Rob folded his arms on the table and buried his face in them. "I'm so tired."

Andreu put a hand on his shoulder. "Once we get things settled here, I'll take you home."

Home. Rosa. He needed her counsel.

* * *

Rosa heard the Nebula. It was Rob. "Is everything okay?"

"Yes. I'll tell you about it when I get home. How are things there?"

She winced at the word "home" and glanced through the window. "Quiet. Your father's watching the news."

"Good. I wish I'd brought you with me. I hope I'm doing the right thing."

"I'm sure you are."

In the background, Andreu said, "They're ready."

"I got to go. I love you."

"I love you."

Greg opened the door, startling Rosa.

"You don't need to stay out here, Ms. Ortiz," he said with a benevolent smile. "Why don't you come in and sit down? I don't bite."

No, neither does a rattlesnake. Yet she entered and took a seat near the door.

"I'm just watching the news. You don't mind, do you?"

"No. Why should I?" *As long as you can't call out.*

"I know I'm under surveillance, but it really isn't necessary."

Rosa laid her book on her lap and opened it.

"I see you are a lover of antiquities."

"You might say that."

"What are you reading?"

"It's a study of the rise of autocracy through the early twenty-first century."

"That's a weighty matter for such a pretty girl."

Rosa's heart pounded. She pretended to study but kept Greg in her line of vision. To her relief, he turned his attention to the screen and ignored her. It was hard to concentrate on her book. Instead, she watched the news.

Disturbing as reports had been in recent days, the newscasters seemed to have abandoned any pretense that the pudientes still maintained control. They gave accounts of security forces turning on their masters, and the reporters themselves appeared to have done the same.

One story described an attack on the compound where Salli lived. Rosa was watching intently when Henry came to relieve her. "Just a minute. I want to hear this." When the segment was finished, she left the office. Henry followed her out. Rosa took a few deep calming breaths. "A friend of mine lives there."

Henry said, "A friend of Mr. Hardman does, too."

They looked through the window. If Greg was disturbed by the news, he didn't show it. Rosa said, "Don't let him leave the office until I get back. I won't be long."

Henry nodded.

Rosa went to their room and sat down. She tried to reach Salli on the Nebula. No response. She left a message. Then she tried to call Rob.

Ramon answered.

"Where's Rob?"

"He's busy giving a speech."

"Oh."

"What's wrong?"

Rosa took a deep breath. "Just the usual. The world's falling apart. When will you guys be back?"

"I think we can leave pretty soon, unless lover boy's words of wisdom backfire on him."

When Rosa returned to the office, Henry was trying to bar Greg's exit.

"I just want to go to bed," Greg said. "It's late."

"It's okay, Henry. I'll take it from here." She followed Greg to his door and sat on the chair outside. It was hard to stay awake.

Rob called. "We're on the way back. Is everything okay?"

"Yes. Your father's in his room, supposedly sleeping. Are you done with your business?" When he paused, her heart sank.

"For the moment. We defused the crisis, but there's more to be done."

When they returned, Ned relieved her. "Ramon, you can take over in about two hours, then Henry can have the next shift. Tell him to wake me if Mr. Hardman comes out of his room."

"I can do a shift, too," said Rob.

"No, we need you to get a good night's sleep."

Rosa took his hand and led him to their room.

He told her about the events of the night and their plan. "I've got my work cut out for me."

"Rob, there's been an attack on Salli's neighborhood, and I'm worried. She didn't answer her phone."

"That's where my friend Morty lives, too. Well, we can't do anything tonight. We'll check on them tomorrow."

They undressed and slipped into bed. Rob didn't seem to notice the clean sheets, but to Rosa, they felt almost as nice as Rob's body next to hers. "Rob, are we ever going to get away from this place?"

"I hope so." He put his arms around her and drew her closer to him. Then they both fell asleep.

CHAPTER 36

Rob thought he was dreaming, lying on silk sheets on a bed as soft as the one in his room at Hardman Hall, a beautiful girl curled up beside him. A sliver of bright light edged through the blinds and into his eyes. "Command: blinds open." The room was bathed in sunshine. He turned his head. Not a dream. Rosa was really there. *How can I be so lucky?* Actually, he'd prefer to be in a mountain cottage between cotton sheets, but wherever Rosa was, that's where he wanted to be.

She stirred, turned toward him, and shielded her eyes. "My goodness, we really slept late!"

"We were up late. Did we lock the door?"

"I don't remember."

"Command: door lock." He heard a click. "It is now. Let's see how long they'll leave us alone."

When they left the suite, Rob saw Leonard sitting on the chair by Father's door. "I wonder what he's doing here."

"Who is he?"

"My old valet. Let me introduce you."

Leonard stood up. "Good morning, Mr. Rob. This must be your new bride?"

"Yes, this is Rosa."

He almost bowed. "Ms. Rosa."

"Leonard, you don't need to address us as Mr. and Ms. Use our first names, please. Why are you here?"

"I need a job, and Amaline asked me to watch Mr. Hardman until I talked to you."

"Okay. I'll get with you after breakfast."

As they walked down the hall, Rosa smirked. "Valet?"

"I feel obligated to help him if I can. Let's stop and say hello to Mother."

As they reached her door, Betsy opened it. "We're going for a walk. Care to join us?"

"Not now. Things to do." He hugged his mother. "You look good today."

"I feel good, too." She hugged Rosa.

Betsy smiled. "She's recovering beautifully."

In the dining room, a curly-haired girl was cleaning up. With a honeyed voice, she said, "Good morning, Mr. Rob. We shore did miss you."

Rob felt his face turn beet red. "Good morning, Cisli. This is my wife, Rosa."

"Pleased to meet you, Ms. Rosa."

"Cisli, we're dispensing with the Mr. and Ms. Call us by our first names. What are you doing here?"

"Ms. Amaline said you might hire me. I need a job."

"Let me have breakfast, then I'll talk to Amaline."

His appetite had been dampened. He looked at Rosa. *Should I tell her?*

Rosa settled his dilemma. "One of your old servants?"

"Yes." He avoided her eyes.

"What kind of *service* did she perform?"

He mumbled, "Kitchen girl."

"I see."

Rob changed the subject. "I don't know why everyone's looking to me for decisions. I have no authority."

"Who does?"

"If Mother recovers sufficiently, she does. I guess that's something I need to settle before we go back to the mountains."

"When are we going?"

"As soon as possible."

"I'd like to find Salli and Morty first."

As if in answer, the Nebula sounded. It was Salli. She wore no make-up and her hair was in disarray. "Rosa, you're alive! I'm sorry I didn't answer you last night. I thought it was Rob Hardman."

"It's his Nebula. We're married now. What about you? I heard your compound was attacked."

"Rosa, it's awful. They robbed us blind. They took all our food. They even took my clothes! Daddy shot one of them. He didn't kill him, but the others beat Daddy up. The hospital took the robber, but they wouldn't take Daddy!"

"How bad is he hurt?"

"He's got a black eye and a broken nose. And he's so distraught. He just sits in his room all the time and cries. All our servants have left. I don't know what we're going to do."

Rosa shook her head. "I wish I could help you, but we have our hands full, too."

"I understand." She wrinkled her nose. "You really married Rob?"

"Yes. And we're very happy. What about your fiancé?"

"We broke up."

Rob leaned in where Salli could see him. "Do you know anything about the Coopers? Are they okay?"

"They got attacked, too. Everybody did. Morty and his mother and sister are okay, but some guys took his father off and we don't know what happened to him. Daddy said when all this is over, some people are going to regret it. Big time!"

Rosa said, "We've got to go. Keep in touch with me, all right?"

"I will."

Rob said, "Do you want me to ask Betsy to go see about Salli's father?"

"No. He got what he had coming."

"Same with Morty's father, if what Ned said is true." And he believed Ned.

Rosa frowned. "I feel sorry for Salli. But she still has a house to live in. And all her money, I'm sure. More than most people have."

Rob thought about his other friends. How many of them were in danger? But what could he do to help them? Whatever may have befallen, they were no worse off than the many poor people who had been suffering for years. "This lawlessness concerns me," he said. "But I have no idea what to do about it."

Rosa said, "The pudientes brought it on themselves. And on the rest of us. At one time, every city and county had their own police force and people were treated equally, in theory, at least. When they privatized law enforcement, they set us up for disaster."

Rob thought about the businesses which had once been his inheritance. "Rosa, I need to check on the Dongtian Palace and Olustee Academy. I feel responsible for those employees."

They carried their dirty dishes into the kitchen. "Set them down," Cisli said. "I'll take care of them."

"Thank you, Cisli," Rosa said.

Cisli smiled at Rob.

He hurried from the room. "I need to let Wannis and Little Greg know about that water plant."

Rosa said, "Little Greg wants to be called Douglas now."

"Oh."

They went to Wannis' suite. After Rob briefed her, Wannis threw up her hands and told him to do whatever he thought best.

Douglas said, "Uncle Robbie, I know I'm too young run things, but I want to learn my father's business."

"Sure. Come with me."

Amaline was in the office. "Andreu located a doctor who can do autopsies. Ned and Captain Miller are taking the child's body there. They also hired a detective. I hope you don't mind—I sent a truckload of food to Tomoka Estates. But, Rob, we can't hand out food forever. We're going to run out. This is a systemic problem. We need to fix the system."

"How?"

Rosa said, "Is anybody in charge out there, or has civilization totally collapsed?"

"Civilization is hanging by a thread," Amaline said. "But all is not lost. Not yet."

"The Cloverleafs," Rob said.

Douglas looked puzzled, "The what?"

Rob glanced at Amaline. "I don't know who they are or what they're doing. They're either bringing civilization down or trying to save it."

"They're trying to save it," Amaline said. "That's all I can tell you."

"Let's show Lit—um, Douglas what's happening with his desalination plants."

"Excuse me," the boy said, "aren't they still Grandfather's plants?"

"Technically, yes," said Rob. "But he's been relieved of his duties. He shut down a lot of the plants for no good reason. We got most of them up and running but we've been giving away the water, not charging anyone."

"Why?"

Rosa said, "Because people don't have money right now. After air and shelter, water is the most necessary thing to stay alive. If they can't get clean water, a lot of them will get sick and die. And the ones who live will riot, maybe destroy the plants, and more people will get hurt."

Amaline said, "Once things get straightened out, we'll start charging again. You won't end up poor."

"I know. I have plenty of money."

Rob looked at Douglas. *Is he really his father's son?*

Amaline continued, "It's good business to care about your customers. If you treat them fairly, you benefit in the long run."

Douglas nodded.

Rob pulled a small jar of water out of his pocket. "This is from last night. How can I get it tested? I wish I'd paid more attention to that side of the business, but I thought it didn't pertain to me."

Amaline took the jar. "I'll have Henry take it over to the Orange Park plant. Their chemist is still working."

"Good. Have Henry go by the St. Johns plant and get a sample of their water, too. Now, if the poisoned waterhole mystery is being handled...Leonard and Cisli are looking for work?"

"Yes," said Amaline. "I don't know what Leonard is qualified for, besides his old position which I don't see a need for now, but he's faithful and trustworthy."

"I agree. We can train him for something. Is he capable of watching Father?"

She nodded. "You underestimate him."

"What about Cisli? I don't think the cook needs help."

"Not if we're able to do a few thing for ourselves." She turned to Rosa. "I agree with you that we all should do our share of housekeeping, but this is a big house."

Rosa nodded. "I know. Why don't we hire Cisli, and maybe someone else, to clean the rest of the house? But paying them—how stable is the financial system?"

Amaline pursed her lips. "Teetering on the brink, but it hasn't toppled yet. I've told everyone we'll pay them by electronic deposit, but we can't guarantee anything. They'd prefer cash, but there just isn't enough available."

Rob shrugged. "We'll do what we can. Meanwhile, I need to tend to a few things." He called the resort.

Angus Wilson said he had it under control. "But we're in survival mode. Repairs stopped after you left. Your father wouldn't send us the materials we needed. In fact, he ignored us. I confess, I've been letting homeless people stay here. Rob, even if we had the place ready by November, I doubt we'd have many customers."

"I know. I'll come out and see you in a few days."

He was unable to reach Olustee Academy. He said to Amaline, "If there's nothing pressing right now, I'll drive out there and check on them."

Rosa, said, "I'll go with you."

Douglas said, "I'll stay with Ms. Amaline so she can show me the ropes."

"Let's take Ramon," Rosa said. "We can swing by Jem's farm for my parents' car."

Ramon was sitting by Father's door. "Where's Leonard?"

"Bathroom break. He'll be back in a minute."

They told him their plans. Rob remembered the last time he went to Olustee without Andreu. "Do you think we should take protection?"

Ramon cocked his head. "Are your self-defense skills any better than they used to be?"

"Not really."

"We're better off unarmed. It'd be too easy for a bad guy to turn our weapons against us."

Rob blushed. "Yeah."

Rosa spoke up. "Don't even think about leaving me here. I've been through thick and thin with you guys."

The men looked at each other. Ramon said, "She's right."

On the way to Olustee, Rosa and Ramon discussed what to do about their parents' and grandmother's ashes.

Rob said, "You can put them in the mausoleum until you decide."

"It would be nice to bury them with Grandfather," Rosa said. "And we should have a funeral."

Ramon said, "I'll call Father Felix, if I can reach him, and when I get a chance, I'll go pick them up."

Rob said, "I don't suppose your house was insured."

"Probably not."

"The lot should be worth something. We'll see what can be done about it."

Ramon said, "They impounded my scooter when I got arrested. I'd like to get it back if I can." He was silent for several minutes. "There's something else I need to settle. That bitch who got me arrested. I need to deal with her and her asshole father."

Rosa frowned at him. "Are they really worth it?"

Rob said, "I think Ramon wants closure." He looked at Ramon. "But violence isn't the answer."

"I know."

Rob reached over and took Rosa's hand. *What would I do in a situation like that? It's not just that she spurned him. She nearly got him killed.*

* * *

Olustee Academy reminded Rosa of her primary school, only better maintained. No one answered the front door, so they went around back. Many classrooms were empty. In one was a woman with a handful of children. She looked up at them with a puzzled expression.

Rob said, "Ms. Marshall?"

She stood up. "Mr. Rob? I hardly recognized you."

"Don't call me Mr. Just Rob. I tried calling, but no one answered."

"Sorry. I saw it was a Hardman calling. Ever since your father fired me, no one from your family has come here to check on us, or even tried to get in touch. Since I had nowhere to go, I stayed to help the other teachers. When they stopped getting paid, they left to look for other jobs. I couldn't blame them." She gestured at the room. "As you can see, most of the students are gone, too. We few have been doing our own thing."

"How are you supporting yourself?"

"The parents help me all they can. By the way, what happened to you?"

"My father disowned me, put me out with the clothes on my back. Then my brother died. I came back and found my father stripped of power, and I've been putting out fires ever since."

Rosa scanned the classroom. "Rob, why don't you put this school back in operation? I'll help you."

"Ms. Marshall, meet my wife, Rosa. And her brother, Ramon. What do you need to get the school up and running?"

"Everything."

"Make a list. Contact the other teachers and see how many can come back. I'm sure a teacher's salary is better than whatever they're doing elsewhere. Of course, actually getting paid is contingent on the stability of the financial system."

"I understand. Is your father in agreement?"

"No. He's no longer in charge." Rob approached a little girl and asked, "Do you remember me? Last time I was here, you were reading *Jane Eyre.*"

"I finished that a long time ago. Now I'm reading *Little Women.*"

"Do you still want to be a teacher?"

"Yes, sir."

Rosa smiled at her. "I went to a school like this when I was your age, and now I'm a teacher. You can do it, too." She thought about the little school in Summer Valley where she'd been offered a position. That was where she wanted to be.

As they left the school, Rob said, "I don't know how to find Jem's farm without getting lost."

Ramon said, "Let me drive."

The farmhouse was occupied. Two strange vehicles sat in the yard. Ramon turned the Backpacker around and parked outside the gate. Rosa wondered why he did that. *Is he expecting trouble?*

"Stay here, Rosa," he said.

She opened her mouth to protest, but Rob said, "Please."

Okay, she'd humor them. She watched them approach the house and go inside. It seemed like forever before Rob returned, alone.

"It's okay. It's Jem's family."

Rosa let out her breath.

They were invited to lunch.

A middle aged black lady was talking on Doug's Nebula, tears in her eyes. "That's Jem's mother," Rob said. "I was able to reach Jem at the mayor's."

Ramon was telling other family members about their adventures.

"We've been using your car," someone said. "But you can have it back."

"My books!" Rosa said. "I put them in the attic. Can we get them down?"

A young man pulled down the ladder and scurried up, returning with the box of books. "I'll put it in your car."

"Thanks."

Doug's Nebula sounded. Andreu came on the screen. "Everything all right?"

"Yes," Rob said. "No problems."

"If you run into any, show them your cloverleaf and call me."

"Thanks, Andreu."

When they left, Ramon drove their parents' car. Now that they were alone, Rosa asked, "Rob does it feel to you like we're married?"

"Yes. What about you?"

"I'm not sure what it's supposed to feel like. I always thought marriage meant setting up housekeeping. We've been bouncing from place to place, apart more than we've been together, making love when we can steal a few minutes alone."

"I'm sorry, Rosa. You deserve better. You're not having second thoughts, are you?"

"Oh, no, nothing like that. I knew going into it we were taking chances. I think about my parents' marriage. They were a team."

"I feel like we're a team. Whenever I don't know what to do, I look to you for advice. I couldn't do it without you."

She scooted closer so he could put his arm around her. "I'd like a little time alone with you. I hope there isn't another crisis waiting for us at the house." She refused to refer to Hardman Hall as home.

By some miracle, Rosa got her wish. Amaline said, "The only news is that Doug's funeral is scheduled for Wednesday. I've notified your relatives and as many of his friends as I could. A lot of them are afraid to come. I couldn't get a preacher to come, either, so I lined up a holo transmission. Why don't you two spend some time together? Go for a walk. It's a fine afternoon."

Rosa smiled at Rob. "Let's go." Hand in hand, they strolled through the park in front of the house. Rosa sat on the edge of the fountain and let the water run through her hands. "I have to admit this is lovely. Didn't you tell me the estate raises most of its own food? I saw the vegetable gardens and orchards on the way in. You have animals, too, right?"

"Yes. Let me introduce you to Cricket."

"Who?"

"My...used to be my horse."

In the backyard, they passed the swimming pool and playground and... "Is that a tennis court?"

"Yes. Do you play?"

There were so many things they still didn't know about each other. "No. I never had the opportunity to learn."

"I'll teach you." He looked at the pool. "You know, I haven't had a chance to go swimming since I got here. We need to make time to enjoy ourselves."

As they approached the stone wall, Rosa felt claustrophobic. Had this been built to keep the world out or to keep family in? Or both? She breathed easier after they passed through the back gate. A handful of horses grazed in a field by the stable. "Which one is Cricket?"

"The most beautiful one." Rob cupped his hands around his mouth and shouted, "Yo, Cricket!" A palomino raised his head and galloped over. "Twice in a row I don't have a treat for him. He's not going to like it."

Cricket nuzzled Rob's empty hands and turned to Rosa. She showed him her hands were empty, too. He rubbed his head against her arm and let her stroke his neck.

"He likes you," Rob said.

"I like him, too. Rob, I never realized how much you gave up when you left here. I don't mean the money."

"Yes, but I found freedom. Most important, I found you." He took her in his arms and kissed her. Then he took her hand and pulled her up the lane. "Come on, I'll show you the best part of the estate."

"These hills are nice," Rosa said. "It was so flat where I used to live." She heard a sound like thunder. A dozen cattle galloped toward them. "Rob!"

"It's okay. They're inside the fence."

"Why are they doing that?"

"They think we're going to feed them." The cows stopped at the fence and lowed at Rob. "You aren't getting anything today," he said. "You have plenty of grass."

They were the biggest cows she'd ever seen. Each had a hump on its back. "What kind are they?"

"Brahmans. We also have Angus and Limousins in other pastures. Brahmans handle the heat better."

A stately creature towered above the rest. "Is that the bull?"

"Yes. Someone with a twisted sense of humor named him Gandhi."

At the top of the hill, more pasture lay before them, dipping down to a creek. Gently rolling hills stretched through meadows and beyond, to woodlands. Rosa looked back. "You can't see the house from here."

"I know." They passed through a gate into a copse of ancient live oaks. One tree had split and a large limb rested on the ground. They sat on it. "I brought Ned up here. He said this would be a good place to build a house. For the view."

"Yes. Not as nice as a mountain view, but good for Florida." Rosa removed her shoes and her toes played with the leaves. "Are there any cows in this field?"

"Don't seem to be right now. We rotate them, let them graze in one pasture, then move them to give the grass time to recover."

"You seem to know a lot about farming."

"I tagged along with the help when I was a boy. I always thought it would be a nice vocation. That's why I was so excited to get a job in Summer Valley."

"Is anyone likely to come here right now?"

"I don't think so." They slid off the limb and leaned against it.

"Are there chiggers in these leaves?"

"I hope not."

The ground was soft. Rosa inhaled the earthy scent and felt more at peace than she had in many days. "I'm glad I married you after all, Rob Hardman."

* * *

By the time they were ready to return to Hardman Hall, Rob's heart was dancing. Whatever the future threw at them, he would welcome it as long as Rosa was at his side. They brushed the leaves from their clothing.

As they approached the stables, Rosa pointed to a line of cows ambling toward the milking shed. "What kind are they?"

"Jerseys. Milk cows."

"It must have been nice to have fresh milk growing up."

"It was. Let's see who's milking them. The couple who used to handle the dairy aren't here anymore."

As they entered the shed, he heard Steven say, "Now, Bossy, be patient."

"Steven, are you doing this all by yourself?"

"Oh, hello, Mr....um, Rob. No, that's too big a job for one person, with everything else I have to do. My grandparents are helping me." He stared at Rosa.

"I'm sorry, you haven't met my wife yet. Rosa, this is Steven." When she stepped forward to shake his hand, Rob noticed leaves sticking in her hair. He picked them off. "Steven, are you able to process the milk?"

"Well, Rob, I never knew the tricks to makin' cheese, and all, so I've been giving away what doesn't get drunk up on the estate."

"At least it's not going to waste. I'll see about hiring some help for you."

"I'd appreciate it."

Rosa said, "Rob, can we stay to watch? I've never seen anything like this."

"Certainly. Maybe I can lend Steven a hand." While Steven handled the milking machines, Rob fed the cows.

Rosa asked, "Are they tame enough? Can I pet them?"

"Sure," Rob said. "You know, we're doing the right thing here, producing good food, but it's more than the estate can use. We need to find a fair way to distribute it."

Steven answered, "You're right, Rob. Even when the place was full staffed, there was more food than we could eat. Mr. Hardman always sold it to his friends, but he doesn't seem to have many friends these days."

The dinner bell rang. Steven said, "Why don't you all go on. Granny and Pappy will be here in a few minutes to help me finish up."

CHAPTER 37

When they crossed the lawn behind the house, Rob glanced at "that spot." The sod had been disturbed. "Oh, no!" He took off running.

Rosa tried to keep up with him. "What is it?"

"Mother."

They found her in a complete melt-down. Amaline and Betsy were trying to comfort her. "What happened?"

Amaline said, "I told her we'd scheduled Doug's funeral. She went through another round of grief, then she went outside."

"I know. I saw it."

Rosa asked, "What are you talking about?"

"She tears up the grass where Michaela died."

"Rob," his mother wailed. "He did it!"

Rob knelt down and took his mother's hands. Her fingernails were black with dirt.

She took a deep breath and tried to control herself. "Your father. He killed Michaela."

Rob grit his teeth. "How do you know?"

"He was ashamed of her. He wanted to put her in a home. He said if I didn't go along with it, I'd regret it. I thought that meant he'd make my life miserable. I didn't know he'd hurt her. And now Doug's gone, too."

"Mother, do you have any proof?"

"No. I just know it. He put me in the hospital until I agreed not to say anything. Dr. Robertson gave me pills to ease the pain, but it never went away." She pulled a scrap of fabric, one Rob had seen her with many times, from behind the seat cushion. She lovingly smoothed the cloth. "This is all I have left of her. He even took her pictures away."

An image flashed in Rob's mind—Michaela wearing her favorite dress.

She began to fold the cloth. "I don't want anything to do with that man!"

"Mother, I'll see what I can do. Amaline, what's that detective's name?"

"Daryl Kaminski."

"I need to talk to him and the medical examiner."

"Come with me."

Amaline got Detective Kaminski on the phone. Rob asked, "What are the chances of solving an almost twenty year old murder?" He gave him the details.

"With no witnesses or evidence, not very good."

"I want to try anyway. Can you come here tonight?"

"As a matter of fact, I wanted to talk to you about the girl who was poisoned. We identified a suspect. I can be there in an hour."

After terminating the call, Rob realized he hadn't asked who the suspect was. When he reached the medical examiner, he asked, "Are you interested in another autopsy?"

"Another poisoning victim?" the doctor asked.

"No." Rob winced. "The body's been in a mausoleum for nineteen years."

"Look, unless there's an open law enforcement case in my jurisdiction, I don't get paid for doing these things. Besides, it's highly irregular."

"We'll pay you whatever you ask. Do you want us to send you the body? Or can you come here?"

"Let me come look at it. It may be too far gone to show me anything."

"When?"

"Tomorrow."

After he hung up, Rob doubled over with nausea. "That was my little sister's body I was talking about."

Rosa put her arms around him and kissed him on the head.

Rob looked at Amaline. "If it's true, what are we going to do about my father?"

After supper, Rob was on his way to the office to meet Detective Kaminski when he noticed Father heading for the holo room, followed by a security guard. He clenched his fists and cursed under his breath.

The detective greeted Rob. "Before you tell me about your new case, let me update you about the poisoning. Captain Miller had already questioned several people in Tomoka Estates. When I showed up, the boy who'd gone with the truck driver to get water broke down and confessed."

"To poisoning the water?"

He nodded. "He poured the toxin into it. He claimed he was told it'd make people sick, not kill them. He was real upset someone died."

"Who gave it to him?"

"Someone at the plant. He couldn't tell me who. They paid him. He said he did it only because his family needed the money. The plant manager is uncooperative, says he answers to Gregory Hardman only."

"I'll see about him tomorrow."

Amaline spoke up. "Last night, I turned off that desalination plant, but the manager apparently turned it back on. I was going to turn it off again, but if the Tomoka Estates water was all that was contaminated, I see no point."

Rob nodded.

Detective Kaminski said, "One problem is, the justice system has fallen apart. There is no law enforcement agency to handle this. I'm investigating on a private basis. If I prove who supplied the poison and set this boy up, I don't know how to proceed, legally, and I'd hate to see vigilante justice take over." He drew a deep breath. "Regardless, I'll help you find your answer."

"Thank you. Now let me tell you about my little sister." He described his efforts through the years to find answers.

"Why do you think it was murder? If dogs got loose and killed the child, it could have been an accident."

"I hope to God it was an accident. But a former groundskeeper said he'd heard that her injuries were inconsistent with dog bites, that she was already dead, and the dogs were let loose to cover it up. I asked the medical examiner to come look at the body."

The detective shrugged. "If he finds something, let me know. Again, even if we can prove someone murdered her, it may be impossible to do anything about it. Say, if you're going to the desalinization plant tomorrow, I'll go with you. I want to get to the bottom of this."

* * *

By the next day, Rosa had found a clothes rack and chest of drawers for their room. Now Rob didn't need to go to the dressing room for clothes. "You have a closet full of shoes. Don't any of them fit any-more?"

"No. I tried them. My feet are wider."

"There will come a time you'll want to wear shoes. Why not buy some?"

Rob looked perplexed. "I don't know how to. Besides, I don't have any money."

"I still have cash. What do you mean you don't know how to buy shoes?"

"Whenever I needed clothes, Leonard would take care of it."

She shook her head. "After we go to the water plant today, let's find a store. I need a few things myself. I've been wearing the same few outfits over and over."

"Really? You always look good."

"Thanks. I'm going to talk to Amaline. All the work you're doing for the Hardmans, you deserve a salary."

"I suppose you're right. You do, too."

"Let me find a useful job, then we'll talk about it."

Amaline was at breakfast with Rhea and Betsy. Rosa brought up the issue of Rob's salary.

"Certainly you deserve pay, Rob. How much do you want?"

Rob said, "The same as everyone else who lives and works here. Put it in Rosa's bank account, since I don't have one." Voices came from the kitchen. "Who's in there?"

"Leonard and a few security guards. I told them to eat with us, but they said it wasn't proper."

Rob got up. "I'll tell them."

After he left, Amaline whispered, "Rosa, I've restored Rob's legitimacy and everything that goes with it, including his bank account, even though he says he doesn't want it. And I put Doug's Nebula under his name, and took his name off yours."

Rosa smiled. "Let's not tell him right away. Put his salary in my account for now, like he asked."

Rob returned with a retinue of hired help. "There's no 'upstairs/downstairs' here anymore. We're all equal. Y'all eat here with the rest of the family." After he sat down, he muttered, "Not that I have any real authority."

Rosa and Amaline looked at each other and grinned.

When Ramon and Ned joined them, Rob said, "I'm going to meet the detective at the desalination plant this morning."

Rosa said, "I'm going, too."

Ramon turned to Ned. "Will you go with them? I have other business to tend to."

Rosa frowned at him. "Don't do anything stupid."

Ramon sighed. "I won't. Andreu's going with me."

* * *

When Rob drove up to the plant, Detective Kaminski stood at the gate. "No one's answering the intercom, but I see cars in there."

Rob pressed the button and said, "This is Rob Hardman. Please open the gate."

Silence.

Rob called Amaline. "Do you have the codes for this plant?" She gave them to him and he opened the gate. When they reached the front door, a security guard stood inside, rifle pointed at them. Rob grunted. "I don't have time for foolishness. I'm Rob Hardman. You don't want to shoot me." He pressed past the guard, who showed a moment's hesitation. Ned deftly disarmed him.

"Thanks, Ned. Where's the manager?"

The guard shook his head. "I don't have to cooperate with you."

"Fine. I think I know the way."

They found the manager locked in his office. Through the window, Ned saluted him with the rifle. The man opened the door and said, "I just called Mr. Hardman. He has security on the way."

"Bullshit," Rob said and charged into the office. "I'm Rob Hardman, and I'm in control. Mr. Kaminski here has some questions for you."

"I won't answer them."

"Detective Kaminski, does Tomoka Estates have a holding cell?"

"Yes. That's where we put the kid who poisoned the water. There's room for another prisoner."

The manager blanched but didn't give in. He went to his desk and commanded his computer, "Connect me with Gregory Hardman."

The computer replied, "I find no such person."

From across the desk, Rob could feel the man's fear.

"Computer, who is Rob Hardman."

Uh oh. How am I going to get him to cooperate now? Rob didn't think it was possible for the man to get any whiter. Rosa moved to where she could read the screen. She caught Rob's eye and grinned. *What's going on?*

The manager collapsed onto his desk, holding his head in his hands. "It wasn't my idea. I told Mr. Hardman about the theft. He sent a man over with a bottle of liquid. He said it would cause nausea and vomiting, but it was otherwise harmless."

Detective Kaminski said, "Mr. Hardman told you that?"

"No. The man who brought the stuff."

"Who was he?"

"I don't know. He didn't give his name. It was dark—I don't even know what he looked like."

Rob took a deep breath. "Where's your assistant?"

"I fired him. He was letting people steal water."

"Call him and tell him to come in immediately. I'm relieving you of your duties."

"Am I going to jail?"

Rob looked at the detective, who shook his head almost indiscernibly. "Not at the moment. Go home until I tell you otherwise."

The computer connected the manager with his assistant. "James? How soon can you get here? You're hired back. I'm leaving."

* * *

Rosa had looked for a clothing store on their way to the desalinization plant, but every one she saw appeared to be out of business. While waiting for the assistant manager, she used Rob's—no her—Nebula to search for one. "Rob, there's a Jensen's department store in Hollister. It's out of our way, but let's go there on the way home."

"Sure. But we can't spend a lot of time shopping."

"Don't worry." *What does he think I am, a spoiled pudiente?*

Ned said, "That's not far from my home in Carraway. I'd like to go by and look at it."

"Certainly."

Jensen's had been looted, but nearby was a used clothing store. Before she looked for clothes, Rosa made Rob try on shoes. "These look brand new," she said.

"They probably came from Jensen's," Rob said.

Rosa chose three pair: dress shoes, sandals, and a comfortable pair of casuals.

"Why do I need so many?" Rob asked.

"Because you do." She chose a few outfits and a swim suit for herself. *I need more underwear, but not second hand.* Fortuitously, she found a new, unopened package her size. *From Jensen's, I'm sure.*

On the way to Ned's, they passed Carraway Correctional, where he used to work. The facility looked abandoned. "I suppose the government's no longer paying Mr. Cooper to keep people locked up," Ned said. "I bet he was pissed about losing money when I let those prisoners out!"

He directed Rob to his house. "Where is it? I should be able to see it...Oh, no!" He jumped from the car before Rob could stop. Then he stood frozen with shock in front of a charred ruin. Rosa put her arms around him. Ned said, "Let me look around." He walked among the ashes, occasionally stooping to pick up, then drop, something. Finally, he returned to the car and said, "Let's go." He was silent for miles. "I bet it was arson."

"A disgruntled former prisoner?" Rob asked.

"More likely a disgruntled former employer."

"If it's any consolation, Mort Cooper got his comeuppance. His compound was attacked by a mob. They dragged him away and he hasn't been seen since."

"Good."

"Was the house insured?"

Ned shook his head. "Couldn't afford it."

"Ned," said Rosa, "You'll always have a home with us."

"Thank you."

When they returned to Hardman Hall, Rosa found Ramon eating lunch with a young woman. She wore expensive clothes, but her face and arms were covered with bruises in various stages of healing. In a not very gentle voice, Ramon said, "Rosa, meet Valerie."

His old girlfriend? The one that got him arrested? Why would he bring her here? Rosa shook Valerie's hand and looked quizzically at her brother.

"I couldn't leave her with her father. You can see why."

"Has Betsy examined her?"

"Yeah. The injuries are superficial. The physical ones, anyway. Rob, do you have a room she can stay in? Until she decides what she wants to do?"

"Cisli's in a guest suite. She can bunk with her."

"Thanks. I'll take her bags up." He picked up his dishes and left.

Valerie set down her fork. Her voice trembled. "He's never going to forgive me."

Rosa was torn between wanting to comfort the girl and telling her off. She restrained herself and did neither. On one hand, she wanted to hear the whole story, and on the other, she didn't want to listen to whatever lies the girl would tell. "If you're done eating, I'll show you to your room."

Valerie got up, leaving her plate on the table.

"Around here, we pick up after ourselves."

Valerie picked up her dirty dishes and waited for Rosa to tell her what to do.

"Bring them in the kitchen." Rosa showed her how to scrape her plate and put it in the dishwasher. "When it's full, someone will run it. If you find the dishwasher full of clean dishes, put them away. We also wash our own clothes and clean our rooms. Cisli will help you until you get the hang of it."

When they passed her door, Rosa said, "If you need me, I'm in here. Ramon and Ned share this suite with me and Rob."

Ramon was depositing two large suitcases in Cisli's suite. "Cisli has the bed. There's a couch you can sleep on." He followed Rosa down the hall to their suite. "I got Mama and Papa and Grandmother's ashes. Haven't had time to call Father Felix yet."

"Ramon, tell me about Valerie."

"I didn't go there with the intention of bringing her back. But you see her face. She claims her father made her say I raped her. When she found out I'd been arrested, she threatened to tell the truth, and that's when the beatings began. The worse the economy got, the more her father took it out on her. He called her a slut, said she was damaged goods, told her no decent man would want her. Like I damaged her? Shit! She was no virgin when I met her. Those pudientes will screw anything."

Rob had entered the room.

"Sorry," Ramon said. "I didn't mean..."

"Yes, you did," Rob said. "Good thing I'm not a pudiente anymore."

* * *

After lunch, Rob asked Amaline, "Any new developments?"

"Yes. I got the report from the lab. The substance is tetrodotoxin."

"What?"

"Tetrodotoxin. Originally it came from pufferfish, but this was synthetic. It can cause nausea and vomiting, among other things. And death."

"I never heard of it. Where would anyone get the stuff?"

"It's used in medical research."

"Dr. Robertson?"

"I don't know."

Rob thought for a moment. "We need to talk to Wannis. I haven't told her our suspicions about Doug yet, either. We also need to notify the detective."

"I already called him."

"Thanks. Will you sit with Mother for a few minutes and send Betsy here? I need her expertise." *I need all the help I can get.*

Rob located Ramon and Ned. "Is Andreu still here?"

Ramon said, "I'll see if I can catch him before he leaves."

"Ask him to come to the office. Ned, ask Alice to join us. Her security guards need to know about this. Where's Rosa?"

Rosa arrived with Betsy.

Once everyone was assembled, Rob told them about the poison. "Betsy, could that have been administered to Doug, too?"

"There's no way of knowing. Since he died under the care of a physician, it would be useless to ask for an autopsy or toxicology, especially in the present state of the world."

"Well, Wannis needs to know these things. Maybe Mother, too. Is she up to it?"

Betsy drew a deep breath and let it out. "She's been overprotected too long. I think we should tell her."

Rob nodded. "Ask Amaline to bring her here." He went to fetch Wannis. This could get ugly, he thought.

With the support of his friends, Rob laid it out: The sickness and death at Tomoka Estates, the discovery of poison in the water, the confessions of the boy and the plant manager.

Wannis put both hands over her ears and whimpered. "I don't want to know this."

"You need to know," Rob said. "It's your business."

Rhea shook her head. "What kind of monster did I marry?"

Rob put his arm across her shoulder. "There's more."

Betsy related her suspicions about Doug.

"No! No! No!" Wannis shook her head violently. Rhea tried to comfort her.

Alice Frees said, "What do you want Security to do?"

"Keep Greg under surveillance. With the present state of things, I don't think we have any recourse, legally." He looked around the room. "Let's keep this to ourselves until we have all the facts."

He left the office with his arm draped over Rosa's shoulders, almost leaning on her. "Rosa, how did life get so complicated? I'm not sure I'm up to it."

"Rob, you're doing just fine."

"I wish my mother would tell me she was an unfaithful wife."

* * *

Rosa and Ramon carried their family's ashes to the mausoleum when Rob took Detective Kaminski and Dr. Spencer, the medical examiner, to it. It was a small Greek revival structure, hidden from the house and yard by a tall row of viburnum. Rob punched in the code to open the door. The place was climate controlled and surprisingly clean. Only three spaces were filled. Plaques displayed the names of Greg's parents and Michaela. *Now I understand "silent as a tomb." Not even a cockroach.*

Rob pointed at an empty shelf and said, "You can put them there for now."

She and Ramon reverently laid their boxes on the shelf. "Do you need us to stay?" Rosa asked.

"No," Rob said. "We can handle it."

Rosa was only too glad to leave. Ramon looked as relieved as she.

When they reached the viburnum hedge, Ramon looked back and said, "If only I'd stayed home. Maybe I could've saved them."

"Or maybe you'd have died with them." She sighed. "I feel guilty, too, for staying at Salli's." If Ramon hadn't gone to jail, if they hadn't died, life would be so different now. And the chain of events that brought her and Rob together wouldn't have come to pass.

As they approached the house, Ramon said, "What's *he* doing out here?"

Greg was peering through the hedge at the mausoleum. "Spying on Rob, I guess. I've never seen him out of the house before."

"Who's supposed to be watching him?"

Leonard stood a short distance away, with Greg in his line of sight. Rosa asked, "Leonard, what's Greg up to?"

"He asked me what was going on and I said I didn't know. I was told to keep him away from Ms. Hardman, and he hasn't bothered her, so I just follow him around."

"Let Rob know if he does anything suspicious."

"Yes, ma'am, I will."

"Ramon, I think I'll sit out here by the pool and keep an eye out."

From the pool, she had a good view of the back yard. Greg watched through the shrubbery for several minutes, then returned to the house, Leonard in tow.

Rosa took a few minutes to think. Despite Rob's promise to return to the mountains, they kept getting more and more mired in events that required his attention. Doug's funeral was tomorrow. They couldn't leave before then.

Rob came around the hedge with his head down. Rosa rushed to him. "Are you okay?"

"Yeah, I'm all right. Just had to get out of there."

Rosa wrinkled her nose.

"Oh, the smell wasn't bad, but I didn't want to look. Once the doc had the casket open, he said he didn't need me to hang around. The detective's there to help him." He wiped his hand across his brow. "I keep picturing Michaela as she was, alive. She was such a sweet little girl."

Rosa put her arms around him. "Do we need to wait for them?"

"No. They said they'd come to the house when they were done."

* * *

Rob overheard Ned and Andreu talking to Leonard in the dining room,

"How did he get away from you?" Ned asked.

Rob's heart raced. "What happened?"

"Nothing, we think," Ned said.

Leonard said, "He was in the holo room watching one of those preachers and said he had to go to the bathroom. I thought that's where he went. I don't know how he got out without me seeing him. When he didn't come out of the bathroom, I went to check on him and he was gone."

Andreu said, "Jerome saw him pokin' around in the garage. I didn't see anything disturbed. I don't know what he was up to, but I think Jerome stopped him from whatever he had in mind."

"Where is he now?"

"In the holo room," Ned said. "Alice is with him. He won't get away with anything under her watch."

"Has anyone checked on Mother?"

"Yes. She's fine."

Rosa said, "When Rob was in the mausoleum, he was watching them through the bushes. He's up to something."

"He knows we're investigating Michaela's death," Rob said. "We need to tighten up. I don't know what he's capable of."

Ned nodded. "From now on, he can't be left alone, even in his bedroom or bathroom. I'll let everyone know."

CHAPTER 38

Later that day, Rob's older sister Sophia and her family arrived, accompanied by her in-laws. Rhea greeted them. "Why don't you get settled in your suite, then we can visit."

Rob helped carry their bags. Sophia said, "Mother's doing well today."

"Yes. We hired a nurse who took her off most of her medications." She stared at Rob. "Was that wise?"

"Yeah. They'd made her into a zombie. You see how she is today."

"What does Dr. Robertson say about that?"

"He's no longer allowed to treat her, or anyone else in the family."

"Really?" Sophia said. "Where is Father?"

"In the holo room."

"I'm going to say hello." To her in-laws, she said, "I'll be back shortly."

After Rob returned to the office, Sophia stormed in.

"Rob, just what are you trying to pull? Father did not authorize you to take Mother off her medication."

"Sophie, a lot has happened lately. I need to bring you up to speed. Betsy showed me what Mother was on, and what they were for. She should have been weaned off some of the drugs years ago, instead, more were added. That's why she kept getting worse instead of better."

"Who is this Betsy to second guess Dr. Robertson?"

"There's more. Doug's death was suspicious. Betsy looked at his medical records and said his condition was serious but not fatal, that he could have lived, albeit with disabilities. At best, Dr. Robertson was negligent."

"Rob, you have really gone off the deep end. Father warned me."

Rob bit his tongue. "Another thing you need to know is that we're investigating Michaela's death."

"What! Who is *we*?"

"A detective and a medical examiner are looking at her body as we speak. She may not have died of dog bites."

"You cannot be serious! And now you're treating Father like a criminal—why? So you can take over the family business? Let me tell you, after the funeral, I'm going to put a stop to this nonsense, and I'm going to help Father throw you out on the street where you belong."

Rob clenched his fists and forced himself to remain calm. "I'm not going to argue with you. The facts will speak for themselves."

She stomped out of the room.

What am I going to do if those facts don't speak? He shook his head. *Oh, well, she may bluster, but she's not in charge here, and there's no lawyer who will take her case against me.... I hope.*

Rosa came in. "What's wrong?"

"Sophie's going to be trouble. She's taking Father's side."

"Rob, don't worry, you can handle her. What I came to tell you is, Dr. Spencer and Daryl Kaminski are on their way to talk to you. They asked that your mother be present. I'll go tell her."

She returned with Amaline and Betsy as well as Rhea. Mother sat by Rob and said, "Shouldn't Sophie be part of this?"

Amaline said, "I'll get her."

"What did you find?" Rob asked Dr. Spencer.

"Let's wait until everyone's present. I only want to say it once."

When Sophia entered, she glared at Betsy. "*She* doesn't need to be here."

"Sophie, it's my call," Mother said. "I want her here."

Sophia scowled at Rosa.

Rob said, "Stop right there."

She sat down and remained silent.

Dr. Spencer cleared his throat. "I performed a visual examination of the body. After almost twenty years, it's difficult, if not impossible, to make a determination. I assume no autopsy was done at the time of death?"

"I don't know," Mother said.

"No," said Amaline. "Greg said it wasn't necessary."

The doctor nodded. "Who discovered the body?"

Rhea took a deep breath and said, "I did."

Rob expected her to fall apart. She clenched her teeth and fists and held herself together.

"How much blood did you see?" Dr. Kaminski asked.

"Not much." She shook her head. "I don't remember any."

Amaline spoke up. "I was the second one there. I hadn't thought about it before, but there was very little blood."

Dr. Spencer shook his head. "I'll have the body transferred to my office where I can do a more thorough job. I understand you have a funeral scheduled for tomorrow. I'll have my assistants come for the body the following day."

Sophia jumped to her feet. "No! I won't have it. My sister should not be disturbed just because someone who is no longer a member of this family thinks he can usurp his father's position!"

"Sophia!" her mother said, "This is not your decision. Nor is it Rob's. It's mine, and I want the doctor to complete his examination. Now sit down."

Sophia looked at her mother. "What have they done to you?"

Mother gritted her teeth. "Better to ask what your *father* has done to me for the past twenty years."

Dr. Spencer coughed. "I don't want to be in the middle of a family feud. Ms. Hardman, unless I hear otherwise from you, my people will be here Thursday for the body." He beckoned to Rob. "I need you to lock the door so no one tampers with anything."

Rob and Daryl Kaminski accompanied him back to the mausoleum. "I'll change the code, too," Rob said. "I appreciate what you're doing, even if you don't find any answers."

"I'm just doing it for the money. I don't know how long I'll have a job, or whether they'll even pay me. Ever since that hurricane, cases aren't being referred to me like they should be. But you have my word, I'll give you an honest answer, to the best of my ability."

Detective Kaminski said, "I'll be in touch, too."

Wannis' family arrived before dinner. It was one of the most unpleasant meals Rob had endured. The relatives didn't hide their disdain when the "servants" were invited to eat with them. Several employees made the excuse that the dining room was too crowded and chose to eat in the kitchen. Rob wished he could go with them.

The meal was served buffet-style. Although nothing was said, Rob was amused by the looks that told him the guests expected to be waited on. He whispered to Rosa, "Should we ask them to pick up their plates when they're done?"

She shook her head and whispered back, "They don't live here."

Instead of catching up on news of one another, they complained about how the deteriorating social and economic conditions were affecting them. Wannis' father said, "We spent three and a half hours on the road to get here. I was afraid to take my copter because the rabble shoot them down."

Halfway through the meal, Wannis' mother asked, "Why isn't Greg eating with us?"

Sophia said, "He's too overcome with grief. He's in the holo room. Praying."

Rob caught a look of disgust on his mother's face.

After the ordeal was over, Rob helped Rosa clean up the dining room. "I don't know how much more of this I can take. How can you be so cool about it?"

She laughed. "I had lots of practice when I was in college. You didn't notice it because you were one of them."

"Why did you even give me the time of day?"

"Because you weren't as bad as most of them."

The next day when Rob tried to dress casually for the funeral, Rosa intervened. With Leonard's help, she chose a suitable outfit and made him wear socks with his new dress shoes.

"Do you think I need to impress those pudientes?" he asked.

"No, you need to show respect for your brother and not be a distraction."

Although the security detail kept close watch on Greg, they didn't prevent him from socializing with guests. The former lord of Hardman Hall enthroned himself in the grand salon to receive their sympathies. Ned, Alice, and Andreu sat discretely where they could supervise him.

Wannis was conspicuously absent, but Sophia circulated among the mourners, talking quietly. "I think she's poisoning them against you," Rosa said.

Rob grimaced. "I don't know what I can do about it."

Amaline said, "They can't do anything as long as I have control of Greg's codes." She looked around the room. "Not as many as I'd expect. Most sent their condolences but said they can't come due to dangerous traveling conditions."

Greg's sister Edwina and her family arrived mid-morning. Shortly after, the funeral home staff brought Doug's coffin. They set it in the holo room, where the chapel program was running. Virtual flowers and somber drapes set the mood. Wannis, dressed in black, sat in the front pew, weeping quietly.

Rob and Rosa went in to pay their respects. "Very nice," Rosa whispered. "In the old days, they surrounded the casket with real flowers. That stopped when the US borders were closed."

"Why?"

"The flowers were from South America, where they could grow fresh ones year-round."

Greg led his entourage into the chapel. The security detail followed.

Sophia stormed up to Rob. "What's that chauffeur doing in here? You're embarrassing Father in front of everyone. Just wait 'til this is over."

Aunt Edwina asked. "Rob, what's going on? Greg is saying strange things to his guests, talking about being kept a prisoner in his own house."

Sophia spat out, "Rob and his cronies are trying to take over Father's business. Did you know Father kicked Rob out a couple months ago? Disowned him? So Rob shows up with a gang of thieves to take revenge on him."

Edwina looked from one to the other.

Rob said quietly, "There are suspicions Father may have been involved in three murders."

"What?"

"Let's step outside and I'll fill you in."

Sophia shouted, "That's right—whisper in corners, don't bring your nasty little conspiracy out in the open where it can be shown for what it is!"

Rob ignored her. They moved out to the hall. Rob said, "The water at one of the plants was contaminated, and a child died."

"What proof do you have?" asked Edwina.

"We caught the guy who poisoned the water. And the plant manager admitted Father sent him the stuff."

"But why?"

"Because they were stealing water."

Sophia's tirade had attracted attention. A few mourners came out of the chapel. Edwina looked for the nearest chair and sat down. "You said three murders."

"Doug was one."

"Doug?"

"He overdosed on a combination of drugs and went into a coma. Our nurse looked at the medical records. She said Doug could have survived with the right treatment. She thinks his life was deliberately terminated."

"Why?"

"Because he would have been disabled. Then there's Michaela."

"I thought the dogs killed her."

"That may have been a cover-up. She may have already been dead. We had a medical examiner here yesterday. He looked at her body and wants to take it in for a complete autopsy tomorrow."

"My God, Rob! If any of this is true, what are you going to do?"

"I don't know. Protect Mother, at least."

Sophia stamped her foot. "Aunt Edwina, how can you take this seriously?"

"Because I know how ruthless and cold-blooded my brother can be."

"Sophie," Rob said, "I couldn't believe it at first, either. Even after everything Father did to me. But the evidence kept piling up..."

Wannis' father approached. "What's this about Doug being poisoned?"

"We're not sure what Doug died from, but he shouldn't have died."

The man frowned. "Wannis told me you had some half-baked theories. Is my daughter in any danger? What about my grandchildren?"

"There's no reason for Father to target them. We've been watching him around the clock."

"That's not good enough. The minute this funeral is over, I'm taking my family and leaving. We're not staying for dinner."

"I don't blame you," Rob said.

"What about these other people? Shouldn't they be told?"

Rob bit his lip. "I was trying to keep some decorum..."

The man returned to the chapel, where raised voices could be heard.

"Sophie, see what a mess you've made?"

"You made the mess, Robert. Nobody's going to believe this charade."

Murmuring funeral-goers filtered in and out the chapel doors, forming loose clusters, exchanging rumors. "Preposterous!" a man shouted. Furtive glances turned Rob's way, some quizzical, some piercing like daggers. Rosa clutched his arm. Ned and Ramon flanked him.

Rob said, "Aren't you guys getting tired of saving me from lynch mobs?"

No one laughed.

Organ music spilled through the chapel doors. "Let's get on with it," someone said.

Rob and his companions entered through a back door where Rob could observe the assemblage. Wannis' parents hovered over her and her children, as far from Greg as possible. Sophia sat beside her father, both speaking animatedly to guests. A few moved away. Others showed solidarity, patting Greg on the shoulder.

Everyone took their seats when the virtual preacher appeared and began his litany. Rob's pounding heart drowned out the words. He remained standing, alert for trouble. Rosa stood by him. "Why don't you sit down?" he said.

When the preacher announced the time for family members to speak, Greg stood up. As he walked to the podium, a door opened. Detective Kaminski entered and sat down. Rob's heart stopped.

Greg Hardman's expression did not change when he saw the detective.

How can he be so cool? He should be a nervous wreck.

But Father seemed unperturbed. He didn't even clear his throat. In a clear voice, he began, "No parent should have to bury his child. Today, in sorrow, I bury my first born son, Douglas Gregory Hardman III, the second child God in his mercy has elected to take from my loving arms. How can a father live on when he loses the companionship of those he loves most? I aspire to the day when I will be reunited with my loved ones in eternal bliss."

Greg reached inside his coat...

Andreu shouted, "Everybody get down!" and rushed toward the stage.

Ned and Ramon left Rob's side and dashed in the same direction. Rob's mouth flew open in disbelief as light glinted off the gun in his father's hand. He pushed Rosa to the floor.

"Get your mother!" she yelled.

Rob climbed over seat backs to reach her, but Amaline and Betsy already had her hidden.

"You're making a perfect target!" Ned grabbed Rob and pulled him down.

The virtual preacher was howling, "What in the name of the Prophet Joachim is going on?"

"Halt!" Greg turned the pistol to his own temple. Time froze. "Grief is too great to bear." In less than seconds, Greg extended his arm and sprayed the audience with several rounds before turning the weapon on himself again.

Rob watched his father's body crumble to the floor like a discarded suit.

Rosa screamed, "Ned!" and flew to where Ned lay in a pool of blood. Rob was shocked into motion.

Betsy shouted, "Don't move him!" Rob knelt at Ned's side. Rosa cradled his head.

"Did you order the lynch mob?" Ned asked, then lost consciousness.

Betsy barked, "Amaline, get blankets. Rhea, run to the kitchen and get towels. Andreu, do you know where we can take him?"

"Yes, ma'am," Andreu said. "Ramon, get the Backpacker. Put the seats down and drive it around to the side door." He moved away from the crowd and took out his phone.

Pandemonium spilled out every exit of the room. Rob looked around. "Is anyone else hurt?"

"No one but your friend," said Detective Kaminski. He wrapped Greg's gun in a handkerchief.

Mother and Amaline returned. Betsy pressed a towel into Ned's side while Andreu and Amaline eased a blanket under him. Ramon came in, followed by Jerome.

Andreu grabbed the boy's shoulder and said, "You see this? This is what happens when people play with guns. Now help me carry him to the car." He and Jerome each grabbed a corner of the blanket, and Rob and Ramon took the other two. Betsy stayed in step with them, holding a towel against Ned's wound. They slid Ned into the Backpacker and Betsy climbed in beside him, covering him with another blanket.

Rob opened the passenger door, but before he could get in, Ramon said, "I'll go. You're needed here."

As the Backpacker sped away, Rosa put her arms around Rob and cried. "Please tell me he'll be okay."

Rob hugged her. "He's in the best hands possible right now."

Arm in arm, they returned to the holo room. The program had been turned off. No more flowers or drapes or preacher. Alice Frees and another security guard stood by Greg's inert form. Despite himself, Rob cried. After he recovered, Alice said, "Detective Kaminski is talking to your guests."

Rob nodded. Rosa handed him a handkerchief and they went out into the hallway.

Some mourners were weeping, many were silent with shock, and a few were arguing. When they saw Rob, several hurried toward him demanding an explanation.

Detective Kaminski said, "Where can we talk to these people?"

"Let's go to the salon." Rob shouted, "I'll tell you what I know."

Amaline descended the stairs as Rob walked by.

"Where's Mother?"

"In her room. Sophia's with her. They're very upset, but they'll be okay. Wannis and her mother took the children out to the play area."

The crowd followed Rob and found seats. No one sat in the chair Greg had recently occupied. Rob remained standing. When the guests began hurtling demands at him, Rob held up a hand and said, "I'll answer all your questions. First, let me tell you what I know. I returned to Hardman Hall last week..." It seemed like a year! "I brought my brother home. He'd overdosed on drugs and was in a coma. His doctor took him to the hospital. My father was in a state of mental dissociation because of the economy. His secretary was running things because he wasn't capable. I tried to help her. Then Doug died." He choked back a sob. "A medical person looked at his hospital records and said he should have lived. If he'd received the proper treatment. But he might have been an invalid for the rest of his life. We think his life was deliberately terminated."

"Why would anyone do that?"

"There's a family history. I had a little sister with Downs Syndrome. My father was ashamed of her and wanted to put her in an institution. She died under mysterious circumstances."

A roar of protest circled the room. "That child's death was accidental!"

Rob waited for the clamor to die down. "We're not sure. A medical examiner is looking into it now." He held up two fingers. "Two children with disabilities, two questionable deaths. We'll know when we get the autopsy report. But there's more. A community that gets water from us was stealing it. People started getting sick and someone died. A poison had been put into the water supply. Detective Kaminski here is investigating it. A young man confessed to being paid to poison the water."

More hubbub.

The detective held up his hand. "The manager of the plant admitted to me that he'd asked Mr. Hardman how to handle the theft, and Mr. Hardman sent the toxin to him. The manager was told it would make people sick. He didn't know it would kill them."

"If that's true, why wasn't Greg arrested?"

"He was on house arrest. That's why we had guards assigned to him."

Sophia's husband said, "You mean Greg didn't kill himself because he was overcome with grief, but because he knew he'd been caught?"

Detective Kaminski said, "That's what it looks like."

Once Rob had answered their questions, guests trickled out of the salon and went home. The funeral director asked what they should do about the deceased.

Rob said, "Put Doug's coffin in the mausoleum. We'll have a private service later."

Rosa asked, "What about your father?"

The detective said, "I'll report the incident to the authorities, such as they are. There's no question as to the cause of death. A few months ago, there would have been an investigation anyway, but times have changed. Do as you see fit."

"Let me talk to Mother and Sophie."

Sophia was still hysterical. Her mother, by contrast, appeared serene. "Let the funeral home take him away," she said.

The cook had prepared food for the multitude, but few remained to eat, and many of them had little appetite. "Take it to the outside gate," Rob said. "Feed anyone who comes by."

Rosa said, "Cisli and Veronica cleaned up the mess in the holo room."

"Thank them for me."

They went up to check on his mother and sister. Sophia had calmed somewhat. "Oh, Robbie, I'm sorry. I thought I knew my father. I can't believe I was so wrong."

Rob tried to find words to console her, but all he could think of was, "Me, too."

Once he and Rosa were alone, he asked, "What do we do now?"

Rosa sighed. "Heal."

CHAPTER 39

Rosa wakened to the aroma of frying bacon. Sunlight streamed through her open window and birds sang in the trees. She stretched and allowed herself to luxuriate between the soft cotton sheets. "Mmm." She could almost taste the bacon. *Thanks, Rob.*

She rolled out of bed and slipped on a comfortable summer dress. Rob poked his head in. "Breakfast is ready. You want to eat on the deck?"

"Oh, yes."

He sat beside her with his coffee. She sipped raspberry tea. Coffee didn't agree with her lately. "Such a beautiful morning. It's so nice to live on a farm."

A gentle breeze rippled the grass in the pasture where the cattle had been turned out to graze. Rob said, "How does it feel to have the summer off?"

"Great. I'll miss my students, but this'll give me time to digitize some of my books and work on my history textbook. I'm so glad censorship is over. What are you doing today?"

"I promised to help at the dairy this morning. In fact, I'm late. Then I'll see what Mother needs me to do."

"Will you be home for lunch?"

"I'll let you know if I can't make it. What are you fixing?"

"You'll have to come home to find out."

He scooted to her side and caressed her tummy. "You are so wonderful." After a lingering kiss, he picked up his dishes and left for work.

Rosa loved her little cottage. Rob had designed it with the help of an architect. It had all the features she wanted, with plans for additional rooms when they became necessary. They didn't have long to wait. Rosa stroked her swelling abdomen and felt for movement. *Still sleeping. After playing all night and keeping me awake!*

Three months into their marriage, Rosa noticed she'd missed a cycle. "I thought you had an implant," Rob said.

"So did I." She talked to Betsy, who told her implants weren't one hundred percent effective. They hadn't planned to start a family so soon, but they were happy. Happy? Rob was over the moon.

He'd worked hard to finish the house in time, doing as much of the work himself as he could. They'd paid for it from Rosa's modest savings and both salaries.

When Rob had learned his legitimacy and fortune had been restored, he converted his wealth into an endowment from which they funded projects such as Olustee Academy and the school where Rosa taught. Hardman Aquatics paid him a reasonable salary for helping manage the farm and businesses.

Rhea had recovered beautifully from her years of stupor. With the help of Amaline and Rob, she took over the family empire. Amaline suffered greatly from years of abuse by Greg. At times she was so overcome by guilt for her perceived wrongs against Rhea that she was barely able to function. Therapy was helping her climb out of the hole.

Wannis had taken her children to her parents' home for a while. Then she decided they were safer at Hardman Hall, where the family was on better terms with the community than at many pudiente strongholds, including her parents'. To everyone's surprise, she enrolled her children in Rosa's school, where they rubbed elbows with working class scholars. In December, she had given birth to a daughter. Rosa was glad her child would have a cousin near the same age to play with.

While Rosa cleaned up from breakfast, Ned appeared at the foot of the porch steps, leaning on his cane. "Good morning."

"Good morning. Would you like some coffee?"

"No thanks. I'd just like to sit with you a while. Carrying out doctor's orders to walk a mile a day isn't always easy."

"Are you hurting?"

He nodded. "I think the weather's about to change." He settled into a rocking chair. "You know, when I told Rob this was a good place for a house, I was thinking of myself, not him."

Rosa laughed. "Sorry. There's still plenty of room. I'm sure Rhea would sell you a few acres."

"Well, I'm not sure what I want to do yet. I still have my lot in Carraway, and now I'm seeing someone."

"If you move away, we'll miss you."

"I never thought you'd give up on going back to the mountains."

"We're settled here. We'll go up this summer for Greta and Hector's wedding. Since she was my bridesmaid, she says I should be hers." She smiled. "Greta's aunt will be there. She has the books I left in the cottage and said she'll bring them to me."

"How are their kids doing?"

"Quite well, considering all they went through. The oldest girl is going through teenage angst, but she's very bright. We may sponsor her for college."

"Speaking of what kids go through, I could hear little Edwina screaming again last night."

"She has a right to her nightmares. Counseling is helping, but it will take time. I worry about Douglas. He handles trauma differently." They were silent for several minutes. "Wannis surprised me. After all her histrionics over Doug's death, she really stepped up for her kids. I can't imagine watching a grandparent commit suicide."

It was bad enough watching a father-in-law blow his brains out. *But why couldn't he have done it in private? Because Gregory Hardman wanted to make everyone else suffer with him.*

Greg must have known what the autopsy on Michaela would show. To complicate matters, a crew harvesting trees in the longleaf plantation had stumbled across a grave. How many more would they find? The recently restored Clay County law enforcement agency, under the direction of Daryl Kaminsky, was investigating.

Greg's body had been placed in the mausoleum but they held no service for him. Rob had wanted to throw away his father's portrait, but Rosa told him, "Don't be too hasty to erase your history." Instead, he stored it away and put Doug's photo in its place.

Rosa and Ramon had found their old priest, Father Felix, who said Mass for their parents and grandmother. They buried the ashes next to their grandfather's grave. Rosa looked forward to Father Felix christening their baby.

Rob had asked Rosa if she wanted a church wedding. "We already had a wedding." Father Felix blessed their union and their wedding rings. Rosa stretched out her hand and looked at the simple gold band, the only ring she wore. A memento box on her dresser, atop Grandmother's doily, held her Citizenship ring. Rob wore a wedding band, but he had never reclaimed his other rings.

Ned stopped rocking. "Guess I'd better hobble back to work." He helped manage the relief center Rhea had established at Hardman Hall and oversaw security at the clinic Betsy ran. Both were funded by Rob's endowment.

After he left, Rosa watered her garden. The cool weather plants had withered weeks ago but she still had basil and sweet potatoes and okra.

"Hey, Rosa." Valerie approached with a basket. "Rob said you needed more eggs."

"Thanks. How's Ramon?"

"He's fine. He's on a Road Department conference with his team in Tallahassee."

"Have you two made any decisions?"

"Not yet. We're still talking about it."

Valerie worked as a housekeeper at Hardman Hall. Her education hadn't prepared her for a vocation, but she wanted to study music, an aspiration her father had discouraged. She and Ramon's hot and cold relationship finally showed signs of healing.

Rosa and Valerie had become friends. Valerie once confided in Rosa, "We were in love and believed love would conquer all obstacles. I knew Ramon didn't want me for my family's money. And I didn't care how poor he was. And now my family's poor and Ramon has a good job. I'm grateful to Rob for helping him get it."

Andreu and Amaline had persuaded Rob to take his father's place in the legislature. Before he agreed, he asked to be clued in on the cloverleaf network. It was no organization, only a confederation of entities trying to keep society on track. As control slipped from the old order, they operated more in the open. Citizen militias were being transformed into public law enforcement departments. Public servants were persuaded to go back to work, and the legislature was making efforts to have them paid. Leaderless factories, farms, and hospitals were put under workers' control.

The new legislature consisted of a few pudientes, elected members of the working class, and others, like Rob, who wanted to restore justice. Rosa couldn't accompany him to Tallahassee when she was teaching. She missed him terribly when he was gone and worried about the dangers he faced. At least they spent weekends together.

Rob had proposed the new citizenship law. Everyone with a high school diploma was allowed to vote, own property and telephones, and use the internet. "Next year," he told her, "I'm going to move forward on free public education. That's the key to a functioning society. After that, I have other ideas. Someday I'll propose reparations for people who were cheated by the so-called currency reform. That won't be easy, but it needs to happen. The biggest obstacle we face is preventing would-be dictators from taking over." Rosa was proud of him.

After Valerie left, Rosa started lunch. They'd had bacon and eggs for breakfast, so a meatless meal was in order. She decided on quinoa salad. The farm had grown a good supply of quinoa last winter.

Rosa had just finished making the salad when Rob arrived. "You're early for lunch."

"I know. Mother suggested I go over to Dongtian with her this afternoon. Since we can't open it as a resort, she wants to start a college for oceanic research. The sciences have been neglected too long."

"I agree."

"Do you want to go, too?"

"No, thanks." It was too close to where her family once lived. She'd returned to the ruins of their house only once to retrieve the books and a few other things she'd left. The house signified too much loss and heartbreak. She and Ramon tried to sell the lot, but no one wanted property in a flood zone.

Whenever she thought about last summer—a rollercoaster ride of desperation and hope—she marveled that she had survived. She'd more than survived. She had found Rob. Moreover, he had found himself.

Rob gathered her into his arms and nuzzled her neck. Then he kissed her down to the curve of her belly. "If you go into labor, call me right away. It doesn't matter where I am or what I'm doing. I'll come straight home."

"Rob, we've got another month."

"I don't care. The only thing more important than this baby is you."

They sat on the porch swing. The day had heated up, but a balmy breeze still blew. A mourning dove called softly across the field. Rosa had never felt more at home.

"Rob, when we were in college, did you ever dream we'd end up like this?"

He took her hand. "No. Not in my wildest fantasies. I thought of you as a treasure beyond my aspirations."

This made her cry. "Rob, do you really mean that?"

"Yes. I do. Besides, this is the life I always wanted, working the land, helping others. You made my dreams come true."

Rosa was quiet for several minutes. "I think I always loved you, but I didn't want to be part of the world you lived in. Now we're making our own world. A better one."

He drew her closer to him. "Yes, a better one."

THE MOURNING DOVE

The morning was a' singing.

Music danced from tree to tree

As a thousand little songbirds

Gaily trilled among the leaves.

Then a song so soft and plaintive

Drifted low among the rest.

T'was a solitary mourning dove,

That was, like a monk, brown dressed.

Then the call, oh, it was answered

By another 'cross the way.

Who-i-whoo-whoo-whoo then echoed

Through the morning and the day.

ACKNOWLEDGEMENTS

I am deeply indebted to the members of my critique pod who kept me straight on the road to the finished manuscript: Allison Durham, Bonnie Ogle, Jessica Elkins, JoLaine Jones-Pokorney, Joy Southwell, Ken Campbell, and Richard Gartee.

To the Reader

Thank you for reading *Season of the Dove*. It has been my pleasure to take you on this journey. If you enjoyed reading this novel, please write a review on Amazon and Goodreads. Reviews help sell books, and sales nourish the writer, physically and creatively, so she can bring forth more stories.

To read more of my work, visit my website, https://marieqrogers.com/ and my Amazon page. I am available for readings and talks on topics related to my writing. You can contact me through my website.

May all your wanderings lead you to better worlds.

ABOUT THE AUTHOR

When not traveling, award-winning author Marie Q Rogers has nothing better to do than wander the woods of North Florida and think about curious things. Her musings have evolved into short stories, novels, and creative nonfiction posted on her website marieqrogers.com.

Other novels by Marie Q Rogers

Trials by Fire

Quest for Namai

Notebooks Hidden in an Abandoned House

As a Contributor:

Local Lives in a Global Pandemic: Tales from North Central Florida